Cast
of Illusions

Ashley J. Barnard

I0565137

Renard Argenté Press

For Alexandria, the Faerie Queen

Renowned duke, vouchsafe to take the pains
To go with us into the abbey here
And hear at large discoursed all our fortunes:
And all that are assembled in this place,
That by this sympathized one day's error
Have suffer'd wrong, go keep us company,
And we shall make full satisfaction.
Thirty-three years have I but gone in travail
Of you, my sons; and till this present hour
My heavy burden ne'er delivered.
The duke, my husband and my children both,
And you the calendars of their nativity,
Go to a gossips' feast and go with me;
After so long grief, such festivity!

- William Shakespeare, *Comedy of Errors*, Act V, scene i

ONE

JONATHAN WILDER HAD died one-thousand, four-hundred-and-thirty-two times, give or take a few. The majority of these deaths had been by stabbing, either with a rapier or dagger. Two hundred had been by poison, sixty by hanging. He'd also been beheaded, thrown from a tower, trampled, choked, smothered, and, on one memorable occasion, simply died of fright. He preferred dying by the sword, as smothering and choking usually occurred when he was a woman. This was not always the case; eighty-four times he'd stabbed himself with a dagger as Lady Macmaren. That was the only benefit of getting older: those days of donning gowns and wigs were behind him. Regardless of the manner of his death, the only ones that mattered were the ones that garnered applause or cries of dismay. The quiet deaths could mean the death of his company: too many and he'd lose his audience to the King's Men. But never had a death mattered more to him than today. The future of his career depended on it.

His feet thundered on the hollow wooden stage as he danced in the choreographed duel with Thomas, and twice he narrowly missed stepping on a groundling's fingers. Six groundlings were sitting on the stage, leaning forward in complete absorption. Thank heaven they were a fairly disciplined crowd; the last thing he needed was for lusty audience members jumping into the final duel, their *real* swords drawn. Usually he welcomed audience participation, but not with this play, not today.

Sweat poured into his eyes but he didn't dare wipe it away and risk throwing Thomas off. And so he let his eyes sting and blur, relying more on his memory of the choreography than sight. When it was time for the killing blow, he "fell" for a feint, throwing his arms up to block a head attack that didn't come. Instead Thomas's dulled rapier sliced under his arm. He gasped and fell to his knees as Thomas yanked the blade free. Blood pooled, a crimson stain on white silk. There was a feminine yelp from the audience, and a deeper, gruffer voice yelled, "No!"

Thomas dropped next to him, pulling his head into his lap. "Forgive me."

It was all Jonathan could do not to smile up at him and say, *Did you hear that woman squeal? Did you hear that yell?* He blinked the sweat out of his eyes. "There is nothing to forgive. She loves you. The strife between our houses is mended in your love for one another. May God...grant you...joy."

Jonathan's eyes closed, and for several moments there was no sound but a dizzying and deafening thumping in his head. He waited, holding his breath. Someone reached out and touched his shoulder, one of the groundlings presumably. Finally there was a thunder of applause. Thomas pulled him to his feet as the cast assembled behind them, waiting for him to lead the bow. But he was still remembering the stage kiss in Act Four, the shock of a woman's lips instead of a ten-year-old boy's. *I will not yield to your will, but by bending yours to mine shall I have you.* The line, written with Gregory in mind, came out more forceful than intended with Miranda standing opposite. He had seized her shoulders and for three full seconds crushed her lips against his; she pulled away with a gasp and dropped her next line.

Behind the curtain it was all awkwardness, none of the heated passion from their onstage exchange. He shook her hand and muttered congratulations, only to go absolutely rigid when Thomas threw his arms around him, picking him up off the ground.

"Well done, a great success!"

"Please put me down."

"Very well, but I doubt your health would suffer greatly if you displayed occasional elation."

"My heart grows weak at this very moment."

He pulled off his blood-stained shirt; the sewn-in pig's bladder wasted with the rent of a sword cut. His ribs were sticky with blood that was still wet to the touch. He heard distant applause above him in the galleries of the Unicorn, and a lady's handkerchief, whether by design or accident, fluttered down in front of him. Thomas picked it up and smelled it, closing his eyes. "Attar of roses." He studied the embroidered letters. "Sweet RF, I am yours."

"And half the ladies in Diernioch," Jonathan said.

Then a page stood in between them dressed in blue and gold livery, his velvet hat hanging over his eyes. "My lord, the Duke of Chauncery, Prince of the Realm, brother to his Majesty–"

"Yes," Jonathan said. "His lordship and I are well acquainted."

He had no choice but to kneel, still shirtless and stained, to kiss the ring of his patron. Duke Leonardis was stork-like in his height and posture, nearly bald with a hooked nose and a pronounced knob of bone in its bridge. He had a very affected manner of speech, something Jonathan would have parodied on stage were it not for the duke's patronage.

"Exquisitely done," the duke said. "Another rousing performance by the Duke's Men, and your first triumph as an author. Rothford would be jealous."

"You are too kind."

"And...quite an improvement in your casting." Leonardis's eye swiveled in search of the improvement in question, and Jonathan felt a surprising jolt when Leon's lips curled in a lewd smile. "Yes. Exquisite. Though the King's Men have two of them now. Women."

"None but Miranda possessed the courage to audition."

Leonardis's gaze did not waver from its target. "Can't bear to watch the boys now. I'll be glad when there are others."

"They'll come. His Majesty's reform is still new; it is frightening for women after centuries of censure."

"I shall relish the day the stage is full of them. Indeed I shall." His eyes glazed over; Jonathan waited patiently until he cleared his throat and shook his head. "Tomorrow. Tomorrow you stage your other new play, yes? *The King of Salsima.*"

"At the Crown. There is too much interest in it to stage it in the yard of an inn."

"Why not stay at the Crown in perpetuity? Seems more sensible than your wild scheme of building your own playhouse."

Jonathan shook his head. "I will not live in Rothford's shadow. And the rent is insufferable. I must have my own playhouse."

"You take on too much. You are player, playwright and manager. You cannot—"

Jonathan pressed his hand to silence him, a gesture, he felt, that did not overstep his bounds after living seven years under the duke's patronage. "Your Grace, I founded this company as you well know. I broke from the King's Men so I would have to answer to no one. I *will* have my own playhouse, if it takes twenty years."

Leonardis nodded; a smile playing at his lips. "Perhaps indeed you shall." He bowed his head. "You have the perseverance for it, and the heart."

"And a bull's temperance. Is that not what Rothford said of me?"

"If it takes a bull's temperance, then so be it. Perhaps he said it with awe rather than disdain."

They broke off at the sound of a shrill voice, both men shuddering. "Jonathan!"

"The lady wife," Leonardis said as Jonathan scrambled into a clean shirt, untucked with laces askew. He barely managed to fall to one knee before she was on him, a predatory sort of peacock with voluminous skirts of red velvet. Upon rising he noted with amusement that duke and duchess wore matching ostrich plumes in their caps.

"Your ladyship."

"Dear Jonathan, your play was splendid."

"Your ladyship is too kind—"

"Though heavy-hearted, yes? Your company is at its best with the lighter comedies; how much I enjoyed Rothford's *Two Brothers of Elkyn*."

"Yes." Jonathan could all but feel Thomas bristle behind him. The duchess wanted to hear the play on every occasion; last year alone they played it thirty-six times at her request. As much as Jonathan hated the play, he knew Thomas despised it more for its banality.

"I find I have a stomach for heartier fare," Jonathan said, treading carefully. "My break from the King's Men was done in part to try my hand at profundity."

The duchess stared at him. "What faults find you with *Two Brothers of Elkyn*?"

Jonathan cleared his throat. In his periphery vision he saw Thomas sidling up to him and knew disaster was impending. "Not fault, exactly, your ladyship…merely…" He glanced at Leonardis, looking for help. The older man's eye's twinkled; there would be no help there.

Thomas snatched the pause and went running with it. "Merely its absurdity, and that of every other Rothford comedy."

Jonathan closed his eyes.

"The – did you say absurdity?"

"Yes. They are good for laughs, I'll grant you. But do you not find their predictability and outrageousness tiresome? Twin boys separated at birth. Each assumes the other is dead, as well as their mother. After a perfunctory hour or two with mistaken identities and the madness that ensues therein, each man wins his true love, is reunited with his missing brother, rejoices the return of his mother from the grave, discovers—"

The duchess's fan snapped open with flick of her wrist, silencing Thomas. "That is precisely why, my dear boy, I find them so endearing." Jonathan watched the frantic waving of her fan over her face; every second he was granted sight of her blotched complexion. "If I wanted a play that reflected true nature, I would simply plant my chair on River Street and watch the vermin."

Now Jonathan could not resist. "But is not the idea splendid, my lady, of a play reflecting true nature in the safety of the playhouse, where one may be transported into the lives of real people for an afternoon only, plunged into troubles that reveal the human spirit, giving one pause to assess his or her own spirit? For two or three hours you are given leave to contemplate the darkness and light of a man's soul, to wonder—"

The duchess stopped fanning herself, and Jonathan saw, through her closed lids, her eyes rolling as if in a swoon. He stopped and waited out the tempest, guilt filling his throat. He risked a glance at Leonardis, relieved when the duke smiled at him.

"Forgive me," he said. "I let my tongue carry me away. I beg your pardon."

Thomas bowed with him, muttering an insincere apology.

"It is precisely that sort of fire," Duchess Isabella said, "that overwhelms me in the playhouse. I come to be entertained, not dragged into hell with the darkness of a man's soul."

"Of course. How may I make amends?"

"By attending my celebration tonight on your behalf."

Jonathan was relieved he was still bowing in order to shield his expression from the duchess. Doubtless she knew how well this command cut him to the quick as she was no stranger to his misanthropy.

His swallow was painful. "Of course."

"And next week is my birthday. I wish to hear *Two Brothers of Elkyn*."

"Yes. Certainly."

When she was gone Jonathan once again pressed Leon's hand. "You will forgive my impetuousness, I trust. I was rash and foolish."

"And that is why I esteem you above so many."

Jonathan gaped at him, his face suffusing with heat. He bowed. "You are too kind."

"I look forward to seeing you tomorrow at the Crown in *The King of Salsima*, which, I trust, is not a comedy."

"Most assuredly not."

"But of course you submitted it to the Master of the Revels for approval?"

Jonathan met his gaze levelly. "Of course."

"Good. So I shall see you this evening at Donchester House."

"My...my pleasure entirely."

Jonathan followed the ostrich plume with his gaze until it bobbed out of view. Thomas pumped his hand up and down, laughing. "Well done! Excellently done. Another performance of our *favorite* play, and a night of frivolities!"

"You were not so brilliant yourself. What with all of your absurdities, outrageousness…what else? Predictability–"

"Everything you have trumpeted a thousand times."

"Yes. But I have the prudence to refrain, for the most part, in the presence of their lordships. Whom, may I remind you, shield us from being lowly ruffians?" He pulled at the liveried banner that covered their cart. Underneath the unicorn and falcon crest were the words *The Duke's Men*.

"Yes, yes! A thousand times yes."

Jonathan could not begrudge his friend overmuch, for it was this passion of his that brought him to Jonathan's attention in the first place. Seven years ago Jonathan saw him stumble into the common room of the Unicorn, already drunk. This was certainly no rare occurrence, and it wasn't until the young man jumped to his feet to snarl at a fellow at a neighboring table that Jonathan took notice. It was his voice that seized the attention of the room's occupants. It was strong and rich, resounding with a strange sort of beauty in the hot, foul-smelling room. Jonathan was transfixed, listening to this voice boom, hearing past the actual words to the timbre and tone of the voice. He imagined what that voice could do in a playhouse, how it would reach the far, upper galleries and even beyond. A voice that could no doubt woo as well as it could rage.

The fellow had a good physique: he was tall with broad shoulders but none of the lankiness of so many of the Unicorn's patrons. His face was handsome with a firm, set jaw, large brown eyes and a goodly nose, an aristocratic nose that belied his stature. Jonathan elbowed his way over to him, unflinching as the man threw a chair. Jonathan shook his hand even as he still raged.

"Filthy son-of-a-whore," he was yelling, to whom Jonathan was unsure. "Senseless braggart. Poxy, ill-begotten, plague-faced coxcomb–"

"Excellent, excellent," Jonathan said, at which point the man noticed his hand being vigorously shaken.

"What in God's–"

"You've a tremendous voice. For the playhouse, I mean. Have you any mind to be a player?"

And the fellow, who looked to be of Jonathan's own age,

seemed to crack open. "By all the stars of heaven. I should love to be a player."

Whatever his grievance, it was now entirely forgotten. Jonathan learned, in a span of three and a half minutes, of this lad's dream of the theatre, how he had conned lines as a boy and performed them for his family. The three fellows at the neighboring table at which he was raging, fell silent and listened, enraptured.

"And where are they now?"

"Mother dead. The others – I know not."

Their kinship was sealed in an instant, for Jonathan saw his own pain of loss in this man's eyes. "I am to start my own company. I have a patron, Duke Leonardis–"

"The king's brother?"

"Even he. Will you join? I have but only five others. There will be more–"

"I would be honored."

"What is your name?"

"Thomas."

"Welcome, Thomas, to the Duke's Men."

And a fine seven years it had been, performing alongside this impetuous, passionate man who fell into violent mood swings and spoke his mind while Jonathan kept his tightly sealed. Jonathan rescued him from many scrapes while Thomas shielded him from society as best he could, for though Thomas was an intensely gregarious animal, he respected Jonathan's lack of social graces. They made an excellent team, and while Jonathan held the sole position of leadership within the company, he consulted with Thomas on every decision.

As promised, the other members of the troupe appeared. Some had come and gone with the years, but of the twelve members that made up his troupe, seven were stock that had been with him since the beginning. And of the current twelve, only one actor stood out as difficult, which was good considering the odds. Though he grated on Jonathan's nerves, Jonathan did not despise Sebastian Roanoke as the others did, as Sebastian had taken a young, orphaned Jonathan under his wing with the King's Men. A boy actor, Jonathan started out playing women, his face obscenely painted. And after playing in hundreds of performances in the plays penned by Henry Rothford, the resident playwright, Jonathan broke out on his own, taking Sebastian with him.

Times were certainly changing. After all this time of using boys to play the ladies, they had a woman in the troupe. She was beautiful, spirited, talented. Though the change was desperately needed – a boy could only convey a grown woman's depth and feeling so much – Jonathan sensed it meant disaster. Eleven headstrong and lonely men, with one woman. He needed no astrologer to read the stars on that one.

As he mused his players came backstage to shed their characters along with their clothing; he watched the pile of blood-soaked costumes rise. It was a bloody play with coups and assassinations, a duel between brothers over a woman. Tomorrow would be worse with *The King of Salsima* which conveyed the brutal murder of two very special women. Jonathan hoped he was up to the task.

First he had to survive a dinner party and Duchess Isabella.

TWO

THOMAS WAS VERY drunk, as was his frequent wont at any social gathering. What was not frequent, however, was seeing Jonathan drunk, which greatly amused Thomas. He watched his friend guzzle wine to endure the lecherous caresses of the duchess as well as the inane conversation of the gentry whose obvious disdain of the lowly players grew worse as the night deepened. Their barbs and oh-so-witty quips would soon be met with fists swinging, patron hosts be damned. Thomas despised them with an acidity that burned through his chest and throat.

To distract himself he danced and jigged and entertained the ladies with merry tales of mishaps on stage. Miranda was his most attentive audience, and after several dances he let his arm drape around her shoulders, perhaps once or twice dropping his face into her generous cleavage. By accident merely. His attempts at flirtation were often hindered by young Gregory, who closely followed Thomas to escape the rough hands of some of the duchy's distinguished guests. When he was pulled into a wardrobe, trapped under the fervent kisses of some courtier or other, Thomas nearly drew his sword. He settled instead for yanking on the gentlemen's short beard as hard as he could. When the courtier fell forward with a yelp of pain, Thomas kneed him in the bollocks.

"I think it is nigh time to get you home," Thomas said, and Gregory nodded. "I'll wager Jonathan is ready too."

When he found Jonathan he looked as desperate as Gregory had in the wardrobe, pinned against the wall with the duchess whispering in his ear. If the duchess would but ease her raptor's grip, Thomas knew Jonathan could have his choice of the ladies. He was handsome enough with large, green eyes, sand-colored hair always tightly pulled back with a ribbon, and a jaw and cheekbones most men would kill for. But such gifts, as far as Thomas knew, were wasted. Jonathan was always quick to dismiss inquiries of past conquests, alluding only to a disastrous initiation that he had little desire to repeat.

Thomas drew a breath and squeezed himself in between the duchess and Jonathan. "I beg your pardon, your ladyship, but I must borrow Jonathan. I have questions regarding tomorrow's staging."

"That can wait, surely."

But Jonathan fell against him, gushing thanks as soon as they were out of earshot. "Thomas, that woman is a viper. Take me home, please, I am very drunk."

Outside the night was warm in late summer, the river stunning with its shining lanterns winking like fireflies on the boats. On the other side he could see the outline of the bankside playhouse, the Crown.

Helping Jonathan into a boat Thomas said, "What will you name your playhouse?"

"I know not. The Scourge of Isabella?"

"Plague of the Duchess."

"Rotten, Stinking Pox of the...Oh, never mind. She gave me more money."

"For what services?"

"I shall bite you."

"Oh, not that."

There was a feminine laugh; Thomas whirled and saw Miranda climbing into the boat after Gregory. Thomas doffed his cap and she smiled in the moonlight.

"Back to the Unicorn, is it?" the boatman asked.

"No," Jonathan said. "Take us to the playhouse."

"Really, Jonathan—"

"To the Crown!"

And so they tripped over benches and gallery railings after breaking into the playhouse. Jonathan took his place on the stage while the others sat in the nobleman's box in the gallery nearest the stage, watching their leader stare up at the stars.

"How about a soliloquy, then?" Thomas called, but Jonathan ignored him. He stepped backwards until he was underneath the balcony, and stared up at the celestial paintings on the ceiling that could not have been very visible in the darkness. Thomas felt the mood darkening and hoisted himself over the railing, landing neatly on the stage. With a hand over his heart, he boomed out one of Sebastian's monologues, imitating the older actor's pretentious, overdramatic voice perfectly. Miranda's hysterical laughter egged him on until Jonathan gave him a push.

"That's enough out of you, you rogue. To bed, to bed."

"Aye, aye, to bed. I'll drink to that."

Thomas helped Jonathan up the stairs at the Unicorn, putting him to bed in the room they shared. He had no sooner kicked his boots off than he felt a small hand slide into his, pulling him toward the door. He would claim later that he had no idea how he ended up in Miranda's bed, against Jonathan's orders, and even as she pulled him he invented various excuses: the wine, the moon, the playhouse. Then his face was in delicious golden hair and he no longer cared.

THREE

"IF YOU WOULD hear us patiently, upon this wooden stage, we would relate to you a story of two kings: one a conqueror, the other, conquered. Believe, if you will, as if by some magician's trick, thirty years reversed themselves. A younger King Edward rules here, his ill-fated daughter not yet born. Stand witness to a momentous occasion and see a monstrous bargain born: a young bride sold to free a people, her virtue enslaved to a man's lust. See a treaty broken, a people damned, a son killed. Upon your patient ears, we attend to you, and give you the *King of Salsima*."

Jonathan stood in the wings through the applause that followed the prologue. As it died down he sucked in a breath and followed Sebastian onstage, the two of them playing royal brothers. Sebastian was too old to be playing King Edward, younger by thirty years, but he alone commanded a voice worthy of the part. Jonathan, at seven-and-twenty years, was the perfect age to play the king's younger brother, Chancellor Thaddeus. They strode to center stage; for a moment Jonathan was allowed a glimpse of the audience.

At two in the afternoon, the sun was behind the stage, though rays shone down on the swarms of flies, and the groundlings crowded in the back of the octagonal theater. The galleries were full, and a glance up right revealed courtiers dressed in red around richly dressed gentry in the noblemen's box. The groundlings, their stench making an almost visible cloud, were packed in more tightly than ever. As usual, several sat on the edge of the stage, and Jonathan felt the weight of thousands of pairs of eyes on him.

Sebastian did a flourish that earned him a smattering of applause. Jonathan bowed.

THADDEUS: I wait upon your Majesty's pleasure. You did send for me?

KING EDWARD: That I did, Thaddeus, my trusted chancellor and my brother. Such news I have would hardly be believed. A fortnight ago I received a letter from King Fallon, ruler of that same heathen people the Selphyn that my ancestor, good King Balon, banished near two-hundred years ago.

THADDEUS: What would he?

KING EDWARD: Why, peace and a reconciliation! (*belly laugh*) As a gesture toward alliance, he did offer me the hand of his sister

Syldonia in marriage.

THADDEUS: That were folly enough. Knows he not you are already engaged?

KING EDWARD: He knows well enough now, as we did meet in secret this very morning to hold conference. But I do tell you, Thaddeus, that upon spying the fair visage of that Syldonia, my mind did tremble and shake, so near came I to accepting her.

THADDEUS: My good lord, you jest.

KING EDWARD: In faith, I do not. Never have I beheld such beauty. She is exquisite.

THADDEUS: And a heathen princess, I remind you.

KING EDWARD: In that moment I cared not. At the last moment did I remember me, and told of my engagement.

THADDEUS: What said King Fallon?

KING EDWARD: He offered an alternative. (*dramatic pause*) He said perchance a brother of mine could be tempted into marriage with his sister, thus ensuring an alliance between our two people. I thought it an excellent idea, and as our brother Leonardis is already married –

THADDEUS: My good lord. I pray you, say you did not promise me in marriage to a heathen Selphyn.

KING EDWARD: I did indeed. And when you see her, mark her beauty, you will thank me a thousandfold.

THADDEUS: Wherefore did you so?

KING EDWARD: So that I might look upon her countenance when so e'r I please. And you will grant me, good my brother, my sovereign right, and give me access to her bedchamber as it pleases me.

A loud boo hissed from the audience. Jonathan used the sound to take a pause, which increased the dramatic effect. As he delivered a monologue on the evils of coupling with demons, his mind wandered to the noblemen's box, where Duke Leonardis was no doubt in attendance. It wasn't until this moment that it really occurred to Jonathan that his play might greatly offend the king's brother, and Leonardis could withdraw his patronage. Or worse, he could take his complaints to the king himself. He risked a glance at the box and saw Leon wearing his cap with the ridiculous ostrich feather which must have been blocking the view of everyone behind him. Even as he had the thought, a hand reached up from behind and snatched the feather, holding it in place while the other hand sliced it off with a dagger.

Jonathan almost dropped his next line, but quickly recovered. In the next scene, his character was to meet his bride. When Thomas and Miranda entered the stage, bedecked in Selphyn silks with their skin tanned with paint, Jonathan's mouth dropped open. Thomas was wearing a wig so that his hair matched Fallon's golden curls, and with Fallon's signature raven feather tied in the locks, he looked so much like his character that Jonathan felt a wave of revulsion. His admiration of Miranda, however, was unfeigned. He did an aside to the audience.

THADDEUS: Can this be my future bride? It cannot be. This angel is no more demon-spawn than I. Yet she looks Selphyn enough. Her hair is of that same golden hue as her brother's, her skin a Selphyn bronze, and her eyes — God, how like bright stars — shine in that unearthly light that all Selphyn share. But she is too beautiful, too lovely to be counted among the damned, the forsaken race that once ruled our holy land of Salsima. Archangel Miken forgive me, but I think I love her. (*to Syldonia*) Good lady, if you will have me, I am yours.

SYLDONIA: You will forgive my trepidation, I trust. I do a sister's duty, not that of my heart.

THADDEUS: May your heart find its duty in mine. I will endeavor all to make it so. Sweet princess, will you allow a kiss to seal our bargain?

FALLON: (*holding off Thaddeus*) In doing so you will remember your promise. Our people will soon be allowed to return to our beloved country of Salsima, where our kind will live in peace alongside yours.

KING EDWARD: Yes, yes, you have heard it sworn from my lips; need you my blood too? Brother, kiss your bride.

It was a chaste kiss from which Jonathan had to force himself away. He exchanged a look with Thomas, and shivered again at the close resemblance. Back offstage he listened to his Chorus, voiced by Toby, inform the audience that ten years had passed. King Edward married Lydia, but had yet to produce an heir. Thaddeus and Syldonia were also wed, and born to them was a half-Selphyn child whom Thaddeus named after his king. If King Edward II remained childless, young Prince Edward would inherit the throne as Edward III. The scene opened with three children playing in the palace courtyard; Gregory was young Edward, and Ralf and Andrew played John and Lauren, children that belonged to Syldonia's maid Anne. Anne herself was played by Roland, who had been very put out when told he must don a wig and dress. He and Miranda looked on the children playing with smiles, while Roland laced up Miranda's gown from the back.

SYLDONIA: Look how they play. Such great friends are they.

ANNE: I am, as ever, grateful you took the three of us in, your ladyship. My children, though poor and fatherless, have a family here, and liken young Prince Edward as their brother.

SYLDONIA: And so he is. And you are like my sister, sweet Anne.

ANNE: Tush, tush. I shall weep if you keep on. There, there, John, what play are you three enacting now?

JOHN: Prince Edward and I are knights, and Lauren is the captured princess. We shall rescue her anon from the evil King Edward.

ANNE: (*freezing*) Surely you mean the gallant King Edward.

JOHN: What you will. He is evil to me.

SYLDONIA: Dear Anne, you need not look so shocked. I know well that the king misuses you as he does me.

ANNE: It is of no matter.

SYLDONIA: Nay, but it is! Where I come from no woman is another man's whore against her will, even if he be the king himself. There are no secret passageways between bedchambers, no lurid looks across the table at dinner. You call us heathens, but methinks we are more civilized.

ANNE: Here comes your husband and the king. But who is with them?

SYLDONIA: Alas, it is my brother, King Fallon.

ANNE: He looks not well.

SYLDONIA: Nor should he. The king has not kept his word.

FALLON: You do not keep promise with me, your Majesty. Ten years have passed since I did give my sister in marriage to your brother, and yet you still refuse us entry into Salsima.

KING EDWARD: I find I have had a change of heart.

FALLON: And so have I. If you will not adhere to our agreement, give me my sister back.

KING EDWARD: Nonsense! She and Thaddeus are married. He is her lord and master now, not you.

FALLON: I was never her lord and master. The Selphyn are no man's slaves.

THADDEUS: You do me wrong. She is my wife, not my slave.

FALLON: Yet she is a slave to your king's filthy bed. If you will not release her from the bonds of marriage, then I shall.

Thomas lunged forward, whipping out a dagger from his doublet. The dulled blade slashed through the pig's bladder sewn into the collar of Miranda's dress. Blood spurted out, showering Thomas's face and drenching the white gown. Even though they knew it was coming, several women in the audience screamed, and out of the corner of his eye, Jonathan saw one even faint. A groundling next to the stage shouted, "No!" As Miranda fell, Thomas lunged again and performed the same action to Roland as Anne. The "children" began screaming and running, and a great sword fight broke out between Fallon's Selphyn attendants and those of the king. As Jonathan knew they would, some of the groundlings drew their own swords and jumped on stage, joining in the fray, their real blades against the company's blunted ones.

Thomas, as Fallon, stopped the duel with a shout. "Stop! Where are the children? Where is Prince Edward?" Jonathan shoved him and screamed, "You shall not have him too!" before thrusting his rapier toward Thomas's chest. The thrust was parried, and Jonathan fell to the ground when a blow to his head was feigned. Thomas carried Miranda offstage while one of his attendants carried off Roland. As the mass of actors gave them chase, Jonathan slowly sat up and then knelt, weeping, as he began to deliver what he hoped was a heart-wrenching monologue of despair.

"STOP!"

Jonathan threw his head up and saw the figure in the nobleman's box stand, throwing off his cloak. There were gasps as everyone in the playhouse clumsily fell to one knee. Jonathan closed his eyes. "Oh, bloody, bloody hell."

FOUR

HE WAS STILL in his kneeling position when they came for him, pulling him up by his elbows before securing his wrists behind his back. It all felt very surreal to Jonathan, as if his play had merely deviated from the script for a new plot twist. It hardly even registered when Thomas threw himself at the guards, attacking with his blunted rapier. His face was still covered with pig's blood, and his wig was askew. It wasn't until he saw the guards arresting Thomas as well that Jonathan fully awakened, shouting protests. Someone clubbed him on the head; this blow, unfeigned, blackened his sight for a moment, and he stumbled to the ground. He was half-dragged off the stage, and the galleries, filled with yelling people, tilted at a grotesque angle.

He managed to right himself and saw Henry Rothford, of all people, at the foot of the stage, his long forehead reflecting sunlight. "Well played, Master Wilder. Well played." Jonathan searched his face for irony and saw only concern, and perhaps a touch of awe.

"I wish that meant something," he said before he was pushed forward.

They passed two bear pits and another playhouse before reaching Prisongate. Jonathan looked up at the wrong time and saw a naked corpse hanging from the gallows, gutted and quartered. The kites were feasting on him and had already taken his eyes. His mouth was open, tongue blackened and half-eaten. Jonathan dry-retched and closed his eyes.

He and Thomas were placed in adjacent cells with fetid straw and the tell-tale sound of scurrying rats. Rusted manacles hung from the far wall, and once his eyes adjusted to the gloom Jonathan could see the carved initials in the walls of former tenants. He was still standing, unwilling to sit in the filth, when Leonardis appeared in front of the bars. Fearing tears, Jonathan said nothing.

"I know you are not mad. And yet…You promised me you submitted the play to the Master of the Revels. Had you done so, all would have been prevented."

"Including the playing of *The King of Salsima*."

"Precisely! Do you know how this makes me look? Your patron?"

"I did not know – I did not think – why was the king there? He has never attended one of our plays."

"I, the great fool I, thinking you meant a tribute, implored him to attend."

"Oh, God."

"Yes. And were you anyone else, under anyone else's protection, you would be tried for sedition, found guilty, drawn, quartered and hanged."

There was a sound from Thomas's cell: a muffled cry or whimper. "But you—"

"Yes. I interceded on your behalf. As I did six times before the king finally interrupted your play. Said I, 'Surely he means to honor you by disproving these rumors he set forth.' Then I could restrain him no longer. What did you hope to accomplish? Did you think he would not hear of it?"

"I knew we would have only one playing of it before it was shut down. Once would have been enough."

"To what end?"

Jonathan met his gaze levelly. "To show the truth, just for once."

Leonardis sighed and massaged his brow, which was when Jonathan noticed he was still wearing the cap with only a stub remaining of the ostrich feather. "The truth no one dares to speak. Surely you knew he would not stand for it, that he would crush not only the play but you as well."

"I…"

"Our brother Thaddeus was also in attendance."

Jonathan almost smiled. "Indeed?"

"He was very taken with your performance of him as a younger man. He…though he could not say it, I believe he was grateful for your show of truth."

"As he should have been."

"He still mourns Syldonia's death, though all but twenty years have passed."

"Does not everyone?"

Leon shook his head. "But to the point. Between the two of us, we perhaps persuaded leniency on your behalf."

"And now?"

"And now you must plead your case. Take some of your honeyed poetry and put it in your mouth. Woo his Majesty as you would a goddess. Convince him he missed some vital scene wherein you cleared and trumpeted his name—"

"God."

"Or hang. It is a simple choice, really."

"Am I – am I to go now?"

"That is amusing. You wait upon the king's pleasure, not him to yours. I would say five or six days before you are summoned."

Jonathan sank to the floor, no longer noticing the filth. Leonardis crouched so that they were level. "And Jonathan, you should know that your days as a player here in Salsima are done, at least while the king lives. I can no longer offer my patronage; it would not be seemly. He may let you live, but your plays will most certainly be banished."

After he was gone Jonathan sat in silence for several minutes. His lack of movement coaxed two rats out of hiding; they sniffed his boots and one even walked over his hand. He did not flinch.

"Thomas."

"Yes."

"I am sorry."

There was a pause, and Jonathan heard his friend shifting position in the cell next to him. "I chose to put myself in danger. You are not responsible."

"Why did you so?"

"You…you are the only family I have."

Jonathan squeezed his eyes shut. "Go to, you rogue. I'll not have you making me feel worse." There was a soft chuckle. "But I meant with the play. I put you all in danger."

"That I chose as well. You know the king is no friend of mine."

"Careful. The walls have ears."

Someone was calling out for water, and another was moaning. It was impossible to know how many people with whom they shared their prison house. When Thomas stayed quiet, Jonathan said, "I pray you, speak. Say something to distract me."

"What? Shall we practice lines?"

"To what end? Nevermore shall we perform."

"You are succeeding admirably in keeping yourself distracted."

"Ah. Here is something for you. Do not think, though we may hang, that I have forgotten your transgression."

"My transgression?"

"Last night." There was another pause, and Jonathan felt a flicker of satisfaction. "Yes. Last night. I know you stole away to Miranda's chamber."

"There was no harm in it."

"Yet I forbade it. What will she when you dally with some other wench? If she loves you she may leave our company and–"

"What company?"

Jonathan sighed. "I speak in hypothetical terms. You broke the rule before we were banished."

"Set your mind at rest. She does not love me. 'Twas sport and nothing more."

Jonathan relaxed – a little. He thought of Miranda's shoulders rising from the lowered sleeves of her gown during his play the day before. His mind flickered to that afternoon when Thomas cut the bladder in her collar, dousing her chest and his face with blood.

"That bladder was too full today."

To his pleasure, Thomas laughed. "Saw you my face? It sprayed me as if from a perfume bottle."

"Is it still there?"

"Yes! What a fright I must be. And here is my wig, hanging like a dead animal."

"Ha. You were a formidable creature, make no mistake. How like Fallon you looked."

"I looked in a glass with my face paint and wig in place," Thomas said, sobering. "I almost could not stand my own visage. I shuddered and nearly wept."

"I – I did not know. I am sorry."

"Should we ever have the playing of it again, in some far-off country, _you_ can play Fallon."

"Fair enough."

"It makes sense with your hair. Your complexion too. You are not so fair as I."

Revulsion crept up Jonathan's throat, imagining himself in Selphyn guise. "You played it better than I could have. 'Twas well done, truly."

"Thank you. Even the bull-faced Sebastian played his part well."

"He did. He was a better King Edward than King Edward."

They exchanged a laugh. There was a rustle of skirts and both men scrambled to their feet. Miranda, wearing a simple gown with her face washed clean, stood in front of Jonathan's cell. She held a fat purse in her hand and her eyes were filled with tears.

"What means this?" Jonathan asked.

"I meant to pay your bail. It was refused."

"Oh, sweet lady. Where did you get the money?"

"My parents."

"Give it back to them with my thanks. I am to stand trial, I think, for sedition. There is no bail rich enough to save me." The look on her face made his throat tighten. "You were excellent today as Syldonia. Whatsoe'r may happen with the Duke's Men, you must find another company. Salsima must not be deprived of your charms and talent."

"Do not say that! It is with the Duke's Men alone I shall act. So many times I watched your company perform, and you in particular, and wished myself upon the stage. There is no one else on the stage with so much passion and presence—"

Jonathan was blasted by a wave of heat like the wind blowing flames all around him. She had her hand clenched around a bar in his door; for a moment he allowed himself to touch her hand. Her skin was so white and soft, like a dove's breast. She had not even acknowledged Thomas, with whom she had spent an evening in "sport." Jonathan feared she would, at any moment, leave him so that she might fawn and cry over Thomas. Yet she pulled his fingers through the bars, and for one blessed moment brought them to her lips.

"Oh, God," Jonathan whispered. He was like to hang in a few days, and yet could still not tell her his heart.

She pulled away from him and he half-expected to see his arm severed at the shoulder, his fingers still entwined in hers. "I must go."

"If – if I should not fare well with the king, will you watch over Gregory?"

"Yes, but you mustn't–" She covered her face with her hands. "I cannot stay."

She ran from him and he lowered himself back to the floor. The stone was freezing now to his overheated skin.

"Like you this?" Thomas said. "She says nothing to me! Not even a dog whose head she might pat, though it was cradled between her breasts only a few hours ago."

"Thomas, I am very glad you are here."

FIVE

IT WAS SIX days before he was sent for, led to the palace by the king's men in their livery of black and burgundy. The king's crest flapped in the wind on the parapets, making the diving falcon with talons outstretched look as if it were actually flying. The soldiers had to fight through a crowd on the bridge; word must have spread that Jonathan was to have his audience with the king. He kept his head down while they jeered at him, many of them demanding his execution. Some of those people, he was sure, had watched the play, rapt and excited, and now that he was pulled down they hated him. Insulting the king is acceptable only if one gets away with it.

They held him in place at the foot of the dais, filthy and half-deranged with exhaustion as he was. A handsome, blond courtier in his mid-twenties stepped into his vision, smirking. "What will you play today? *The King's Whore?*" Jonathan sighed while the others laughed, and was relieved when the king arrived so that the chamber fell silent. He went down on one knee, silently screaming at the pain in his stiff joints. His kneecap hardly touched the ground before he was wrenched back up to his feet.

"So. This is our seditious playwright," King Edward said, sitting on his throne, his palsied hands trembling on the armrests while his ample girth sagged over the edges of his seat. His eyes were rheumy and bloodshot, and Jonathan could not help but hope he would conveniently drop dead. Chancellor Thaddeus and Duke Leonardis stood to his right; Jonathan could not look at either one.

"Your Majesty."

"Well? And what have you to say for yourself? My brother, your patron, is most assured I interpreted your play in error. You may explain."

Jonathan sucked in a breath. A few nights before he had prepared a speech; now, as he stood trembling before the king, all rehearsed words fled. He said, "I do apologize, your Majesty, that I caused offense with my play."

"Your terrible play, I might add."

Jonathan met his gaze squarely. When he spoke again, his voice was steel, and the king smiled. "Yes. My terrible play."

"Before you explain what you *did* mean to convey by insinuating relations between myself and Lady Syldonia, I believe you owe my chancellor an apology for calling his wife a whore."

Jonathan snapped his head in Thaddeus's direction; the king's chancellor looked just as stunned as Jonathan felt. "My lord Chancellor, I – I never called your wife a whore, and would suffer a thousand torments before doing so. Did I not present her in a pleasing light?"

Thaddeus's eyes softened. "Perhaps–"

"You implied, by no discreet means, that I had relations with my brother's late wife," Edward said. "In doing so, you called his wife a whore. Can you deny it?"

Jonathan's face flushed with heat. "I can and will. Forced relations, against a woman's will, do not a whore make."

Snickering gave way to gasps, and out of the corner of his eye Jonathan saw Leon's head drop. Thaddeus was staring at him with an expression he could not read. And the king's face was the color of congealed blood.

"What say you?"

He would die for it, but there was no going back anyway. He realized he may as well go out with courage. "Rape does not a whore make."

Edward was on his feet, pointing and bellowing. "How dare you! How dare you! You make this assertion on what grounds?"

"On the grounds that I was there. I saw it, heard it. I know you took her *and* her maid against their wills. You are a damned–"

Someone clubbed him hard in the head. He fell to his knees and saw stars. Over the roaring of his head he heard the distant echoes of the king's screaming, the orders for his death first by beheading, then hanging, then the king's own hand. He considered struggling against his captors to ensure he died a swift and merciful death, but lacked the strength.

Hands grabbed at him as he was dragged out of the audience chamber, the shouts in his ear deafening. He assumed they would take him back to Prisongate and execute him right then and there, stringing him up next to the limbless corpse that was still hanging. Instead they were stopped in the courtyard by Leonardis. Jonathan could not hear what he told the guards over the din of the crowd's yelling, but he was taken back into the palace through a side entrance, forced to climb stairs though he could hardly walk.

He once had the run of the palace, and though it was almost twenty years ago that he had been inside he still knew they were taking him to Thaddeus's chambers. That he was left in there alone with the chancellor seemed miraculous; as the chancellor studied him he took in the rows and rows of books on shelves that covered almost every available wall space.

"I know who you are," Thaddeus said. Jonathan's pulse accelerated. He blanched when the older man approached him and reached for his face, and then relaxed when he felt a soft handkerchief on his temple. "You are bleeding."

"I was not aware of it."

"Are you hurt badly?"

"Yes. No. I'm…I'm not sure."

Thaddeus stepped back to take him in. Reluctantly Jonathan met his gaze. "For a wild moment, I allowed myself to hope you were my son in there. I wanted it so badly I nearly died. You look like him well enough, though you always did. The servants were always confusing the two of you, particularly when you were both wearing costumes."

"My lord?"

"You need not feign confusion. Leon has known ever since he offered you his patronage who you were. It was I who needed convincing. And after your impassioned display in court, I believe."

He sat down in a plush armchair and offered Jonathan its twin into which he fell. He closed his eyes to let a spell of dizziness pass; when he opened them Thaddeus was smiling at him. The youngest of the three brothers, Thaddeus was also the shortest. He lacked Leon's gauntness and prominent joints; like his eldest brother the king his face was round and tended to be rosy, as if perpetually caught in a blush.

"You are John Warden, son of my late wife's maid, Anne. You have nothing to fear from me; you may speak candidly."

"I – I do not know what I should say, my lord."

"Say I am right, for one."

"Very well. I…I lived here as a child, and I loved you and your wife very well."

Jonathan's brow kneaded to see the chancellor's eyes fill with unexpected tears. "Forgive this display. I miss my son exceedingly; you make me think on him."

"I miss him also."

"You found his body."

"Yes."

Thaddeus looked out the window; Jonathan followed his gaze and saw a gargoyle holding up a stone ledge, its forked tongue extended. "Why did you both hide under the church? Why did you not come to me? I was mad with worry."

"Forgive me. It was Prince Edward's idea. He feared his uncle Fallon meant to kill him too along with our mothers. He bade me hide with him in the Selphyn ruins under the cathedral, where none were sure to find us."

"Did he not know his father would protect him?"

"You forget we were but ten years old. We were young and frightened; we just witnessed our mothers being murdered. He meant to come to you within a fortnight, when the danger was sure to have passed. But…"

"It was you who sent word to me of the plague? It was a child's hand."

"Yes. He bade me sneak into the palace for food and blankets. When I returned the trapdoor leading down was locked, and days passed before I regained access. I found him covered in boils and sores, and it was very much too late. Forgive me. I see it pains you to hear of it."

A tear slid down Thaddeus's cheek. "It was bad enough losing Syldonia. And then my only son …" He wiped the tear aside. "Why did you remain hidden? Why did you not come to me yourself, rather than send the letter informing me of Edward's death?"

"I heard the king's men were looking for me."

"Yes."

"I never knew what they wanted of me. I was afraid."

"Your sister, she too fled."

"Yes."

"And where is she now?"

"I do not know. I never saw her again."

"Miken's sweet life. So many lives ruined that day."

"Do you know why they were looking for me?"

"The queen sent them."

"The queen?"

"She was expecting the king's heir. She could not have any bastards threatening her child's claim to the throne."

In spite of his pounding headache, Jonathan jumped to his feet. "I am no son of the king, my lord. I object most heartily."

Thaddeus raised his eyebrow. "How can you know for sure?"

"My mother's womb was quick before she was taken in by Syldonia."

"You have but her word for it."

"And you abuse her honor by suggesting it does not suffice! She was four months gone, and showing."

Thaddeus laughed. "Sit down, boy, sit. No one is threatening your mother's integrity. But there was speculation that the king knew her, in the religious sense, before she became my wife's maid. It is said he used his influence to secure her employment here when she told him she was carrying his bastard."

"How you all love to talk! Nobles with their rich blood, high and mighty above the rest, yet they'll gossip worse than a dairymaid."

Thaddeus was silent a moment. "Do you know who your father is?"

"No. He died before I was born."

"Well, then. And she an unmarried widow at the time. You can see how such rumors are started."

"She was an unmarried widow after I was conceived! Lauren and I share the same father; she remembered him, a fishmonger or some sort. Leave off."

"Such informal speech to your betters. Tsk, tsk." Jonathan spun and saw Leonardis standing behind him, smiling in a way that now infuriated him. "You and Lauren looked nothing alike, she with her dark hair and eyes, and you with your light hair and green eyes. And looking so like the prince. As if you shared the same blood."

Jonathan dug his nails into the chair's arm; the brothers heard it and exchanged a glance.

"I think you can understand now why such conclusions were born in certain people," Leon said. "And anyway, such speculations just may save your pathetic life."

"Good sir. I am in your debt for all the service, protection and money you have afforded me. But now I see it is quite clear the king was not in attendance by mere chance. Nor was I, I think, in your protection by chance. This is but some grandiose scheme I have not the cleverness to understand. Because I think I am ill-used in your hands, I will beg you not to insult me. I am not that bastard's bastard."

Leon waved his hand. "What you will. It matters not if you are or not. It is merely the possibility that you could be that matters. When I tell the king who you are, he may grant you clemency."

"Let him hang me. It were better than claiming he is my father."

Leon moved up closer. "Have you ever attended a public execution for treason or sedition?"

"No. I do not find sport in violence."

"Well. It's not the hanging that kills you." Leon settled into a third chair, arranging his robes until he was comfortable. "If your executioner is skilled, you will still be alive when the trapdoor drops. Still alive when he slices you open from nave to chops. Still alive when he cuts off your privates. And alive still when he shoves his fist into your chest to rip out your still-beating heart. You'll be dead of course when he pulls out your guts and cuts off your arms and legs. Or wait. Do I mistake me? Thaddeus, does he pull out the guts first and then the heart?"

"Enough! I am grasping your point vividly."

"You'll see it all first-hand. I'll have him do your friend Thomas first."

Jonathan's head fell forward and a heaving sob constricted his chest. "In God's name, what will you have me do?"

"Nothing, really. Just commit the most vile treason imaginable."

SIX

LAUREN STOOD IN a line with the other servants, their hands held out, palms down, for inspection. Her nails were deemed unclean, so she scrubbed them again in scalding water. This time, when she offered them for re-inspection, her fingers were raw and red. She was given leave to serve wine at dinner, expected to wait in the corner should any goblets go dry. Because she had to scrub her hands again, the guest for dinner was already seated, his goblet empty. Lauren blushed under the filthy look from her mistress, and her hand trembled as she poured the wine for Gideon Ambrose.

Once the other goblets were filled she took her place in the corner, staring straight ahead while her hair felt hot and sweaty under her cap. She was not in the least tempted to steal glances at Master Ambrose, though the other girls called him devilishly handsome. He wore his light hair short and wore gold hoop earrings in each ear. He had started the fashion of sporting long sideburns with just a tuft of hair on the chin, and whatever his cut of doublet was that week became the same cut among most gentlemen of the court.

It was rare for her master and mistress to have only one guest for dinner, but if Gideon Ambrose felt honored he did not show it. He monopolized the conversation, laughed loudly, and showed entirely too much ease with the duke and duchess that outranked him. His loudness made it difficult for Lauren to let her mind wander, and snatches of conversation forced themselves into her attention.

"And to him said I, 'What will you play today, *The King's Whore*'?" Gideon said. The duke and duchess laughed politely. "And then he – I still doubt my ears. I doubted my very sanity when next he spoke."

"It was absolutely shocking," Duchess Isabella said. "That my dear Jonathan, or whatever his name is, should have spoken like that to the king! When I think how often he was our guest, in our confidence...I am sure we are the laughingstock."

"Hardly, my dear," Duke Leonardis said.

"I expected to witness his execution right there," Gideon said. "And yet now you tell me he is not to be executed at all? On what grounds, I ask you?"

Gideon finished his wine and Lauren was instantly at his side with the decanter.

"He is that same John Warden whose parentage has always been in question. He may very well be the king's only surviving heir."

Lauren's hand shook and the wine spilled on the white tablecloth. Gideon stared at her until her face caught fire. She curtsied and mumbled an apology, slinking back to her corner.

"With what proof?"

"Well, he looks like a Boussard, for one. For another, it was widely known that his mother was the king's mistress." Leon laughed. "And here he is, writing a play about it, yelling at the king that he *raped* his mother, and yet he refuses to acknowledge the possibility he is the king's bastard."

"Where is he now?"

Lauren was unaware she had spoken aloud until three pairs of eyes turned incredulously in her direction. Isabella gasped and contorted her face, as if Lauren had defecated on the floor.

It was Leon who finally spoke. "Who?"

"The playwright. J-John." She dipped into another curtsy. "I beg your pardon. I forgot myself."

"Indeed you have," Isabella said. "You are dismissed. Send Sarah in your place."

"Yes, ma'am."

She turned to go, her ears burning. In the corridor she heard Leonardis say, "What is her name?"

"Lauren," Isabella said. "Since when do you show an interest in the names of your servants?"

"Have we had her long?"

"Oh, only seventeen years!"

Forgetting completely about Sarah, Lauren ran upstairs to the servants' quarters to change her clothes. It never occurred to her that bursting out of the house without leave might jeopardize her employment; her only thought was that after seventeen years she finally knew that John was alive. And just barely by the sound of it.

She stripped off her uniform and wrenched off her cap, setting loose a cascade of long, straight chestnut hair. She put on the only dress she owned apart from her uniform, the muslin scratching her bare calves. Then shoes, a cloak and her purse; she had saved most of her wages which would hopefully pay John's bail, or at least bribe a guard.

She flew down the stairs, taking the corner at an alarming speed. A hand clamped over her forearm, spinning her so that she nearly fell. She screamed and dropped her purse as fingernails dug into her skin. Gideon Ambrose pulled her in against him, his breath stinking of wine.

"In a hurry, are we?" His fingers tightened and tears sprang to Lauren's eyes.

"Please—"

"Off to sell my ring? I think not."

He released her to pick up her purse. He turned it upside-down and shook it; coins clattered and bounced on the floor, the sound echoing through the house like hail. He threw the empty purse to the ground with a curse before grabbing each of her forearms and shaking her.

"Where is it? Where?"

"I – I don't—"

"Gideon? Lauren! What on earth—"

Gideon released one of her arms so he could turn to face Isabella. "Some clever thief you have here, madam. She slipped my signet ring so deftly I felt nothing. And now she is off to pawn it though it be hidden somewhere in her person—"

"Nonsense," Leonardis said. "She is no thief. Your signet ring was already missing. I marked its absence when we shook hands upon your arrival."

The blood drained from Gideon's face. "You – you are quite certain?"

"Yes. Completely."

Gideon looked at her and Lauren blushed fiercely. If only he would let go so she could pick up her money and be gone. Isabella stepped in front of her, her shoes grinding against dropped coins.

"Lauren? What are you playing at? Stealing away in the middle of dinner, without leave? Where did you think you were going?"

"Prisongate. To see my brother, if he is there."

"Your brother?"

"Yes, my brother. John."

Isabella gasped. Leonardis said, "He is not allowed visitors."

Tears spilled over her cheeks. "I have to try!"

Isabella snatched up a handful of coins and hurled them at Lauren. She pulled out of Gideon's grasp to shield her face; the edge of a shilling hit her forehead.

"Go then! Do not let *me* hinder you. Only the gracious duchess who took you in when you had nowhere to go. Please. Feel no obligation or concern for *me*. I shall endeavor to help by dismissing you. Permanently."

Lauren knelt to retrieve her coins, listening to the departing click of Isabella's heels. A beat later Gideon was kneeling beside her, dropping coins in her purse. They worked silently, and once all the coins were replaced she glanced at him. He looked at her forehead, his lips parting. "You're bleeding."

"It is but a scratch."

He pulled a handkerchief from his sleeve and dabbed at her forehead. She saw the blood smeared over his initials as he pulled it away. "I owe you an apology."

"Please. It is unnecessary."

"No. My behavior has no excuse. And now you are without employment."

She shook her head, and they rose to their feet. "That was not your doing."

"Still. I wish to make amends. I could use another servant, someone to send messages and other such trifles. Will you accept?"

She was flabbergasted, and could barely manage a curtsy. "You are too kind."

"This may be the last moment you experience such a sentiment." She might have laughed, had she not seen he was in earnest. "Will you come? I find I have no stomach after discovering the loss of my ring."

She took a step forward and then paused. "I shall. But...I must attend to this business with my brother first. May I have your leave?"

Leonardis, who watched their exchange with mild interest, said, "As I said before, he is allowed no visitors. The guards have strict orders."

"If nothing else, I can send him a message. I must go to him."

Leon nodded. "Very well. I am sorry...my wife..."

"I expected no less," Lauren said, and dropped into another curtsey. "My lord has always been kind. Thank you."

On the cobblestones outside, they waited for Leon's groomsman to retrieve Gideon's horse. A half moon was reflected in the fountain, and a heron slept on one foot in the water, its silhouette majestic in the moonlight.

"He mocks me," Gideon said. "The Ambrose crest is a heron, and he comes to mock the theft of my ring."

"Perhaps it will turn up."

"Perhaps. Now, this business with your brother. He is the king-slandering playwright?"

"As I understand."

"Sweet Miken." Gideon laughed. "Be grateful you are not attending his hanging. He should on all accounts be in Prisongate." Lauren nodded, and Gideon sighed. His black gelding was led forward, his hooves echoing on the cobblestones. "And this cannot wait until morning?"

"Please, I – it's been seventeen years–"

"I suppose we can make a stop on the way to my estate." He swung up in the saddle and held out a hand. The groom gave her a boost, and she landed neatly on the back of Gideon's horse. After some hesitation she put her hands on his waist to keep her balance.

The horse's trotting gait made her teeth clatter, and within minutes, her legs, unaccustomed to riding, began to ache. Gideon did not speak, and soon they were riding over the bridge on the Reyne River. Dozens of boat lanterns lit up the water, bobbing up and down in a gentle current. Several bats flew overhead, and beside them were two carts carrying bears in cages. Overtaking a third cage, Lauren expected to see another bear. Instead a wolf stared at her with amber eyes, and she jumped before settling down with sympathy. The wolf's head hung dejectedly, and tufts of fur were missing, no doubt from fights with dogs or bears. She longed to touch it, and imagined reaching through the bars to scratch his head behind the ears. He slunk to the floor, head between his paws, and closed his eyes. Then Gideon's horse overtook the cart, and the wolf was out of sight.

Gideon tethered his horse on a post outside Prisongate, and nodded across the road at a tavern. "You shall find me there when your business is concluded."

Leon's prediction proved true, and Lauren was not granted admission. The guards were not swayed by her tears or even the whole of her purse, but finally assented to delivering a message. Growing up with the prince of the realm yielded some advantages, for unlike most servants, Lauren had been schooled, and could read and write. The guards were amazed to watch her scribble out a letter with an old, moldy quill. She told John she would keep trying to see him; in the meantime, she was now in the employ of Gideon Ambrose, should he need to find her. In her frustration to be so close to him yet unable to see him, she began to weep again.

She was still wiping her eyes in the common room of the tavern, looking through throngs of seedy people in the dim lighting for Gideon. He was at a table by himself, finishing off a mug of ale. "Back already?" He tripped over a chair and Lauren rushed to his side to hold him up. "Thank you, Katherine."

"Lauren."

"Yes, Lauren. I am in my cups after Leon's wine and now a cup or two of sack. I may need assistance in getting to my horse."

"Of course." She allowed him to put his arm around her shoulder.

"Did you find your brother?"

"They would not let me see him."

"That is because he is a traitorous villain."

Lauren sighed.

They rode a good fifteen minutes through town, the horse deftly picking his way through drunk peasants, mangy cats and heaps of dung. Lauren was surprised Gideon's estate was on the other side of the river from most of the noble houses, but when she saw that it was a stone's throw from the palace she understood. Gideon, as the king's favorite courtier, must always be available to attend his Majesty. Lauren felt a tumultuous turning of her stomach at the thought of the king; Gideon straightened when her fingers tightened on his waist.

As if it were the most natural thing in the world, Gideon's footman caught him as he slipped sideways out of the saddle. Lauren was forgotten, and had to dismount while the horse was being led to the stable. She caught up with Gideon only to dance backwards as a sleepy woman with wild, blonde hair fell into his arms. He kissed her nosily while Lauren blushed; when she cleared her throat the woman, buxom in a low-cut nightgown, broke away and stared at her.

"Who the bloody hell is that?"

Her dialect suggested Diernioch peasantry, and though Lauren was of the same stock, she learned her dialect growing up in the palace. And as Lauren predicted, the woman's gaze narrowed when she heard her speak, as if Lauren were pretentious. It had been a problem anytime a new servant was employed in Leonardis's household, but like animals they soon sensed Lauren's submission, and tolerated her elevated manner of speaking.

"How do you do, miss?"

"My new servant. Katherine."

"Lauren."

"Right. Meet my mistress Helen."

He nuzzled her throat and she laughed, not at all affronted by his off-color introduction. Lauren curtsied, which went ignored. She relaxed when the housekeeper was sent for, and listened to a no-

nonsense lecture on the way to the servants' quarters. Occasionally Mrs. Givens would glance behind her to take in Lauren's dress and her unkempt hair. She was shown to her bed which Lauren would have gratefully fallen upon were it not for the loaded look in Mrs. Givens's eye.

"You may think, miss, with your fancy manner of speaking, and because the master fancies you, that you're better than the rest of us."

"No, no. I was simply raised in—"

"We won't be having that here. I've been the master's housekeeper for nigh twelve years, and I won't have a highfaluting hussy thinking the rules are beneath her."

"I assure you—"

"Well. Here's your bed, then. I expect to see you at dawn in the kitchen."

"Yes, ma'am."

"Don't know what the master was thinking. You're not even pretty. Or young."

Lauren's cheeks ignited. "Goodnight, Mrs. Givens."

The housekeeper snorted. "Offended, are you? You're highfaluting, all right. See you in the morning."

She took her candle with her, leaving Lauren alone in the dark. She sensed eyes on her in the darkness, and her hands trembled as she unclasped her cloak. Her head on a cold, scratchy pillowcase, she thought of John, who must have been cold and lonely too in his cell. Something Duchess Isabella said suddenly materialized in her mind and she froze. *That my dear Jonathan, or whatever his name is, should have spoken like that to the king! When I think how often he was our guest, in our confidence…*

Their *guest*. She had made inquiries all over town, questioning nearly every servant and shopkeeper, in her search for her missing brother. And he had been a guest in her mistress's house, and several times by the sound of it. He had been within a hand's reach, and now she could not get to him. She wept until she fell asleep, dreaming of him.

SEVEN

THOMAS WAS THE first one to see him, walking like the dead through the yard at the Unicorn. Thomas was sitting on their stage which rested on tied barrels, a sad-looking thing after performing on the grandiose stage of the Crown playhouse. When he saw Jonathan he vaulted off the platform and ran to him, squeezing out his breath.

"Thank God you're alive! How came you to be released? They sent me home and would not say if you were to be hanged or no — we have been beside ourselves with worry. Why look you so glum? What happened?"

"If you would but stop your mouth, I shall tell you all."

"Oh. Sorry."

He was glad to see the whole of his company on the stage, as if waiting for him to arrive to position them and give them lines. Which was, more or less, what he had come to do.

"Sit down, everyone," he said when they surrounded him, pulling on him, embracing him, demanding answers. "I will explain. Do but sit down."

They crowded on the edge of the stage, looking up expectantly at him like children at lessons. He sighed and massaged his forehead. He was terribly thirsty and hungry, but refused to indulge himself until he had this rotten business taken care of. He felt like the father of eleven large and wonderful children, who was tasked with the burden of telling them an awful truth about nature, one that would forever rob them of their innocence. For a moment he blinked back tears.

"I'm afraid...I'm afraid I've gotten you all into a spot of trouble, and your only wrongdoing is your association with me. It is hardly fair, for I must ask of you a terrible favor, one which, I fear, you cannot refuse." He paused to get his bearings and found he could no longer look his players in the eye. "You have, no doubt, heard something of my outburst in court?"

There were nods, and Thomas was the only one comfortable enough to call him mad. He smiled ruefully.

"I should have hanged for such an offense. And yet I have been released. Our good patron, Leonardis, is to thank for that, though I use the word lightly. What I am about to relate to you is highly confidential. If you repeat it, I am assured you will be killed. If you would not be privy to such information, leave now, and perhaps I can persuade Leonardis to leave you be."

No one stirred, and he felt both gratitude and guilt. He looked pointedly at Miranda; she held his gaze and nodded. He released a breath.

"Very well. I thank you, though you may yet regret your decision. My life has been spared because the king thinks I may be his bastard." Over the noise of their reactions, he continued, though he kept his voice low in case of passers-by. It was still early enough in the morning that the tavern was not yet stirring, but he had to be careful. "It matters not why he thinks so; I will not waste time telling you a long story that does not relate to the matter at hand. The story that I must needs tell you, is about the Selphyn and the king's daughter."

He was met with a stony silence, which he predicted. Leonardis had also used this dramatic tactic when he related the particulars to Jonathan, and achieved the same result: utter amazement and complete attention.

"You all know this bedtime story, at least part of it, yes? When Queen Lydia gave birth to their daughter, the midwife kidnapped the infant and stole away in the snow. Her body was later found, ravaged by wolves, with the child missing and presumed to have been carried off. What you do not know, is this. After killing his sister, King Fallon returned to Salsima some months later to claim his nephew, Prince Edward, in order to raise him, so we are told, with the Selphyn. He found instead a corpse, rotted with the plague. He blamed the king. When he discovered that Queen Lydia was in her lying-in to give birth to their only child, he bribed the midwife to take the child in revenge."

Miranda gasped and covered her mouth. Thomas's gaze was hardened, and Jonathan knew he had already grasped the situation, and had probably jumped ahead to guess what Jonathan was going to ask of them.

"The wolves that attacked were white wolves, and you all know they are the demonic agents of the Selphyn. They killed the midwife, but preserved the child. She lives still. She resides with the Selphyn, on their island of Rowan."

Sebastian pushed off the stage, his face bloated. "Raised with heathens!"

Bored already with Sebastian's predictable reaction, Jonathan closed his eyes. "Yes. Raised with heathens. And now they want to send her back."

Again there was a merciful silence. Miranda looked star-struck, caught up in the romance and drama of the whole thing, not yet grasping the implications. The others were beginning to shift uncomfortably.

"A letter was sent to Chancellor Thaddeus. Fallon claims he sees the error of his ways, and wishes to make amends. He wants to reunite the princess, now seventeen, with her parents." He quickly put up a hand when Sebastian started to bellow. "Yes. It is an obvious ruse. He means to put a Selphyn sympathizer on the throne of Salsima, who will one day allow the Selphyn to return."

When it was clear they were no longer listening, Jonathan entered the quiet tavern through a side door, helping himself to a decanter of wine. He managed to drink a full glass before Thomas dragged him back outside to finish his narrative. By then they had calmed considerably, though their eyes shone with apprehension. Jonathan cleared his throat.

"If the king and queen were to discover that their only child lives, they would welcome her back with open arms, undoing two-hundred years of progress. Leonardis and Thaddeus will not let that happen. They mean to send false emissaries to Rowan to escort the princess home. Only she will not be coming home. You understand now, I think, the severity of the situation."

"Oh, God," Miranda whispered. "We?"

"Fallon requested one Gideon Ambrose, by name, to be ambassador. He knows of the courtier's reputation as the king's favorite, and may be aware of Gideon's basic attributes: he has light hair and green eyes." Jonathan bowed. "According to Leon, I am the perfect candidate. I was raised in court – another story, some other time – and am aware of courtly ways and behavior. I am not loyal to the king, nor do I bear the Selphyn any love. I have good reason to hate them both. But more than that, Leonardis has my head on a platter, and he knows it. If I fail, I shall die. And now you too."

Ralf was shaking and stood up, pointing at Jonathan. "Why us then? Just you. You with your rash, importunate mouth! Why should we be punished?"

Thomas answered for him. "One man cannot escort a princess home, you fool. There must be others. Guards, a lady-in-waiting…"

Miranda's eyes filled with tears and Jonathan's heart lurched. He should have sent her home to her parents.

"Thomas has the truth of it. A monk was also requested, a

Brother Dominick." He glanced at Sebastian whose countenance transformed. Jonathan knew what he was thinking; Sebastian would see no delineation between himself and his character. He would try to convert the Selphyn. "And a bard, no doubt to witness this grand occasion and compose a ballad celebrating the many charms of the Selphyn. Fallon requested his Majesty's favorite harper, Horatio. Thomas, I fear this is your role. You have a pleasing voice and can alone play the harp."

"You fear?"

"Horatio is foppish and terribly dull. It will not be pleasant for you. For either of us, really. I am told Gideon is famous for his reputation of being rash, impetuous, passionate and arrogant. Gregarious and lively. Everything I am not."

"Would that we could change places," Thomas said.

"My life upon it. The rest of you will be guards. Leonardis will be coming presently to provide you with the king's livery, and horses for all of us. We start for Rowan today."

"No. No, no," Ralf said, still standing. "I won't. I refuse. I will not endure the Selphyn because you offended the king."

"Ah, but your friend has not spoken of the rewards."

All heads turned to take in Leonardis. As promised he brought with him eleven horses – Jonathan had his own – on a large cart, along with a trunk ostensibly filled with clothing. He made a grand gesture, as if Master of the Revels. Jonathan despised him.

"If you succeed, you shall have your playhouse, name it what you will. And a grand house to live in. Several-hundred pounds for each of you."

Jonathan thought of his face when asked how he would afford such promises. *When I am king, I can afford anything I choose.* The chill in Jonathan's spine returned. Though Leonardis might keep promise with the others, Jonathan did not expect to survive. After all, a possible heir, bastard or no, would interfere with Leonardis's plans for the throne. And King Edward thought him still safely locked up in Prisongate. They could not keep up this ruse forever.

Back in his role as wise and generous benefactor, Leonardis handed out clothing from the trunk, taking pains to compliment each actor and provide wardrobe assistance. He was especially attentive to Miranda, holding up beautiful dresses against her body. She touched silk and velvet, her eyes shining with longing. Leon gave Jonathan a lascivious wink.

"It is no secret Gideon has a lover, a certain Helen Devorak, one of her Majesty's ladies. You play the role of the lover well. You should have no trouble making your affections for this lovely lady convincing."

Jonathan was too angry to blush, but he saw the color rising on Miranda's cheeks. He turned his attention to Sebastian, who was belting his monk's robe and looking completely at ease with his attire. Leonardis pulled out a velvet doublet slashed with gold silk and handed it to Jonathan.

"Only the best for Gideon Ambrose. Ah, I nearly forgot me. Here." He pulled a ring from his pocket and dropped it in Jonathan's hand. He squinted and saw the tiny letters spelling AMBROSE under a heron in flight. "Gideon's signet ring. It is the little details that will ward off suspicion."

"You stole this?"

"It is of no consequence. He can afford to have another made. And here is a map that will see you to Zirnich where you may seek passage to Rowan. I estimate your journey will take ten to fourteen days, and you must not delay your departure. He is expecting you within a fortnight."

"This is madness," Jonathan said. "Will you not call an end to this farce?" He gestured at his actors, young Gregory in particular. "You cannot expect us to succeed. Someone will drop his guard."

Leon patted Jonathan's shoulder. "I have the utmost faith in your company's abilities. And there is too much to be gained in your success, and too much to lose in your failure. Now. There is one last thing. See yonder fellow in black? Yes. He. His name is Richard and he will be accompanying you. He will be *attending* to her Highness."

"He is an assassin?"

"You need not look so scandalized. You have your trade, he has his. There is food and provisions packed in each saddlebag. Leave at once, and report back to me upon your return to Diernioch." He saw the look on Jonathan's face and softened. "Someday you will not despise me as you do now. As a gesture of my good faith, I will have construction started immediately on your playhouse. It may even be finished by the time you return."

"The playhouse I can never use."

"The king is ill, and daily grows more weak. I think you can come out of hiding within the year."

Thomas strummed the harp Leonardis gave him, singing a song from one of Jonathan's plays.

Depart, O Death, cold mistress
Your lover bids you adieu
Let us not meet
Whilest still the yew tree grows
And maidens dance upon the earth
Until then I would not have you
Though you beckon and woo
Get you gone; I'll no more of you

"Miken's wounds," Jonathan said. "Can you not sing something of a more cheerful note?"

Thomas gave him a stony glare. "You did write it, not I."

The biting tone cut him to the quick. He turned to Leonardis. "You see how well they love me for this."

"They will thank you when all is done."

"And with such encouraging words, I leave you."

"God's speed, my lad." He held out his hand for Jonathan to shake.

Quoting his song, Jonathan said, "'Get you gone; I'll no more of you.'"

"Ha, ha, but I do like your spirit. Here's money for you; see it well spent. I look forward with great eagerness to our next meeting."

Jonathan tied the purse to his belt, using the action as an excuse to look away when Leonardis turned to leave. He walked through actors trying on black and burgundy tunics; for a moment he pretended they were dressing for a performance. He paid the innkeeper for the month's rent, then went to the stables to saddle his horse. He passed by the stalls that held their props, costumes and set pieces, and could not look at them. His mare, whom Thomas christened Saucy Wench, threw her head over the stall door when she smelled him coming. He pressed his forehead against her brown one, thinking of the many times he found solace in her company. Like many misanthropes, he preferred the company of animals over that of man.

"There's a good lass," he said when she nuzzled his neck. She sniffed his jerkin for apples, and finding none, tossed her head up and down. "Your master is remiss. I brought no treats, only the promise of a long journey. Ah, but you love me still. I am not betrayed in you."

He led her out of the stables, looking past his players to the road that would lead them out of Diernioch. He followed it with his eye until it disappeared behind a tall hill's zenith, creating the impression that it simply led to the sky. And it may as well have, for all Jonathan cared.

To the right of him he could see the distant outlines of the playhouses along the river. As he watched the sunlight washed over them, slowly creeping up so that they glowed in the late dawn.

Sebastian, cowled and pious, walked toward him with his hands folded. "Master Ambrose, the day grows late. Shall we depart?"

Jonathan sighed and straightened. "Yes, Brother Dominick. By all means, let us depart."

EIGHT

SIR FRANCIS RATHNAR just completed the finishing touches on his appearance when there was a frantic knocking at his door. He took a last glance at his reflection in the tall glass, ensuring all was in order. He was dressed in black velvet and hose, his long hair immaculately combed, single hoop earring in place that matched the heavy gold medallion he wore on a thick chain. He gave a nod of satisfaction; he looked ready to sit for a portrait. He wrenched open the door, as the knocking did not cease, and stared at Thaddeus's short steward Claude.

Claude started at his appearance though he was no stranger to their Majesties' principal secretary. Rathnar was accustomed to this reaction, often overhearing superstitious remarks to ward off evil. He used people's fear to his advantage in running affairs of state for the king and queen, earning the informal title of the realm's spymaster. Well over six feet tall, Rathnar knew he was imposing, with his white skin, long, gaunt face and midnight-black hair. Some called him vampire, others phantom. His reputation so preceded him that when suspects were brought in for questioning, they often spilled everything they knew before Rathnar could even form a question. Torture devices were rarely necessary.

"Well?"

"Sir. You requested intelligence pertaining to the Selphyn."

"You have – come in."

Rathnar gestured toward a chair in his antechamber, choosing to stand while Claude obediently sat. He was aware that Claude was lightly shaking.

"I have a letter–"

"Give it me."

Rathnar read the letter three times, his disbelief increasing each time. "Why was I not informed? This letter concerns me; I am requested by name along with Gideon."

"Sir. Ah, yes. They – I do not believe Master Ambrose was informed either. In fact, he was heard railing in court late last night that his signet ring had gone missing."

Rathnar stared at Claude until the latter began to squirm. "They are sending false emissaries in our place."

"It would seem the case. At least in Master Ambrose's place."

"Your meaning?"

"I caught sight of a draft in my master's hand addressed to Fallon. He regretted you were indisposed for such a journey, which Gideon alone would make with the necessary escorts."

Rathnar's laugh was a short bark. "Because Fallon knows me and would recognize an imposter. But Gideon...Upon my life, they mean to murder the princess, no doubt."

Now Claude was trembling with excitement. "What will you do, sir?"

"You are going to help me. Gather a group of trusted men, but tell them no particulars. Have them search for travelers: a Gideon lookalike, a harper, a monk, a lady, several soldiers. Detain them until I can question them." He pulled Claude up by his collar, wrinkling his nose when he smelled the short man's fear. "You will tell no one of this. If you do, I shall put you on the rack. You understand?" Claude nodded mutely. "I will not tell their Majesties until their daughter's safety is secured, otherwise they will only suffer the agony of losing her twice."

Rathnar lowered him and shoved coins in his hand. "For your pains. You've done well; I'll see you well rewarded."

"Yes, sir. Thank you. The king and queen, they are lucky indeed to have you in their service."

"Go!"

"Yes, yes, yes."

Alone in his chamber, Rathnar checked his appearance again. Sweat had erupted at his temples, ruining his careful preparations. He would start again with his toilet, and then he would deal with treason.

* * *

Jonathan tried to make a game of it. Each day they would set aside a few hours pretending to be their alter egos, adding an hour daily, so that by the time they reached the harbor at Zirnich they would be completely immersed in their characters. Anyone who slipped out of character during the allotted time would set up camp if there was no inn, or sleep on the floor if there was. To get them acclimated, he chose three hours for the first day, thinking this would be easy. For the others it may have been; for him it was torture.

They pushed him relentlessly, all eager to talk to the lively, passionate, gregarious Gideon Ambrose. After just fifteen minutes, he was sweating profusely, and after an hour all of the cuticles on his fingernails were ripped or chewed off.

To shift the focus off of himself, he reined in next to Sebastian, knowing the would-be monk would dominate the conversation if given the opportunity. He ignored Thomas's look of appeal, and attempted a playful poke on Sebastian's arm.

"How now, Brother Dominick. What sermons of fire and brimstone have you concocted in your mind to deliver to those heathen Selphyn?"

Sebastian stared at him from under his cowl, glaring at the offending hand that pushed him. "There is hope to escape the eternal fires of damnation. It is not too late for them. If they embrace the holy Father and beg for forgiveness for their ignorance, the Almighty may be merciful. An eternity in Purgatory is vastly preferable to one in Hell."

This remark was delivered with perfect execution; Jonathan had no doubt that Sebastian was not only acting like Brother Dominick, but thinking like him as well. For a moment he started, worrying that by the time they completed their enterprise, Sebastian would be no more.

"Ah. And so they have no hope of reaching the kingdom of Heaven?"

Sebastian reined in closer, giving Jonathan a scandalous look. "Certainly not. They *murdered* God's only son, the Archangel Miken, who humbled himself to be born of man that we might be saved. They rejected his embrace and killed him, claiming his holy land of birth to be theirs. For this offense God cannot forgive. Anyone who believes otherwise is a fool."

"And what would you say for those few who bear but a portion of Selphyn blood? What of Prince Edward? Your philosophy would have him condemned to an eternity in Purgatory."

"Purgatory at best. I do not know how much influence his pagan mother had over him. He would have only escaped the eternal fires if he devoted himself fully to the Lord, and begged Him for forgiveness for the taint in his blood."

Jonathan wheeled his horse in front of Sebastian's, forcing a halt. "Have a care, Brother Dominick. You – you tread on treason."

"Treason! What care I for treason? God alone governs me. What care I for the fate of a prince dead and gone? I did not know him, and could have been no help to him. Whatever his fate is now, it cannot be undone."

"I *did* know him, and well. He was pious and kind. I tell you his soul is in Heaven."

"And I tell you it is in Purgatory, if he is lucky. And his damned, heathen mother is in Hell!"

Jonathan's hand flew to the pommel of his rapier. Sebastian brightened, and Jonathan recognized the look of paternal pride before Sebastian caught himself and replaced it with a look of sanctimonious scorn. It was enough to center Jonathan and recall him to his purpose. His hand dropped, and Sebastian made the sign of God over his head and heart. Jonathan pulled his horse aside to let Sebastian pass, ignoring the looks of the others. Thinking this gesture dismissed the subject, he clenched his jaw shut when Sebastian kept talking.

"I see you are one of those lovesick fools who exalt in the memory of Lady Syldonia."

"Do not taunt me with this."

"Many forget she was a member of the race responsible for killing our Lord."

"She was different. She was all goodness."

"She was a *Selphyn*. Men still sing her praises, I well know. They were blinded by beauty, tricked by a honeyed tongue. Her blood alone condemned her, and then adultery only intensified her sentence. If they could but hear her tortured screams–"

Jonathan flung himself out of the saddle, and dragged Sebastian off his while his horse bucked and whinnied. The heavy actor fell against Jonathan, nearly knocking him down. Jonathan shoved him backwards and drew his sword, his vision red.

"I care not if you are acting or no. I would not hear it from the king, nor will I hear it from you. Draw your sword, you damned scoundrel! I said I would have satisfaction!"

Sebastian lifted his hands and laughed. "I am a man of the cloth. I carry no weapons."

"Oh, for heaven's sake," Jonathan said, slamming the rapier back into its sheath. "Enough of this foolery. I have had enough of being Gideon Ambrose for an eternity."

Sebastian looked up at the sun. "A whole hour by the look of it. And you were doing so well, so convincing! Now you will be the first among us to sleep on the floor of the inn."

In his mind's eye Jonathan saw himself strangling Sebastian with the cord that tied his robes. There was nervous laughter as he remounted his horse; they did not know what was real and what was not. He was sickened by the realization that he almost killed his benefactor, *would* have if the man had been armed and took up his challenge. To distract himself he studied the scenery passing by, the lush forest that flanked their path. Mountains, glowing purple by the setting sun, jutted above the treetops, the clouds overhead turning dark pink. He tried to think of a profound remark worthy of Gideon, something to denote appreciation of nature's beauty and his marked passion. Then for an instant he *saw* it, truly saw the beauty in the moment, and was briefly overwhelmed. He turned in his saddle to observe other things in his heightened awareness, and his eyes met Miranda's. She too was stunning, glowing though dusk was settling around her. He opened his mouth to tell her when the spell was broken, and everything settled back down into his dull perception. The sunset was like any other ordinary sunset, and she was just another human being to upset his equilibrium.

Because he looked at her she spoke, further jarring his nerves. "I did not think it would be you, Jonathan, to be the first among us to fail."

"I was provoked."

"You think the Selphyn will not provoke you?" Sebastian said, and Jonathan refused to acknowledge him. Instead he turned to Thomas, who was consulting their map.

"How far to the nearest town?"

"We're almost to Lowden. There is an inn there, the Blue Duck, I believe." He folded the map and slipped it in his doublet, carefully avoiding Jonathan's gaze. His stomach flipping, Jonathan adopted a light tone to his voice.

"I ruined our game for today. You may release Horatio."

"I was not *being* Horatio."

"What have I said to cause offense?"

Now Thomas looked at him, and Jonathan flinched. "It's what you have *not* said."

Thomas kicked his horse into a trot, taking up the lead. With a whispered curse, Jonathan kicked the sides of his mare to catch up with him. Her sudden lurch forward was clumsy, and her left front hoof slipped into a gopher hole. An equine scream ripped through the air; Jonathan clamped his hands over his ears as Saucy Wench went down, bringing him with her.

He rolled out of the way before he was crushed, and did not have to inspect her leg to know it was broken. Before her scream he had heard the sound of a bone snapping, twisting his gut. Now she was lame, and he knew what was expected of him.

He took two steps toward her, his rapier extended, and her eye rolled and landed on him. He heard her sharp, shallow breaths, and large, brown eyes that adored him now waited for rescue. Tears flooded his eyes and his throat seized.

"Oh, God. I cannot, I cannot do it. She is my friend, she trusts me, I cannot–"

Thomas wordlessly took his sword and Jonathan whirled, covering his eyes with his hands. "Make it quick," he whispered, and did not move until there was a hand on his shoulder. He turned, expecting to see Thomas, and was mortified when Miranda stood there instead, seeing his tears.

"I am so sorry."

He nodded, wiping his face. "I raised her, from when she was but a foal. She was my family."

He would not accept any offers to ride double, determined as he was to serve his penance by walking.

"It will be dark soon," Thomas said. "Don't be a fool."

"Go on. I'll catch up."

"Wolves, bandits–"

"I care not. Please. I need this time alone."

For an hour the silence was blissful. Then blisters formed in his heels where his boots rubbed, and the temperature dropped considerably. As if Thomas conjured them, wolves began howling, and the hairs on the back of Jonathan's neck stood on end. There was only a sliver of a moon, and all he could see was the dark outline of the trees and mountains, and the ground directly beneath his feet. When he turned a bend and saw Lowden's lights, he heaved a sigh of relief.

Thomas met him in the Blue Duck's yard, with Jonathan trying not to look at the egregious bare spot where a stage would normally be erected to honor their arrival. There was likewise no cart, bearing Leon's livery and overflowing with props and costumes. He had never before been an ordinary *guest* in an inn.

"The innkeeper said he has a horse for sale," Thomas said.

"Good. Thank you."

"You'll be sharing a room with Gregory and me. Your bed is already made up on the floor."

Jonathan smiled. "How thoughtful."

When Thomas turned to go Jonathan put his hand on his arm. "I would have this business with you resolved, if I can. I like it not when we are at odds."

As if waiting for such an invitation, Thomas did not hesitate. "Why did you not tell me of this business with you growing up in court? I did not think there were secrets between us."

"I was not withholding information from you, per se. It is simply that I let John Warden go when I was ten years old, and have been Jonathan Wilder ever since."

"John Warden!"

"I simply don't think of him anymore. Or me rather. Me as him – blast it. You get my meaning."

"You mean the boy in your play?"

"Yes."

"You…that…you did not think it important to mention?"

"I told you, I let him go. John Warden is dead, and I would prefer it stay that way."

Instead of placating him, Jonathan sensed this intelligence only enraged Thomas all the more. "What will you do when we get back? Assume the throne?"

"There is no need for nastiness."

"I am quite serious. The king thinks you are his son, does he not?"

"According to Leonardis he thinks it a possibility. He does not remember that my mother was already carrying me when she undertook employment with Syldonia."

"And so…does Leonardis expect you to assume the throne?"

Jonathan made a flippant gesture. "He means to stage my escape from Prisongate, and I will never be heard from again."

He all but felt the rage dissipate from Thomas, like air from an accordion. "But…our company, the plays–"

"Will be well managed under your care."

"Jonathan!"

"I cannot stay in Diernioch. If I were to try, even under a different name, I fear me that Leonardis would feel the need to dispose of me once and for all. He may do so even before I am safely out of town following our return."

The bells for evening Vespers began to ring at a nearby cathedral, and Jonathan stared at his boots. He wanted nothing more than to go to bed, on the floor or not.

"Then why are you doing this for him?"

"I'm doing it for you. And Miranda, and Sebastian. A little for the others, though you know well they do not hold my affection the way the three of you do. Especially you."

"But...you could disappear."

"And what would happen to the rest of you if I did? If you showed up in Rowan without Gideon Ambrose? I will not desert you."

"Good God. And here have I been, a little rude to you—"

"A little rude? You have been a downright coxcomb."

"Well, I—"

"A plague-faced knave."

Thomas burst out laughing. "Go your ways."

"Yours first. To bed, scoundrel. Wastrel. And some other –rel thing."

"Whosoe'er you be, I am glad to be in your company."

"Ah. You see how quickly he takes my role as playwright. Now he speaks in rhyming couplets."

"What a terrible rhyme!"

"All in due time."

"But I will fore'er be thine."

"That does not rhyme."

"'Tis close enough."

"Come. Let us buy my horse and get to bed! I have had enough of your face."

NINE

UNDER THE EVER watchful eye of Mrs. Givens, Lauren swept and dusted the dining room, working around Gideon and Helen while they broke their fast. She felt intrusive, but had learned very fast that an idle servant is not allowed under Mrs. Givens's supervision, and the dining room was the only place left to clean. She tried to avoid looking at them whenever possible, but could not resist sneaking glances at Helen. Her low-cut nightgown was thin and slightly transparent, and the light coming in from the window shone on her bed-rumpled hair. With the exception of her lady's maid, Duchess Isabella never allowed the servants to see her before she was properly attired and groomed. This peek of intimacy in the life of a woman she hardly knew was as shocking as it was fascinating.

"What is the gossip at court this morning?" Gideon asked, buttering a roll.

"It is all of that John Warden."

Lauren was careful not to pause in her sweeping.

"Ah, yes. What of him?"

"The king sent for him for questioning, where it was learned he did escape from Prisongate two days ago."

Lauren whisked the broom with extra fervor to cover her gasp. She was unaware of having swept the same tile seventeen times.

"Two days! I thought…Well, and what now?"

Helen shrugged and her nightgown slipped from one shoulder. As if there were no one else in the room, Gideon reached over and squeezed a heavy breast, and Helen sighed. "The queen consented."

Gideon froze. "Consented to what?"

"Marriage. If I so wish."

In the pregnant pause that followed, Lauren nearly screamed in frustration. Her brother was missing, and they were focused on breasts and marriage.

"Well. I am glad to hear it," Gideon said, and the corner of his mouth twitched. Over Helen's shoulder their gazes met, and while she blushed he blinked several times. "John Warden–"

"Oh, very well. I see you are bent on hearing the story. Edward sent for him to determine if he was truly his bastard. He is gone, none knows where. There. That is all I know."

There was a knock on the door, and Lauren, being the closest, answered it. An older teenaged boy, scrawny and travel-worn, let loose a torrent of information that Lauren could barely follow. She tried to interrupt him when Gideon appeared behind her, demanding the story from the beginning. Relieved, Lauren stepped aside but remained in earshot.

"So he says, 'Go to that Master Ambrose and tell him –'"

"Wait. Stop. Who said?"

"My master, sir. The innkeeper at the Blue Duck. In Lowden, sir."

"The Blue Duck."

"Yes, sir."

"Why does that sound familiar?"

Helen called from the dining room, and Lauren half-expected her to appear at the door with her nightgown falling off and all. "We stayed there some two years ago. You broke a chair."

"Ah. It comes back to me. And your master finds he wants more recompense?"

"No, no. I know nothing of that, sir. There was a gentleman, sir, a gentleman come to the inn with your ring."

Lauren shot a glance at Gideon and saw the blood drain from his face.

"Go on."

"He bought a horse, sir. And stamped the bill with the Ambrose heron. My master, he says to me, 'I know Gideon Ambrose. That rogue be not he.' "

"Good man. And where is the scoundrel now?"

"He stayed the night, sir, he with a bit of company. I rode all night at my master's orders, sir. I know not if they mean to stay another night or no."

"What did he look like? Who is he traveling with?"

"He looked a bit like you, sir. Same years, belike. Same hair color. Wore it tied back. He was with some ten other men, one lady. Some of the men wore the king's livery, sir. Soldiers, like."

Gideon gave the man several coins. "Go your ways then, and take to your master my thanks. I'll follow anon."

He closed the door and stared at Lauren, ignoring Helen's inquiries from the other room. "You're coming with me."

"I – why?"

"I will relate to you my suspicions on the road. Get your cloak."

She rode behind him again but without the easygoing gait from two nights previous. She considered reminding him that forcing a furious pace for a day's journey would only necessitate a long rest for his horse, but then thought better of it. The landscape passed by in a blur, and she was glad she brought her cloak. Though it wasn't chilly now, it would be on the ride back that evening. Unless he meant for them to stay the night, which Lauren knew would not settle well with Helen. Already Gideon's mistress was cross; he refused to elucidate his intentions even to her.

When they stopped to water the horse at a brook, Lauren slipped off and cupped water to drink herself, her throat dry from the dusty road. The early-summer sun was warm on her back where it stole in through the trees, and as she washed her face, Gideon began talking.

"I have heard many a play in which your brother performed. I did note he bore a passing resemblance to me, and many have remarked in humor that I ought to play his twin in those Rothford comedies." He paused to look at her still crouched at the brook's edge. The seriousness in his eyes made her stand, her legs trembling. "We know now your brother was not, in fact, in Prisongate the day you petitioned to see him; the guard belike was bribed to cover up someone's mistake, or someone's ill intention."

"You think—"

"My impersonator is traveling with ten other men, and one woman. If I do not mistake me, this configuration matches that of Jonathan – or John's -- troupe, the Duke's Men. *Leonardis's* men. Leonardis, who noted the absence of my ring, whom I now recall shook my hand with unusual vigor the day I dined at his house."

Lauren covered her mouth, her words muffled. "Oh, God. But why?"

"I cannot say. Some political intrigue of some sort. I mean to find out, if we can overcome the troupe at the inn. They may have moved on and all will be for naught. But I suspect treason, and will do what I can to defend his Majesty's interests. I brought you in case some influence can be gained over our friend John."

Lauren shuddered. "I hope you do not mean him harm."

"Not until I know his intentions."

"But you will allow him to explain—"

Gideon's sigh cut her off. "Perhaps my bringing you was not wise after all." He mounted his horse and held out his hand to help her on.

They took a slower pace, and just when Lauren assumed there would be silence for the duration of the journey, Gideon began talking. He spoke of trivial things, fashion and entertainment, and she understood at once that she was not expected to answer, only to listen. It was clear Gideon loved the sound of his own voice, and remarked, on more than one occasion, on his renowned wit. He spoke well of Helen, but Lauren couldn't help recalling his expression when Helen told him the queen consented to marriage.

Twice Gideon referenced something in his rambling monologue that reminded him of his purpose, and both times he fell into a petulant silence that lasted a few minutes while he ostensibly vented his angry thoughts on John. Then he took up his narrative once more, as if having forgotten the entire affair. Lauren never said a word.

They reached the Blue Duck at twilight, with Gideon slamming open doors and marching in with bluster. The innkeeper was out, and Gideon ordered a serving girl to check upstairs to see if the rooms were still occupied. They were not, and with a snarl Gideon gave himself permission to search the rooms. Beyond empty tankards and rumpled sheets, nothing was found until Lauren spotted parchment peeking out from under the bedclothes. She was able only to determine it was a map before it was snatched out of her hand.

Gideon said, "There are marks here, notations…they chose a route that would appear to end in Zirnich."

They stared at each other, neither willing to pronounce the words *Rowan* or *Selphyn*, though it was clear they were both thinking the same thing.

"What do you mean to do?"

"Drink a pint. Then we will follow this route, without rest, until we overtake them."

Back in the common room, Lauren sat close to the fireplace while Gideon drank not one, but three pints. The door opened with a howl of the wind, and Lauren looked up, seeing it was completely dark outside. Five men stood in the doorway, surveying the room's occupants. Though she could not have said why, she went cold all over, and put her hand on Gideon's arm. He followed her gaze, and the men, all armed and stout, saw them. Their leader narrowed his eyes and approached them; Gideon stood up, and Lauren was dismayed to see how much he swayed on his feet.

The man looked Gideon up and down before asking his name.

"Gideon Ambrose, if it be your business, which I doubt." When the fellow's eyes lit up, Gideon's widened. "You have information for me? You know the rogues who stole my signet ring?"

"Missing your ring, eh? Convenient, that is."

"What? Someone–"

"Where are the others? I see the girl; where are the others?"

Gideon grasped the back of his chair for balance, his smile uneasy. "Ah. I see you have reached a misunderstanding. *I am Gideon Ambrose.* I'm looking for–"

The man laughed, a low, loud noise that vibrated in Lauren's ears. He made a gesture at Gideon's appearance, and Lauren saw him through this man's eyes: hatless, with his shirt half-tucked, his doublet missing, forgotten in that morning's haste, his eyes bloodshot, and his hair uncombed and disheveled from their furious ride. "So might my nag outside be Gideon Ambrose." He glanced back at this group, who began advancing. Lauren shrank back, pinned against the corner of the fireplace. Gideon stood his ground, though he continued swaying. "Shame the others are missing. But you're the one he really wants."

"Now, wait. I tell you there is a mistake–"

The men closed in on them. Gideon reached for his sword, a desperate cry escaping when he discovered that that too had been left behind. He threw an empty tankard into the group, clipping someone on the forehead, and lowered his head before launching himself forward like a battering ram.

He never stood a chance, and when they finished clubbing him on the head with meaty fists, they came for Lauren.

TEN

THREE DAYS IN a row it was his fault, his mistake, thus two nights were spent on the floor of inns, and the third he set up camp while the others watched and laughed. In spite of it all being his idea, it did not stop Jonathan from grumbling as he untied bedrolls and blankets from the saddles. What irked him the most was not his penance for losing focus, but that he was turning out to be the weakest of them all. It did not occur to him when they set out that he would be the one constantly losing his temper or composure. He was determined to set the example from then on; he would not be the one to risk their lives once they were in Rowan. As he drifted off to sleep on a bed of leaves, shivering under a cool, late-night fog, he resolved to be Gideon for the entire next day, beginning with the first opening of his eyes in the morning.

At first light he sprang out of his blankets, stretching and inhaling the pine scent, wide awake and oh-so-happy to be Gideon Ambrose. The others moaned and shifted in their bedrolls in protest; all but Miranda were still cocooned in bed. He glanced around for her through pine needles dripping with dew, and when he didn't see her he wandered through a nearby meadow.

Wheat-colored weeds blazed in the sunlight, the dew reflecting the light so that it blinded Jonathan. He threw an arm over his eyes and squinted, finally catching sight of Miranda kneeling at the river's edge. He crept up behind her, smiling as she splashed water on her face, the rush of the river concealing his footsteps.

"Good morrow, Helen."

She gasped and spun; as she straightened he caught her in his arms and planted a hard kiss on her lips. There was a muffled squeak, and when she tried to pull away he held her close. She yielded and softened in his grasp, twining her fingers in his loose hair. Electricity crackled down his spine, and it was all he could do not to break away.

She released him with a throaty laugh. "You caught me by surprise."

His shyness kicked in immediately. To cover for his lack of loquaciousness, he threw her over his shoulder and carried her back to the camp. He dropped her rather roughly on her blankets, and by this time most of his actors were at least sitting up. Thomas blinked at them before a slow smile spread over his face.

"Helen is lively this morning," Jonathan said. "I found her cavorting with faeries."

Miranda flopped back on her pillow and smiled at him. The whiteness of her throat commanded all of his attention. "Not fairies. 'Twas was a horned god."

Before a blush betrayed him, he began rolling up his bedroll. He felt eyes on him, and knew his success was already precarious. No. He would *not* be sleeping on the floor again.

"I hope he gave you a tumble worthy of your appetite."

Her mouth dropped open and he laughed. He kicked Thomas's foot. "Give us a song, harper."

Sebastian, belting his robe, said, "I hope, young Gideon, you have not sinned. You and Mistress Helen will restrain yourselves until you are properly married, I trust."

"Have no fear, Brother. I do not mean to marry her."

The laughter was all he needed; now he was in his element. He swung up on his saddle and gave Miranda a wink, letting fly a string of Gideon-worthy jests. Thomas picked up his harp and strummed.

Now that she hath tumbled me I would see her no more.
That is until the babe she left a-wailing at my door.

"A goodly song, Horatio," Jonathan said. "I will have no songs of love and death this day. Let it be mirth and merriment, or I'll none of it."

"Here, here."

"You are in fine spirits today," Miranda said, reining her horse in line with his. His new mare was old and slow, a nag that insulted the memory of Saucy Wench. He vowed to look for another in the next town, though he would direct someone else to sign the bill of sale. He had not liked at all the look on the innkeeper's face as he looked from Gideon's signature and seal to Jonathan's face and back again. Though he completed the transaction without a word, his look of suspicion lingered in Jonathan's memory, and he would not risk being caught out before they reached Rowan again.

"Indeed, I am. And you are looking very, very well, good mistress."

"I thank you."

"I trust you would alert me if...something were amiss." He gave her a hard look which she dismissed with a wave of her hand.

"I will, but do not worry. I am well. These arrangements suit me." Her smile threatened to unnerve him.

"Ah, ha. I should have but named you Saucy Wench. 'Tis a better fit for you." She squeezed his knee and he caught her hand, bringing it to his lips. "I daresay these arrangements suit me well in kind. Methinks your eyes flash like the flames of a bonfire."

He heard her hard swallow, and his eyes moved back to the delicate arch of her throat. He gave himself permission, as Gideon, to touch it, his finger trailing down toward her collarbone. He was aware her breathing changed, and his own quickened.

Thomas spoke and Jonathan snatched his hand away. "You would do well to remember others are in attendance." He was grinning, his eyes shining with approval. "Though I daresay a certain someone is not to sleep on the floor tonight."

"But of course," Miranda said. "He will be in my bed."

Thomas sang, "And he shall be Gideon forever more," and plucked his harp while Jonathan recovered himself, whistling "Merry Mistress" under his breath.

He avoided Sebastian when he could, and took attention off of himself without notice by encouraging the "soldiers" to speak about themselves, forcing them to create names, histories, interests and the like. He was worried about Gregory, who withheld enthusiasm while inventing a past for himself and how he came to be in Gideon's service as his page. Gregory's expression was reminiscent of a boy waiting for his parents to live apart, or even abandon him. He wanted to give him reassurance but didn't know how without deviating too much from his character, but felt Gregory was not mature enough to understand the nuances he used with Miranda and Thomas. Finally he rumpled the boy's hair and said, "And you have served me well ever since, and shall continue to do so, without worry for welfare."

"Thank you, sir." He gave Jonathan a clandestine wink, which the other returned before relaxing. If anything, Thomas would look after him when this whole business was done.

A shadow fell over the road and Jonathan looked up, seeing a cluster of ominous clouds spreading. He endured conversation for the next several minutes with an inward smile, knowing soon he would be saved. A fat raindrop landed on his hand, and Thomas felt the top of his head with a curse. Everyone looked up except for Jonathan, who knew he could count on nature to give him an out, and when the downpour began he smiled still as the others pulled their hoods on and kept to themselves.

"Lovely weather," he said, confident it was a Gideon-esque comment. "Ah, but I do love the rain."

"And I know why," Miranda said. Hoodless, she was holding her cloak over her head like a tent. "Saved by the rain."

Jonathan shrugged. "You needn't look as though I caused it. Indeed, I am quite saddened by this reprieve from conversation."

"And you lie not well."

They moved off the road so that the canopy of tree branches overhead would shield them somewhat from the rain. Footing around the trees was awkward and slowed them down. Reining his horse tightly to avoid a tall shrub, Jonathan's nag stepped into the path of another horse. Each rider reined sharply in the opposite direction but a collision was unavoidable. Jonathan's knee was pushed against that of the other rider. Jonathan pulled back his hood to apologize and found himself staring into Richard's face. The assassin's eyes were the color of a frozen lake; they penetrated Jonathan's gaze like cold steel. Jonathan remembered himself at the last moment and gave him a quick nod.

"Soldier."

The corner of Richard's lip turned up in a mocking smile. He stopped his horse to give Jonathan lead, his eyes watching every move. He was not hooded, and his face and hair were drenched. He did not blink when raindrops hammered into his eyes. Jonathan looked away, hoping his shudder was imperceptible in the rain.

For hours they rode in near silence, shoulders hunched and heads lowered. Though there were still two or three hours left of daylight, Jonathan called an end to traveling for the day when they reached a town called Sterling, which was bound to have at least one inn. There were murmurs of relief and gratitude, and Thomas spotted the Boar. They came in like bedraggled kittens, leaving puddles on the floor while Jonathan procured rooms for them. Informed there were only two vacancies, Jonathan winced, imagining the eleven men pressed together in one room. Miranda put her hand over his and smiled.

"I need not a room of my own. I know my virtue is in good hands."

Thomas laughed and put his arm around her. "There's a good wench."

She shrugged out of his grasp and made her way up the stairs. Jonathan resisted a look of admonishment at Thomas, though his need to convey *I-told-you-so* was very strong. Instead, with only precious seconds remaining of his day as Gideon, he divided them into two groups, ensuring Sebastian and Richard would not be rooming with him, Thomas and Miranda.

In their damp and drafty room, Miranda had already claimed a bed at the far end, and Jonathan dropped his satchel on the bed next to hers. Thomas shook his hand.

"Well done, Jonathan. And all day too. Enjoy your bed, though you'll have to share it with me. I suppose no one must sleep on the floor?"

Jonathan smiled. "Just you." In response to Thomas's blank stare, he said, "I never said we were done." He clapped Thomas on the shoulder and pulled off his wet doublet and shirt, aware of Miranda watching him. "I'll give you an extra blanket. That looks to be a cold, hard floor indeed."

Thomas sighed. "Rat-faced villain."

ELEVEN

THEY DROPPED HIM into a room; he fell from a considerable height and landed on a bed of straw that did little to cushion the stone floor underneath. It was all he could do not to scream; he did not want them to know he was awake. When Lauren was dropped on top of him, however, he gasped and arched his back. Her head was on his chest, hair fanned over his neck and part of his face. She was rigid and then went limp. The two of them played possum with their eyes closed, listening.

"Well. Enjoy your stay," Gideon heard a man say. He sounded like the large one, the one who first approached them. Gideon flashed on the man's huge fist coming down, and his head throbbed smartly from the thrashing he received. "There is wine, at least."

"What about the others?" said another voice.

"They'll turn up."

"The innkeeper said—"

There was a loud creaking that drowned out the voice, then the boom of doors slamming shut, followed by the unmistakable sound of a bar sliding in place to brace them. Gideon pushed Lauren off and sat up, wincing at the flash of pain that speared through his head. It was completely dark, only a small, rectangular window provided any light, which was but a thin sliver of moonlight. The window was high, too high to reach, and as he stared at it Gideon noticed the pair of heavy doors underneath. They were slanted, and like the window, too high to reach.

"We're in a cellar," he said.

He took a step backwards and his heel collided with something hard. A bottle fell and rolled in front of him, and he remembered his captors mentioned wine. He turned and saw the outline of dozens of crates behind him. Without speaking to Lauren, he stacked the crates until he could reach the doors. Balancing precariously, he pushed on and then pounded them, yelling. The crates shifted under him and he froze, willing the nauseating sway to stop. The window too proved locked, and the glass was at least an inch thick, too thick to break. He doubted they could fit through the narrow opening anyway.

He jumped down from his tower of crates, jarring his head once more. The topmost crate, swaying dangerously now from his jump, slipped off and crashed down on his toe. His scream was muffled by the sound of dozens of bottles breaking, and wine seeped from the broken crate, soaking a good deal of straw. With a howl Gideon picked up the crate and hurled it against wall, wine flying everywhere. He picked up two loose bottles and smashed them, uttering every curse he knew. He stopped only when the pain in his head was blinding. Sinking to his knees, his breath ragged, he cradled his head.

"Are you quite finished?" Lauren said.

"You will speak so to me?" He waited for an apology. When none was forthcoming, he pulled his arms down and stared at her. "What?"

"Perhaps we ought to determine if there is a sensible means of escape."

He fell back on his rump, his breeches instantly soaked with wine. "Please. Let me not deter you with my insensibility."

He saw her silhouette as she sat down on a crate. He would die before admitting he admired her composure. Helen would have been shrieking.

"On the way here they spoke of an old woman who would provide for us," she said. "Perhaps we can overtake her when she comes?"

Again she surprised him. "Perhaps. But not if she means only to drop provisions in through the window. It's too narrow."

"Have you any theories as to why we are here?"

Gideon shook his head before realizing she wouldn't see it in the dark. "No. Someone knows I am being impersonated and sent men to apprehend the traitorous rogues. And…then they were mistook."

"Mistaken identities, like the plays my brother enacted."

"The irony has not escaped me. Nor does it amuse me."

"Think you someone will come and recognize you?"

"It is likely, yes. Unless they simply mean to kill us."

"Oh."

Anticipating a surge of feminine weakness on display, Gideon preoccupied himself with a bottle of wine. When no opener could be found he broke the neck on the edge of a crate, and tipped the bottle upside-down so that wine gushed onto his face and into his open mouth. He took long, loud swallows until only a trickle remained. He threw the empty bottle against the other broken ones, aware of Lauren's flinch when the glass shattered. He sensed her fear of him but lacked the energy and desire to reassure her.

"Good vintage, that. Lansing wine." He broke open another bottle. "Care for a drink?"

"No, thank you."

When he was stumbling, slobbering drunk he felt much happier, and the pain in his head was now bearable. The dilemma of a privy was soon apparent; he took some straw and placed it in the far corner of the cellar. Relieving himself of two and a half bottles of wine flooded the small amount of straw; he was stricken to see it, though just barely in the darkness, float away on the current of his urine. He relaxed when it congealed with the pool of spilled wine.

Lauren was already curled up on her cloak on a pile of straw. He collected what remained of the dry straw to make his own bed, grateful for the wine that would soon knock him out. There was just one brief moment when he entertained the possibility of entreating Lauren to cradle him with her body, and then dismissed it. She was too plain, and her breasts too small to provide any real comfort. Old, too – thirty years if she was a day. In the harsh light of the morning he would have to see her aged-scarred skin with sags and wrinkles. He shuddered and thought of Helen's ripe plumpness.

Shrieking or no, he ought to have brought her instead.

TWELVE

CLAUDE BOWED DEEPLY. "We have secured them, my lord."

It was the closest he had ever seen Rathnar come to a smile. "Excellent. You have them all?"

Claude had rehearsed his speech at least twenty times; outside Rathnar's chambers he felt almost confident that all would be well. Now, under that incinerating gaze, he completely lost the thread of his thoughts, and no words came. Rathnar stood from his chair, and Claude began to tremble.

"Who is missing?"

"So please your lordship, my men found only two of them. But the man we have is the one impersonating Gideon. The others are meaningless, yes?"

Rathnar walked toward him while Claude blinked furiously. He could not look at that white, pasty skin in close proximity, and Rathnar's eyes, a blue so dark they were almost purple or black, were like the eyes of a warlock. It was easy to understand why so many broke down under the weight of that gaze.

"The others possess dangerous knowledge, do they not?"

"Yes? Yes. Yes, sir."

"And now they could be anywhere."

"Well, I – yes."

He put his hand on Claude's shoulder and propelled him out of his chambers. Claude walked numbly, his vision blurred.

"Where are the ones you found?"

"An old woman's wine cellar, outside the Blue Duck."

"And where are the men who captured them for you?"

"They...they are mercenaries I hired...I found them at the White Stag in Chauncery."

They reached the end of a corridor and descended a flight of stairs. The stairwell was cold and unlit; when they reached the bottom Claude was shivering violently. He glanced around the chamber they now occupied, a cavernous room encased in stone that was even colder than the stairwell. His eyes lighted on machinery that at first glance made no sense. And then he knew.

"Oh – oh – I did as you asked–"

"You did. You did. What a disappointment it was when documents were found in your chambers that suggest you are conspiring with the Selphyn to put an imposter on a throne, a girl pretending to be the king's dead daughter. I am afraid I will need a full confession."

Claude's eyes filled with tears. "I served you well. You know there is no such–"

"There is no shame in confessing before the torture. No one would think less of you."

"Thaddeus. Ask him! He knows I am no traitor."

"Thaddeus was heartbroken when he learned of your deceit, after all your years of so-called loyal service."

Claude was weeping freely now. "I did what you asked, now you...how could you?"

Rathnar patted his shoulder. "Politics. If you are going to play with men of power, you had better take care. It was clumsy, leaving that correspondence in your chambers where anyone could find it."

"You...you know there was no..."

"Which should we try first? That one is always a favorite. But then I'll have to change my clothing again."

"Oh, God..."

* * *

"I am not attending church."

"You are my flock. I must care for the salvation of your souls."

"As it is Sunday," Jonathan said, "a day of *rest*, I decree a day of rest for us, to be ourselves. And so, you may put Brother Dominick to bed for a day."

"We will reach Zirnich tonight."

"Sebastian–"

"There is no Sebastian. I am Brother Dominick. And you *will* go to church with me. All of you."

"Why did I not make you a jester?"

"Well, I am not being Horatio today," Thomas said.

"Then you can *not* be Horatio in church."

Jonathan jumped in between Thomas and Sebastian before the argument could begin. "Enough. We will go to church. But in God's name, I pray you, let us be for the rest of the day."

Sebastian nodded. "Though I would recommend confession after mass."

"Where I shall confess to murder!" Thomas yelled.

Jonathan looped his arm through Thomas's, pulling him toward the cathedral. "Come. Let us not do this. This is our last day to be ourselves; let us enjoy it."

A group of monks spotted them and Jonathan went rigid. He watched incredulously as Sebastian held out his arms to embrace each of them, introducing himself and receiving a hearty welcome from the other monks.

"This is wonderful," Thomas said. "We leave him here. He will not notice our absence as he will be too busy fasting and praying in the monastery."

"We'll leave him here on the way back," Jonathan said. "Come on. They are waiting for us."

When Sebastian joined them in the pew, he was glowing. "They have heard of me! Imagine. My reputation extends well past Diernioch."

"They have heard of Brother Dominick, you mean," Jonathan said.

"It is all one."

"Miken's wounds. Why did you become an actor if your heart belongs to the church?"

"I understand not what you mean. And attend to your blasphemy in taking our Lord's name in vain."

Kneeling, Jonathan admired the architecture of the cathedral rather than listening to the sermon of avoiding temptation and a life of sin. The cathedral reminded him of St. Bartholomew's in Diernioch, with its stone angels battling devils. He wondered if this church was also built on top of Selphyn ruins like the ones he had hidden in as a boy. It was quite likely as most of the churches in Salsima were. Selphyn holy days were claimed by the Mikenite Church, just as some of the pagan rituals were adopted and then changed to fit the church's doctrine. All was done in an effort to make the transition of conversion easier for the Selphyn, but the Selphyn would not be converted.

"Forgive us, Lord, for worshipping false gods, and for being led astray by a heathen princess whose beauty seduced men into an eternity in flames."

The priest would of course be referring to the Lady Syldonia, who defied two centuries of prejudice. No one who met her could help loving her, regardless of the strength of their faith. Jonathan did not think she was of this earth; perhaps she was born a Selphyn to remind mankind of God's glory in every living thing, even heathens.

After church they gathered in the courtyard, around a massive statue of St. Miken the Archangel, God's warrior and then His only son, who lived and died for the sins of mankind before resurrecting and ascending into Heaven. Here he was depicted in his angelic form, armed with a broadsword and dressed in armor. One outstretched wing as large as a boat; Jonathan stood in its shadow and prayed that he and his troupe would be protected in the company of the heathens.

They mounted their horses and prepared for their last day of riding. In the morning they would sail to Rowan, a two-day's voyage across the channel. After that there would be no more chances for mistakes; if any of them slipped their fate would be far worse than spending the night on a hard floor.

They reached Zirnich at dusk, and had to all but crawl through the congested streets to find an inn. Apparently they arrived just in time for some sort of festival, for everyone was costumed and masked, many already roaring drunk. Minstrels played on every street corner, and there were flame throwers, belly dancers and jugglers. Jonathan couldn't hear himself think, and when he dismounted near the Swan, a woman in an elaborate peacock mask fell into his arms and kissed him. She was roughly wrenched away, and Jonathan saw Miranda say something sharp to her, her fingers digging into a feathered arm. When he raised an eyebrow at her she blushed.

"I forgot I wasn't Helen," she yelled above the noise, and Jonathan laughed.

They learned, once inside the Swan, that all the rooms were let, and it was doubtful they would find any vacancies anywhere in town.

"What is the occasion?" Thomas asked.

"It is our summer festival."

"On a Sunday?" Sebastian said, pushing forward. The innkeeper blanched.

"We celebrate the same day every year, Brother. It happened to fall on a Sunday this year."

"Is there anywhere you can put us?" Jonathan said, showing the innkeeper his full purse. "We will pay handsomely."

A few minutes later they were arranging what few blankets they could find in the innkeeper's own room. He and his wife would sleep in the stables, after happily draining Jonathan's purse.

Miranda looked out the window and bounced on her toes. "I want to dance."

"We must rise early, and there is a long—"

She looked at him. "We do not know what will happen to us there. What might befall us. I want to *dance*."

It turned out they all wanted to, save for perhaps Sebastian, Jonathan and Richard. When he realized he would be left alone with only those two, Jonathan changed his mind and allowed Miranda to drag him down the stairs. A street merchant outfitted them with masks, capes and feathers; when Jonathan consulted a looking glass he found himself dressed as one of the faerie folk, complete with iridescent wings. His mask was green and silver, sequined and glittered. Miranda had white feathers around her eyes, on her head rested a full-size swan, its long neck curved in repose.

"Fitting, that," Jonathan said. "You match our inn."

She laughed and pulled him into the street before he could wait for the others to finish with their costumes. Night had fully descended at this point, though all the shop windows were lighted with candles and lanterns. Long torches blazed in holders set up every ten feet or so, and many walked with hand-held torches or candles, making the night appear as though it were on fire.

Miranda's great swan hat reflected the light as she pulled Jonathan deeper into the crowd until they were simply swallowed up. Still the vendors with their mulled wine found them, seemingly materializing whenever they paused to catch their breath. Jonathan lost count of how many cups they drank after seven, and refused more when three swan hats began to spin in a sickening circle. While they danced he was pushed against Miranda several times, and sometime after midnight she was jostled so hard that her swan hat was knocked loose. Jonathan dove forward to catch it, and as he righted it he found that his arms were around Miranda. He put his hands on either side of her face to stop it from spinning, and it was ever so easy from this position to release resistance and drop his head forward so that his lips were on hers.

Her lips were burning from exertion and spiced wine; he caught them between his teeth and gently bit. She grabbed him by the back of his head and pushed against him so they were molded together, throngs of people dancing obliviously around them. She ran her hands on his face, turning it this way and that, and their masks collided and pushed against each other so that they both fell off. Jonathan broke away to retrieve them before they were trampled, and halfway up he looked at her with her mask off and felt his own bare and vulnerable face.

"Come. We should retire. It's late, and…the world is spinning."

He wasn't sure if she heard him or not, and grabbed her hand to pull her out of the street. It took several minutes to cross a few feet, pushing their way through the crowd, and once they were safe on the porch of the inn, he paused to let them both catch their breath. When she reached for him he instinctively pulled away.

"Why is it you will only kiss me when you are being someone else?"

He had no answer for this. She stared at him, waiting, when Thomas stumbled up the stairs and fell against them.

"Good God. What are you wearing on your face?"

"A nose."

This "nose" was six inches long and bright blue. Jonathan laughed. "You will kill someone with it."

"Tell me you are not yet going to bed."

"We are going to bed. And if you were wise, you would go too."

Miranda pulled off her swan hat and left them standing on the porch. Before going in she threw Jonathan a look of disappointed longing.

Thomas said, "If you are not going to bed her, may I?"

"No. You have done damage enough. And you may recall, we are all twelve pressed in one room together."

"There is a kitchen, wardrobes, cabinets. I would find a place."

"It is no wonder the ladies swoon over you."

They stumbled in together, and in the dark Thomas's blue nose collided with the wall. They were still laughing in the innkeeper's room, though Jonathan sobered when he saw Sebastian's one eye glaring at him by candlelight. Angry at this silent chastisement, Jonathan said, "Forgive me, Brother. I have sinned."

"The Lord will only forgive when you are in earnest."

"Oh, go box your ears," Thomas said. "Brother."

Another round of laughter ensued, and Jonathan, knowing his comrades would be in worse conditions than he, made his bed as close to the wall as possible. As he predicted, as they staggered in at various intervals, they tripped over sleeping bodies and stepped on hands and feet. The laughter and cursing were however a soothing balm to his anxiety regarding tomorrow's passage. He did not resist when Miranda snuggled in close to him, and it was only when he had his arms around her, his nose in her hair, that he was finally able to fall asleep.

THIRTEEN

FOR FIVE DAYS the old widow dropped food and water for them through the narrow window. She never spoke to them and ignored their pleas and Gideon's curses, and so for five nights they shivered in the damp cellar, their backs and necks aching from the stone floor. To pass the time they talked – or rather, Gideon talked and Lauren listened. She now knew the names of his childhood pets, his favorite color, each and every pastime, the favorite of which was painting, and intimate details of his relationship with Helen. When asked when he would marry her, he laughed and confirmed her suspicions that he had no intention of marrying so far beneath himself. He assured her that Helen suffered no illusions on the subject, but Lauren could not help but recall the look on her face when she told Gideon the queen consented to their marriage if they wished it.

"Then…you will lose her when you marry."

"Not likely," Gideon said, breaking open another bottle of wine. Empty bottles were stacked in a huge, misshapen tower behind them; whenever Lauren looked at them she was stunned anew by their multitude. "She will remain my mistress."

Lauren wondered if Helen would agree with such certainty.

On the sixth morning the cellar doors were opened.

They threw their arms across their eyes against the blinding sunlight. Lauren was desperate to see their rescuer, but each time she started to lower her arm the light seared into her eyes like a hot poker.

"Who – who's there?" Gideon said.

Lauren heard a gasp. "Gideon?"

"Yes! Who's that? I cannot see."

"Oh, for the love of Miken. It's really you."

Lauren did not understand the blatant disappointment in the voice of their visitor. She took her arm away and looked at the floor to give her eyes time to adjust. Gideon was doing the same, his face contorting. "That sounds like Rathnar. Is it?"

"Yes, it is I."

The voice was very distinctive: low and deep. Lauren was not surprised Gideon had no trouble placing it.

"Thank God! Here, give us a hand, will you?"

They both blinked up into the light, and Lauren saw the outline of a kneeling figure in black. A ladder was lowered, and Gideon climbed out first. As Lauren stepped onto the ladder, Gideon was pumping Rathnar's hand.

"How did you find us?"

Rathnar had not yet replied by the time Lauren reached the cellar doors. Forgotten, she stepped off the ladder and into the grass, still unable to look around without squinting. She inhaled the fresh, blessed air and stretched, her back screaming.

"Rathnar?"

"Forgive me. I was not expecting you."

"You were expecting – *you* sent the men after us!"

"After the imposters. Apparently a mistake was made."

"You think so? God's wounds. We've been here for *days*. What took so long?"

Lauren turned to better study Rathnar, and took an involuntary step backward in revulsion. He was now standing upright, all six feet and more of him. His deathly white pallor was a shock against all of that black – his black clothes and the long, black hair that he wore loose around his shoulders. She knew who he was, of course; *everyone* knew of the famous spymaster that no one dared trifle with.

"As I thought I was dealing with villains, I did not hurry. There was business in Chauncery that demanded my attention; a small coup that needed stifling. I beg your pardon."

Rathnar glanced at her and then shifted his attention back to Gideon. He terrified her and she took another step back. The way he stooped, along with his white skin and black hair, made her think of the mythical vampire. Looking at him, she could almost believe they existed.

"I will if you tell me what you know. Who is impersonating me and why?"

Rathnar's head dropped and he sighed. "The situation is very complicated...I will tell you all, but not now. You are both, I think, in want of a bath?"

Lauren surprised herself by speaking. "Yes. Very much." A sharp look from Gideon reminded her that she was to restore their former dynamic of master to servant, and forget such intimacy ever existed between them. She was not surprised, but very disappointed. She followed the two men from a respectable distance toward a cottage, ostensibly belonging to the old widow.

"The woman who fed you is guileless," Rathnar said. "She was paid to care for whom she thought were traitors, but she is now set to rights." He threw open her door without preamble, and when Lauren entered she saw her cowering in the corner. The men ignored her and headed with authority to the kitchen. Lauren paused and said, "Thank you for providing us with food and water."

The old woman turned her head and covered her face as if Lauren would strike. Lauren wondered just what Rathnar had said or done, and felt a flash of anger. While they waited for the water to heat, Rathnar packed his saddlebags full of food from the woman's cupboards.

Watching closely, Gideon said, "We are going somewhere?"

"Yes. I am afraid necessity forces me to bring the two of you with me. As it concerns the man who is impersonating you, I am sure you will not find this proposition disagreeable."

"I cannot think but to get my hands on the villains."

"I guessed as much. Now. Shall we let the lady bathe first?"

Lauren turned crimson while Gideon guffawed. One look from Rathnar silenced him, and with a sneer he gave his acquiescence. As Lauren carried buckets of hot water to the tub in the widow's bedchamber, she caught snatches of their conversation.

"Who is she?"

"My new servant. She has interest in this matter; I believe her brother is involved."

"Her brother?"

"John Warden."

Lauren paused to hear Rathnar's response, but when none was forthcoming she emptied the last bucket into the tub. She peeled off her soiled dress, filthy and stiff, and slipped into the heavenly water. Knowing Gideon would be impatient for his turn, she did not pause to luxuriate, but scrubbed her skin fiercely with soap and then washed her hair. Clumps of dirt floated free, and after rinsing it three times she pulled her fingers through it to work out the tangles. After some hesitation she pulled a sheet off the woman's bed and wrapped herself in it, creeping with increasing embarrassment out to the kitchen.

Gideon saw her and glared. "Oh, and thank you for filling the tub with fresh water for me. Will you stand there like a mute ape?"

"Gideon," Rathnar said. "Let her be. Fill the damned tub yourself."

There was no contradicting Rathnar, but Lauren felt no satisfaction as Gideon brushed past her with a bucket of hot water, fuming. Rathnar resumed packing his bag, so Lauren edged in closer.

"Excuse me, Sir Francis, but it occurred to me I have no clean change of clothes. My dress is…well, it is not wearable until I have such time as to wash it."

"Please. 'Sir Francis' is quite loathsome to me. Rathnar will do."

He looked up at her and froze. Mistaking his look, she sucked in a breath of fright and began to tremble. His hands dropped to his sides.

"Forgive my staring. I did not realize until this moment how beautiful you are."

He spoke so plainly and directly that she would have laughed, had she not been so frightened. When he did not smile, her mouth dropped open. "Do you…do you mean to insult me, sir, with this jest?"

"Jest? Jest? Ha, I never spoke with more sincerity in my life. You do not mean, you *cannot* mean, to imply that no one has ever said this to you before."

"I am not beautiful by any means. I am under no illusions."

"If you do not think yourself beautiful, then I fear I must tell you that you are greatly disillusioned. Who told you that you were not?"

"I need only to look in a glass to know. And it is not what has been said, but what has *not* been said, if you take my meaning."

"Then…then the world must be mad. There is no other accounting for this."

Her whole body on fire, Lauren was still standing there when Gideon came back for another bucket of water. "Ah. She is *excellent* in being useful. Lauren! Dress yourself already."

Neither of them responded as Gideon took another bucket, pausing to look at each of them with impatience.

"You are Lauren Warden?" Rathnar said when Gideon was gone.

"Yes."

"I remember you as a child. You and your brother."

"Do you? Forgive me if I do not recall."

"I was but newly appointed secretary when you…when your mother was killed."

"Oh. I see."

"She was a kind woman."

"Yes."

"And your brother is…he is—"

She could see him floundering, searching for a noun or adjective that was not insulting. She decided to help him.

"He is the actor who insulted the king, yes. And may be the man who stole Gideon's ring and identity."

"Ah. Yes. He."

"I have not seen him in all these years. I very much hope to see him soon. I – I must beg of you to be merciful, if you can, though I know it is not in your nature to be so."

He softened under her gaze, almost like a flower wilting in the heat. Her eyebrows lifted. "Never before have I cared to be thought merciless. How strange that...I would not have you think so for all the world."

Again Gideon tramped through for another bucket. He guffawed with exasperation, seeing them still locked in their former positions. "*Excuse* me!" No one took notice of him. "Next my dog will sprout wings." Water sloshed down the hallway his wake.

"For your sake," Rathnar said, as if they were never interrupted, "I will let him plead his case. For now, that is all I can promise."

Lauren smiled. "For now, it is enough."

Rathnar nodded and then cleared his throat. "Clothes, yes. I do not think the dwarf widow will have a gown to your size." Lauren giggled, and he rewarded her with what she knew instinctively was a rare smile. "You will have to content yourself with a shirt and breeches of mine, until we reach the next town. I do not have the leisure to ride back into Lowden as it lies in the wrong direction."

He pulled out a white shirt and black breeches from his bag and handed them to her. "I fear they will be a trifle large."

His prediction proved to be an egregious overstatement. She had to roll the sleeves several times before she found her hands, and the breeches, knee-length on Rathnar, dragged on the floor. Though he was very lean, she still had to belt the waist, and the hem of the shirt reached her knees. Still, it was a vast improvement over her soiled dress, which she washed while Gideon took his bath. Unlike her, he languished in his bath until Rathnar ordered him to hurry.

Once they were dressed and packed, and after Rathnar helped himself to two horses from the widow's stable, they mounted and awaited orders.

"We ride to Zirnich," Rathnar said, and Gideon nodded impatiently. He too was wearing Rathnar's clothes. The black velvet doublet was ill-fitting, but he did his best to maintain dignity.

"This information I have already gleaned. Tell me something of which I am ignorant."

"On the way."

Rathnar reined his horse toward the road, and Gideon kicked his in a trot to catch up. Lauren rode behind them, keeping close enough to hear. As they rode through a grove of apple trees, she reached up and snatched an apple overhead; Rathnar glanced back and caught her in the act. When she blushed he smiled, so she relaxed and ate her apple. Gideon threw her another exasperated look, and reached for an apple of his own. The branch held steadfast; he was nearly pulled off his horse before wrenching the apple free. The branch snapped backwards, and Lauren had to duck before it hit her in the face.

He took a loud, crunching bite of his apple just as Rathnar began to speak. "The imposters are going to Rowan. If we don't catch them in time, they are going to kill the king and queen's long-lost daughter Kassandra."

Gideon spit out his bite, showering his horse's ears and head with apple bits. Lauren's eyes filled with tears. The sudden reappearance of a dead princess meant nothing to her. Her brother, and now she, would be sailing right into the arms of the Selphyn, the race that killed their mother.

FOURTEEN

THE TOWN OF Zirnich the morning after the festival resembled the aftermath of a great siege. Trash littered the streets, along with broken glass, shredded costume pieces and empty wine cups. Tattered ribbons clung to tree branches, and crows and blackbirds darkened the road, picking at discarded food. A vendor's cart was turned sideways, the wood split down the middle, and looked as though it were alive with the dozens of crows that crowded in to feast on sausage. With the exception of their cawing, the streets were quiet, a sharp contrast to the raucousness of the night before.

The horses carefully picked their way through the litter, down the road that was dyed red from spilled wine. No one spoke, though Jonathan almost wished they would, just to distract him from the inevitable. A fierce breeze blew from the west, bringing with it the smell of salt water and seaweed. Jonathan closed his eyes and tried to ignore the nauseating turn of his stomach. Wine and anxiety did not mix well.

As they crested a hill they caught sight of the harbor. Dozens of ships were anchored, with even more approaching, their sails billowing in the wind. Crewmen and fishermen were shouting, and cargo was transported back and forth on pulleys. Instead of crows, the sky was filled with seagulls and pelicans, and across the beached landscape was evidence of abandoned bonfires from the night before.

Jonathan stopped the group and turned to face them, seeing reflections of his pale face and anxious eyes in each of them. "I do not need to tell you that from henceforth you do not exist, only the character you are meant to portray. Though we will not meet the Selphyn for two days, we must needs be well prepared. We cannot afford a single slip. Do not address each other by your given, Christian names. Do not allude to our plays. If you speak of our mission, speak of it as your character, and in terms of what responsibilities your character has. We are here to escort a princess home. You will concern yourself with naught else." His gaze met Richard's, and he resisted a shiver. "Any questions or concerns before we leave the life of players behind?"

No one spoke, but Gregory nudged his horse to move in closer to Jonathan's. Jonathan put a hand on his head, and whispered, "Think of it as but a game, young Gregory. Better yet, a play. Your best role yet."

"And when we return, perhaps I can play a prince. Or a soldier."

Jonathan looked away. "As it pleases you. I promise a reprieve from women."

"Thank you."

He waited for the others to speak, but not even Thomas had anything to say. Miranda pulled her cloak tightly around her throat against the wind, small beads of moisture gathering on her forehead from the ocean breeze.

As he led them down the hill toward the harbor, Sebastian intoned a prayer for their safe passage there and back again, which Jonathan found slightly comforting. He wondered if it occurred to Sebastian how blasphemous it was for him to be impersonating a monk.

The closer they were to the harbor the worse the wind was. It whipped their cloaks and hair and stung their eyes. The ships rocked violently, not an auspicious start to their journey across the channel. Jonathan dismounted and approached the closest ship while the others waited. Crewmen were busy loading crates, and Jonathan faltered until a man in a striped shirt noticed his hesitation and approached.

As if it were an everyday occurrence, Jonathan calmly said, "We seek passage to Rowan, and will pay handsomely." He jiggled his purse for emphasis.

At worst he expected a laugh, but this fellow's darkened countenance was worse. "There's no ship, no captain here who will take you to Rowan."

"But I have gold—"

"No one. You understand? Unless we have a Selphyn onboard, we are expressly forbidden, by pain of death, to sail there."

"But we're expected—"

"Ah." He pointed down the harbor, and Jonathan followed his gaze to a ship with a dolphin figurehead. A cloaked figure sat on the stern railing, facing their direction. Jonathan went cold. "Oh, God."

"They have been here some three days or so, waiting for you."

"No, no, no. We cannot — we cannot sail on a Selphyn vessel. Please. I will pay you the entire contents of this purse—"

"You said they are expecting you. What objections have you to sailing with them?"

Jonathan closed his eyes. "Two more days of peace, safety. Sanity. There is nothing I can do—"

"No. She saw you anyway."

"'She'?"

"Selphyn girl. They are not so terrible. We do an amiable trade with them. Mind, off these shores, not those of Rowan. They are a quiet sort of folk, but courteous. Better mannered than pirates."

He walked back to tell the others, his legs all but numb. Through their protests and Miranda's tears he kept his eyes fixed on the sea, at the gray smudge on the horizon that was their island destination. He had no patience for Thomas's yelling, and did not react when Ralf reined his horse backwards to retreat. Richard grabbed the reins and yanked the horse in close. Whatever he said to Ralf ceased his struggle, and when it was quiet Jonathan motioned for them to follow. They dismounted and pulled their horses, boots and hooves sinking in loose sand.

"Dignity, above all," Jonathan said without turning. He heard a snort and ignored it.

The figure on the railing leapt down to the pier and met Jonathan halfway. The hood was pulled back, and he saw it was indeed a woman. Like all Selphyn her hair was the color of spun gold, her skin bronze, her face long and angular. Her eyes were a bright turquoise, wide and intense; when they fixed on Jonathan he saw them shift with surprise.

"Gideon Ambrose?"

"I am he."

While she contemplated him he folded his hands behind him so she would not see them shaking.

"I thought you…" He held his breath and did not exhale until she said, "Well met," and offered her hand to shake. He surreptitiously wiped a sweaty palm on his breeches before taking her hand, which was slender. The skin was rough, fingertips callused from some sort of manual labor.

"I am Corrine, and welcome you aboard *Transcendence*."

"Thank you." He turned to introduce his companions but Corrine had already leapt back onto the railing, directing them to board on the gangplank with their horses. Jonathan expected the horses to balk when handled by a Selphyn crew, but they followed with their natural calm. He wished he could say the same about the humans. The horses were taken below deck, and Jonathan stood with his company on the forecastle deck, staring at an equally curious Selphyn crew. All were cloaked, and when the wind picked up, snatches of bright silk and satin were revealed underneath. Most were barefoot, the hems of their trousers gathered in tightly around their ankles. Gold and silver anklets and even toe rings winked in the sunlight, and two men had animals tattooed on their bare ankles. Jonathan could not resist and looked down at Corrine's feet, shocked to see their blatant bareness all the way up to her anklebone. She too wore anklets and toe rings, and had black spirals tattooed on the tops of her feet. He looked back up at her face, expecting to see some evidence of the knowledge of her impropriety: a blush, shifting, guilty eyes. She met his gaze evenly, her bright eyes outlined with thick, black kohl.

A man emerged from the cabin and smiled broadly, taking Jonathan aback. He wore a blue silk coat over trousers and a shirt with billowing sleeves of the same color and material. He too was barefoot, and his hair, long and golden, was curled at the ends. His eye kohl matched Corrine's, and braided into his hair was what appeared to be red fur. He pumped Jonathan's hand.

"I am Uthen, captain of this vessel. I welcome you and your companions most heartily."

Grateful there was no language barrier – King Balon, who conquered the Selphyn over two-hundred years ago, adopted the language of Miken's holy land and made it his own – Jonathan thanked him, wondering if he had imagined the fleeting look of shock that crossed over Uthen's face just before he grabbed Jonathan's hand. He wondered if somehow they knew and were playing dumb. Was there some glaring physical characteristic that he had or lacked that betrayed him? If this turned out to be the case, and somehow he survived, he was going to murder Leonardis in his sleep for his carelessness.

"Corrine can show you to your quarters, unless of course you would prefer enjoying the fresh air and beautiful scenery as we set sail–"

"Our quarters, please. Yes. I thank you."

Uthen shook his hand yet again, and Jonathan felt a wave of revulsion. "You are invited all to join me for dinner in my cabin."

"So please you, we are weary from our long ride here and would prefer to dine below." He was going to make himself at home below deck and never resurface again until they reached Rowan.

"As you wish. We are happy to serve your every need."

Below deck, alone, there was a massive, unified sigh of relief. They each claimed a cot, grateful for the wooden partition that divided them from the crew. They heard the loud clanging of the chain as the anchor was hoisted, and everyone sat down when a large swell rocked the boat with an unforgiving violence. Jonathan looked at Miranda and saw her lying down, her face positively green.

"Oh, no. You suffer seasickness?"

"I never knew till now. My first passage, this. Oh, God. A bucket, please."

He held back her hair while she vomited, deciding he would suffer this indignation with her a thousand times before joining the Selphyn. He brought her a wet cloth and placed it on her brow, softening when she moaned under the force of another swell.

"Perhaps if you slept."

"Yes. But I am too anxious as yet. Will you talk to me and distract me?"

"What shall I say?"

"Talk to me about – bucket, please." When she was finished, she completed her sentence as if never having left it. "—Your family, your days as a boy in the theater. Anything."

He chose the latter, and spoke of the time he joined the King's Men as a boy. Sebastian put a hand on his shoulder; he looked up and smiled, thinking the older man meant to contribute to the discussion and reminisce. "You have forgotten already. That man no longer exists."

"Oh, hang it! This is a special situation."

"Perhaps you ought to tell her about your days as young Gideon."

"Go to. I can make an exception here."

"You risk us all!"

"I shall whisper. Go."

She made room for him on her cot, and soon she was spooned in front of him, his mouth just behind her ear. As he told her the story of his first role as a kidnapped princess, the others lay on their cots, their eyes closed. Jonathan envied them in their escape, but soon found that he was enjoying this, the smell of her hair, the curve of her body against his, her soft laughs in between groans at something he said. He talked until he was hoarse, and there was a chorus of snores around him.

"It was helping. Talk a little more."

"Perhaps if you talked…"

"Yes. All right. Ask me something."

He meant to ask her about her childhood, her parents. Instead he said, "Why did you bed Thomas?" She stiffened against him and he sighed. "Forgive me."

"I…"

"Do you love him?"

"No. Well, as I might a brother."

He was quiet for a long time. "Why then risk your prospects? Actors talk. Terrible gossipmongers, we."

She laughed. "I have no prospects. What prospects could I have, as a player?"

"But your family…your parents, I think, must be rich. How else came you by that bail money, and so quickly too?"

"They are rich. My father is a very wealthy merchant."

"Then you could have married well."

Again there was a long silence. The rocking of the ship lulled him though he was anxious for her reply. Just as he thought she had drifted off to sleep, or at least meant to ignore the statement, she said, "My prospects were ruined before I turned player. I was…engaged."

"Engagements often end. Your virtue still intact, you could have found another suitor—"

"And passions often conquer sense. My virtue was sold for a honeyed tongue filled with words of love. He took my dowry and my maidenhead; I stood in my bridal clothes in a full church, all accounted for, save the groom."

"Oh, God. Miranda—"

"Their scorn I could live with, and other suitors did press their suit. But before long my folly was visible to all."

"You were quick."

"Yes. And my family dishonored. My father's trade destroyed. We moved from Chauncery to Elkyn, to make a fresh start."

"You might have pretended—"

"And lived my life in fear that the truth would be learned? No. I found myself at the playhouses in Diernioch, day after day. I could lose myself in the fantasy lives of others."

"But the child?"

"Did not live."

He heard the catch in her throat and pulled her in closer. He wanted, more than anything, to tell her none of it mattered, it did not alter his opinion of her, but the words caught in his throat. Then she was sitting up, vomiting into the bucket. Her shoulders shook as she rose to wash her face.

"I cannot sleep, I cannot escape it, this terrible rocking."

Thomas, on the cot next to them, propped himself up on one elbow. "Below deck is the worst place to be for seasickness. She needs fresh air."

"I'll take you."

He hoped this gesture would atone for the turn their conversation had taken at his prodding; he hoped she understood the sacrifice he was making on her behalf. He followed her up the narrow stairs to the deck, each of them sucking in deep breaths of blessed, fresh air.

"I did not realize until now just how rank the air is below," he said, and she nodded, her face instantly wet with moisture. It was almost dusk; they had been talking for hours. He walked with her to the railing, careful to avoid eye contact with any of the Selphyn crew. She closed her eyes, face in the wind, and he noticed her color was better.

"She is ill?"

He jumped, and saw Corrine behind them. "Yes."

"I have medicine that will help."

"Thank you, but I do not think—"

Miranda turned. "I would be most grateful, madam."

When the Selphyn was gone, ostensibly to retrieve the medicine, Jonathan said, "You ought not to drink anything – it could be poison."

"And to what end would they poison me?"

"Very well, an accidental poisoning if you will. What is harmless to them could be toxic to us—"

But Corrine was back with a purple vial; Miranda ignored Jonathan's imploring looks and drank it down without so much as smelling it. An eagle flew down low over the ship, and Corrine lifted her hand, lightly brushing the golden wingtips with her fingers while her human companions cowered for fear of stray talons. She laughed at their reaction, but did not offer an explanation.

Miranda said, following the distant eagle cry, "Is it possible to feel the effects so soon? I feel much improved already."

"Yes. You must be hungry."

"Famished!"

"Please do us the pleasure of dining with us. Both of you. The captain would be honored."

Jonathan took Miranda's elbow, incredulous when she resisted. "I think I should like that," she said.

"Are you mad?" he whispered.

"If I go back below, I may get sick again."

"And that would be preferable." To Corrine, he said, "Forgive us, but we are still much fatigued—"

His mouth dropped when Corrine pulled his hand from Miranda's elbow. "The laws of your land have perchance made you her master. Here, there are no such bonds of gender, stature or wealth. She may do as she pleases."

"How dare you—"

"Further, when we land there will be no such hiding in your chamber from your hosts. You would do well to acquaint yourself with our—"

Jonathan put up his hand, surprised by how easy it suddenly was to be Gideon. "No. If I can put off the inevitable, I will endeavor to do so as long as possible. If Helen wishes to dine with you, she may. I am not her master."

The corner of Corrine's mouth turned up. "No? Then I misread you, and the pull of your arm. I bid you good evening. Someone will be down shortly with meals for you and your men. Shall we, Helen?"

Miranda threw an apologetic look over her shoulder as she followed Corrine, and Jonathan put up his hands in surrender. He had not anticipated losing control so soon. He watched the women until they disappeared into the captain's cabin, ignoring the stares of the Selphyn crew on the rigging and at the helm. A lurch of the boat threw him off balance, and he grabbed the rigging to balance himself, wishing it were as easy to balance the turbulence of his mind.

FIFTEEN

IN THE NEXT town Gideon and Lauren purchased new clothes, and Gideon bought a rapier, dagger, bow and a quiver full of arrows, to arm himself against the Selphyn. Rathnar watched these proceedings with exasperation, buying nothing for himself save the services of a courier. He noticed Lauren watching him write, and surprised her by explaining himself.

"A letter to King Fallon. In his letter to Thaddeus, he instructed that all correspondence be sent to the Swan in Zirnich. I fear me though, that not expecting a letter, no one will be sailing to Zirnich unless it be to conduct trade."

"I thought the Selphyn were forbidden to enter Salsima."

"And I would expect that the merchants in Zirnich rob them blind anyway."

Lauren colored, though she could not say why. By this time Gideon was tapping his foot, and Rathnar raised an eyebrow. "You are finished packing your arsenal?"

"You mock me, but will be glad of my defenses once we are in Rowan."

"I will be sure to hide behind you."

"Ha."

Back on their horses, Lauren smoothed her new black skirt and admired the matching bodice. It was a fine material, finer by half than anything she had ever owned before. She caught Rathnar watching and blushed again.

"You are pleased?"

"Yes. Very. I cannot ever repay you—"

"Nonsense. Call it a gift from the Crown."

"How reassuring," Gideon said, "to know the royal treasury is in such good hands."

"You like your velvet doublet well enough."

"For which *I* can repay."

The cobblestoned street gave way to a dirt road, and as they rode out of town they found themselves flanked by an array of wildflowers, each more beautiful than the next. Their perfume sweetened the air, mixing with the delicious scent of pines. A shadow fell over them and Lauren looked up, spotting a convergence of dark clouds. Soon the smell of rain would comingle with the others, creating an olfactory sensation. She was not surprised when Gideon observed the clouds and complained, negating her appreciation.

When no one responded, he forced the subject at hand back on them, the same theme he had harped on ever since they left the cellar. Lauren wished he would just remain silent so she could enjoy the beauty of the day, but knew it was not at all likely.

"My mind still spins in disbelief of this whole affair. That Leonardis and Thaddeus would – the king's own brothers…Have you told the king?"

"No," Rathnar said.

"And why? Are you not his secretary? His most *exalted* spymaster? Is that not your duty, to keep their Majesties informed?"

"My duty is to fix the problem. Then report."

"I think in this instance they would prefer–"

"Their expectations of my duties are very clear, especially those of the queen. I will offer an example. My business of late in Chauncery, that same which detained me from finding you, was to halt a coup in progress. Some distant cousin or other of the queen, deciding he had a claim to the throne, sought to build an army and overthrow their Majesties. I shall report to the queen, upon our return, that her cousin Sir William is dead, and the plot overturned. It will save her the agony of sentencing her own kin to death, as well as the anxiety and fear of a planned assassination. So have I dealt with treason these near twenty years, and so I will continue to do so."

Gideon was about to speak but Lauren beat him to it. She ignored his hostile look. "You killed her cousin? He will not receive a fair trial?"

"Good mistress, I intercepted correspondence between Sir William and his cohorts for months. His guilt was clear."

"Yet…is that not murder?"

Rathnar turned back in his saddle, and she was still unable to look at his face in full view. She looked down while he spoke.

"He was killed trying to flee."

"Poisoned? Stabbed in his sleep?"

When she dared to look up he was smiling at her. "I admire your persistence."

"It is for my brother I worry. Will he be not 'killed trying to flee'?"

His expression sobered. "I promised you I will be merciful. I keep my word."

He turned back around, and a minute later Gideon leaned in

toward him, though Lauren had no trouble overhearing him.

"You contradict your reputation. Sir Francis does not go soft, even for a woman."

"Gideon, have you *looked* at her? She would teach these flowers beauty."

"Ah. I think this business has overtaxed your brain."

Lauren, her head down, smiled.

"What plan you to do with Leonardis and Thaddeus then?" Gideon asked.

"Dealing with the king's own brothers is a different matter entirely. I will have to allow their Majesties to decide; I can only present the evidence. That is, only of course, if the princess is still there and alive when we arrive in Rowan. If she is dead, the king and queen must know nothing of this."

Gideon turned sharply to face Rathnar. "Who — who else knows? Claude, surely, and—"

"Claude is dead, or will be by the time we return."

In the ensuing silence, Lauren heard the buzzing of a swarm of bees in the flowers. She stared at the mass of them, their movement blurred, while Gideon attempted to ask the question she dreaded.

"But...Lauren and I..."

"No one will miss an annoying steward, especially Thaddeus, now that he knows he was spying. The king's favorite courtier, on the other hand...Let me ask you this: what purpose would it serve to tell the king that his daughter was alive all this time, but because we were not fast enough, she is now dead? Again?"

"You mean...we would be to blame?"

"Yes, in part."

"Oh."

"And so I think I have nothing to fear in your confidence." He turned again to look at Lauren. "Either of you."

She met his gaze and nodded. "And my brother too—"

"Lauren." The way he said her name was enough, and she began to cry. "The man is committing the worst treason imaginable. If the princess lives, I will bring him back to be tried in court. If she is dead...I will give you but one hour with him, that is all. He may choose the manner of his death, and I will endeavor to see it as painless as possible."

"You said you would show mercy—"

"As for the others — never sun shall they see again, and will wish, when I am through, that they never lived to see it at all."

* * *

Out of the corner of his eye Thaddeus saw Leonardis approaching and turned his attention away from the king's sentencing of Claude. There would be no surprises. The evidence against him was overwhelming. In spite of himself Thaddeus had to applaud Rathnar, though the man terrified him. Especially now.

"Do you think he knows everything?" Leonardis asked.

"Yes. Claude was missing two fingers. Regardless of which evidence he was gathering – real or feigned – Sir Francis undoubtedly heard everything."

"Then why protect us by planting false evidence?"

"Why think you? He's going after her himself."

Thaddeus heard his brother's sharp inhalation. "To bring her back? Selphyn-raised?"

"Rathnar's duty lies in protecting the interests of the king and queen. Getting their daughter and only heir back, regardless of her upbringing, is in their best interests."

"And disastrous for the realm."

Thaddeus took a breath. "There is more."

"Oh. What a relief."

"I questioned Helen regarding Gideon's absence. He left days ago to follow the trail of his impersonator."

"Oh, God! How–"

"Some innkeeper or other, Helen knows not much, sent word that a man was using his name and ring. Gideon was supposed to return the following day, and she has not received word from him since."

"Do you think he and Rathnar–"

"Very like. Yes." Thaddeus met his brother's eyes. "Can you send word to someone? In Zirnich perhaps?"

Leonardis straightened his robe and paused during the shouting of the court, the cheering for Claude's execution. "Yes. There is someone in Sterling, actually, who can stop them."

SIXTEEN

AT A FIRST glance, it was an ordinary captain's cabin, with nautical instruments, the ship's log, flags and a wine decanter. There was nothing to delineate it as a Selphyn cabin, save for the dining arrangements.

They were already seated when Miranda approached, and no less than fifteen Selphyn, seated at a table long enough to serve as a seafaring vessel itself, stood upon her arrival. The party was made up of mostly crewmen, a practice that was unheard of in Salsima where none but distinguished guests would be invited to dine with the captain. Their bright eyes, intense and penetrating, regarded her with warmth while she eyed them in return with suspicion. She accepted a vacant chair next to Corrine, and sat down, her hands trembling, wishing she had stayed with Jonathan. And then dinner was served.

Succulent lamb and pheasant, coated with a garlic and butter cream sauce, was heaped on her plate. Every bite was a near religious experience, and Miranda was unable to quell a few moans of appreciation. Captain Uthen smiled, and she blushed when she realized the Selphyn were not yet eating.

At Uthen's signal, the others bowed their heads as their captain spoke. "We thank you, spirit of lamb, pheasant, rabbit and fish for your sacrifice."

Something bumped against Miranda's foot under the table and she jumped. As she reached her hand down, teeth gently closed around her shoe and began to chew playfully. Her fingers touched a cold nose and a long muzzle; the chewing stopped when her hand reached pointed ears behind which she began scratching. Paws landed on her knees, and a head began wiggling upward to find purchase on her lap. Expecting a dog, Miranda grinned and looked down.

The fox, paws and head on her lap, climbed up her skirted legs, squeezing itself like a weasel to fit between the table and her waist. Sitting completely on her lap now, it put both paws on her shoulders and began licking her face. She laughed and scratched its ears again.

"I do beg your pardon," Uthen said. "That is my friend Belcastro. I'm afraid he is easily excitable with new guests. Belcastro, do give this kind lady some room."

Although his voice lacked command and firmness, the fox still jumped down as if having received a sharp reprimand. He sat on Miranda's feet, the weight and warmth of him a lovely reassurance in this room filled with heathens.

Miranda smiled at Uthen to indicate no offense had been taken, when she again noticed the red fur woven into his hair. Its origin now obvious, she searched the heads of the other Selphyn, looking for animal fetishes. She saw black-and-white fur – skunk? – bear claws, feathers, snakeskin, brown fur and white fur among other things woven into the hair of her hosts. Corrine, watching her make her observation, had a large eagle feather tied into her golden locks.

"That's why Fallon wore a raven feather," Miranda said, and Corrine, following the train of her thought, nodded.

"We Selphyn each have a totem animal, and we wear a symbolic token to honor our relationship with that animal."

Enthralled, Miranda said, "How do you choose which animal will be your totem?"

"We do not choose. They choose us."

"Oh." When no further explanation was offered, Miranda said, "Syldonia. Did she have an animal totem?"

"Hers was the dolphin. I believe she wore shells hidden behind her neck when she lived in Salsima."

Miranda imagined the Selphyn princess playing with a dolphin and smiled. It fit perfectly.

"How do you find your dinner?" Uthen asked.

"I believe I have had none better."

"Excellent. I am sorry your companions could not join you. We will bring them plates once we have finished here."

The fox shifted on Miranda's feet, curling up to sleep, his warm tail draped over her ankle. "The more sorry they, if it were known what they missed."

Corrine smiled at her, and Miranda experienced the oddest sensation. It eluded her for a few minutes, but as she fell into easy conversation with Corrine, she realized what it was: a sense of companionship, for the first time, with another female. It was as welcome as it was shocking, and for the first time since they boarded the ship, she began to relax.

* * *

It rained for three days in row.

They rode quietly, not speaking except out of necessity, huddled in their woolen cloaks. Gideon fell ill on the third day, sneezing and coughing, but otherwise mercifully quiet, allowing Lauren to enjoy the sound of rain pelting her hood and the ground. The horses trudged through mud and deep puddles, and the northern mountains were shrouded with low clouds and fog so that only their gray bases were visible. Rathnar was more imposing than ever, with his hood pulled as far down as it would go over his face, giving Lauren only glimpses of the white skin underneath. He looked positively ethereal in the swirls of fog and rain, a great bent and hulking figure, like Death itself.

They slept in inns where they could, but spent one rainy night camped in the forest. Rathnar made a tent of cloaks and blankets and was not heard from until morning; Lauren thought of a cat that despised water, enraged if just one paw fell in a puddle. His reticence was appreciated as Lauren preferred keeping her distance from him.

The rain abetted the morning of the fourth day, though the fog and low clouds remained, perpetuating the wetness on the branches and pine needles. They just broke camp, riding back on the muddy road, when Lauren heard a noise in the brush. She glanced over with mild curiosity, thinking she might see a rabbit or a startled doe. A mass of thick, black fur moved next to her, with only a bush separating them. She caught sight of a yellow eye and a pointed ear just as her horse stomped and shied away with a neigh of fright.

Gideon and Rathnar looked back, both of them with their hoods lowered.

"There's a – there's a wolf—"

It darted into the trees as Lauren fought with her reins. Gideon began to unharness his quiver, while Rathnar regarded her with an impassive expression.

"He's been following us for some time."

Gideon's bow was caught on the saddle and he nearly dropped it. "What? And you said nothing?"

"A lone wolf will not attack three people with horses," Rathnar said, and Lauren heard a sigh of impatience. "And if he meant to harm us, he would have attacked in the night. I did not want to cause any unnecessary fright."

Lauren shivered, thinking about a wolf sniffing around while she was asleep in her bedroll. Gideon now had his bow and quiver loose, and slipped off his saddle, heading for the trees. Rathnar reached down and caught Gideon's head between his thumb and ring finger, the way one might grab a large, dead rat.

"Wolves are exquisite creatures, and that one means us no harm. Leave him be."

Gideon scowled but obeyed, and they were soon back on their way. Lauren nudged her horse forward so that she was riding alongside Rathnar, whom she sensed was purposefully avoiding her. She studied his profile which confirmed her suspicion when he looked back at her when she saw the wolf.

"You are not well."

His skin had taken on a slight yellowish hue, and there were circles under his eyes. He lowered his head so that his long hair obstructed his face from her view. "I am well enough."

"No. You look terrible."

She heard what sounded like an amused sigh. "I have been called worse."

"You ought to sleep a day or two at an inn–"

"No time."

"But–"

"Your concern touches me more than you will ever know. But we cannot delay."

"At least tonight?"

"Yes. We should reach Sterling by dusk, the last large city before Zirnich. We can find an inn."

Lauren was surprised by a sudden eagerness to share her history. "I have not been to Zirnich since I was a very young girl. I am anxious to see it with a woman's eyes."

"You were born there, perhaps?"

"Yes. My father was a fisherman, my mother a seamstress."

"Why the move to Diernioch?"

"She needed help when my father died, and she again with child. She heard the Lady Syldonia was kind and generous, taking in ladies to attend on her regardless of their stature."

"And the lady did take her in."

"Yes, unheard of as it was: hiring a maid with a child and another on the way. We were very well cared for -- educated, clothed and fed. But my mother's sanctuary soon proved to be her hell."

"The king misused her."

"Yes. As he did Syldonia, and very like countless other ladies of the court. Oh, dear. I suppose that now you must dispose of me for treason. I shall be but a footnote in your report: *killed while attempting to flee.*"

He rewarded her with a genuine smile, one that showed a row of meticulously cared-for teeth, white and straight. The smile transformed his face, softening his eyes and those hollow, high-boned cheeks. She could not help but smile in return.

"You would do well to smile more." Blood flooded her face when she realized what she said.

"And ruin my reputation? Never. You ought to speak your mind more. A beautiful hue blossoms in your cheeks, and your eyes dance with radiance."

Gideon, on the other side of Rathnar, sneezed loudly. Grateful for the distraction, Lauren said, "God bless you."

"And God bless the both of you if you truly find the other attractive. Miken's second coming."

"I do much wonder how Gideon survived being locked up for five days in the wine cellar. Had I been his constant companion, I would have cut his throat with a glass shard before dawn of the second day."

"Oh, how my sides heave with laughter," Gideon said.

Lauren stifled a giggle. "I made good use of the bottle corks."

Rathnar laughed out loud, a startling noise that frightened his horse. Gideon pointed at her. "So safe you are with the king's spymaster between us! I ought to have you flogged for that."

Rathnar instantly sobered. "Say that again and I'll see your head on a pike, greeting visitors as they cross the bridge to the castle."

Lauren's stomach flipped and she casually reined in her horse so that she fell behind the two men. Rathnar's shoulders fell forward, as if in disappointment. She silently chastised herself for fancying herself the cause.

As Rathnar promised, they arrived at the outskirts of Sterling at dusk. Like Talsin in the neighboring country of Lansing, Sterling was a valley town famous for its vineyards. Twice a year it hosted wine festivals that attracted thousands of visitors, and it was home to many rich lords and ladies. As such, it was well fortified and fully enclosed by a towering wall. Sentries were posted at every entry gate, and the three travelers were asked for their names and purpose at the eastern gate.

When the guards grouped together to quietly confer upon hearing their names, Lauren shifted uneasily in her saddle. She saw Rathnar's face, illuminated by the torchlight, tighten. When the guards descended the stairs, leaving the portcullis closed, Gideon dismounted and demanded an explanation before there was anyone present to give it.

Rathnar said, "Gideon. Get back on your horse. We need to ride out."

Gideon threw him an incredulous look over his shoulder. "I refuse to sleep out-of-doors again tonight. And we have to pass through here to get to Zirnich."

"I think it will be better reconciled in the morning. Something is wrong."

Gideon ignored him and advanced on the soldiers. "I demand to know–"

"Goddamn him," Rathnar said, and Lauren gasped. "He will kill us all."

He pulled back on his reins, as if to flee, and then paused with a resigning drop of his head. He dismounted and did not resist when two soldiers approached to bind his wrists. Gideon threw a punch at one of the soldiers, yelling. Only Lauren remained on her horse, who was stomping and breathing heavily.

"Dismount," a guard said. She glanced at Rathnar who nodded. Gideon was still struggling.

"Gideon," Rathnar said, "there is a time for action and a time for prudence. A wise man knows the difference."

"But they have no claim on us!"

Lauren dismounted and offered her wrists for binding when a guard holding Rathnar said, "We have been instructed by Lord Riordan to detain you. He has been sent for, and will answer your questions if he pleases."

They waited fifteen minutes while Gideon raged and the sun descended. When Lord Riordan arrived, riding a stunning and spirited black horse, it was dark. Lauren saw by torchlight that he was near thirty and handsome, with black, curling hair and a short beard. Like Gideon he wore gold hoops in each ear, and sported an array of rings. He dismounted, ignoring Gideon, and shook one of Rathnar's bound hands.

"Sir Francis."

"Lord Riordan."

"Bartholomew, please. I beg you to forgive this harsh welcome."

"We'll do none of the sort," Gideon said. "How dare you!"

"Master Ambrose. How good to see you again. How fares their Majesties?"

"May the plague rot your nose. What means this?"

"I have orders from Duke Leonardis to take you into custody

until such time as he bids me release you."

Rathnar appeared completely unsurprised, while Gideon let loose a tirade of foul names.

"On what grounds said he?" Rathnar asked.

"On suspicion of treason."

Everyone ignored Gideon's outburst to this intelligence, and Lauren was impressed by Rathnar's calm. "I think you know well enough how unlikely that is."

Bartholomew nodded. "Indeed. You are the royal hound, sniffing out treason. Not the one who commits it."

"And so—"

"And so I am afraid I must obey the duke regardless. He is the king's brother and a prince of the realm. I cannot do otherwise."

"Yes, yes. I see. Perhaps a large purse?"

"Thank you, but no. A large purse is useless if I am imprisoned in the Tower."

"Well spoken."

"Please. Do not make trouble for me, and I will make your stay as comfortable as possible."

"How long?"

Bartholomew shrugged. "We are at the mercy of Leonardis and his whims. I know not."

"I will make one last entreaty. I swear to you, upon my life and that of their Majesties, that I know of a terrible plot. Leonardis has interest in its outcome, and I fear me will endeavor anything to prevent me from uncovering it. I beg you, from one loyal gentleman to another, to release us. I will see you protected and well rewarded."

Lord Riordan smiled. "He warned me you would say as much. I must obey. I am sorry."

"Very well. I can do no more."

At Riordan's order Gideon was gagged. The lord looked him over with his hands on his hips. "You honor your reputation, Master Ambrose. You would do well to remember you are the son of a baron, and will one day inherit his title. Do justice to your parentage, and act a gentleman. Know when you are beaten and surrender with dignity."

There was nothing but muffled curses behind the gag. Lauren was actually embarrassed for him.

Their horses led away, they followed the guards on foot, allowed at last to enter the city. Rathnar caught Lauren, in spite of his bound wrists, when she stumbled. She turned to thank him and was silenced by the terrible look of dejection on his face. He saw her looking and misinterpreted her expression. "I am sorry you are involved in this."

She smiled and shrugged her shoulders. "I find it is rather superior to sweeping floors."

"If we survive all of this, I will see you compensated enough to never sweep again."

She had no words to thank him as she found no joy in his assurance. Her whole life had been spent consumed with worry over her brother and his whereabouts. When John was dead, she would have no aim or purpose in life but to mourn him. And such a life as that was not worth living.

SEVENTEEN

THEY ARRIVED AT the island at midday, and the crew and passengers were rowed to shore in two longboats. The passengers were pale and fighting off the sun from staying holed up below deck, all save for Miranda. She was refreshed and bright-eyed, and while Jonathan envied this, he did not envy the many hours she spent on deck. Before going to sleep each night, she entertained her fellow actors with tales of dining with the Selphyn – their strange habits and connection to animals. Jonathan remembered Syldonia's seashells after Miranda mentioned it; he recalled the Selphyn princess's passion for dolphins but did not know how deep her passion had run.

Now, as he was rowed to shore, he realized he was at the point of no return. He stared longingly back at the ship; the horses were there, and though Corrine assured them they would be well cared for, he was still worried about them. They had not been told until the last minute that the horses would remain on the ship throughout their visit.

Rowan was a rocky and rather unattractive island with an inactive volcano at its center. Most of its surface was covered with volcanic rock from eruptions centuries ago, and where trees and plants should have grown, there were only black lumps, like so many burnt loaves of bread. Instead of a stream there was a long lava bed that reached to the shoreline; they walked alongside this blackened path, through sparse trees with misshapen trunks.

No one spoke: the humans were too intimidated by their Selphyn guides, and the latter kept silent out of respect for this intimidation. Jonathan studied them, looking for the animal fetishes. Sebastian had of course ruled this Selphyn-to-animal relationship unholy and unnatural, but Jonathan found he rather liked the idea of intimacy with animals. Uthen and his fox Belcastro certainly made an endearing example; for awhile the fox trotted alongside his feet and then put up his paws like a child reaching for a parent. Uthen obligingly scooped him up and put the fox on his shoulder, where he faced backwards, watching everyone march behind him. Jonathan continuously fought a smile watching their exchange, lest he meet with disapproval from his peers.

All was proceeding well until a pack of white wolves burst out of the shrubs.

Miranda screamed, and Jonathan's "soldiers" unsheathed their broadswords. Jonathan was too stunned to retrieve his rapier, and stumbled backwards. A wolf was on him in an instant, knocking him over onto his back. He cringed and tried to protect his face; after a few seconds of struggling he realized he was being ardently licked and not eaten at all.

He pushed himself up on his elbows, laughing when the wolf put its front paws on his shoulders and licked his ear. The wolf slid off and rolled, offering a belly to be rubbed, and Jonathan saw his attacker was a she-wolf. He rubbed her belly, smiling when her rear leg kicked in frenetic ecstasy. He looked up, ready to say that this wolf was not so unlike a pet dog, when he saw he was the only one – the only human, that is – that had been jumped on.

The Selphyn had taken no notice, as they were hugging and scratching the wolves that were writhing at their feet, but the actors were frozen, gaping at Jonathan with expressions that ranged from surprise to disgust. Jonathan cleared his throat and stood up, pushing the she-wolf gently down when she tried to jump on him again.

"Odd," he said. "I suppose they can sense an animal lover."

Three more wolves joined the first, and he could barely walk for all of their prancing and jumping around his feet. Thomas fell into step next to him, neatly kicking a wolf out of the way that came too close.

"They are said to be demonic. You recall the midwife they tore to shreds?"

"Good God, I did forget."

He leaned over to push them back, but the she-wolf would not be separated from him. When he walked she pressed her side against his calf and kept pace with him; when he stopped she sat on his boot. She looked up at him adoringly, tongue lolling out the side of her mouth, and Jonathan found he could not summon a sufficient amount of revulsion. He put his hand on the top of her head; the fur was as soft as a baby rabbit. She pushed her nose against the inside of his wrist and he ran his hand down her soft throat to her chest, feeling the steady beat of her heart. She wrapped her paws around his arm and held on with a lover's tenacity, dancing on her back legs.

Uthen's fox scrambled down and joined the wolves, rolling and playing as Jonathan pried his arm loose. He tried not to look down at his companion, though he felt her rub against his leg, undoubtedly leaving behind a carpet's worth of white hair on his breeches.

As they drew closer to the volcano the trees increased, the

ground below them spared when the lava ostensibly projected far beyond the volcano's base. This change in scenery afforded little reassurance as the trees were more of the same on shore, twisted and bent. When they were led to a path that cut through, Jonathan felt as though they were walking into the belly of a beast as the trees formed a natural tunnel. Stepping out, however, was like traversing into another world. The trees here had been cleared to make room for a golden palace built in the fashion of an immense temple with columns, archways and statues. Behind it the purple volcano stood like a protective god, a vengeful one that was now sleeping.

The humans followed the Selphyn, and their white wolves, into an open-air courtyard decorated with animal statues. In the center, where one would find a fountain in Salsima, was the most stunning statue of Miken the Archangel Jonathan had ever seen. For a moment he was too absorbed in the beauty of his extended wings and glowing armor to understand the significance, and then he heard Sebastian mutter a prayer. Jonathan had always been under the impression that, while the archangel had been born as a human in a Selphyn land, the Selphyn never believed in nor worshipped him. As he admired the statue more closely, his mouth fell open. The archangel's face was long and angular, a telltale Selphyn trait. As Sebastian chanted *blasphemy* repeatedly, Jonathan glanced at the Selphyn sea captain. Uthen smiled and shrugged, as if to say, *What did you expect?*

And then their host appeared from a tall doorway at the far side of the courtyard, the Selphyn king whom Jonathan instantly recognized. Fallon appeared virtually untouched by the seventeen years that separated him from the younger version Jonathan knew, and yet it was impossible. The man must have had fifty years if not more, and yet his face was unlined, as smooth as the golden statue of St. Miken. He was dressed in sparkling gold trousers, tapered tightly at the ankle, a matching shirt, and a long, billowing coat made of purple silk. His feet and head were bare, matching those of his fellow Selphyn, and as he approached, Jonathan and his companions pulled off their caps and knelt.

"Please, please," he said. "We do not kneel upon ceremony here. Rise, and be welcome."

As Jonathan straightened he found himself face to face with the Selphyn king. His hair, almost the same color as shirt and trousers, fell in loose curls to his shoulders, the raven feather still there. Fallon's eyes, outlined in thick, black kohl, were large and bright, a color that could only be described as violet. There was no denying that, with his high cheekbones and strong chin, he was absolutely beautiful. Jonathan, even as he succumbed to a violent wave of rage, was mesmerized.

As Fallon extended his hand to shake Jonathan's, his smile began to fade. His heartbeat accelerating, Jonathan shook his hand, the skin of which was cool and smooth, and fought to keep his expression impassive. When Fallon's grip tightened, his smile completely disappeared. Jonathan's breath caught, and he waited to be denounced.

"You are Gideon Ambrose, yes?"

"Yes."

"I am...so pleased..."

Fallon's voice trailed off and then he seemed to recall himself, and cleared his throat. "I am very pleased indeed to have you here as my guest. Honored, indeed."

"Thank you."

Jonathan was aware his hands were shaking, and gently pulled his hand loose from Fallon's grip. When the king moved on to greet the others, Jonathan wondered if the Selphyn king merely wished to avoid a scene, and would arrest or kill him later on, without so many witnesses. He must have known Jonathan was an imposter, as Jonathan could not otherwise account for his stunned reaction.

In case he was mistaken, Jonathan grounded himself and listened carefully to his other actors reciting their rehearsed lines. Fallon shook each and every one of their hands, even the soldiers and page. When Sebastian refused to shake hands, Fallon actually laughed and forced the issue.

"Brother Dominick, let there be no hard feelings between us. I respect your religion and promise not to inflict ours upon you."

"I hope you will listen to reason. It may not be too late to save your souls from eternal damnation—"

"Ah, you must be Mistress Helen. Gideon has excellent taste, and I know you will be a valued addition to the party back to Salsima."

Jonathan saw Miranda's curtsey out of the corner of his eye. She was quiet but firm. "Thank you, your Majesty. I am glad to be included."

"Call me Fallon, please, the lot of you. You will find we are not so formal here. You are hungry, yes, from your journey? Come inside and feast with us."

As they walked through the towering twin doors, Fallon moved in and put a hand on Jonathan's shoulder. "We will speak after the feast, you and I, of a matter of great urgency."

Jonathan could only nod. He entered the great hall, limbs all a-tremble, and wondered if this was to be his last meal.

* * *

If he knew they were imposters, Miranda thought Fallon was hiding it well. He was gracious and smiling, and insisted that she sit next to him at a ridiculously long table in the great hall. Like the one in the captain's cabin, only on a much larger scale, the table seated Selphyn of no discernable rank. Jonathan made a good show of being appalled when told there were no servants, that even the king served himself. She smiled when he looked down the table for Gregory, thinking it a good character choice for Gideon to find someone to serve him, until, discovering Gregory too far down to be within hearing, shifted his gaze to Miranda. She narrowed her eyes in warning and he gave her a small, apologetic shrug.

"Helen. Be a dear and fill my wine glass."

Fallon looked amused. "The wine is imported from Lansing, and I hope you find it to your liking. We have heard, even here, of your great appreciation of wine."

Miranda made sure everyone heard the grating sound of her chair as she shoved it backwards to stand. She had to walk several feet to round the end of the table and reach Jonathan who was sitting directly across from her. She snatched a wine decanter on the way, spilling some on the white lace tablecloth. He did not acknowledge her as she poured, which befitted his character but irked her nonetheless.

Back at her own seat, she heaped more lamb and pheasant on her plate, already knowing how exquisite it would taste. Prior experience, however, gave her pause to wait for the Selphyn to do their prayer, which interrupted the eating of the others.

Fallon bent his head and led the prayer; Miranda saw, through the curls that fell over her eyes, that Jonathan remained upright, watching his host's every move.

"We thank you, spirit of pheasant, lamb, rabbit, deer and pig for your sacrifice to nurture our bodies."

There was a loud clearing of a throat, and Miranda groaned

inwardly as all eyes shifted to Sebastian. "Bless us, dear Lord, for the food we are about to eat, from your gifts and generosity."

"Amen," the actors said in automatic response. Fallon's eyebrow arched, but he said nothing.

There was silence as everyone ate their food, though Miranda's eyes were restless. She saw that, bereft of their cloaks, the Selphyn all wore bright silks. Some of the women, when they straightened to take a drink or gather more food, revealed a bare midriff, causing Miranda to choke on her wine when she first saw it. She looked at Jonathan to see if he noticed, but he was locked in a game of cat-and-mouse with Fallon, as they guardedly watched the other in between bites.

At length Fallon paused and straightened, a smile playing on his lips. "Gideon. You've not yet asked about the princess."

Jonathan froze. "Indeed, I have not. I confess that…I forgot about her entirely."

"Is that not the purpose of your visit?"

Rather than make a sheepish response, Jonathan shifted in his chair and lowered his tone. "At which mention I should inquire as to our arrangement here. We are to sail back with her on the morrow, yes?"

Fallon burst out laughing. "Goddess, no. You have only just arrived, after traveling many days. I would not hear of it."

"Yet…I believe I speak for all of us when I say we would prefer making our visit here as brief as possible."

Fallon leaned forward. "This is my only opportunity to show your kind that we are not the savages you think us. I mean to keep you here until I have significantly altered your perception of our people. I would have you, along with your harper here, singing our praises upon your return."

"You mean to keep us forever, then?"

"Ha. Gideon, you do your reputation well. I know that within five days I can soften your opinion."

"Through sorcery?"

Fallon ignored him. "If at the end of five days you are still immovable, I will bid my adieus and wish you good sailing."

"Five days with you be like an eternity indeed."

"Good Gideon, why should you harbor such venom?"

Jonathan drained his glass and slammed it hard on the table. "Oh, I know not. Perhaps it were the killing of your sister, one of the kindest, most generous—"

"Oh, oh, you will – you think I do not…" Fallon paused and sighed. "I had but hoped we could avoid this subject–"

"Because you know what a heartless villain it makes you!"

Miranda inhaled and stared at her plate.

"Helen, my *wine*, please."

She threw her head up and discovered the wine decanter had been passed down to the far end of the table. She shot him a poisoned look which he missed, his focus entirely on Fallon. She blinked when she saw his expression; either he was acting very well, or not at all.

"You do not understand the ways of my people."

"You mean the ways of sibling-slaying, cannibalistic–"

"Cannibalistic!"

As Miranda reseated herself, she saw that Fallon's expression of shock was completely unfeigned.

"Oh, come now. It be but common knowledge that you sacrifice your infants in your sordid, bloody rituals–"

Fallon's loud laughter cut him off, and several people, Selphyn and human alike, paused to stare at them. "We? Sacrifice our own infants? It is no wonder to me now why we are so despised. By Miken's sweet – to what end would we kill our own kind? We whose numbers are so depleted? We sacrifice nothing, be it Selphyn or animal, for our rituals. Our only sacrifice – and that be of animals only – is for our sustenance, just as you do."

Miranda caught Thomas's eye and saw her own look of concern reflected there as Jonathan took several gulps of wine. She, after drinking only a half a glass, knew how potent the Lansing wine was.

"An exaggeration, then, perhaps. But of the slaying of your sister, and her maid, *that* you cannot deny."

"Nor should I like to. What you do not understand, is that my sister wrote to me of the abuse she suffered at the hands of the king, and *begged* me to take her life–"

"And her maid?"

"*And* her maid, Syldonia's greatest friend, who suffered equally."

"And did *she* beg you?"

"No. It was my sister's wish. The only way to free her."

Suddenly Jonathan was on his feet, his half-full wineglass knocked aside so that it spilled crimson liquid over his plate, making his pheasant appear newly slaughtered. "You orphaned their children!"

Thomas half-rose and pulled Jonathan's arm. "Master Ambrose.

Sit down. You're drunk."

Jonathan wrenched his arm free just as Fallon rose from the other side, leaning forward with his palms on the table. "It was my sister's wish that I should bring them back with me, all three! She wanted them raised here, with our peaceful, loving ways–"

"*Murderous* ways–"

"The Selphyn are no man's slaves! We serve no one, we submit to no one. I did what she wanted–"

"The hell you did!" Jonathan, reaching for his wine glass, found it spilled. His eyes, filled with rage, flashed on Miranda. "Helen. My fucking wine glass is empty!"

The decanter rested between them. Without thinking, Miranda stood and launched three glasses' worth of wine in Jonathan's face.

"Here!"

He froze, the wine dripping from his hair, ears, nose and chin. It completely saturated the white collar of his shirt, no doubt ruining the fine velvet and satin of his doublet. He did not blink. "Helen. Come here, please."

She was shaking all over, but held her head high as she came around the table to face him. His back was to Fallon, completely shielding Miranda from the Selphyn king's gaze. Jonathan's eyes were now soft, but his jaw was set. He said, "You forget I am your lord and master. If I command you to be my servant, so you shall be. If I command you be my whore, so you shall be too. If you defy me, you shall suffer."

She recognized the lines from *The King of Salsima*; Sebastian had said them to her as King Edward to Syldonia. She understood now what he was playing at, as what followed was a feigned blow. She gave him her next line to show him she understood and was prepared.

"And suffer will I but gladly. For I shall forever defy you."

The back of Jonathan's right hand came flying at her face. At the last moment she turned her head and held up her hand so that he hit her palm, creating the loud slapping sound necessary to pull off the desired effect. She fell to her knees and cried out, covering her unmarked cheek with her hand.

Jonathan made almost as if to smile, when Fallon reached over the table to snag his doublet. When Jonathan turned Fallon caught him by the throat, almost lying across the table in order to reach him. His face was a mask of rage.

"We do not tolerate violence to women here!"

Jonathan pried his fingers loose. "Nay, only the murdering of them. I pray you, do not ever touch me again."

Fallon's facial muscles loosened and he slowly righted himself. "Forgive me. We have all, I think, indulged in too much wine."

Jonathan wiped off his face with a napkin, while Miranda stood, still covering her face. He glanced at her and she saw that he recognized her dilemma of keeping her cheek hidden. "Get you to bed. I'll no more of you, until you are in a better humor."

She bobbed in a curtsey, grateful when a Selphyn rose to lead her to her chamber.

"Perhaps we should all to bed," Fallon said, "and recollect ourselves in the morning. Gideon, I would still have conference with you. Once you are changed and refreshed, please meet me in my chambers."

Jonathan threw down his soiled napkin. "I will go now, so please you."

"Very well. This way."

Miranda was led in an opposite direction, and was grateful when Thomas came with her. She was shown to a richly furnished chamber, with a bed large enough to accommodate two. As soon as their Selphyn guide retreated, Miranda threw herself in Thomas's arms and burst into sobs. He was awkward in comforting her, and they were both relieved when Jonathan joined them only five minutes later.

Jonathan was shaking, wiping sweat from his brow. Miranda's heart leaped as he sagged to the floor, leaning against the wall.

"What means this? Does he know you are not Gideon?" Thomas asked.

"No. He is well convinced I am he."

"And so?"

Jonathan looked at them and gave them a crooked a smile. "He knows I am part Selphyn."

EIGHTEEN

BARTHOLOMEW RIORDAN WAS as good as his word. They were each given a comfortable chamber to sleep in, and their wing, in his immense estate, was locked by two heavy oak doors. At meal times they were released to join Bartholomew in the dining room, while guards were posted at every corner to prevent their escape. Servants attended to their needs, and Lord Riordan was a gracious host, though he ignored entreaties and questions, pretending his prisoners were guests on a social visit.

Lauren, trying to make the best of the situation, kept to her room and read from the many books on the shelves. Gideon stayed drunk, the servants only too happy to keep him in his cups lest he lose his temper. Rathnar, however, often acted like a caged wild animal. Lauren heard him pacing the hallway late at night, and sometimes he hammered on the oak doors, demanding release. He begged, bribed and threatened the servants to no avail, and was barely civil to Riordan at supper. Watching his behavior, and Gideon's drunken lethargy, it was almost as if he and Gideon had switched places. Always so meticulous with his appearance, he now appeared with disheveled hair and wrinkled clothes, his eyes bloodshot.

In the middle of their third night, hearing him pacing in the hall, Lauren opened her door and asked him in. Wearing only breeches and his shirt, the latter untucked, Rathnar sat in the armchair next to her bed at her direction.

"You must try to relax," she said. "What is being accomplished while you are in this state? Nothing but your own declining health."

"I thank you, but you do not understand—"

She sat on the bed and opened a book, angling the page toward the candlelight. She felt his gaze and stumbled with her diction at first before falling into the rhythm of the words. She read twelve pages, glancing at him on occasion to see if he was listening. Each time he was rapt with attention, often staring at her face, illuminated with candlelight, while she read. At the end of the twelfth page, when she looked up, his head was hanging forward, hair eclipsing his face. After a moment of hesitation she put a pillow and blanket on the floor, and clumsily dragged him off the chair.

He did not stir, not even when he fell with a loud thump onto the floor. She rolled him into position with his head on the pillow, and covered him up. For several minutes she lay in bed staring at him in candlelight until she too could not keep her eyes open. She extinguished the candle and watched his silhouette, vaguely silver from the moonlight spearing in through her window, as he breathed deeply. She fell asleep feeling more content and secure than she had since she was a child, still with her mother.

* * *

Jonathan was shaking and sweating freely as he entered Fallon's antechamber, his doublet suddenly stifling. Fallon directed him to an overstuffed chair upholstered in velvet, and he sat in another, on the other side of a desk made of dark-red wood. Wanting to look at anything other than his host, Jonathan saw a fireplace with a gilded mantel, shelf after shelf filled with books, and animal tapestries on the walls. It was not unlike an antechamber one would find in the royal court of Salsima.

"You look surprised at our level of sophistication," Fallon said. "You did not think we could read?"

"I...I did not wonder one way or the other."

"We write too," Fallon said, smiling almost playfully. "Books, love letters. We truly are not so different, you and I." Jonathan knew better than to reply. Fallon sighed. "To begin, I must first beg your forgiveness. My behavior was uncivilized and uncalled for. Please accept my apology."

Jonathan forced the words out. "If you will accept mine."

"Of course. We now know, if we are to coexist peacefully, to avoid certain subjects."

"And that is convenient." Jonathan saw Fallon's jaw tighten and felt his own temper flare again. "Well, and what would you say to me?"

"I know...I observed something upon your arrival, and in my great surprise, nearly announced it without prudence. Then it did occur to me that your companions very like do not know, nor would you appreciate my alerting them. Further, it struck me that perhaps *you* do not even know." Jonathan pulled out a handkerchief from his pocket to mop up the sweat on his brow. "What is your parentage?"

Jonathan picked his way carefully through the brief history Leonardis gave him. "My father is a baron, my mother the niece of a countess. Why is this a concern?"

"You'll forgive my asking, but…could there have been a dalliance? On either side?"

Jonathan threw down his handkerchief, grateful to have a reason to rage rather than tremble with fright. "I will certainly not forgive it! How dare you suggest such a thing? Perhaps dalliances among the Selphyn are common enough–"

"Stop." Fallon put a hand on his brow. "I am too weary to argue yet again, for our mating habits are not of the issue."

"And what is then? The faithfulness of my parents?"

"Here. Come here, stand up."

Fallon directed him to a full-size looking glass. They stared at each other and then themselves reflected in the glass. Fallon was just under an inch taller than Jonathan, his bright purple coat a dazzling contrast to the drabness of Jonathan's doublet. Jonathan saw his wine-stained collar, and patches of skin still purple, and sighed.

"You bear Selphyn blood."

Jonathan saw the blood in question drain from his face until he was a deathly white. "This jest does not appeal to me."

"I jest not. We can sense the blood in each other the way you might feel a needle's prick. I know, with all the certainty in my being, that you are part Selphyn. You truly did not know?"

Jonathan shook his head. "This – no. You mistake quite."

"No. The others knew it as soon as they saw you. Corrine shared her surprise with me before we were seated for dinner, validating what I already knew from shaking your hand."

"No. No, no, no."

"Gideon, look at you. Your skin is not much lighter than mine, nor is your hair. Your eyes are bright, your face is angular–" Jonathan turned his back on the mirror. "You are at least a quarter, if not half, Selphyn."

"Go to the devil."

"According to you, I am he."

"True enough. You – this is some trick. You wish to gain my sympathies–"

"No. I promise you, I would not be so hard-hearted, especially as I see now how distressing this is to you."

Jonathan whirled to face him. "Distressing? It is *devastating*, if it is true. You have yet to convince me of it."

"Very well. The white wolves." Jonathan went cold. "Did they greet you upon your arrival? Shower you with affection?" He could not deny it, and sat down before Fallon would see him trembling. "They will only interact with those with Selphyn blood. I am sure you noticed they ignored your friends."

"Because they are your demonic minions. Your familiars."

"They are our link to the faerie realm, the faeries from whom we descended."

Jonathan laughed. "Ah. I am man, demon and now faerie. All in the matter of a moment."

"You may laugh. But again I jest not."

Jonathan stood abruptly. "If that concludes this evening's entertainment, I will take my leave of you."

Fallon softened. Jonathan saw his back reflected in the looking glass, surrounded by an almost imperceptible golden aura. He blinked and looked away. "Can you think of how it may have happened? I think it is useless now to continue denying it."

Jonathan stared at the floor, at the crooked grooves in the wood. "My grandmother resided for a time in Zirnich. I understand...I understand the Selphyn do a handsome trade with the human residents there. Perhaps..."

"Yes. That seems likely. I – forgive me, Gideon, for causing you so much pain. I strongly felt you should know."

Jonathan looked up. "To what end? My life is in ruins. I must return to court and live with a terrible secret, one that is punishable by death. You know this?"

Fallon nodded.

"Then why tell me?"

"Because you will continue to be miserable until you free your passions. Otherwise the Selphyn in you will go mad."

"And what can a Selphyn possibly know of passion?"

"More than you could ever imagine. We draw our energy from the earth, exalt in nature's bounty. We love fiercely, the way a mare loves its colt. We find more joy, passion and sensuality in a flower petal than most humans find in a lifetime. We are passion itself."

The worst thing happened then, worse than the terrible argument at dinner, worse even than the confrontation that followed. Jonathan's eyes flooded with tears that spilled over onto his cheeks.

Fallon straightened. "Gideon, let me help you–"

Jonathan slammed the door in his wake, leaning against the wall to catch his breath. When he found sufficient composure, he wandered the hall until he found Uthen, who was glad to direct him to his chamber.

"You are sharing a room with Mistress Helen."

"What?"

"I trust this is satisfactory. It is no secret here that you and she are lovers."

"Yes, but—"

"Then do you not sleep together?"

Uthen's fox Belcastro rounded a corner and found them, trotting with his tongue hanging out to greet Jonathan, who danced out of reach. "No. It is not our custom – not openly–"

"Ah. You must marry?"

"Yes."

"Here is your room. We do not believe in marriage here."

Jonathan shot him a look of disgust. "Why does that not surprise me? Ah. I know. Because you are all savages." He opened the door to his chamber and all but fell in. When Miranda and Thomas began questioning him, he knew he could not bear the weight of his secret any longer, and told them what Fallon knew.

When they both drew away from him, almost as if he confessed to having the plague, he felt the threat of tears again. "If you two shun me, I do not think…"

He closed his eyes, wishing almost that he could fall asleep and escape from the night's horrors. He opened them when he felt a hand on his shoulder.

"It…it does not signify," Miranda said, and smiled. He blinked several times to clear his vision, and then caught sight of Thomas standing at the far end of the room, his arms crossed.

"And? Do you care to explain?"

"My mother lived in Zirnich before she came to court, this I think you know. She was a seamstress, her husband a fisherman. He died sometime after my sister was born. There was…a love affair. I alone know of this."

Thomas said, "And can prove you are not the king's bastard."

Jonathan laughed. "They will simply behead me for my Selphyn blood." He was slightly satisfied when Thomas's face turned white.

"To think you and Prince Edward both were half-Selphyn."

Jonathan knew Thomas would be shocked, but he did not expect the level of malice that was in his tone. "Syldonia knew; she was in my mother's confidence."

"And so you shared a special bond. Lovely, that."

"Thomas, why–"

"Perhaps because you belie our friendship by telling nothing but lies."

He stormed out, leaving Jonathan alone with Miranda.

"I apologize for the arrangements. I can sleep on the floor."

"I will share the bed. You need a comfortable sleep."

"You are not...you are not repulsed by me? Afraid we might touch in the night?"

Miranda knelt down beside him and gently kissed him. "No."

He might have wept except that she pulled away and gave him a disapproving look. "Do not think you need not atone for your wickedness this evening."

He touched the ends of her hair, wrapping the silky strands around his fingers. "If you only knew how you saved me. Another moment and I would have betrayed us all. Forgive me for treating you badly."

She withheld her forgiveness until he explained everything. He spoke of himself in third person, and told her the story of the three children who were raised in court, the two boys best friends and practically brothers who witnessed the slaying of their mothers. When his head started slumping she brought him to bed and allowed him to lay his head on her shoulder, murmuring the rest of the story into the softness of her throat. He fell asleep spooned against her, his last coherent thought consisting of Fallon's warning, that if he did not release his passions, the Selphyn in him would go mad.

NINETEEN

THOMAS DUCKED OUT on the way to the great hall, having no stomach with which to break his fast with the Selphyn. He wandered gold-colored halls for several minutes before finding a passageway that led outside, and sucked in deep breaths of fresh air. The day was perfectly clear and beautiful, a reassurance when he realized he was lost, having exited the palace from a new location. He followed a spiral path laden with flagstone, and at the path's end was a spectacular array of wildflowers. He sat down on a bench and took in brilliant reds, blues and yellows, colors so bright they were almost blinding.

He considered several different ailments that he might claim, something severe enough to keep him bedridden whose symptoms he could feign. Last night had proved more difficult than he anticipated. Flanked by Selphyn on either side of him at the long table filled him with such revulsion that he managed to eat only two bites of what should have been the most delectable meal he ever tasted. He settled on a terrible cough, an easy illness as his hatred of the Selphyn was so profound that he nearly choked on it.

He heard a rustle of skirts and went still, heart pounding when he saw a young woman enter the garden across from him with a basket. She was dressed in a blue velvet gown, long auburn hair tied back with a matching ribbon. When she spotted him he fell forward onto one knee, head lowered.

"Your Highness."

"Please rise. I suppose my gown gave me away."

"That and your uncanny resemblance to your mother."

Princess Kassandra smiled, and her whole face lit up. Thomas felt something flip in his lower abdomen.

"I am so pleased to hear it!"

He took a couple of tentative steps as if trying out his feet for the first time. He didn't trust his balance and stayed where he was, forcing her to approach. Her eyes were the Boussard green, her skin a lovely white compared to the ubiquitous bronze of the Selphyn. Her hair was very thick; Thomas imagined it would feel like a goose-feather quilt lined with mink on his face.

"I am Horatio Inglan, his Majesty's harper, at your service."

She curtsied and he bowed. "A harper. And do you sing?"

"Tolerably, I am told."

"Perhaps you will sing for me."

His tongue seemed to swell. He ransacked his mind for just a trace of wit or eloquence; when none could be found his mouth clamped shut.

"No? Perhaps then you will help me gather flowers."

Grateful for a purpose, he pulled random flowers and placed them in her basket, jumping once when her hand brushed his.

"Surely a Selphyn can pick his own flowers, without employing a princess."

"Oh, but I enjoy it. Just but look at these colors. They use them, you know, in their dyes."

"I can see that now," Thomas said.

"Our silks and satins are in high demand in Zirnich."

Thomas noted her use of "our." Their eyes met before he looked away, and he saw that her hands were stained red, as if she held and squeezed his heart until it burst, staining forever her fingers.

"Your hands are now of my color," she said. He held up his hands and blushed. "What else do you, to pass the time in Diernioch? I wish to know all I can before going home."

"I...I was an actor once."

She straightened, brushing her hands off on the skirt of her gown. "Indeed? I have never heard a play."

"No?"

"The Selphyn are unfamiliar with theater."

"It is a grand thing. The author, a playwright some call him, writes the play, some many verses of comedy or tragedy to reflect the human heart. In three hours you may witness the plight of star-crossed lovers, a king overthrown, a melancholy prince, or the antics of a clown." He smiled. "Or watch separated twins reunite."

"I should love to see it."

"And at court you shall. Players often come to perform for the king and queen." He stopped, realizing what he was advocating. It was unthinkable that she should return to court. But then he thought of her dying, the candle extinguished at a mere seventeen years, without her so much as ever witnessing a play. He could not hold the two thoughts together, and so instead blurted out, "For our amusement, to pass the time on our long journey, my companions and I conned the lines of a very good play. Perhaps we could perform it during our sojourn here."

"Oh, how I should love it, how we all should! Please say it may be so."

And what could he say but, "It may be so"? He smiled faintly when she all but swooned. Jonathan was going to kill him.

"There you are, Harper Horatio! And I see you found our princess." Thomas whirled, sputtering, when he saw Fallon leading Jonathan and the others toward the garden. "Now you may join our tour."

His plan of feigning a cough destroyed, he could do nothing but nod and slink toward them, his head hanging while Fallon introduced Kassandra to the others. He saw her fairness shook all of them, save for Richard whose cold eye never faltered upon studying her. Even Sebastian was unhinged.

"And now," Fallon said, "I would show you something special indeed."

Thomas followed, ignoring Jonathan's imploring look. He forgot his discomfort upon entering a massive chamber whose domed ceiling was decorated with angels and faeries. Dark oak bookshelves lined the room, and the centerpiece was a glass display holding what appeared to be an ancient manuscript of some sort. Fallon gestured to the ceiling.

"You see we are not so uncivilized. We too have a passion for art and all of its splendors. Tell me Gideon, what artistic medium most pleases you?"

"Plays." Jonathan blinked, having been caught, as Thomas was, spellbound by the glory of the room. "That is—"

"Ah. Plays. We have heard of them, of course, but never witnessed such a spectacle."

Seeing what was probably to be his only opening, Thomas said, "As it would happen, I just now spoke of plays to Princess Kassandra."

Jonathan's eyes narrowed. "Did you so?"

"Indeed. I told her of how we conned lines for our own amusement." Jonathan's jaw shifted forward and Thomas heard his teeth grind together. "Upon her excitement, I suggested that...perhaps...we could perform an amateur rendition of the play."

Jonathan did not blink. Fallon said, "A splendid suggestion. We should be honored. What, pray, is the play?"

Jonathan turned to him and said, "*The King of Salsima* written by a rather brilliant playwright, Jonathan Wilder. Perhaps you've heard of him?"

"Indeed not. Henry Rothford I know of."

Jonathan's eyes briefly closed. "Yes. Everyone knows of Rothford."

"But by such title, I should think, the play may be found offensive by our people."

"I think you shall find it a fair representation of the past. Master Wilder sought to portray the truth of what transpired between Syldonia and King Edward. Now he may hang for his sedition."

"A terrible shame for an act of such bravery. We shall hear the play in two days, if that is sufficient."

Jonathan leaned in toward Thomas. "I'll see your balls roasted for this."

"Now, come and look upon this, our prized possession," Fallon said. They followed him to the heavy glass centerpiece. The manuscript was open, revealing ancient lettering and beautiful illumination. "The original *Book of Miken*."

"You can have no such thing," Sebastian said.

"But indeed we do." Thomas saw the light glinting in Fallon's eye and sensed his urge for ecclesiastical battle. He took a step away from Sebastian. "Two-hundred years ago, when our ancestors were driven from Salsima, they took our most sacred possessions with them, one of them being this book that has always been in our care."

Sebastian took a step and then withdrew it, like a child debating whether or not it should witness a hanging.

"Fear not, you may read all. I had copies placed in all of your rooms. You may find them underneath your beds."

"I will not read your lies."

"My dear Brother Dominick. This is your only opportunity to read Miken's own words writ in his own hand. *Your* version of the book has been altered so many times that I doubt there is one original statement."

"*Our* version was written by Miken's disciplines, which is the only version—"

"Begging your pardon, Brother," Jonathan said, "but even I know that our version has been much changed. Our own king has removed material, reworded—"

Sebastian spun on him, his face crimson. "How dare you—"

"Come, come," Fallon said. "You may believe what you will; I see there is no swaying you. I do but beg you to look upon it at your leisure. I think you may find the material much to your liking."

"I would sooner believe a freezing-over of Hell."

Fallon laughed. "Very well."

"Next I suppose you will say that Miken was a Selphyn."

"Of course he was." Fallon's smile only widened at Sebastian's choking sound. "Did you not ever find it strange that he would be born to a human in a Selphyn community, hundreds of years before the humans invaded? He was born to a Selphyn woman and man–"

"Of all you have said, that is the most blasphemous. Miken, God's only son, was born to a virgin woman–"

Like a child stifling a giggle in church, Fallon covered his mouth, his shoulders shaking. Sebastian's face turned even redder.

"A virgin *human* woman, sent by God, to save your heathen race–"

"Oh, my. That is amusing."

"And when he was slain by your people, he resurrected and ascended into Heaven–"

"With his physical body?"

"Of course. And–"

"His bones are buried underneath your cathedral in Diernioch. In the ruins of our temple. Unfortunately we were unable to save those." Fallon ignored Sebastian and addressed Jonathan. "Our people did not slay Miken. We loved him. He was no son of God, no more than any of us, but a prophet, a loving healer, who had, I doubt not, many incarnations before that one, and belike has had many since."

"You…are mad," Sebastian said.

"I have proof," Fallon said. "Left in our care is a trunk. Miken prophesized there would be a Day of Reckoning when a man, bearing the blood of both human and Selphyn, will reveal this proof. He alone can open this trunk and reveal what is inside, of which even I remain ignorant. It will restore the truth, and bring our people and yours together." Fallon softened. "I had hoped my nephew would be that man." With a casual glance in Jonathan's direction, he added, "There may still be such a man, who can one day unite our races."

"A goblin damned," Sebastian said as Jonathan looked down.

"Well. I promised you all I would leave you to your own devices following our tour. You may spend the day in leisure, and join us once more in the great hall this evening for dinner. Our lovely princess Kassandra will be joining us."

Thomas snapped to attention; he must have gestured or jerked for Jonathan was watching him with a raised eyebrow. Insulted, Thomas said, "You have naught to fear from *me*." He lifted his chin to brush past Jonathan, but when no one was looking he raised his hand to his nose and inhaled his stained fingers, straining for just a trace of perfume from the flowers he helped her pick.

TWENTY

"I SHALL GO mad. Nay, I am mad already, and will only rave and claw at my eyes unless we can escape."

Lauren pulled Rathnar into her room, gasping when he abruptly laid his forehead on her shoulder. "I need you to help me think. I cannot think anymore. He says there is no news from Leonardis. He has no hope or inkling as to when we may be released. We must secure his key to our wing. Time will run out and–"

"Hush."

Lauren stroked his hair as she might her brother's. He sighed against her and did not stir. She wondered, with awe, at which point they had formed such intimacy, and how she had all but ceased to fear this strange pale being famous for torturing spies. She pulled him down the hall to Gideon's chamber; they found the courtier at work on another painting, a stack of finished ones resting against the wall.

Rathnar repeated his entreaty, but Gideon, drunk as usual, did not look up from his painting. His fingers worked deftly despite his handicap, and Lauren peered over his shoulder.

"Is that Helen?"

"Yes."

Lauren studied the windblown hair of her master's mistress as she walked on a beach. He had slimmed down her contours and softened the rough edges of her face. "She looks lovely."

Gideon shrugged. "I did but enhance a beauty there already."

Lauren froze. She looked at Rathnar, her mouth open. "You once said I was beautiful."

"And so I did."

"Did you speak truthfully, or did you seek to manipulate me?"

He frowned. "I manipulate enemies. Never friends. I spoke truthfully, though your beauty were a hundred times greater today."

"Oh, God," Gideon said.

Lauren started to blush and then recalled the matter at hand. "'Enhance a beauty there already,'" she said meaningfully, and Rathnar's eyes widened.

He snatched the color palette from Gideon's easel. "I must needs borrow this."

Gideon began to protest, but Rathnar was already pulling Lauren through the door. "You have hit upon something. Those doxies he dotes on will be no match when I am finished with you."

Her heart racing, she allowed him to pull her into her own chamber, where he closed the door. He studied her from head to foot while she fidgeted. "Your hair…if you were to pull it back away from your face…"

She lifted the sides and the top, pulling them back while he cut a ribbon from the quilt on her bed. Once it was tied back she felt immediately vulnerable without her mane of hair to hide behind.

"Oh," Rathnar said. "Your cheeks and your eyes; I can see them now. No, do not look away. You are lovely." She fought the urge to pull her hair loose while he continued studying her. "Your dress. If we can but…" He mimed lifting her breasts on his own chest and her face ignited. Trembling, she slipped her hands into her bodice and lifted her breasts. Rathnar tightened the cords of her bodice while she held them aloft; when he gestured for her to release them they practically sat on top of her bodice, well above muslin blouse underneath. She watched Rathnar's Adam's apple bob as he swallowed deeply, and drops of moisture appeared on his brow, making him look even more waxy. She dared to look down and saw the deep crevice of her cleavage, the rounded tops of her breasts.

"My God. I look like–"

"A goddess. Now, before we finish, I must know what your intentions are. How far do you plan to take this?"

"As – as far as I must. Even…even if I must wait until he sleeps."

"Then I must ask you: are you yet a maid?"

She did not trust herself to speak and nodded.

"Then I cannot allow you to fully compromise–"

"I am under no disillusionment. I have thirty years and am well aware of my prospects. Or lack thereof.   I am resigned to spinsterhood."

He opened his mouth to speak and then seemed to have thought better of it. "Now to your face."

He sat her down on the bed and knelt so that she was slightly taller than he. She looked at the widow's peak his black hair made on his forehead, a black spearhead in a pool of marble. He dipped his thumb in blue paint and lightly brushed her eyelids. Then he dipped his index finger in red paint and made circular motions on her cheek. While he worked his mouth was slightly open and she could see just the tip of a very normal-looking tongue.

"This is none of your stage paint, I fear," he said. "It may stick for a few days."

"Did you ever see one of them?"

"What?"

"Our plays. When we were children."

"Yes. Two or three. There was one about a faerie queen that I particularly liked. You played the title role, naturally. And wrote it, if I remember me."

"Yes! You flatter me by recalling it. And yet..." He dipped his finger into more red paint while she searched for the right words. "Why do I not remember you? I had thirteen years, and if you will pardon me, yours is not an easy face to forget."

"That was seventeen years gone."

"I would have remembered you. Did we never speak? Never encounter each other?"

He paused, his finger red in midair. "You once needed assistance with stage combat. I made you two wooden swords and taught you how to fence."

She gasped. "I *do* remember you! But...I did not fear you, which is why I did not think we ever met. How can that be?" He smiled faintly and rubbed the paint into her other cheek. "Perhaps because I was a child, I sensed the goodness in you. I was able to see through your frightening – forgive me – exterior."

His finger, in mid-rub, froze on her cheek.

"I know why else. Syldonia was very fond of you, and because I loved Syldonia and trusted her well, I too could be fond of you."

He resumed painting her cheek, his finger lovingly tracing her skin just below the cheekbone. His eyes were moist. "I meant what I said days ago. When this is all behind us, I mean to see you an independent woman, who need not serve anyone again."

"But without my brother, for what have I to live?"

He lunged forward and seized her shoulders, causing her to cry out. He wrenched her to her feet and pushed her toward the window, spinning her around. She felt his fingers digging in her shoulders. "What do you see?"

"I – trees."

"For their beauty alone would I have you live. We do not live solely for another person, be it a brother, mother, lover or daughter. We live to experience every sacred minute of the beauty of our world, and to experience its every succulent delight, from biting into a tangerine to making love."

She wrenched out of his grasp to face him. "You speak of beauty but what beauty can there be in a life spent rooting out traitors, killing and torturing men? What *succulence* can there be in such a life?"

"My God. Your passion is stunning."

He grabbed the back of her head and pulled it forward, kissing her hard on the lips. Her sharp inhalation yielded yet another surprise. An acrid, almost chemical smell burned her nostrils. She broke away, gasping for breath.

"What – what is wrong with your face?"

"Nothing."

But before he could turn away she saw a smudge of white paint on his lip. The only paint on her face was red and blue. She reached out and touched his cheek. He flinched and slapped her hand away. The tip of her finger came away white, and when she rubbed it against her thumb it was moist and waxy. Looking up, she saw the lines of her finger imprinted on Rathnar's cheek.

She dipped her finger in a glass of water and reached for his face.

"Do. Not. Touch. Me."

But he did not prevent her. She ran her finger down the length of his cheek, the water revealing a streak of golden skin. She gasped and pulled a handkerchief from her skirt pocket, dropping it in the water. He held perfectly still, unblinking, while she washed the white paint off of his face. She was not sure what was more surprising: that he was beautiful, or that he was not human.

"I do not…I do not understand."

"The dinner bell. We must hurry. Tell Gideon of your plan and I will meet you both downstairs."

She paused at the threshold of her door long enough to see him produce a canister from his doublet, no doubt filled with white face paint. Then she slammed the door shut and ran to Gideon's room, trying not to cry and spoil her makeup. When she wrenched open his door, Gideon's mouth dropped open.

"By all the stars in heaven. You are beautiful."

"Thank you. I must give the semblance of being drunk while keeping my head clear. Can you help?"

Gideon nodded in a circular motion. "Slip your glass to me under the table. I will drink for both of us. You mean to seduce him?"

"Yes and snatch his key. Be my dinner partner."

He took her by the elbow to escort her down the hall. Their wing was unlocked and open, with a handful of guards standing watch. She held onto the railing for dear life as she descended the stairs, nearly pulled off balance several times by Gideon who kept stumbling. Bartholomew, already seated at the dining table, saw her and lit up.

"Dear Mistress Lauren. You are a lovely creature this evening. What is the occasion?"

"We – we were in want of amusement."

"And you agreed to play dress-up. How delightful."

To keep his suspicions at bay, Lauren giggled and kissed Gideon once they were safely off the stairs. Her lips landed on the corner of his mouth, and like an infant teased with a nipple, his lips sought for greater purchase.

"Later," she said in his ear, a loud stage whisper.

"Your breasts are beautiful," Gideon said, his head dropping forward as if he simply meant to bury his face between them. Lauren danced out of reach.

"I must agree, if you'll forgive my impudence," Lord Riordan said.

Lauren curtsied and took the seat he offered, relaxing when Gideon sat next to her. Rathnar then made his appearance, and the recent past came slamming back to Lauren. Her breath caught in her throat and she could not look at him. When he sat across from her she raised her eyes, studying the hastily applied white paint. It was dusk and the candelabra was blazing in the dim room, casting flickering shadows that reflected on his white face. Their eyes met and hers filled with tears.

"A toast," said Bartholomew, "to fine guests, and the surprise of a beautiful companion."

Their glasses clinked together, Lauren's shaking. She took one sip and waited for Bartholomew to look down at his plate before slipping her glass under the table. Gideon's fingers brushed against hers as he grabbed the stem, quickly lifting it and draining it in one gulp. The process was reversed, and when she brought her glass back down it was empty. Riordan saw and smiled.

"My lady is thirsty tonight. Here. Have another."

His voice dropped and Lauren knew he was taking the bait. It was obvious Gideon was already drunk, and once overset, Lauren would be free for claiming. Her hands began shaking again as she took another sip, her eyes darting between Rathnar and Riordan. She was unsure which of them now scared her more.

She barely tasted her dinner, but concentrated on plundering the reserves of her acting days to play the coquette, leaning against Gideon and flashing Riordan her bosom while feigning a drunkenness worthy of four glasses of wine that Gideon actually drank. He also drank from his own glass, and by the time dinner was done, his face was resting on the table.

"I fear your friend is incapacitated," Riordan said, his eyes drinking Lauren in. She let the corner of her mouth arch upwards and lifted her shoulders, pushing her breasts out in the lord's direction.

"Perchance I shall not be lonely."

"Perchance not."

Riordan was also in his cups, his cheeks a dark red from the wine. He licked his lips. "Rathnar. I think you wish to retire."

"Yes. I believe so."

Lauren did not look at him, but kept her gaze fastened on Riordan, though it faded in and out of focus in her fear.

"Take young Ambrose with you."

"Of course."

Out of the corner of her eye, Lauren saw him half drag and half carry Gideon up the stairs, who moaned but never opened his eyes. Bartholomew never moved his gaze from her.

"Leave us."

The servants and guards disappeared, with one following the men upstairs, ostensibly to lock the two men in. Lauren knew Bartholomew possessed a copy of this key; he had released them from their wing several times himself. She hoped, and assumed, the key would be in his chamber where she could easily find it.

He barely waited to ensure their privacy before launching himself at Lauren. He yanked her out of her chair, burying his face in her bodice while pawing at her backside. She gasped, seeing he meant to take her right there at the table.

"Not so fast," she said, lifting his face to kiss him. She immediately remembered the feel of Rathnar's lips on hers, and the smell of his face paint. His lips, she was surprised to recall, had been warm and soft. Bartholomew's were cruel and intrusive; she squirmed when he bit her lips.

He pulled back and fumbled with her bodice, yanking loose the stays. A summer-night wind blew in from an open window and the thin curtains swirled and billowed as if in a dance.

"Would we not be more comfortable in your bed?"

"Nay. I'll have you here, bent over the table."

Then her blouse and bodice were yanked down, her breasts free. While he feasted on them she closed her eyes and tried to will herself away. All of this might be for naught, for when he was finished with her at the table he would very likely send her up to bed by herself, never granting her access to his chamber. Her eyes filled with tears and overflowed on her cheeks when he pulled her dress off, leaving her trembling naked before him. He turned her around, put a hand on her rear and the other on her back, pushing her over.

And quite suddenly he screamed.

His hands fell away rather than lifting from her body, followed shortly by a loud thump. She straightened and turned, and saw him lying on his back, a huge, black wolf on his chest. Her heart in her throat, she gathered her clothes against her. When she looked at the wolf, and he at her, he actually began wagging his tail, tongue lolling out in playful regard. Bartholomew was making a strangling noise and regained her attention.

She lifted a trembling arm and forced her hand to rest on the wolf's head. He lifted his nose in order to lick the inside of her wrist. "This beast is under my power." Riordan breathed a half-strangled word that might have been *witch*. "Tell me where the key is."

"I -- in my bureau."

She dressed quickly, never taking her eyes off the wolf lest he attack. The wolf was clearly distressed, torn between keeping Riordan down and jumping off in order to lavish what she hoped was affection on her. It was like watching a puppy learn the command to stay as the wolf was now wiggling its entire body and whining. Dressed, the stays of her bodice loose, Lauren gave the wolf a pat on his head. Then she was running toward Bartholomew's chamber.

Two minutes later, after ransacking his bureau, she was dashing up the stairs with the key. From the floor below, Riordan gasped, "Get him off! Please!"

"A moment only."

As she predicted, servants and guards were abed in order to give their master privacy, and she had no trouble unlocking the door. Rathnar was there, their satchels packed and over his shoulder. Seeing him unsurprised and prepared clicked something into place.

"He's yours. The wolf."

"Yes. I cannot rouse Gideon and need your help."

"Oh, no."

She followed him into the chamber where Gideon was lying on his back, his body half hanging off the bed. He was singing. They each took an arm and pulled; he fell hard onto the floor and laughed.

"You were magnificent," Rathnar said. "And so beautiful. A goddess indeed."

"You saw – through the wolf?"

"Help me lift him. Yes."

Oddly enough this intelligence did not embarrass her. As she put her head under Gideon's arm, following Rathnar's lead, she said, "Thank you. For sending him."

Somehow they managed to get Gideon to his feet. His head fell against Lauren's. "Good mistress. Another cup of wine."

"Not on your life. Can you at least *try* to walk?"

"In faith, you are a cruel mistress. I would but sleep."

In the futility of it all, Rathnar pushed his shoulder into Gideon's stomach and lifted. As he fell over Rathnar's back, Gideon let loose a flood of wine-drenched vomit that Lauren narrowly avoided.

"I will be avenged for this," Rathnar said, and carefully negotiated the stairs. Lauren followed, smiling when the wolf was still standing on Bartholomew's chest. He saw her and wagged again.

"Witch! Whore! Villains!"

"Thank you for your kind hospitality," Rathnar said.

Outside the wind whipped at their hair and cloaks, and it wasn't until Lauren stepped on cold, wet hay in the stables that she realized she was barefoot. They found their horses; Rathnar rode behind Gideon to hold him up while Lauren led Gideon's horse from her own saddle.

"If we ride all night, we may reach Zirnich by dawn," Rathnar said. The moon was behind him, casting a pale light over his silhouette. His long, black hair fanned out in the wind, and he looked more like a vampire than ever. But now Lauren could only see golden skin with her mind's eye, and wasn't sure which was worse.

"You cannot ride like that all night. And I must rest."

"We must not waste another moment!"

Lauren shook her head. "Four hours, please. That is all I ask. I can sleep, and perhaps Gideon will recover enough to ride."

It didn't seem very likely, however; the man in question was slumped over the neck of Rathnar's horse, completely asleep.

Rathnar lowered his head. "Four hours. For you I will deny nothing."

"Where then? An inn?"

"Not here. Riordan will be searching."

They rode out of the city easily enough, as the soldiers were concerned with people coming in rather than those leaving. The road was deserted, and the forest on either sides of the road was menacing in the dark, a sanctuary to nocturnal creatures and bandits. They rode until they reached a farmhouse off the road; at Rathnar's suggestion they took refuge in the barn with their horses and four others plus two cows. The shuffling and lowing were loud, but Lauren took comfort in the animal noises and smells. She spread her cloak in the hay after helping Rathnar pull Gideon down.

When Rathnar was sitting next to her, his posture indicating he did not intend to sleep, she said, "The wolf – will he be all right?"

In the dark she could not see his expression, but did see his head turn toward her. "He is out, and not far from here."

"Your minds…they are joined?"

"Lauren. Sleep. I will answer your questions on the ship."

She closed her eyes and tried to relax. She imagined how reassuring it would be to have the wolf there with her, curled up in her arms, her nose in his fur. She could almost feel the warmth of his body and hear the sound of his breathing. When she fell asleep she dreamt of him, of his yellow eyes that were filled with devotion and love, not at all the eyes of a killer.

TWENTY-ONE

THE MOMENT HE was on his own, the little she-wolf appeared and sat down on his feet. Jonathan tried shooing her off, but every time he gently pushed her away, either with his boot or his hand, she instantly clambered back on. He surrendered and allowed her to walk with him. He was intent on catching the Selphyn unawares, wanting to witness activities that were not scripted or rehearsed for his benefit. He wanted evidence to throw at Fallon's feet with a laugh of triumph: you are the savages I knew you to be. Fallon's eloquence and sophistication were confusing him, and he needed to be righted.

His journey brought him to their village, less than a mile from the palace. They lived modestly in thatched houses, and he soon realized their choice in location. It was one of the few areas untouched by volcanic rock, where it was possible to grow and cultivate food. He watched them gathering wheat in a field, corn in another. The corn filled him with nostalgia; he remembered watching Syldonia teach the servants how to plant it. Wary of Selphyn food, the people of Diernioch nevertheless trusted Syldonia, and began to grow corn in earnest. Now the royal city was flanked by rows and rows of cornstalks.

He sat down on a bench to watch a group of Selphyn children playing with a litter of kittens. The wolf sat on his feet and made no move to attack what ought to have been tasty little morsels of fur. She simply was not interested.

The children played like ordinary human children, their little voices calming and sweet. Jonathan caught himself smiling on several occasions watching their antics, and let out a yelp of surprise when a hand came down on his shoulder.

"I see you found Zartha," Corrine said.

"Rather, she found me." Jonathan scratched the wolf, grateful for a reason to keep his gaze averted from Corrine. "Zartha, eh? A rascal, this one."

"Your lady Helen wanted to see our children. I brought her, you see."

Miranda took no notice of him; her attention was fixed on the infant in her arms. Jonathan blinked, startled to see a Selphyn baby with its soft, golden skin and hair. It kicked and gurgled in Miranda's arms, and she was nuzzling it and cooing, gently bouncing in the rhythm all new mothers have, an instinctual knowledge of calming babies. What ought to have been endearing filled him instead with unease. He was abrupt and unapologetic in his exit, and continued his search for unseemly behavior.

He found a temple, a shrine dedicated to their goddess. This too brought back memories as the architecture resembled the ruins he hid in as a boy under the cathedral. He smelled incense and watched two Selphyn women in crimson robes lay gifts at the feet of the goddess statue: a winged, Selphyn woman made of stone. He waited for something to be killed as a sacrifice, or to witness a clandestine ritual of fornication or black arts. Instead he was lulled into calmness watching them pray and sing; when they began beating drums he nearly nodded off.

When Sebastian arrived, blowing in like an unwanted gust of wind filled with pomposity, Jonathan's first instinct was to grab him and silence him before he ruined the sanctity of the moment. He caught himself at the last moment, and watched with increasing dismay as Sebastian railed at them for their blasphemy.

One of Rothford's more famous plays depicted an aging king on the brink of madness. Sebastian had played the part to perfection, ranting, hollering, filling the playhouse with bombast. He was engrossed in that same character now, only as a mad monk rather than a mad king. When Jonathan realized he was becoming ill, he pulled Sebastian aside. The priestesses had not moved during his tirade, and when Jonathan silenced him, they quietly resumed their drumming and singing.

"How dare you interrupt an attempt of salvation!"

"Sebastian. Stop."

"You will do well to remember to address me respectfully as Brother Dominick."

"No. I need to know that Sebastian is still in there. Can you find him for me? I would like to speak with him."

"You've gone mad."

Jonathan laughed. "No, *you* have. Oh, irony, you are cruel. I came here to find abominable acts, shameful practices to appall me. All that appalls me is your behavior."

"They have tainted you!"

Jonathan grabbed a fistful of monk robe and pulled. "*Stop.* Give me hope that my friend and benefactor Sebastian is still alive. Give me assurance he will return once this business is finished. *Please.*" Sebastian stared at him sullenly. Jonathan softened his tone. "Do you recall the day we met? Do you? Where did you find me? Come on, man. Think. Where was I?"

A large cloud passed over the sun, shading the temple. For a moment the drums stopped, in the silence Jonathan could hear the sea crashing against the rocks and the cry of seagulls. The breeze picked up, carrying in it the overwhelming scent of musk-wood incense. Sebastian was staring at the ground, and just when Jonathan did not think he would speak, he said, just above a whisper, "In the cart. With the props. You...were covered with wigs and costumes."

Jonathan released a breath. "What was I doing?"

"Weeping."

"And what said you to me?"

"I said...I said, 'Here, now, lad. Where be your parents?'"

"'Dead,' quoth I."

"'What is your name?'"

"'John. John Warden.'"

"'Ah. I know you now, poor laddie. And the king's men are searching for you. You'd do well to...you'd do well to change that name.'"

"And you gave me a new name," Jonathan said. "And when they came looking for me you put me in a dress, painted my face and covered my hair with a wig. You told Rothford I was your nephew, and you pushed me out on stage with two lines."

"...Yes."

"You cared for me. Tutored me. And I trusted you."

Sebastian blinked several times. "Yes."

"Now. I need you to remember. This is a role you are playing. You are my friend Sebastian. You are playing a monk. When this is over—"

"But they might be saved. It is my duty—"

"Oh, a God's name, I have done with you."

He nearly tripped over Zartha, whom he forgot was sitting on his feet. Sebastian saw her and pointed, his face crumpling. "Get it off! It is a demon—"

"It's just a damned wolf!"

Without thinking Jonathan reached down and scooped Zartha up in his arms, feeling smugly satisfied when he saw the expression of horror on Sebastian's face. He carried her all the way to the palace, letting his encounter with Sebastian fuel his rage. He threw open the door to the great hall where preparations were already being made for that evening's feast.

"Where be this king?"

Fallon came from the direction of his chamber, a large raven sitting on his shoulder. Jonathan blinked.

"I demand you release us at once. Ready the crew of *Transcendence* and hand over your princess. I am weary of your game. I insist we sail *now*."

Fallon sighed, as if disappointed to hear of a shortage of carrots. "I understand. You fear you will find nothing with which to condemn us. You fear that there *is* nothing."

"I – I wish to go home. I can and *do* condemn you."

"On what grounds?"

"You...you commune with devils."

"Like the one you are holding?"

Jonathan looked down. Zartha was snuggled in his arms, panting. When their eyes met, she wagged her tail. Jonathan snarled and tossed her to the floor, but not without surreptitiously glancing back to make sure she was unhurt.

"Enough. Let us go."

"But I could not possibly. Not now. Not after your sublime promise of a theatrical performance, just for our benefit." Jonathan mentally said a dozen curses in Thomas's name. "And anyway, I cannot possibly let you leave before you have been made acquainted with your totem animal."

Jonathan went cold. "What totem animal?"

"The one who has undoubtedly been trying to connect with you your entire life. And I will help you discover which one it is. Tonight."

* * *

Miranda pretended she did not see the Selphyn baby's mother following her unobtrusively in her tour with Corrine around the village. Whenever the woman entered her peripheral vision, Miranda would feign interest in something, turning her back on the mother. The baby's warmth and the press of her weight against Miranda's heart were sublime, and she wasn't going to give her back until she absolutely had to.

Inevitably the baby grew fussy and stopped gurgling against Miranda's throat. She started off with an occasional cry and wiggle, which soon developed into full-blown wailing and flailing. This time the Selphyn mother shed her politeness and stepped into Miranda's vision, arms outstretched. Her vision blurring, Miranda slowly handed her the baby, and then could no longer stand to be in the woman's company. She would have fled the village, but Corrine fell into stride beside her.

Miranda squirmed under the intense gaze of the Selphyn and blurted, "I did not expect her to feel just like a human baby. I did not know she would be…"

"You've lost one."

Miranda wiped away her tears. "Yes."

"Can you not have another?"

"I – no. I am unwed."

"Gideon–"

"We cannot wed. He must wed someone of his own stature. And I – I am spoiled goods."

Corrine stopped, forcing Miranda to do the same. "What barbarism is this?"

"Barbar—it is our custom–"

"And I say your custom is barbarous. You are denied love and companionship if you lack sufficient wealth or rank? You are denied the divine gift of motherhood if your maidenhead is taken outside the bonds of marriage? And your society will shun you?"

"It – we are governed by laws that transcend the realm of man–"

"Ah. Your god dictates these laughable laws?"

"Some of them. Otherwise – otherwise the system will fail. And people would…they would–"

"People would revert to their natural instincts."

"Precisely!"

When Corrine smiled, Miranda blushed. "When you tire of this custom, you are welcome here."

Stunned, Miranda followed the pathway back to the palace. She would never tell anyone, but in her mind she could see it: living among a people without judgment, raising babies and loving Jonathan without marriage. If she could have that and still act…if God, or even the Selphyn Goddess, offered her that life as a gift, she would have snatched it up in an instant.

TWENTY-TWO

THEY REACHED ZIRNICH by midday. Gideon was upright but green, and forced them to stop several times so that he might vomit. He was not, however, so sick as to quiet his gregariousness. He complained about his treatment, about the road conditions, about his horse, about his stomach. He demanded to know the full details behind their escape, and when Rathnar grew vague, he directed his inquires at Lauren. She gave him a condensed version of the truth that still included the wolf, but did not explain where he came from nor his friendliness toward Lauren. She sensed Gideon suspected withheld information, but didn't quite know how to articulate his questions to catch her out. He knew something was missing, but not exactly what.

When they reached the harbor he was still questioning her, and was oblivious to Rathnar's tension. Lauren was watching him carefully while trying to answer Gideon, and saw him searching the horizon and piers for any signs of their human predecessors. As far as Lauren could tell there were only crewmen and fishermen at the docks, no passengers. Rathnar chose a galleon bedecked with wine, catching Gideon's interest, and demanded to speak with the captain.

While they waited Rathnar metamorphosed back into Sir Francis, royal spymaster, torturer, killer. He was all tense muscles and hard lines, eyes cold and unforgiving. When the middle-aged captain appeared on deck, Rathnar boarded the deck without permission, and stood in front of the captain. The effect was amazing: Rathnar *loomed* over the captain in his average height, no match for this tall, imposing and hulking figure.

"I am Sir Francis Rathnar, Principal Secretary to their Majesties, King Edward and Queen Lydia."

The captain bowed. "I am honored. How may I serve–"

"I am here on official business, and have been charged by their Majesties to apprehend traitors whom I understand have sailed to Rowan. You can aid me to the best of your ability, or you can suffer the consequences."

"With all due respect, Sir Francis, as Principal Secretary you are no doubt familiar with King Fallon's decree that no human may sail to Rowan without a Selphyn onboard–"

"I am familiar. But we are expected. And I mean to pay

handsomely."

He pulled a heavy moneybag from his doublet and dropped it at the captain's feet. Two gold coins spilled out the top, which, for a moment, seemed to captivate the captain.

"A generous, appreciated gift. One that will, I regret to say, do me no good if I am dead."

Lauren saw Rathnar's jaw slide forward. In spite of herself, she shivered.

"I *command* you, in the name of the king, to grant us passage to Rowan."

"Then you will have to arrest me, and my crew. No man is fool enough to sail to Rowan. We are given to understand archers will fire upon us—"

"We are *expected*. You will not be attacked. Upon my word, you will not."

"If you are expected, why did the Selphyn not await you with their own ship, as they did the others?"

Rathnar closed his eyes. "Then they took the others."

"Days ago."

"They are imposters. You must allow—"

"Forgive me, Sir Francis. I cannot. My men will mutiny otherwise. I wish you good day."

Rathnar's hand, white and bony, flashed up, catching the captain by his collar. "I will give you but one last warning. Take us there. *Now.*"

"Release me at once. Their ship will dock here eventually, either for trade or to return the human passengers. You may wait upon their leisure."

"It will be too late."

"I care not. You will put me down this instant."

The bewilderment of defeat filled Rathnar's face. He slowly lowered the captain. "If there is a Selphyn onboard, do I have your word you will grant us instant passage?"

The captain rearranged his coat. "Yes. God grant you luck in that enterprise."

"So be it."

Lauren knew what he was going to do, and slipped off her horse without thinking. "No! Do not do it!"

Rathnar cast her a glance with a rueful smile. "Thank you. But there is no other way."

There was a crewman with a mop and a bucket; he had paused

in his swabbing to watch the curious exchange between his captain
and Rathnar. When Rathnar strode toward him, he dropped his mop
and scurried backward until his back hit the railing. Rathnar knelt and
splashed handfuls of dirty, soapy water onto his face. Lauren could
not bear to watch the indignity of using foul water, and closed her
eyes. When she opened them Rathnar was back in front of the
captain. Streams of white paint dripped down his face and from his
hands. His skin looked mottled, disease-ridden. Lauren started to
weep.

The captain's mouth dropped open but he made no sound.
Gideon, trying to scramble off of his saddle, got tangled in the
stirrups and fell. His face bloated, he took two steps toward the ship,
arm outstretched, when Lauren caught him by the elbow.

"Not now."

He wrenched her loose. "And you *knew*! You *knew* his filthy little
secret and you – how could you?"

"I have known but for a few hours. And his filthy little secret
saved my maidenhead, and is about to grant us passage which we
would otherwise be denied."

Gideon's mouth twisted into a snarl. "My God. You *love* him.
How…how revolting."

She ignored him, for she did not know herself whether or not
his assertion was true. Onboard, the captain finally managed to find
his voice. "I – I shall ready the crew. I beg your pardon, Sir Fran–"

"Rathnar."

"Yes. Rathnar. Please – I beg your forgiveness."

Rathnar looked back at them once, as if to say, *Are you coming?*
before he disappeared below deck. Lauren and Gideon unfastened all
three saddlebags, and, without the wisdom of their leader, left their
horses behind.

The crew scattered in their wake, as if they too might at any
moment metamorphose into Selphyns. Lauren stood at the railing,
letting the wind blow her hair, and refused to look at Gideon who
was staring daggers into her back. When Rathnar reappeared on deck,
he was washed clean, and utterly transformed. With no white paint
on his hands or face, he simply glowed in the sunlight. He was
wearing a white shirt, the open V revealing a golden, smooth neck
and chest. Lauren's mouth dropped open as she stared at those long,
sharp features that were rendered poetic rather than vampiric in their
natural color. Gideon wasted no time in striding forward to deliver a
hard slap across Rathnar's face.

"How dare you?" Lauren said. "Four minutes ago you were too afraid to of him to utter one cross word. And now you think—"

"Shut up. Selphyn whore. He has no power, no—"

He cut off when Rathnar clamped a large hand around his throat. He lifted Gideon into the air. "Call her that again. I beg you. Then I may forever rid myself of your irksome, tiring, prattling voice."

He dropped Gideon when his face began turning blue. Gideon gasped and clawed at this throat. In a strangled voice, he said, "How dare you—"

"Until I am dismissed as such," Rathnar said without looking down, "I am still their Majesties' Principal Secretary."

"Until you are beheaded you mean."

Rathnar ignored him. Gideon stood and coughed several times, clearing his throat. "They *trusted* you. You knew every secret, every weakness…all to exploit them."

"I will not explain or justify myself to you. I would prefer if you simply did not speak to me."

"My pleasure entirely!"

By this time the ship was ready to set sail. Rathnar stood at the bow, his gaze fixed on the sea. The wind blew hard into his face, blowing back his hair. Lauren, creeping in closer, tried to imagine it in its natural, golden color. She had no doubt he would look magnificent.

When he turned to acknowledge her, she said, "Forgive my staring. I did not realize until this moment how beautiful you are."

He rewarded her tribute to his own words with a ghost of a smile. He turned his gaze back out to sea, and Lauren's eyes abruptly filled with tears. She must have made a sound for his shoulders sagged, as if with disappointment that he would now be obliged to comfort her.

"Why do you weep?"

"Because you have given me cause to hate you. And that I never wanted."

"How did I give you cause? By lying? Pretending? Or being a repulsive creature?"

"I watched my mother die. Her blood spilled on my face. I watched a golden monster kill her, and you must have known it was coming."

Rathnar softened. "I knew, yes. I was to…I was to help gather the children, to bring them to Rowan, where you were to be cared for."

"Cared for by my mother's murderers?"

He sighed. "It was Syldonia's wish."

"And my mother?"

Rathnar turned to face her full on. His eyes, she discovered, were the color of a dark sea whose depths contained either treasures or deadly creatures. He took hold of her forearms. "I swear to you, on my life, and on yours, that your mother knew what was planned. She put her fate in our hands and was in full agreement."

"No. She would not have abandoned us."

"She meant for you to come with us—"

"She would not have made us orphans! She would not have left us without a mother!" Lauren was sobbing now, and pulled free in order to pummel Rathnar's arms. "You sicken me! All that talk of beauty and sacredness. Why do you spy and kill for a king you must despise?"

He caught her wrists. "What care I for the affairs of man? If they want to kill each other, I will gladly help. I won their trust so I could watch over my sister. And—"

"Your *sister!*"

"And when she was dead, the children scattered, my nephew dead — what had I to do but avenge myself on those who destroyed my family?" He squeezed her wrists until she cried out. "And yes, I have enjoyed myself immensely. Here, allow me to cut off your fingers, break your bones, rip out your fingernails until you confess to I care not what! Every limb severed, every bone snapped, and my lust for revenge is a little more sated."

"It can never be sated. You are a *monster.*"

He spoke through clenched teeth. "Then why do you not fear me?"

"Because…because you love me."

He dropped her wrists and snatched at her hair, pulling her forward until her lips were smashed against his. This time when she inhaled, she smelled not the acrid, chemical smell, but a sensual, intoxicating musk. Seconds streamed past and they were immovable. The wind snapped at their hair, water splashed their faces and crewmen shouted in their nautical language, but they were frozen. When he pushed his tongue in her mouth she gasped, reeling, and then all but swooned when his taste filled her mouth and his lips devoured hers.

She was flooded suddenly with a warmth that started between

her legs and spread throughout her body. The sensation grew and became frenzied, when suddenly she threw her head back and cried out, her vision dark. When she could see, everything was throbbing and scorching hot, and she was panting for air. She took a step backwards and put her hands on her cheeks, horrified.

"What – what just happened?"

Understanding dawned on Rathnar, and to Lauren's shock, his own eyes filled with tears. "You...I believe you felt the pleasure most men, but few women, experience...do you understand?"

"No. And why do you weep?"

He touched her cheek. "Because you detest me and will find men who will only paw at you, or worse, no man at all, convinced as you are of being unworthy. If you were mine...I would have you collapse in my arms everyday."

She found that her muscles were limp, as if she had been exerting them for hours in some strenuous activity. When he reached for her she stepped backward. "No. Please, I...I need to lie down."

On her way to the hold a thought occurred to her, and she paused. "You cannot go back now, can you?"

"No."

She could not make sense of her feelings, and left him standing there, watching her go with a look so mournful, that for a moment he looked more human than humans.

TWENTY-THREE

THERE WERE A number of things that Jonathan had wanted to ask the princess, most of them intrusive and merciless to trick her into revealing her true motivation in returning to her family. But Fallon's enigmatic reference to a Selphyn ritual after dinner completely distracted him so that he could barely eat, much less question Kassandra.

The princess was seated at Fallon's right, directly across from Thomas. Jonathan was not so distracted, however, as to miss the subtle glances between the two of them, and Thomas's occasional innuendos. And when Fallon requested Thomas sing after they ate, Thomas actually blushed. Thomas never blushed before a performance of any kind, and his first notes were off-key. He closed his eyes and found the rhythm, and Jonathan relaxed when he sang the ballad with ease. There was hearty applause following the song, and Kassandra's complexion was flushed, her breathing a little heavy.

"Well played, harper," Fallon said. "I hope by the time you return you will have ample inspiration to compose a ballad of your visit here."

Thomas's gaze honed in on Kassandra. "I have found inspiration enough."

Jonathan sighed, and Fallon laughed. "Oh, but it is a shame that among your people one must marry according to one's station. If you would all marry for love, I should think people would find themselves much happier."

"And you are the expert on such things," Jonathan said. "Though you would have us kill those we love."

"Must we?"

Jonathan shrugged. "If I recall, it was you who brought up the subject of customs and love."

"Love and custom should never be forced to coincide. The nature of one will crush that of the other."

Jonathan could feel the rage simmering, just waiting for an excuse to boil. He was both relieved and annoyed when Kassandra deflected the conversation, turning her attention on Miranda.

"Speaking of custom, dear Mistress Helen, I do hope we can become friends. There is so much I wish to know about your traditions and etiquette. Perhaps you would be so kind as to instruct me how to behave properly as a lady of the court?"

"I should be happy to."

Jonathan heard the slight tremor in her voice, audible, no doubt, only to him. It was unlikely Miranda had ever set foot in court. He also felt certain that she could fake her way through describing it to Kassandra, long enough to get them through their visit. Kassandra's sweetness seemed genuine enough, but Jonathan hoped it was not. It was quite preferable to imagine her as a conniving temptress, a schemer who was putting on a show as much as they, who would show her true, vicious colors as soon as she took the throne. Regardless, he was extremely glad it was not up to him to perform the deed. Glancing down the table at Richard, he saw the assassin looking as cold as ever, a constitution that no sweetness of breath or smiles could melt.

Fallon entreated all of them, soldiers included, to describe their activities that day, and Jonathan listened with increasing dismay as an animated discussion ensued, wherein his actors had seemingly enjoyed themselves. Gregory went deep-sea fishing with Uthen, and caught several enormous fish. Ralf and Toby hunted with falcons, and they laughed, as if recounting stage mishaps at the Unicorn, as they explained how their falcons brought down six rabbits, which just happened to be the totem animal of a Selphyn named Raziel. Raziel took their teasing in good stride, dramatically reenacting his dismay with each conquest. "The birds know well enough, at least, to spare my special friend Eckyl."

"Eckyl is a very fat, well-loved rabbit," Fallon explained to Miranda and Jonathan, the latter feigning disinterest. "He and Raziel share a mind link, as do we all with a specific animal of our totem." To Jonathan he said, "Earlier today you were made acquainted with my raven Tiben. He and I have been joined some six years now, following the death of his beloved predecessor."

Miranda uttered an empathetic gasp. "How very difficult it must be for you when your animal dies."

"You cannot conceive of it," Fallon said. "It is akin to losing one's own child."

The animation seemed to seep from Miranda's bearing. Her shoulders slumped and her head tipped forward. Jonathan's nails dug into the table as Fallon reached across to take her hand.

"I see you can conceive of it after all."

"Please spare us your metaphysical sensitivity," Jonathan said.

Fallon withdrew his hand. Jonathan could see the retort

mounting an aggressive campaign on his lips, but he held it in. Jonathan was impressed, and a little sheepish.

"Master Ambrose," Kassandra said, and Jonathan, by now, no longer had to remind himself to look up. "You know my parents well. Can you tell me about them?"

Your father is a fat louse who raped his brother's wife.

"They are just rulers, wise and merciful. Your mother is quiet and kind. I think you will find them overjoyed to meet you; 'twas said they never recovered from when you were taken."

He met Fallon's gaze challengingly, and the latter was smiling faintly, drumming his fingers on the table. He did not rise to the bait.

When Jonathan did not get the reaction he wanted, he said to Kassandra, "How long intend you to wait before bringing the Selphyn back during your rule?"

The blood drained from her face. Fallon chuckled, and when Jonathan looked at him he saw his violet eyes shone with a feral glow in the candlelight.

"You are very ill-tempered this evening, Gideon."

"Why? Because I will not nod and smile and pretend that I believe her intentions and yours are honorable?"

There was a hush over the table as heads swiveled in their direction.

"Will you always sour our digestion with this malice at dinner?"

"Will you always evade this subject?"

Fallon stood. "Come. Enough. I will have you see what you are meant to see. I will no longer listen to this childish and spiteful speech, when you have no inkling of what we are about."

Jonathan was still formulating a refusal when Sebastian stood. "I will not have you tainting a member of my flock."

Fallon's face was a wall of stone. "Methinks you would do well to inspect your sheep. Oft times a wolf will slip in when you least expect it."

Jonathan imagined how satisfying it would feel to launch across the table and plunge a cleaver into Fallon's chest.

"What mean you by that?" Sebastian asked, and Jonathan jumped to his feet.

"I will answer this challenge then. Do your worst."

"Gideon, I must advise against—"

But Jonathan was already following Fallon, grateful for the anger that overpowered his fear. He faltered a little when several Selphyn, including Corrine, rose from the table and encircled him, almost as if they meant to prevent his escape. He allowed their momentum to carry him outside and down a spiraled path of flagstones. A three-quarter moon illuminated their passage, as well as tiny fragments of quartz glowing in the flagstone. In looking down the length of the path, it appeared to be made of stardust.

No one spoke as they walked, and he was not surprised when the path ended at the temple he had visited earlier that day. Winged angels in the columns now took on a nefarious atmosphere in the dark, and their imposing stone goddess appeared to be more like a destroyer than a creator. Bats flew overhead, one of them lighting on a Selphyn's shoulder and startling Jonathan. He had a fleeting fear that his animal, if indeed there was one, would be revealed as something equally vile.

Fallon opened a trapdoor in the floor of the temple, and as they descended a stone stairway the other Selphyn lighted the torches on the walls. Above the faint traces of incense, Jonathan could smell damp and musty earth, a smell that instantly took him back to the Selphyn ruins underneath the cathedral.

As if reading his mind, Fallon said, "You are no doubt aware of our ruins underneath your cathedrals. We prefer being one with the earth, and often build our temples, or at least some chambers, underground."

They reached the bottom of the stairs and stood inside a cavernous chamber that was easily fifteen degrees cooler than the surface. The room was more or less a cave, with no flooring, furniture or décor. At Fallon's gesture they all sat on the dirt ground, forming a loose circle. Corrine lighted four torches before she joined them, and as Jonathan took in their faces, their golden, angled features seemed to melt together, their animal fetishes spinning. He closed his eyes and breathed deeply to center himself. He heard Fallon's light laugh and tensed his jaw.

"See how eager our friend is to begin! Gideon, as I mentioned previously, we have brought you here to connect you with your totem animal."

Jonathan said, "I do not have one. I am only a quarter—"

"It matters not. All those with Selphyn blood, no matter how slight, have an animal waiting to bind itself to them."

Corrine handed him a slim vial from inside her cloak. As he dubiously eyed the opaque contests, the vial shook in his hand.

"It is sometimes difficult to make the first connection," Fallon said. "This mixture will help you relax your mind."

Jonathan offered the vial to Fallon, who made no move to take it. "Please. I have no wish to participate in this. And I fear me that you hope to convert and manipulate me—"

"Gideon. I swear to purely altruistic motivation. I want to help you."

"Help those in need. I lack nothing, wish for nothing, save to go home."

"I think you know how untrue that is."

Jonathan ignored his intrusive gaze, staring again at the murky contents of the vial. He tried to imagine what the real Gideon Ambrose would have done in this situation, assuming the courtier was part Selphyn. He would have thrown the vial in Fallon's face, hurled obscenities, stormed out. Or, no. He never would have allowed them to bring him down here in the first place. For that reason alone, never mind his fear, he knew he should refuse. He was about to stand when Fallon's voice stopped him.

"Imagine, if you will, for the sake of example, that your friend Horatio suffered a blow to the head. Upon awakening, he could not remember anything: his name, situation, interests. Various friends help him recall these mundane things and restore him to his home. Days go by and he says to you that while all should be well, he feels hollow. Or perhaps is filled with a burning desire that he cannot name, and so is miserable."

Jonathan's hands began trembling again. "Make no comparison to—"

"Perhaps his fingers pluck at the air in listlessness. Perhaps he sighs and is filled with a terrible melancholy. You know what he lacks, do you not? And how simple it will be for you to help him. In fact, you feel you would do him a great disservice by ignoring his pain."

"Please—"

"You need only slide a harp into his hands, and show him where to place his fingers. Once he hears the music, his fingers will remember what to do. And his passion will finally have an outlet. With such a simple gesture, you will have set your friend free." Jonathan sighed. "And so it is for us to see you silently suffer. For we know what you need, and it is simple for us to guide you."

"But I fear a visible taint," Jonathan said, at once repulsed by his weakness in confessing. "I will be marked for life as a Selphyn, with no hope of going back."

"Hm. Yes. I see. Let us revisit the wolf-and-sheep scenario. A wolf raised among sheep must someday discover his true nature and run with the wolves. But he can still choose to live among sheep. They are dull animals and may not notice a change of heart."

Jonathan smiled wryly at this comparison to his countrymen. "They will notice when he eats them."

Fallon burst out laughing. "A poor metaphor, then, I confess it! But you understand my meaning. You may nurture this new aspect of yourself in secret. I promise you that your skin will not darken."

A thought occurred to him then, that perhaps it wouldn't work. Yes: he could resist it and then exult in triumph that he was not, by nature, one of them. The thought was so appealing that he opened the vial and drank it without further pause. He gagged on the bitterness of the concoction that tasted like dirt, tree bark and roots, and fought to keep his stomach from rebelling. He closed his eyes to resist the nausea, and heard Fallon softly speaking.

"Yes. Relax. Clear your mind. Release your resistance. And then search for him in your mind; seek him out, and ask permission to join. He is not far; he will be waiting for you."

Breathing deeply, Jonathan attempted the opposite, and recited lines in his head from various plays. He thought of Miranda, how her skin smelled, and of the playhouse with the constellations painted on the ceiling. He was becoming very groggy and finding it increasingly difficult to stay focused. Just a few minutes more, he thought, and he could declare failure.

His head was extremely heavy and fell forward. He tried to raise it but lacked the strength as he fell into the in-between land on the edge of sleep, where one could dream but with awareness. Something pushed at his mind and he recoiled, suddenly frightened. There was another push, a gentle nudge of inquiry like a soft hand on the side of his face trying to rouse him from a nap. He knew instinctively if he took hold of this hand there would be love and compassion, like that of a mother. He tried to resist but then felt this love, a tumultuous outpouring, and gave way.

His body was flooded with warmth. Had he been fully awake he would have wept with gratitude, and embraced this incomparable feeling. In the back of his mind he remembered Fallon's instructions, and mentally asked permission to join minds. There was a moment of violent disorientation. He felt his physical limbs flail as he fought to ground himself, but like being carried away in a strong current he eventually stopped fighting and allowed himself to be swept away, a wonderful, buoyant feeling once he stopped resisting. Then he felt as though he were being slammed to the ground. He inhaled sharply and realized he was no longer smelling the dirt of the cave, but an overpowering scent of grass. Eyelids – not his own, he realized – lifted, and he saw the open night sky drowned in stars. In the distance he saw the outline of trees and a fence, and beyond these were pinpricks of light, perhaps from lanterns shining in windows. He heard crickets chirping and leaves rustling in the wind, both sounds nearly deafening.

Then he was running. The dark landscape blurred past as he listened to hooves pound into the ground. His sinews pulsated with life and fire; he never dreamed how much ecstasy could be found in running. His heart felt as though it were tearing open, no longer able to contain this overwhelming zest, passion and vitality. Then he – they – reached the fence and came to a screaming halt. His body, young and virile, reared upwards as his head was thrown backwards. A vibration began in his abdomen and carried through almost his entire body, rattling his throat as it erupted into a roar, or what he foolishly heretofore thought of as a whinny. But that sound and vibration was grossly insulted by such an innocuous word, a child's word. This shriek of life could only be compared to a lion's roar, and would never, Jonathan knew, be thought of again by him in such domestic terms as a neigh or whinny. It was a howl, a scream, a bellow.

Then they were running again, back the way they came, having found their exit blocked by a fence. Grass was ripped out by the roots in large clumps by these deathly hooves that were capable of killing a man. The wind filled his ears, blinded his eyes, and was sucked in by his nose. Again the muscles in his legs sang with ecstasy with each pounding leap. Abruptly he lost his hold on this mind, likening the feeling to dropping his quill after hours of writing, the muscles in his fingers spent and aching. And yet here he had only been holding on for a few precious moments.

Once again he felt that sickening disorientation, followed by the slamming home of his mind into his own body. His eyes snapped open, and he took a huge, gasping breath of air as if he were drowning. He fell forward, directly into Fallon's arms. Because he was still reeling with love, he crushed the Selphyn king in an embrace, bursting into heaving, gasping sobs.

"Yes, yes, I know," Fallon said in a soft, soothing voice, patting Jonathan's back. "It was thus for all of us the first time."

"It – I–"

"Yes. I know. You have not words for it."

"No."

He sobbed, with embarrassing audible whimpers, for almost two minutes before he was finally able to quiet himself and catch his breath. Fallon gently released him. "Gideon. What were you?"

"A – a horse."

"Ah! A noble, passionate creature. Well done!"

Jonathan wanted to describe the encounter, but fearing another onslaught of tears, said nothing.

"Do you know where he is? Far? Was he wild?"

"There…was a fence. He belongs to someone, but still…wild. At heart, at least."

He considered his statement and felt a wave of rage. This spirited creature *belonged* to someone. He nearly retched.

"Oh. That is…difficult. He will try to find you, and you him. You will both–"

"Stop at nothing, I know," Jonathan said. "I *will* find him."

Fallon gave him a lopsided smile. "Yes. Welcome, Gideon. You are home."

It was, of course, the worst thing the Selphyn could have said. Jonathan looked at all of them, their exultant, happy faces, and realized how much he had failed in his initial plan to foil them all. Though he would not have given back his experience for the world, he was still horrified at how much they witnessed.

He stumbled to his feet and nearly fell, his legs rubbery as if he himself had done all of that running. He was also still drugged, and this sudden defiance of gravity made him violently dizzy. He lurched and stumbled until he fell against the cave wall. The ground tilted and he clung to dirt wall for dear life. Fallon's anxious face swam in and out of focus.

"Gideon. Do not fear. Sit down and recover."

He ran, this half-disembodied monster, for the entrance, tilting and swaying. Someone grabbed at him but he shrugged them off, and heard Fallon say, "Let him go."

Somehow he managed to get up the stairs and stumbled through the temple, tripping over an ill-fitting stone in the floor. He inhaled breaths of fresh air, and kept running to avoid them when they emerged from the cave. Tree branches whipped at his face and snagged in his hair and clothes, and a bramble with thorns cut open his hand. When he finally burst into a clearing he was covered in dirt and leaves, his hand and cheek bleeding. He looked around and realized he had no idea where he was, nor was there any structure he could see.

He started to take a step when a howling of wolves pierced through the silence. He froze, his heart thudding. They were close but it was impossible to tell in which direction as the howling bounced off the volcano and echoed. The sound continued, deafening, and he put his hands over his ears with his eyes tightly squeezed shut. He remembered something Fallon said, that the awful concoction he drank was necessary only for the initial contact, which led him to assume he could now connect with his animal link on his own. He was so shaken and distracted that he doubted he could focus, but the moment he tried reaching out with his mind, searching for that warm, familiar tug, he was flooded with love and then the sweeping disorientation.

Again they were running as one, and he forgot the wolves and his fear and felt only wild exhilaration. Then something pushed on his physical, human legs and the connection was abruptly severed, slamming him home.

He opened his eyes, amazed to find himself still standing, and wind-milled his arms to keep his balance. Zartha, tongue lolling out, was sitting on his feet. He jumped and did fall then, landed hard on his rump. Zartha jumped on his chest and began wagging incessantly, licking his face. The howling of her comrades persisted, but was fortunately farther away than before.

He put up his hands to ward off her tongue. "Oh, go to, you little goblin. You terrified me half to death." He sat up and she nuzzled him. "Help me find my way back?" She chewed on his doublet laces. "Home?"

He set her down and said the word again, hoping she could understand. When she trotted toward the trees he exhaled with relief and followed, still dizzy. She led him back through the trees he had crashed through earlier; he saw signs of his desecration in several snapped branches and trodden flowers. He moved branches gently this time, but quickly as Zartha was still trotting. He was soon out of breath, panting, and wondering why he suddenly felt more disoriented than before when the effects of his drink should have been wearing off. There was also the disconcerting sudden manifestation of fog.

He stumbled into it headlong, feeling the chilly dampness of it permeate his clothes. It was so thick that he could no longer see Zartha leading the way, and when the ground was swallowed up he stopped. "Zartha?" He heard a distant flute playing and followed the sound, moving blindly with his arms outstretched to ward off unseen tree branches. After several feet the sound of his boots on the dirt disappeared. He knelt and was startled to find soft grass, and no trace of the trees. The music was louder so he resumed following it, though he was having trouble keeping his eyes open as the air felt oppressive and heavy. Finally the fog began to thin and then disappear; he found himself in a clearing covered with grass. Hilltops shone silver in a moonlight that was much brighter than before, and there was an intoxicating smell that was sweet and yet animal at the same time.

Something touched his hand and he whirled, or at least tried to. His movements were slow and heavy, as if he were trying to walk underwater. A woman stood before him, lithe and naked. She was amber-colored, her face an exaggeration of the long, angular Selphyn features. Her eyes were the color of ice tinged with blue, and as Jonathan took her in he saw the iridescent wings that sparkled in the moonlight.

"Oh," he said. "I'm dreaming."

Her arms, all bone and skin, reached for him, and she touched his face. Fingers like the long, thin legs of an insect grazed his skin, tingling. She stepped in closer and he endured a wave of extreme dizziness. His swallow was hard and painful.

"Where's – where's Zartha?"

The woman – faerie? – smiled. The sound of the flute grew louder, but Jonathan could not see who was playing it. "Here."

"Ah. Yes. Dreaming."

She pulled him in and he no longer cared if he was dreaming or not as limbs entwined around him, wings gently vibrating to hold the nearly weightless body aloft. He did not protest when his clothes were removed, nor when he was bitten and scratched. The last coherent thought he had was that he thought he could hear someone calling his name from very far away, a muffled sound like they too were underwater.

He had no idea of how much time had passed when he opened his eyes and saw the anxious Selphyn faces, illuminated by torchlight, looking down on him.

"Gideon, thank the Goddess," Fallon said. "Are you well?"

Jonathan giggled and then sighed like a lovelorn boy. "Very well indeed. I humbly thank you." He lifted his very heavy, pounding head. He was naked, lying in the grass. The moonlit, shining hills were gone.

Fallon laughed. "I think our friend has been cavorting with faeries."

TWENTY-FOUR

LAUREN WAS SURPRISED when the ship's captain invited them to dine with him. He was obviously terrified of Rathnar, who did not react to the captain's shaking hands and voice. Rathnar was all grace and calm, sipping his wine and avoiding Gideon's murderous gaze. He was still dressed in his white shirt, his golden skin on display. Lauren was having a difficult time not staring at the opening in his shirt, at the smooth skin and delicate hollow of his throat. Whenever their eyes met she would look away, heat flooding her face.

In between bites Gideon talked as if the captain were not in attendance. "How long have you practiced this ruse?"

"Since my sister was sold into slavery."

"I understand you not."

Rathnar took a long drink of wine, and Lauren silently admired his serenity. "Since Syldonia was married off to Thaddeus."

"She...you..."

"I worked my way up as quickly as I could. I was not admitted to court until it was too late, and there was nothing I could do for her."

While Gideon absorbed this, Rathnar ate grapes and bread. Lauren watched his every move, mesmerized by this new creature that had hatched from a dull, dark chrysalis. No one else shared her fascination; they were too afraid or enraged to be curious.

The captain, seeing a break in the conversation, took a shaky breath and said, "I – I will not betray you, my lord. My men and I – you can be assured of our secrecy."

Rathnar almost smiled. "I know better than to believe you. I give you my word that I will not harm any of you."

"I will tell!" Gideon said as if Rathnar hadn't spoken. "I will tell them all what a dissembling, foul creature you are. And what will you? Will you not kill me now?"

He sounded like a schoolboy taunting a younger child, and Lauren nearly told him so. The conversation seemed to finally take its toll on the captain, who excused himself from his own table and cabin. No one marked his exit.

"No. I will not kill you," Rathnar said.

"But you cannot ever go back. For I will tell the king."

"Gideon. You may do as you like. I only ask that you first help me secure the princess with her rightful parents. This may require my return, as brief as it may be."

Gideon looked thoroughly confused. Then he gasped and half rose out of his chair, pointing his finger at Rathnar. "I see you now! You mean to put her on the throne so that she might allow the Selphyn to return. You have no loyalty to the king."

When Rathnar ignored him, Lauren said, "You cannot go back. They will kill you."

"I must see this through."

"How noble," Gideon sneered.

"What does this all mean for my brother?" Lauren asked, hoping that now that Rathnar's weakness was exposed, he would be less likely to follow through with his original plan. He looked at her and she felt tears welling up when she saw his expression.

He gestured to his face. "This changes nothing. If he means the princess harm he must be dealt with."

Lauren slammed her goblet down and stood, taking immense satisfaction in Rathnar's blink of surprise. "How dare you issue judgment on him before you know the circumstances! You are hardly now in a position to *deal* with him."

"Who are you to strip me of my power?" Rathnar said softly. "Whether I am acting on behalf of King Edward or King Fallon, my duty is to see this girl reinstated as heir to the throne. Whoever opposes me is mine enemy."

Her lower lip trembled. "Then I am your enemy."

"Again you put your brother before all."

"And would not you do the same?"

She left the table before he could respond. Gideon's triumphant "Ha!" enraged her, and she nearly whirled to assure him that she was *not* allied with him. She climbed into her hammock below deck and sobbed, oblivious to the rats she sent scurrying. She wished more than ever that she could banish the memory of his lips on hers, the way he tasted, looked and felt. But her body betrayed her, and even as she fought to forget, warmth surged through her, and she positively ached for him.

* * *

Thomas followed her through the garden, watching her pick flowers and drop them in her basket. When she caught him looking, he broke into song and capered around her like a jester.

O, say you, sweet lady
Where will thou be gone?
My love follows thee
And will have thee anon.
I take up thy hand
And will sing thee this song
Be mine now and ever
Be thou never gone.

She laughed and he bowed. "Sweet music, that."

"It is extempore from my dazzling wit. Good lady, see what brilliance here you conjure from me." He snatched a handful of flowers from her basket and flashed an exaggerated look of innocence. "Here are pansies for you. I spent all the morning picking them. I would have picked roses too but alas, they were withered."

"Indeed?"

"Indeed. For they saw not your face these three days gone, and that were too long."

Color bloomed in her cheeks and Thomas's pulse accelerated.

"Such pretty words."

Her tone contained a touch of facetiousness, so Thomas threw himself onto one knee in front of her and she rewarded him with a laugh. He was well aware that he had completely broken character, but thought it well worth the risk. Horatio the Harper was not born to woo.

"What say you, lady? Let us forget this business, and run away together."

She put her hands on her hips. "And would you have me disappoint my mother and father? My future kingdom?"

"They who know not what they miss cannot be disappointed."

"I am ashamed of you, Horatio."

He put his hand over his heart. "Oh, she wounds to the quick! Such arrows of spite hit my breast. My poor little heart."

"Methinks it will heal quickly."

"Only a kind word from you can save me."

While she pretended to deliberate, he looked at her face. The morning sun was behind her head, casting a brilliant halo of light around her hair. "How she glows in brilliant contemplation."

"Be quiet, you. I am thinking."

"Think but on me. Oh, do not frown, dear lady! I would not

have you frown nor knead your brow for the world. And when you are queen, you shall do much of both. See why I would spare you from such a life? Run away with me."

"I could not so fail my people."

He stood up, now taller than she. She looked up into his eyes, her smile faltering.

"And which people would that be, my lady? The Selphyn or the humans?"

He heard her swallow, and saw her look of uncertainty as to whether or not he was still in jest. When he did not smile she paled.

"Good sir. I think you do me wrong."

"Do I?"

"I think – I think you do."

He took her hand. "I think my thoughts do echo those of my friend Gideon. How long *do* you intend to wait before you bring them back?"

She tried to pull away but he squeezed harder. Her hand twisted in his. "I ask you to release me."

Harder still. She gasped. "I asked you a question. I entreat you to answer."

She wrenched her hand loose. "And you forget your place!"

He bowed mockingly to hide his alarm. "She is a princess, after all! They have trained you well."

"Good – good day."

She shrugged past him. He felt and heard her skirt brush against him, and it was all he could do not to grab the hem and kiss it, begging her forgiveness. Then he remembered that it did not matter – none of it. In his mind's eye he saw her sinking down in dark waters, her hair and skirt fanned out beneath her. Her mouth was open, as were her eyes, though sightless. Her arms were floating above her, fingers gently bent, though perhaps the index finger of her right hand was extended, as if pointing. He shuddered and left the garden, his eyes lighting on the abandoned basket that held a dozen murdered flowers.

TWENTY-FIVE

MIRANDA WAS AWAKENED in the middle of the night when they brought Jonathan to her bed.

If she hadn't seen the flash of their bright clothing, she would have thought his escort consisted of humans. The uncharacteristic way in which the Selphyn bumbled into her room, laughing and whispering, was strongly reminiscent of her fellow actors, drunkenly stumbling into their rooms at the Unicorn.

She certainly suspected drunkenness on Jonathan's part, at least, with the way he groaned and muttered in his sleep. He threw his arm and a leg on top of Miranda; when she went to push him off, she was shocked to discover he was naked. While her instinctual reaction was to blame the seductive arts of a Selphyn woman, she quickly reminded herself that she knew nothing of their rituals. Perhaps this initiation he participated in required a cleansing or baptism of some sort, and depriving oneself of clothing was a necessary preparation. However, it did not explain why they brought him back that way.

Still, she gave him the benefit of the doubt until dawn that morning. Then, in the soft gray light of morning, she saw the bite and nail marks on his chest and neck. Pulling the coverlet down a little farther, she saw these marks extended well below the level of modesty. She threw the coverlet back up, hitting him in the face. He groaned and rolled over while she slid out of bed, fastening the stays of her bodice with the loudest sighs she could muster. When he blearily opened his swollen, bloodshot eyes, he saw the look on her face and said, "What?"

"Did you enjoy your transgression with some Selphyn hussy?"

"Wha—"

"I hope it was magical."

Slamming the door behind her, it occurred to her that the hussy in question might have been Corrine. The thought plunged her spirits even farther; she liked and trusted the Selphyn woman whom she recently learned was none other than Fallon's own daughter. The fact that they appeared to be of the same age was explained: the Selphyn, upon reaching adulthood, aged much more slowly than humans. She wondered how much this would affect Jonathan, and this thought led to one of envisioning Jonathan in domestic bliss with his new Selphyn wife – or rather, companion. Enraged again, Miranda decided to make a statement of displeasure with her Selphyn hosts by skipping breakfast.

Outside, she realized, upon stepping on a pinecone, that she had forgotten her shoes. She stepped gingerly on the needles, gasping and wincing, when she heard a laugh from behind. Whirling, she saw Fallon watching her. He was dressed in an azure coat with silver satin on underneath, and appeared, unlike Jonathan, to be well-rested.

"I see those tender feet have never seen the light of day."

She glanced at his own feet, unsurprised to see him barefoot. A silver anklet on his right leg caught her attention, and she thought she could see a tiny goddess charm hanging from the chain.

They studied each other for a moment in silence before Fallon said, "It is not as you think."

She immediately bristled. "No? I suppose some animal scratched and bit him."

"In a way."

Miranda crossed her arms. "I know you have no regard for fidelity here—"

"Now, just a moment, Mistress Helen. When we have chosen a companion, we are faithful and loyal. We do not rut and conquer every female that crosses our path."

"Then why—"

"This was…a very special situation."

"Some initiation? I am still betrayed."

And surprised, she discovered, that she was not acting in the least.

"The…creature…in question was not a Selphyn. Nor a human."

The hairs on Miranda's arms rose. "I don't – I don't understand. He didn't – surely – not an animal—"

Fallon laughed and she blushed. "No, we are not so barbaric as that either. Not an animal. I should allow him to explain. But you said 'initiation.' Am I to understand, then, that he told you?"

"That he is part Selphyn? Yes."

"Ah. Excellent. I see it has not affected your esteem of him, and for that, *my* esteem of *you* has grown significantly."

She blushed again and pulled a wayward strand of hair away from her face.

"There is something I would like to show you. Wait here a moment, and I will fetch your shoes."

She waited, grateful for an excuse to stand still and spare her feet the pain of walking. He returned a moment later with her shoes, though still without any of his own. As she slipped them on, he said, "Gideon is anxious that he caused you distress. I would beg you to put these fears of infidelity to rest, for all will be made known to you later."

Reserving the right to maintain anger, she sniffed and said nothing. Fallon grinned and took her arm. "Come."

While they walked she surreptitiously studied his profile. The Selphyn king was nothing short of beautiful, and that coupled with his charisma made him almost irresistible. She reminded herself that his daughter was older than she, and he ruled a race that she had been taught to despise. Yet the longer they remained, the harder it was to maintain this opinion that was making less sense by the minute.

For a while they followed the dried lava bed and then veered away, walking carefully through large rocks. She could hear the sound of the ocean crashing, and when they reached a cliff she sat down to watch the waves splashing against giant rocks below. Assuming this was the object of their destination, she said, "It's lovely. Thank you."

"Oh, no. This is not what I would have you see. Watch a moment."

For two minutes she followed his example and stared at the waves, wondering what she was supposed to be looking for. Without warning a giant head emerged from the surface, and she covered her mouth and gasped. A humpback whale surged upward, revealing at least two-thirds of its massive body. It rotated, fins dripping, and fell sideways back into the sea with a deafening splash. As a final gesture, it flung its tail up, showering the tops of the rocks with water. Miranda applauded.

"Most wonderful!"

Fallon was beaming. "A friend of a friend. Come down, if you can. There's more."

She half walked and half slid down the least steep side of the cliff, now envying Fallon's barefooted grip on the loose dirt. Without hesitating he walked into surf, drenching several inches of his coat and trousers. Miranda kicked off her shoes and followed him in, gasping at the iciness around her feet and ankles. She pulled her skirt up to her knees, but the waves lapped at the hem, and much of the back. When a nose gently bumped into her shin, she let out a cry and dropped her skirt.

Three dolphins circled their legs, splashing and playing. Delighted, Miranda splashed with them with a childlike abandon, occasionally catching glimpses of Fallon's satisfied expression.

"This was Syldonia's animal, you know."

"I don't doubt it," Miranda said, laughing when water splashed her face from one of the dolphin's blowholes. "They are regal and yet so very lovable."

Completely forgetting decorum, she sat down in the water, soaking her dress all the way up to her shoulders. She hugged each of the dolphins, loving the way their fins beat against her hair and cheek. They were softer than she ever imagined, and tireless in their energy. After an hour Miranda forced herself to stand, instantly appalled when she saw the way her dress clung to her. Fallon only laughed.

He helped her onto the shore, and she waved farewell to the dolphins, who were doing their backwards dance on the waves. Fallon led her down the beach until they found a much milder slope to climb. Back on solid ground, she was acutely aware of the indignity of her appearance, particularly her sodden skirt, now covered in sand, dragging behind her. Fallon bore his dishevelment with grace, as if the soaked, sand-covered bottom of his coat dragging behind him was part of his magisterial train.

Thinking about him in kingly terms shifted her perception of their easygoing walk together, and she began to view his bestowed favor on her as absurd. To him, she was nothing but an attendant. In reality, she was even less than that.

"Why did you bring me there?" she asked.

"I'm wooing you." He laughed when he saw her stunned expression. "No, no, you misunderstand. I am wooing you with a lifestyle. You see, I am growing quite fond of your Gideon. I admire his passion and fire, his courage in challenging me. And last night I had a glimpse of a side of him he keeps well hidden."

Miranda's heart accelerated; she wondered if all of this was a sadistic setup to reveal he had caught them out, or to trick her into admitting it.

"I began to think how much happier the two of you would be here, living free of your constricting customs. As outrageous as the idea would seem to both of you, I imagined the two of you joining us and raising a family."

The blush worked its way up her neck, and she would have died before admitting she had entertained the same thought.

"Do you think me mad?"

"No. And I am quite flattered. But..." She closed her mouth against the impertinent question that sprang to her lips; he saw it and stopped.

"Nay, speak. You may be plain with me."

"But do you not mean, my lord, to…"

"Return to Salsima?"

She exhaled. "Yes."

He looked away, giving her a chance to study the violet brilliance of his eyes unnoticed.

"This is the great fear you all share." She did not bother to confirm it. "I have no intention of marching my people back into Salsima to claim our birthright."

Just as he turned back to look at her, her head tilted in an angle that declared, *You don't expect me to believe that, do you?*

"I speak truly. But I do wish for there to be peace between our people. I would like to be able to perform a decent trade without fear of being beheaded. I would like to visit *friends*–" He looked at her meaningfully – "as it pleases me. I wish for all of this bloodshed and animosity to be behind us. I want acknowledgement that we are not savages. Someday, perhaps, though I doubt it would be in my lifetime, we may live amongst you."

"But when you…when you *took* her, did you not do so for the purpose of–"

"It was done in a blind rage. I had no intentions beyond causing King Edward the greatest grief possible." He resumed walking, and she fell into step beside him. "I blamed him for my nephew's death. I was still so very angry, you see, over his treatment of my sister. It was her fervent wish, and mine, to raise Edward here. And when I returned to find him, and learned he died in our ruins, I blamed everyone save the one who was responsible."

The palace was in view, and Miranda slowed her pace so he could finish before they were joined by anyone who might stop his narrative. As if having the same thought, he stepped in front of her and stopped so that she nearly ran into him. He put his hands on either side of her face, forcing her to look him in the eye. Her breath caught and she began to tremble.

"I was to blame, of course. I alone. The death of his mother drove him to such lengths, as to hide away where death and disease found him. I was wild with grief and rage. And young – the greatest folly of youth is to find blame beyond one's self. I blamed the king, and when I learned he was a proud father, I wanted to give him my pain. And now I want to make things right. Are my intentions completely selfless? No. I do hope that because she was raised with us, and knows we are not the savages your people would have us be, that she will give us the opportunity to prove ourselves. Miken prophesized a Day of Reckoning. We may not have such a day without someone opening the door."

She did not blink once during this speech, and under the intensity of that gaze she completely believed him. He smiled and released her face, and as he turned to address someone approaching, she was flooded with horror at the great deceit they were all playing at.

It was Jonathan, dressed but disheveled, with his shirt untucked and doublet unlaced. Hair was falling from his usually tight and prim ponytail, and his eyes were still bloodshot. He allowed Fallon's vigorous handshake with no enthusiasm of his own.

"How I envy you!" Fallon said. "Many a time have I visited, but never have I been treated to such...amorous attention."

Jonathan's mouth dropped. "You never–"

"No, no. You are special indeed. And I should tell you that such an initiation was not my doing. It was all Zartha."

Zartha!

Fallon laughed at her expression and said to Jonathan, "I shall leave you to your explanations. Find me anon and we shall discuss today's performance."

"Oh, God," Miranda said when Fallon was gone. "The play. I forgot."

Jonathan massaged his forehead. "As did I. Listen, about last ni—"

Miranda grabbed his arms as tears filled her eyes. "I cannot proceed with this deception."

"What–"

She repeated what Fallon had said, though there was no duplicating the gleam of sincerity she saw in his eyes. "I believe him, and even more, now that I have met her, I cannot just...before she was just..."

"Just an idea. Just a character," Jonathan said, and Miranda nodded miserably. "She was not flesh and spirit, as she is now."

"And she is kind." Jonathan nodded, and she felt lighter with a surge of hope. "Will you come with me and warn her? Or shall we simply tell him–"

"Wait, wait! What are you suggesting?"

She blinked. "Are you not with me in–"

"Think of the implications. You cannot just admit our ruse.

They may easily kill us."

"Then what—"

"I am not convinced we should do anything." He took her by the arms. "We must think of the good of our country. And though he is very persuasive, you cannot believe everything Fallon tells you."

"You will just let them kill her?" she whispered.

"I do not know. I cannot tell you how much…"

"What?"

"How much I wish I could just stay here and do nothing…let them do what they will do, and I will have no responsibility with the outcome."

"Jonathan…"

"I know. Look, here she comes. Do not tell her anything. Promise me."

Miranda wiped away her tears. "I promise. But—"

"Shh."

Miranda curtseyed and Jonathan bowed as Kassandra approached and took Miranda's hands. She was dressed again in blue velvet, her bodice and sleeves slashed with cream-colored satin. Miranda wondered if she always dressed like that, or if, when no humans were about, she paraded around with her mid-drift exposed in ruby-colored silks.

"My dear friend, I was hoping to find you. As my remaining time here grows short, I would ask you to teach me to dance in the manner as befits my station. My friends here are ignorant, but I know you will be well-versed in such things."

"I should be honored to do so." Miranda threw Jonathan a glance, and he put up his hands in sympathy. "We ought to find Horatio and his harp—"

"Oh."

Miranda kneaded her brow. "Have you quarreled?"

"No," Kassandra said, without meeting Miranda's gaze.

"He means well, but he can be…impetuous. Come, we will find him, and all will be well."

Looking for Thomas gave Miranda a much-needed distraction away from the feel of Kassandra's tiny hand in hers, and the way her face had flushed at the mention of Thomas, reminding Miranda of just how young she was. Her heart, already aching, ought to be mended and broken at least a dozen times before she reached Miranda's age. Remembering her promise to Jonathan, she resisted taking Kassandra into her confidence. But if Jonathan did not act, or at least formulate a plan she approved of, she would not just stand by to see this girl murdered.

This thought was doubly strong by the time they collapsed in a heap of laughter after three hours of dancing to Thomas's harp, and whatever tension had existed between him and the princess was now absent. Twice he bade Miranda sing while he swept Kassandra into his arms to dance. Seeing the look of mutual adoration in their eyes, Miranda hoped she could at least find an ally in Thomas. But later, after Kassandra had taken her leave, he reacted to her suggestion with incredulity.

"You do not know what you are saying."

"But you cannot wish her ill. You lo—"

She shrank back from him, terrified of the sudden rage that leapt into his eyes. "Do not speak to me of her again!"

She was alone in the garden, gently weeping, wondering if she would have the wherewithal to fight off twelve men. Then Gregory came capering in, taking her hands and pulling her into a dance. "Teach me!"

She laughed in spite of herself and pulled him in for a hug which he fiercely returned.

"Just eleven men then," she said while he eyed her quizzically. At the very least, she would take Fallon into her confidence. She trusted him, and though it might earn her the hatred of this company whom she loved like a family, it would be worth it not to have the blood of a princess on her hands.

TWENTY-SIX

THE LAST THING he wanted to do before a three-hour performance was to take a long walk with Fallon. He had hoped to crawl back into bed and sleep off his headache and aching limbs, but the Selphyn king wanted to show him a potential venue for the performance.

"It makes a natural amphitheater, this slope," Fallon said. "You will be at the base of the mountain, which will provide a lovely backdrop as well as containing the sound, and the slope of the hill in front of you will provide us with many a good seat." He looked up and gestured to the cloudless sky. "I daresay you could not have chosen a better day."

Jonathan sighed. "I am not adverse to performing out-of-doors, but did you consider staging us in your hall? It is customary in Salsima to perform for royalty in the court."

"I did consider it. But I realized only half of our number could be squeezed into the hall, so why not perform in the trees and the grass, where we might all enjoy it?"

Jonathan was certain he misheard. Trotting to catch up to Fallon's long-legged gait, each step a dagger to his head, he said, "Surely you do not mean half of your total population could fit in the hall."

"Yes. That is what I mean. 'Twould be difficult indeed to fit more than five thousand. And even then they would be sitting on each other."

Jonathan came to an abrupt halt. Fallon, a step ahead of him, paused and turned, his eyebrow arched.

"Do you mean to say you number only ten thousand?"

"Some ten or twelve. This cannot be a surprise to you."

Jonathan had trouble swallowing. "How...how many..."

"I estimate we lost some six million when King Balon invaded two-hundred years ago."

A long silence stretched as a breeze picked up and lifted their hair, gently, as if invisible faeries were at play. Two hummingbirds zoomed in front of Jonathan's face making a loud chirping sound, and three plump rabbits, unperturbed at their presence, chomped off the heads of dandelions. Life was as it should be, yet if felt so egregiously off-kilter to Jonathan that he had trouble keeping his balance.

Finally Fallon spoke. "We have always been a peaceful people. At the time of the invasion, the only weapons we had were those for hunting: spears and arrows. We had no swords, no armor, no crossbows. We would have welcomed the humans, had they but given us the chance."

Jonathan, finding it increasingly difficult to speak, managed to say, "And yet you – you seem to bear us no ill will. And what a fool I must seem, shouting for blood over the death of but two people. Why do you not despise us? Despise me?"

"Gideon. You could learn all you needed to know, all that Miken preached, by learning the ways of these rabbits." Jonathan started to smile. "No, no. Watch them, how they enjoy their meal of dandelions, and the warmth of the sun on their heads. And yet they know, somewhere, there is a hungry falcon or wolf – in our case, many wolves. They bear their destroyer no ill will. They understand how we are all connected. Miken knew it; he preached to any who would listen that we are all one with the universe. It is all in the book I left for you; take it with you and read it. Physical life, yes, is fleeting, but our souls are eternal. Hating you would be hating me, hating life, hating all. I cannot deny moments of weakness, when I forgot this very basic lesson. When I offered my sister in marriage, only to see her enslaved, and then lost my nephew…then I knew hatred and rage. And even now…no human is allowed on our island without my invitation or a Selphyn escort. And I will kill them if they come." He looked shrewdly at Jonathan, as if welcoming a challenge. "I could not bear to lose any more of our people. And I have learned, finally, not to trust humans."

Lest he give himself away, Jonathan quickly steered the conversation from dangerous waters. "I would have thought, after two-hundred years, that your population would be greater than it is."

"We are very careful lest we outgrow our island and food supply. It is hard to grow crops here, and we rely, too much as it is, on our illegal trade with the people of Zirnich." He smiled. "We know some tricks to avoid overpopulating, while at the same time sating our passion."

Jonathan resumed walking rather than giving Fallon the satisfaction of seeing his scandalized expression. But as he feared, the reference to passion led to questions he would rather avoid.

Slowing down his pace to keep in stride with Jonathan, Fallon said, "Last night. Will you not tell me about it? What was it like?"

Jonathan tried to summon a vivid memory, but could remember only snatches of images and sensations. If not for the physical evidence on his skin, he would have attributed the bizarre events to dreams and drug-induced imaginings. And yet he felt the pressure of living up to a reputation, almost as if he were a schoolboy trading exploits with an older, more experienced boy. He was rather aghast to discover that he was loath to disappoint.

"How does one describe the stars? Or the kiss of a beautiful woman? Can you do justice to describing those first sensations when you joined with your totem animal?"

Fallon sighed dreamily. "Ah, like that, is it? I thought as much. You are lucky indeed."

"Did you speak truly when you said you had never..."

"Oh, yes. We are all jealous. To the extent of my knowledge, you are the only one to whom such an honor has been bestowed. The wolves, of course, have been our guides to the faerie realm for centuries – our link to the blood of our ancient ancestors. We visit from time to time, but this..."

"Why should they bestow such favor on me?"

"I do not know. To help you release your passion, perhaps?"

Jonathan shrugged, wishing he could confide to Fallon that the night was made all the more extraordinary because the majority of his life had been spent in abstinence. He had lost his innocence at fourteen in a tavern to one of Richard Wellington's whores. In addition to managing the King's Men and Henry Rothford, Wellington operated a brothel, offering his actors discounted rates. The experience was awful. The beds, stinking of old, crusted semen, were rat- and flea-infested, and his Rosalind, teasing and mocking him, was missing teeth with her cheeks obscenely painted red. He would later recount to Wellington that she wore more face paint than Jonathan did playing a female role. He remembered coarse and yellowed fingernails, caked with dirt, that undressed him and squeezed him too hard. There had been no love that day, and little passion, and Jonathan never again sought the bed of a brothel whore. Others made solicitations, many of whom were avid playgoers, but Jonathan was holding out for a sanctity he instinctively knew should be present for such an act, and yet he himself avoided finding the prerequisite intimacy at all costs.

There was a noise of scattered dirt behind them, and Jonathan turned just in time to be tackled by Zartha. He caught the wolf in his arms, allowing his face to be devoured until he remembered. Blasted with heat, he put the little wolf down who instantly took her customary seat on his feet.

"Zartha, you wicked, wanton wolf," Fallon said, and Jonathan's embarrassment became agonizing.

"So, she…"

"They cannot maintain their faerie forms in our world," Fallon said, "and only those with Selphyn blood can follow them into their own realm. There they can transform into their natural states." He grinned. "She has taken quite a liking to you, to be sure."

Zartha whined and jumped up, putting her paws on Jonathan's shoulders. "Easy," he said. "I'm taken."

"Yes, you may have some atonement to do with Helen."

They walked on, Zartha keeping up, and began their ascent of the hill in question. Halfway up Tiben swooped down, landing neatly on Fallon's shoulder. The Selphyn king gently rubbed the raven's breast with the back of his index finger, a gesture Jonathan knew was habitual. It made him jealous with longing for his unknown horse, the force of whose presence remained in the back of his mind.

"How will I find my animal link?"

"He will make himself known to you, if it is at all possible. You said he was stabled. You may have to allow your instincts to guide you to him."

"It is strange, this need pressing on me. Nothing else seems remotely as important as finding him."

"I cannot imagine being separated from Tiben."

Jonathan did not want to know what would happen if and when an animal link died. He could not now imagine having that cord between them severed.

They reached the top of the hill and Jonathan looked down, breathless. Below them was indeed a perfect, natural amphitheater, with enough room on level ground in between the mountain and the hill to properly stage his play. The only deficiency lay in the question of wings, as there was no place to hang curtains. He had no idea what to do with his actors when they were offstage.

"Come. Sit for a moment and catch your breath," Fallon said. Jonathan was no sooner on the ground than Zartha was curled up in his lap. There was nothing to do but pet her exquisitely soft fur. He looked into her eyes and tried to visualize her natural form, but nothing clear materialized, just amber-colored skin and sharp, pointed joints. Without warning this image metamorphosed into that of a dead midwife, throat brutally torn.

"These wolves," Jonathan said carefully, "have killed before."

Fallon did not look at him. "Yes. The wolves, lovable as they may be...you mustn't entirely trust them. They can turn on you with viciousness, if it suits their needs."

"You speak of a peaceful race, being one with the universe. And yet you killed three women."

"I did not ask the wolves to kill the midwife, only to bring me the child. That was unnecessary bloodshed that I have always regretted. As for the other two, that was different, and you know why. Or at least, I should think we have argued enough for you to understand."

"Try again."

Fallon's violet eyes met his. "No. If you do not understand it now, you never will." Jonathan was stunned into silence. "I have never killed out of rage or revenge."

Fallon's eyes turned back toward the mountain, unblinking, even when Tiben cawed loudly in his ear. At length he spoke again, his voice just above a whisper.

"I have a brother who is lost to me. He went to Salsima many years ago, disguised as a human." In spite of his shock, Jonathan did not make a sound for fear any interruption would stop Fallon's voice. "And too long has he lived among them. He has forgotten our ways, and is consumed with rage and hatred. Many times have I implored him to return, only to be met with abject refusal. I desperately wanted him present for this momentous occasion, and was told that he was simply too busy to be bothered."

He lowered his head. "For him I try doubly hard to find forgiveness in my heart, as if mine can make up for his lack." He looked up at Jonathan. "If he knew, in his youth, what future awaited him, he would have implored me to take his life. And I would have. For like our sister, he is a slave to human baseness and depravity, only he chooses to be so."

Abruptly he stood and Jonathan scrambled to his feet, knocking Zartha off his lap.

"Come. This is enough dark talk. I will not further sully your day. And you have much to prepare, I am sure."

Jonathan followed him back down the way they had come, his mind spinning. He was still trying to imagine how a Selphyn would successfully disguise himself when Fallon said, "I am glad, Gideon, that you are here."

"Thank you."

"I very much wonder how different things would be if Sir Francis had come with you."

Jonathan stumbled, aware, as he tried to catch his balance, of Fallon stopping. He wind-milled his arms to keep from rolling down the hill. When their eyes met, Fallon advanced on him until their faces were just inches apart. Whatever he didn't know about Sir Francis, Fallon was aware of it. There was no point in trying to pretend his question hadn't thrown him, and so he played it to the best of his ability.

"Sir Francis? As in Sir Francis Rathnar? Why should he be here?"

Fallon searched his eyes before answering. His response was slow and carefully articulated, as he studied Jonathan's face as if watching for the slightest muscle tick or shifting of his eyes. "I asked for him, along with you. Did you not know?"

"No. Thaddeus said nothing."

"He did not show you the letter, then?"

"No."

"Did you not find it strange I should ask only for you, and not the king's secretary of state?"

Jonathan gave him a crooked grin, hoping the Selphyn king could not smell the terror on him. "Naturally you would ask for me. I am his favorite. I need no secretary of state to assist me."

"Yeeeeeees."

In the silence that ensued, Jonathan realized how far he had strayed from Gideon's arrogant and brash persona. Too much happened in the last day, and Jonathan had grown careless in Fallon's increasing approval. He also could not believe Leonardis failed to mention Sir Francis's involvement. Jonathan had only a vague picture of the stooped and pale spymaster in his head, but enough of one to make him especially glad he was not there to be reckoned with.

Evidently satisfied, Fallon broke away and continued walking down the hill. "Ah well. It does not signify. Apparently he was too busy to be bothered."

And that was when it clicked into place. Jonathan reassessed this mental picture of Rathnar, bringing into focus the long, angled face, unnaturally white skin. He would have laughed out loud if he didn't fear Fallon murdering him for his discovery. The king, so frightened of Selphyn infiltrators all of these years, to have one directly under his nose, searching out treason! It was too absurd to be believed.

He was grateful when Fallon never paused in his long strides to look back, blissfully unaware of what he had let slip.

TWENTY-SEVEN

HE WAS OUTSIDE, busy sewing in the bladders filled with pigs' blood into the collars of Miranda's donated gowns, when Thomas found him. His shadow fell over Jonathan, and when Jonathan looked up he dropped a pile of clothing on the ground in front of him. Jonathan looked from his frowning face to the clothes and back again, narrowing his eyes.

"Fallon's clothes?"

"He left them for you. He thinks you are playing him."

Jonathan shuddered. "I would not put on these clothes for all the—"

"I think you should."

It was bad enough, him greeting Jonathan with such a sour expression after days of no communication, and now this. Jonathan's throat tightened. "Because I am half-Selphyn?"

"Even so."

"And I was thus when you played the part weeks ago. This is not a sudden disease like the plague. Nothing has changed."

Thomas guffawed. "You can say this? After they took you to some cave and brought you back half-mad with delirium? Raving about horses and faeries?"

The thought that he and Miranda were discussing him, mocking him even, made him bristle. He fought to keep his voice even. "You know I cannot play this part."

"Perhaps you might care to recall that you promised me you would, after our last staging of it."

"Yes, but that was said when I believed we would never again stage it!"

"At least you are consistent with your trustworthiness."

"Forgive me, but I cannot do it. Not after what he—"

"You think you are the only one who has suffered at the hands of the Selphyn!"

Jonathan reared back at the vehemence in Thomas's voice, putting up a placating hand whose fingertips were stained with blood. "What—"

"You are so consumed with your own misery, you see not what is in front of your eyes. Well I will not do it again. Not with him here, watching. All of them watching! I refuse."

"It is because of you that we are doing this. Can you not just—"

"No. For once, do something for me."

"As if I never have—"

"Please."

"If it means I might regain your love, for what reason it fled I know not, then I shall endeavor to do it."

Thomas's eyes filmed over, and when he spoke his voice trembled. "You have ever had my love. It is my trust that is in doubt."

"Then may I attempt to redeem myself?"

"You may."

Jonathan sighed, and tried not to think how he was going to endure it himself. "Can you play Thaddeus? Do you know the lines?"

"I know all the lines. You know I am a sponge."

"So you are."

He picked up the clothing, seeing the purple coat and matching silver pantaloons and shirt. A black raven feather swirled to the ground; both men stared silently at it as if it were an omen.

Jonathan cleared his throat. "Can Sebastian play the king?"

"Yes. Only he is Brother Dominick playing the king."

Here Jonathan saw a ghost of a smile. "So long as someone plays him. Can you finish here? I must needs…prepare."

He was glad Miranda was gone when he returned to their shared chamber. He did not want anyone to see him transform, especially her. Slipping into the cool silk was like dipping into milk, or dressing in clouds. It was so thin and soft that he felt quite unmanned without the reinforced material and laces of his breeches. His delicate feet, never once feeling the grass or dirt, would now be bare for the duration of an entire play, and his ankles felt constricted in the tight tapering of the pants. The shirt likewise floated over his head and around his shoulders, the silk like a cold whisper. The coat, he discovered upon donning it, was for show only. It was too thin to afford any warmth, but its effect was stunning. Tight around the shoulders and mid-back, it widened as it fell, ballooning outward with the slightest hint of air. Jonathan strode around the room several times just to watch and feel it billow behind him. It lent him the perfect amount of magisterial atmosphere. And now for his hair.

Sitting in front of a glass, he pulled his hair loose from its tight ponytail, gathering it forward, his fingers combing through it. It fell just past his shoulders, about two inches shorter than Fallon wore his. But it was nevertheless completely effective. His ancestry now seemed to scream its presence; he looked almost full Selphyn with these golden waves gathering around his neck. When he tied in the raven feather, he began to doubt his own existence himself. The black eye kohl was the finishing touch, and staring at his reflection, Jonathan saw only a younger version of Fallon. He was both fascinated and repulsed, and had to touch his face several times to prove he was still looking back at himself.

Apparently he overestimated the time he had to prepare. Outside the palace it was eerily quiet; he no longer heard Gregory heralding the performance, nor the excited chatter of actors and Selphyn. He looked up at the sun and felt a jolt; it was near enough two o'clock that he might have even missed his own entrance. He began trotting toward the appointed venue, all professionalism now. A performance was a performance, regardless of whom it was for, or who Jonathan was pretending to be. It had to be a masterpiece, or else there was no point in doing it at all.

His breathing was ragged when he reached the top of the hill that he and Fallon had climbed only a few short hours earlier. And then he simply stopped breathing when he saw the swarm of thousands of Selphyn gathered on the slope below him. They covered the entire hillside, plus the ground directly in front of and around the stage area. Like miniatures positioned in a model, he saw the back of Fallon's azure coat and Kassandra's blue dress as they sat in front, just inches away from the play. Poles had been erected on either side of the stage area, and banners, serving as wings, hung from them and gently rippled in the breeze. The actors were performing the dumb show, which was a great relief, though someone had to step in as Jonathan's masked double. He watched them, all wearing white masks, as they moved gracefully in their mimed dance, performing a ten-minute rendition of his play, entirely without lines. Thomas played his harp off to the side, and as Jonathan circumvented the audience to make the least intrusive entrance as possible, he saw the masked "Fallon" miming the slaughter of his sister and her maid. The Selphyn audience was completely silent, and Jonathan heard only the swish of his trousers as he trotted down the hill. No one else moved.

The two masked women fell to the stage, and the masked "Thaddeus" crumpled in grief and gesticulated toward heaven. Jonathan was running in full stride now, and ducked behind the wings on stage left, gasping for breath. The dumb-show actors divided themselves between the wings, and as Jonathan was panting, several of them took off their masks to first admonish him for his tardiness and then gape at his appearance.

"My God," Thomas said. "You look just like him."

"Never mind that. You are about to make your entrance."

Toby was already onstage, as the Chorus, setting the time and place. His heart in his throat, Jonathan jumped when a hand took his. He turned and saw Miranda, dressed as he was: as a Selphyn.

"Oh, sweet Miken. What a vision you are."

She was in orange silk, her feet and stomach completely bare. His eyes drank in every inch of exposed flesh, including her shoulders and the tops of her breasts. Every line from the play simply vanished.

"From Corrine," she said, smiling uncertainly. Her eyes too were outlined in kohl, and with her hair, almost the same color as his, they looked indeed like brother and sister. "You look incredible."

"I should say the sa—"

She broke him off with a kiss. "For luck," she said, breaking away. "There's our cue."

"Oh, God."

She grabbed his hand and pulled him onstage. Sebastian and Thomas, as King Edward and Chancellor Thaddeus, respectively, awaited them. Jonathan used Thomas's monologue regarding the wonder of Miranda's beauty to ground himself, but when he looked up, waiting for his cue, his eyes met Sebastian's.

Miranda said, "You will forgive my trepidation, I trust. I do a sister's duty, not that of my heart," just as Sebastian pointed his finger at Jonathan, his face white.

"You! They have made you one of them."

Jonathan's heart roared in his ears. Sebastian advanced on him, still pointing, like the harbinger of death.

"They will make you their pawn!"

After three false starts, Jonathan finally managed to improvise a line. "Do you know me, my lord?"

"Aye, aye, and well too. They mean to make you their savior. I read their filthy book! They would have you be the one to bring the two races together. You!"

There was now uncomfortable shifting in the audience as, even to first-time playgoers, they knew something was amiss.

"I – I have brought my sister as we did agree. Is she not beautiful?"

"They turned you into one of them with their savage rituals. But you can still be saved!"

It was Thomas who rescued him. He neatly cut in between them, a dancer claiming his partner, and said his line to Miranda at Jonathan's side. "May your heart find its duty in mine. I will endeavor all to make it so. Sweet princess, will you allow a kiss to seal our bargain?"

For a terrible moment Jonathan's mind was a blank, but he managed to pull his line out somewhere in the recesses of his brain. Then it was Sebastian's turn. They waited, with baited breath, as he stared at Jonathan, his arm still extended. Jonathan gave him his cue line once again, and he blinked. His tongue darted out, as if tasting his lips. Then slowly he lowered his arm.

"Yes...yes. You have heard it sworn from my lips; need you my blood too? Brother, kiss your bride."

There was a collective sigh of relief, and Thomas swept Miranda into his arms. Jonathan felt a stab of jealousy but soon forgot it under the heat of Sebastian's stare. He was supposed to be fawning over his brother's fiancée, not staring at Fallon as if he were a ghost. Then Jonathan was blissfully excused from the stage until the last scene. He sat behind the makeshift wing and took several heaving breaths. Once he was sufficiently calm he peeked out to watch his play unfold, pleased with Thomas's impromptu performance as Thaddeus. Sebastian and Miranda remembered to change their lines before the staged slap in case Fallon recognized the words from the banquet their first night there, when Jonathan feigned hitting Miranda. Then as the Chorus took the stage and described the passing of time, he readied himself for his big scene.

Roland stood next to him, looking, Jonathan had to admit, ridiculous in one of Miranda's skirts and bodices. There were no wigs in Rowan, and his short hair and late-afternoon stubble destroyed any illusion as to his gender. Then he took the stage along with the "children," Gregory, Ralf and Andrew, and Miranda, now dressed in her own clothing as she had been sufficiently "humanized." Jonathan's palms were sweating as he silently mouthed their lines as they spoke them, and the dagger in his hand was slippery. It was real: blades were not dulled on a play-less island. He would have to be careful.

He heard his cue and met with Thomas and Sebastian upstage, their positioning re-blocked to make allowances for their limited staging. Their argument ensued, and Jonathan was relieved to see Sebastian fully in character. In fact, he was so much so that Jonathan began to fear he was once again absorbed in his character, this time as King Edward. Not a prudent choice in the company of thousands of Selphyn.

And then it was time. He delivered his line: "Yet she is a slave to your king's filthy bed. If you will not release her from the bonds of marriage, then I shall." He turned his back on the audience, striding toward Miranda. Her lips parted, and he could see the blueness of her eyes. Her hair shone like gold in the sunlight. He put his left hand on her shoulder to steady both of them and brought up the dagger. He paused, the blade less than an inch from her collar where the pig bladder was hidden, and looked into her eyes. Abruptly his own filled with tears.

"I cannot do it," he whispered.

She licked her lips. "Do it."

His face constricted, and he remained frozen in place, dagger hanging in the air. He thought, absurdly, of his horse, locked away somewhere, a prisoner though his heart was wild. He thought of Zartha, and even Belcastro, and how some animals, like foxes and wolves, will chew off their own legs to free themselves from a trap. If the thought occurred to them, would they not do the same for a loved one in the same predicament?

"Do it," Miranda whispered again, and when he did not move, she put her hand over his, the one that held the dagger. Slowly she guided his hand toward her throat, essentially inserting the dagger herself into the collar of her dress. He gasped when the blood burst free, some droplets hitting him in the face while the majority seeped down her throat and all over her chest. And still she guided him, until the dagger had made a complete sweep across the bladder. Then she rolled her eyes backward and fell.

Roland, looking more like his obscenely painted Rosalind than Anne, was easier to deal with; Jonathan did not hesitate dragging the dagger across his collar. He was ready for the duel, having belted on a rapier just before his entrance. Unlike his human patrons, the Selphyn audience members did not jump in to join the fray. He caught glimpses of them out of the corner of his eye and saw them frozen with rapt attention. Fallon's mouth was open, and, when Jonathan got a closer look, his face was streaked with tears and smeared kohl. The observation nearly caused him to miss a choreographed riposte. Again they were all being careful with their real blades.

In the midst of pandemonium he yelled out his line, "Stop!

Where are the children? Where is Prince Edward?" and shoved actors out of his way to look for the three children who had fled offstage. Then Thomas was charging at him, yelling, "You shall not have him too!" and Jonathan barely managed to parry the cut coming in toward his head. Toby, doubling as a Selphyn attendant, feigned a blow to Thomas's head that would keep him out of the way until the bodies were cleared. Jonathan scooped up Miranda in his arms while Toby picked up Roland with a groan. Roland was dropped unceremoniously backstage, while Jonathan gingerly set down Miranda. She stayed in his arms as they listened to Thomas, now recovered, belt out his heart-wrenching monologue.

"He stole your fire," she whispered. He nodded, not trusting himself to look at her while she was still covered in blood. He was indeed envious that Thomas had taken the best speech in the play, and yet he could not deny that his playing Fallon had been the best choice possible for the production.

After Thomas finished his monologue, all was silent. The rest of the actors, crammed behind the wings, leaned in, waiting for the applause. When none came they glanced at each other apprehensively. Then Miranda brightened and said, "They don't know what to do!" She led the applause, the actors following, and soon there was a thunderous echo of it rippling off the hillside. They hugged each other and cheered, and Jonathan tearfully commended all of them.

He grabbed Miranda's hand and together they led the actors back out to take their bow, opening up to allow Thomas into the line. Thousands of Selphyn were on their feet, clapping and hollering, their bright silks shining like a vast array of wildflowers in the sun. Jonathan's throat seized as he led a second bow.

Thomas said, "Jig?" and Jonathan shuddered.

"No." A post-performance jig, he knew, would detract from the poignancy of the play. He wanted to end on a profound note, not with a frivolous dance though it was often customary.

Fallon stood and strode toward Jonathan, putting his hands on either side of his face. Then he kissed both cheeks, and even pulled Jonathan's head in against his chest. Mortified, Jonathan gently squeezed loose, and Fallon congratulated the rest of the cast.

"Not bad for a bunch of soldiers and courtiers," Thomas said.

Jonathan smiled. "Not bad at all."

Kassandra threw herself into Thomas's arms, and Jonathan took a step backwards, alarmed at the color that blossomed in both of their cheeks. He fell back, a little at a time, as the actors shook Selphyn hands and answered questions or accepted praise. No one took notice of him, and soon it was as if he were watching another play taking place all around him. Conversation jumbled together and faces melted into each other. He wondered if this was what it felt like to be God, looking down on His creations and trying to make sense of everything before giving up and letting it all merge together into one loud, cacophonous mess.

Someone shouted for a feast, and this many-headed creature began to move in a solid mass up the hill. At length Jonathan realized he was not the only one who fell behind.

Fallon stood across from him, staring silently. For nearly a full minute the two of them stared at their almost mirror image, both with tear- and kohl-stained cheeks. Jonathan also had blood on his face, which Fallon did not. But he once did, and looked just as Jonathan did now, stricken. Fallon was the first to speak.

"I tried to find them. I tried to find the children."

"I know. I was there."

If Fallon heard this, he gave no indication that it garnered suspicion. His voice was thick with tears. "Not to hurt them! To keep them safe."

"I think…I think they thought you meant to kill them too."

"I understand that now. Of course they would think that! They just witnessed me murdering their mothers." The tears were flowing freely now. "It was not supposed to be that way. What folly…what utter folly."

"Fallon. I have something to say." The Selphyn king wiped away his tears and waited, fighting for composure. Jonathan swallowed. "I am ready to leave in the morning."

"Yes. You are repulsed by me, having stepped in my shoes. Or rather my bare feet. This Jonathan Wilder is as cruel as he is gifted. I have seen myself in glaring light; I am forever blinded and will now always see with that spot of blackness one gets from looking too long at the sun. The blackness that is my folly. I will not keep you here."

"Moved as I am, I must tell you that you misunderstand me. I am ready to leave because you have won your wager."

Fallon's face softened. "Can this be true?"

Jonathan nodded, suddenly unable to speak. Finally, through the beginning of a sob, he said, "It was what she wanted."

Fallon took him by the shoulders and their foreheads touched. "It was because I loved her so well that I could do what she asked."

"Yes."

"And even now as you are understanding it, I have never regretted it as much as I do in this moment. The children."

"Yes." Jonathan sighed and sniffled loudly. The fingers around his shoulders suddenly locked down, and he gasped.

"The play. You wrote it."

Their eyes, bloodshot and smeared, met. There was no looking away, and no more denying. "Yes."

"You were there, as a child. And you made up this name. This Jonathan Wilder."

"Yes."

"Does the king know?" Jonathan blinked. "Does he know his favorite courtier is a ghost playwright?"

Flooded with relief, he nearly smiled. "No. That play would have seen me hanged. He is even now searching for this Jonathan to have him drawn and quartered."

Fallon released Jonathan's shoulders to laugh. Jonathan's body went limp as he breathed in several deep and joyous breaths.

"Most wonderful! His faithful, loyal courtier! I am delighted." He pumped Jonathan's arm. "A brilliant play and brilliantly rendered. Even your Brother Dominick performed excellently. Do not monks frown upon acting? And he was wonderful!"

The rest of his accolades went past in a rush as Jonathan could no longer focus on anything but his own relief. But as Fallon escorted him up the hill to the feast, he was dismayed to find himself drowned in guilt as he fabricated the life of the secret playwright Gideon Ambrose.

TWENTY-EIGHT

LAUREN KEPT AN eye on the empty hammock next to her, drifting in and out of sleep, until the wee hours of the night. Exhausted and frustrated, she put her cloak on, brushing past Gideon who hadn't stirred since the two of them came below deck hours ago.

She found Rathnar by starlight, keeping vigil at the bow. He half turned to acknowledge her presence but said nothing. She joined him at the railing as they watched dark waves. When she shivered in the damp wind he said, "If you are cold, you should go below."

"I should say the same for you. You have not slept. Did the crew not tell you they were keeping watch?"

"If the ship were to pass us in the night they may not see it. I have better night vision than they."

"Because...because of the wolf?"

"Yes."

"What do you call him?"

"Stojak."

She tried the word out, liking the sound of it. It frustrated her that Rathnar had not once directly looked at her. "I never did thank him for helping me." She heard Rathnar's sigh over the sound of the waves. "I do hope he knows how grateful I am."

His hands gripped the railing. "He knows."

"Even so. I should like to thank him personally someday, perhaps with a kiss on the nose—"

"This is anguish for me!"

She took a step backward. "I – I will leave you."

She blinked furiously and waited for him to turn. When he did not, she fled, furious more with herself for her weakness than anything else. Back in her hammock she lay on her side, her back to Rathnar's empty hammock. Free from the burden of checking on him, she finally slept. In the morning Gideon had to shake her awake.

"We are almost there, your Laziness. If you think you can manage to rise."

A burst of adrenaline lent her clarity, and she slipped on her shoes and shouldered her satchel. Rathnar's hammock was still empty, and she guessed he had never once graced it with his presence. It had been thus the first night as well; she could only hope he had caught snatches of sleep on deck.

Up on deck the sky was gray, covered with dark clouds. Land was shockingly near, immense in its proximity. Surely the island had risen from the ocean depths while she slept, and its towering purple mountain commanded her attention as if it were embodied by a god. Seagulls circled above them, parting abruptly to make way for a huge golden eagle. Lauren gasped as its shadow passed over her, and Rathnar, standing just above the ship's figurehead, threw up his head in alarm when the eagle cried out.

"Everyone," he said, "stand back from the prow."

The crew scuttled backwards without question, their captain included. Gideon guffawed and strode forward. "I do not take orders from you."

Rathnar pointed. "Do you see this eagle? He sees with another set of eyes, beside his own. They know now we are here. You are all in danger until I make my presence known to them. Get you back."

Gideon's finger cracked against Rathnar's sternum, and Lauren saw the Selphyn's jaw tighten. "You wish to communicate to them some treachery. A word or glance to seal our fate. I will not allow you to—"

"Gideon, for the love of God!" Lauren said, her patience frayed. "Do not be a fool! Stand back."

He rounded on her. "And now *you* will presume to give me orders? You forget you are my servant—"

"Think you I can be your servant? That after all of this, I will simply return home with you and resume sweeping your floors?"

"What else have you to do?"

"I do not know. And I do not care. I am grateful that you took me in, but I can no longer be your servant."

Aware of Rathnar's heavy gaze, she looked at him and saw him smiling. "Whatever I must endure," he said, "it will be worth all for this."

Gideon, in the meantime, was purple. As he shouted at Rathnar, his fist full of Rathnar's shirt, Lauren was deeply embarrassed for him. Rathnar towered over him, and in his quiet dignity he reduced Gideon to a raving fool.

"…And from a Selphyn and a woman at that! You are not the leader of this expedition and never were! You will take heed—"

Lauren screamed and pointed, knowing she had no time to tell them of the crossbow bolt that was singing through the air. Without looking at her, Rathnar dove into Gideon, throwing them both hard onto the deck. He made no sound when the arrow embedded itself into his upper arm, the arm that had shielded Gideon's chest. Sputtering, Gideon scrambled out from under Rathnar, the blood draining from his face. For once at a loss for words, he stared as Rathnar stood and yanked the bolt free, grimacing without a sound. Blood soaked his shirt and he ran back to the prow, lifting his good arm.

"Selphyn onboard! Hold your arrows!"

"What ho!" a disembodied voice called from shore. "Who comes?"

"Rathnar."

Lauren squinted, searching the coastline for the speaker. She saw only the beach, volcanic rock and a dried lava bed. Then two figures emerged from the dried brush, one in bright turquoise, the other in yellow. Rathnar called for the captain.

"Drop the anchor here."

"And lower the longboat?"

"No need. The water is shallow." He leaned in toward the captain, who could not take his eyes off of the blood pouring through Rathnar's fingers as he clutched his wound. "That purse I gave you. Its contents will be doubled if you wait here for us. *Transcendence* is obviously not here; I must have missed it in the night. I must first speak to Fallon, but then I will in all probability need you to be ready to take us back to Zirnich in an instant. Have I your word?"

The captain nodded. Rathnar glanced at Lauren, his face tight. "I need Gideon with me. But if you wish to remain here—"

"My brother is there. Of course I am coming."

Rathnar sighed. "Of course." He looked at Gideon who was still lying on the deck, stunned. "Well. If the leader of this expedition would be so kind, I would like to get to shore."

Without looking back he hoisted himself over the railing, landing with a loud splash in the surf that came up to his waist. He lifted his arms when Lauren peered over the railing. Sweat poured down his face, and his lips were white. "I will catch you."

"Your arm—"

"Is nothing."

But he screamed as his hands caught her waist, though to his credit he did not drop her. The water was much colder than she anticipated, and she gasped as it swirled around her legs and splashed her chest. Together they waded toward shore, neither looking back when they heard the loud splash of Gideon following.

On shore Lauren twisted her skirts to ring out the water, and on impulse ripped out her petticoats. Twice she ordered Rathnar to sit on a large volcanic rock before he finally acquiesced, keeping his face averted while she tied her makeshift bandage of petticoats around his arm. She saw the two Selphyn approaching out of the corner of her eye, their crossbows lowered. They ignored Gideon, who recovered enough of his equilibrium to yell at them, and fastidiously tied a sling from the remaining material. They were both men, both golden and beautiful.

"Why did you not send word you were coming?" the one in turquoise asked Rathnar.

"I did. There is a letter at the Swan. But no one has come to find it."

"A recent letter then?"

"Yes." Rathnar looked at him meaningfully. "There was a change in plans."

The three Selphyn took the lead, and when Lauren saw Gideon's face bloat up in readiness for another verbal assault, she put her hand on his arm. "He just saved your life."

His jaw tightened but he kept quiet, falling in stride next to Lauren behind the Selphyn as they followed the lava bed toward the mountain. Her breath quickened as she realized she might be moments from finding her brother; there could be a number of reasons why the Selphyn's ship was missing. She would have preferred not seeing him with her dress soaked, wrinkled and without petticoats, but it would have to do.

She was too focused and impatient to sufficiently admire the palace, which, were she at leisure, she would have found breathtaking. Instead she trotted to keep up with Rathnar and their two Selphyn escorts. A raven flew over them, cawing, and a moment later the double doors within the courtyard were flung open. Rathnar threw Lauren and Gideon a glance and said, "Wait here."

For once Gideon obeyed while Lauren wrung her hands together. Over Rathnar's shoulder she saw the exquisite Selphyn man dressed in purple silk, and saw the range of emotions that passed over his face. Delight prevailing, he smiled broadly and threw his arms around Rathnar, carefully avoiding the sling. She would have known him anywhere; in her mind's eye she could see him dragging his dagger across her mother's throat. And the blood, everywhere, the blood.

"Rathnar, well met! How glad I am you came in spite of—"

"When did they leave? They did leave, yes? And took the princess with them?"

The smile fell from Fallon's face. "Yesterday, late morning."

"*Damn.*"

"What—"

Rathnar made a half turn. Fallon's eyes landed on the humans, his expression blank. "I have Gideon Ambrose with me. The *real* Gideon."

Fallon's eyes swiveled back to Rathnar. "Who were they?"

"Actors."

"Actors." The Selphyn king closed his eyes. "Actors." His face twisted into a snarl, and Lauren took a step backwards. He turned to slam his fist against the heavy wood door. "*Actors!* O, Goddess, I am undone."

The door opened and a Selphyn woman emerged wearing rose-colored silk. Lauren gaped at her bare stomach. "What is this noise?"

Fallon grabbed her arm. "Where is she? They were imposters – where is she?"

The Selphyn woman pointed to the open door; Fallon leaned in, his teeth bared. Like a magician reaching in his bag of tricks, he pulled a woman out by her hair. She was human, and crying. Lauren watched, mouth hanging open, as Fallon seized her by the throat.

"And should I not kill what I love?" He squeezed and the woman made a horrible choking noise. Seconds passed as the woman gasped for air in a manner that suggested she could still at least partially breathe. The tension sank from Fallon's face and his shoulders sagged. He released her throat and crumpled.

"I cannot."

"Still too soft," Rathnar said, and Lauren stared at him, incredulous.

The human girl fell to the ground, gasping. She was trying to say something through her ragged breath; at length Fallon slowly lifted his head to listen.

"He...he's changed. He will not – hurt her."

"How do I know? How do I know these are not more lies?"

Seeing an opportunity to defend her brother, Lauren stepped forward. "It is true! My life upon it that he will not harm anyone. He is kind and noble and good, enmeshed in this for good reasons, I am sure, if you would but hear them."

Fallon, noticing her for the first time, stared. Rathnar sighed yet again. "May I present Lauren Warden. Her brother John was your

Gideon."

Fallon straightened, his eyes huge. After a moment they filled with tears. "Had I but known. If I had only known. I would have told him. It might have made all the difference."

When he paused, Gideon threw up his hands. "For God's sake, told him what?"

Without taking his eyes off of Lauren, Fallon said, "That his mother is still alive."

TWENTY-NINE

"COME, CAROUSE WITH us! It is Midsummer and we would celebrate before you leave us in the morning."

There were so many of them, imploring, pleading, and Miranda could do naught but laugh and agree. Jonathan, as she knew he would, made his excuses after dinner, claiming exhaustion following the performance. She did not even have the chance to ask him to stay. She looked around the table, seeking a companion with whom she might infiltrate this Selphyn rite. Thomas was doting on Kassandra – did he not recall their purpose? – and the other humans begged off, likewise claiming exhaustion. Now she was sorry she agreed to join them.

Corrine took her arm. "Come with me."

In the Selphyn woman's chambers, Miranda sank onto an impossibly soft mattress and took in her surroundings. Dozens of eagle feathers hung from the bed's canopy, and shields and drums, painted with eagles, covered the walls. Corrine dropped the familiar orange silk into her lap.

"Don this again. You were ravishing in it."

"Oh, I do thank you, Corrine, but I spoke in haste. I ought to retire before we set sail on the morrow."

Corrine narrowed her eyes. "If you had seen his face when he first beheld you like this. Trust in me, and wear it."

Now she stood outside her own chamber, trembling. Exposing most of her skin had been difficult enough before, but now she did not have the excuse of wearing a costume. Jonathan would probably be asleep anyway, making it all for nothing.

She opened the door and saw him sitting on the bed, a candle glowing on the table beside him. A large book was open on his lap; she glanced at it and guessed it was the Selphyn's version of the *Book of Miken*. He raised his head slowly, eyes indeed shadowed and dark with fatigue. The book, forgotten, slipped from his lap as he rose from the bed. Through his open window they could hear the drums starting.

"The – there is – I thought you might dance with me," Miranda said, her face on fire.

He came toward her, his eyes locked on the thin gold chain around her bare waist, a gift from Corrine. "Close the door."

She stepped back to grab the door handle, and the tiny bells on her anklet rang softly, like faerie bells. The drums were louder now, vibrating in her sternum. "You will not dance?"

"No," he said, and fell to his knees at her feet, his hands enclosing her hips. He put his lips on her navel, just below the gold chain. She gasped and grabbed a fistful of his hair.

As if they had been on intimate terms for years, indeed like Gideon and Helen, he slipped his hands inside the thin silk and stood, crushing her mouth with his. When he moved to her throat she said, "I cannot rival the faerie folk."

She felt his laugh in a blast of hot air against her skin. "She set me free to love you–" he paused to kiss her throat, her ear, the corner of her eye – "with all the passion, fire and fury you deserve." His hands, still roaming under her silk, emerged to grab her hips again. He pulled her against him. His jaw tightened and his eyes hardened; she inhaled sharply and felt her knees go weak. "Are you ready then?"

"Oh, yes."

His hair, still loose from the performance, glowed in the candlelight, as did the fine, Selphyn features of his face that accentuated his cheekbones and jaw. The drums, louder even still, drowned out her thought. The fingers on her hips dug in.

"Please," she whispered.

"Please what? Say my name."

She put her lips on his ear. "Jonathan."

The back of her head hit the door, and she used one hand behind her to brace herself. Closing her eyes, the hands that tore at her clothes and the mouth on her skin felt multiplied, as if she were enduring the assault of a pack of animals. The drums pounded, filling the room, filling her head. Up against the door they became one, and she was ever so grateful for the deafening drums that drowned out the sound of her cries.

* * *

Light filled the room and she was blinded by the sunlight pouring in through the still-open window. Jonathan's head was pillowed on her breasts and when she stirred, he groaned and held her fast.

"Not yet."

"They will be waiting for us."

He lifted his head and touched her cheek. "Stay here with me. We will raise seven Selphyn babies."

"Seven!"

"Their population is low."

"And who will see the princess home safe?" He sighed, his hair brushing her chin. "Promise me you will not let them hurt her."

"I promise. We had best get up then, if I am going to fight off an assassin."

They actually were waiting for them, assembled on the beach with a large entourage of Selphyn to see them off. The longboat was tied off but bobbing in the water, and *Transcendence* shimmered in the light, waiting to take them home. The actors playing soldiers stood apart in their livery, their expressions solemn and then suspicious as Fallon made his affectionate farewells. Whatever changed Jonathan had not affected them in the slightest. It was clear it would not just be Richard opposing Jonathan, but the majority of the company who, despite witnessing the civility of their hosts, was still dead set in their opposition. Miranda looked into the faces of Toby, Ralf, Andrew, Roland – men she had drunk and laughed with – who were watching her and Jonathan with hardened, unforgiving eyes. She could see it as plainly as if they had drawn a line in the sand to divide them.

Only Gregory seemed oblivious of the tension, playing with innocent enthusiasm with Uthen's fox. Belcastro wallowed in the attention, making his way to Miranda when the white wolves appeared and distracted Gregory. She scooped the fox up into her arms.

"He is ready for another voyage," Uthen said, smiling at her.

"He shall again be my dinner partner."

Jonathan set down his satchel to pet the wolves, and only Miranda saw the slender little wolf slip inside when no one else was looking. She gasped, and the white head poked out for a moment, eyes lighting on Miranda as if to say, *Don't say a word.* She clamped her mouth shut and then smiled. Jonathan was certainly in for a surprise.

Kassandra stood by, hands demurely folded in front of her, as they made their farewells. Thomas was keeping his distance, and Miranda wondered what might have transpired between the two of them last night, during the drums and the bonfire. She smiled to herself when she remembered how it had affected her, and caught Jonathan staring at her while absently scratching a wolf behind its ear. He grinned and she felt a wonderful flip in her stomach.

She hugged Corrine warmly though awkwardly as Belcastro

would not be put down. The two women laughed, and Miranda graciously accepted another gift from her Selphyn friend: a beautiful eagle, carved in stone. To Thomas they presented a silver axe, slender and artfully crafted, which he turned over awkwardly in his hands, muttering thanks. Then Corrine fastened a ribbon around Jonathan's neck; when she stepped back Miranda saw the tiny onyx horse hanging there. The color rose in his cheeks as he kissed Corrine on the cheek. Sebastian was the last to receive his gift, and everyone laughed but him as he was given a leather-bound copy of the Selphyn *Book of Miken*, the edges gilded. He held it with two fingers and dropped it into his satchel. Abruptly Miranda remembered the crazed look in his eye during the performance, when he turned on Jonathan. *I read their filthy book!* She shivered and took a step back.

"Come, you two," Fallon said, opening his arms. Like obedient children Jonathan and Miranda approached. She shifted Belcastro into one hand and gave the other to Fallon, whose right was already holding Jonathan's. "I have come to love you both as I would my family. You are both welcome here." He looked each of them in the eye. "To stay, if it would please you, should you ever tire of your constricting customs. We would be overjoyed to have you."

Jonathan looked down but smiled. "Thank you."

"Before you go, Gideon, I would have your word that you will see my princess safely home." Jonathan threw up his head, all solemnity now. "You have it."

"Swear that you will keep her safe, and do whatever is necessary to see her into the arms of her parents."

Miranda saw the difficult swallow in his throat. "I swear it."

Fallon grinned. "Then let us part as friends!" He dropped Miranda's hand to embrace Jonathan. For a moment Jonathan's wrists hung limply in the air before gently patting the Selphyn king's shoulders. Miranda smiled.

When Fallon turned to her she threw out her right arm to him, shifting Belcastro more to the left lest he get squeezed between them. Fallon's eyes followed the fox's progression. In a low voice, he said, "Drop the fox."

Miranda frowned, completely disarmed by this uncharacteristic vehemence against an animal. Belcastro, sensing this animosity, obliged her by jumping out of her grasp. Unsure now, Miranda took a half step toward Fallon. He pulled her in against him, his chin on top of her head.

"There. Now I have a better hold of you."

And that was when she understood. She pulled back but his grip only tightened, pressing her nose against his chest and forcing her to breathe through her mouth. Tears stung her eyes. To Jonathan, presumably, he said, "You love this one, yes?"

"Yes. Very much. And did I mention I am very possessive?"

She heard his forced laugh. There was none in return from Fallon. She squirmed until she felt cold steel against her throat. She froze as the dagger point rested just below her chin. Fallon shifted her so that she was standing in front of him, the dagger now visible to Jonathan. "Then you will take extra care to see that Kassandra is safe."

Jonathan drew his rapier. "What villainy is this?"

The "soldiers" immediately drew their own swords, but the Selphyn, many of whom wore daggers at their waists, closed in. The humans were vastly outnumbered.

"Mistress Helen is invited for an extended visit. She will remain here with me until you return bearing a letter written in Kassandra's hand assuring me she is safely united with her parents. And I will know if it is written under duress. I will know from her very punctuation."

Miranda sought out the princess with her eyes, careful to keep her body completely still. The princess was looking down, her guilt in this arrangement evident.

"That will take *weeks*!"

She felt Fallon's shrug. "It little matters to me. I hope your horse is fleet of foot."

Jonathan advanced and Fallon pressed the dagger against Miranda's throat. She felt the slender stream of blood, and Jonathan stopped, the rapier blade shaking.

"I *trusted* you."

"I will do what I must to ensure Kassandra is unharmed. And if I do *not* receive word within six weeks, or if I catch wind of any deceit, I will kill your lovely Helen, as much as I will regret to do so."

"You are every bit the heartless villain I thought you to be when we arrived. But your sorcery clouded my vision, and I was blinded by you. God, I am such a fool."

"Do what I ask, and you will find me to be fair and prudent. You will understand the necessity of this."

"No. I will not. For you are of the same ilk as these wolves here, ready to turn on anyone with viciousness to achieve their ends." He sighed and sheathed his rapier. "Let me say goodbye."

The blade was mercifully lowered from her throat, but he did not release her. Jonathan had to awkwardly embrace her, slipping his arms in between her and Fallon. He kissed her and then said into her ear, "I love you. And I will come for you."

She wept and said nothing. Their exchange was sullied enough by Fallon's close proximity. She glanced at the others, smiling ruefully when she saw the love they had for her. Gregory was openly weeping, and Thomas was stricken. Jonathan's eyes looked dead.

She would have stayed and watched until the ship was out of sight, but Fallon pulled her away before the actors were even situated on the longboat. Corrine lifted a hand in her direction, her face twisted, but Miranda glared at her before looking away.

"There is little point in prolonging your agony," Fallon said, pulling her by the hand. She yanked out of his grasp, spitting in his face when he turned.

To her astonishment, he smiled. "Your Gideon is a lucky one. I truly hope I have not lost him forever."

"You never had him."

"Then I am all the more sorry. Come. I will see that you are treated well. You have nothing to fear."

"Unless six weeks come and go."

"He will keep his word. I have no doubt of it. Come. Please. And I shall woo you like a lover until I am back in your good graces."

"You were better to woo the moon."

He laughed. "Yes. He is a lucky man indeed."

THIRTY

AS IF SHE were four years old, Lauren sat curled up on her mother's lap, her head resting on her shoulder, the long, thick, brown hair, like Lauren's own, under her nose. If her weight bothered her, the petite Anne did not complain. She sat on Fallon's oversized chair in his antechamber, her arms around her daughter. Both were hoarse from catching up – the questions and answers volleying back and forth like a game. When dinner was served they both demurred, content to sit in each other's very close company next to the fire.

Three hours ago the rain started, now it was drumming relentlessly on the roof, and subsequently the temperature dropped dramatically. And even if their ship had remained to take them back – Lauren was secretly glad it had not – their journey would have been detained by this sudden storm. The news, however, that their human escorts had pulled anchor to make a quick exit as soon as possible had a devastating effect on Rathnar, whose composure was barely in check. For the most part, during their convergence in Fallon's chamber, he stood with his back to them, leaning against the mantel, his forehead resting on his wrist with his wounded arm hanging in the sling at his side. But Lauren took all of these extraneous goings-on with little interest, her focus, of course, being on her mother.

That Anne Warden was holding her in her arms had not decreased her amazement, even in the several hours that passed. Lauren looked up into her face, to make sure it was really she, at least sixty times. And now she was content listening to her familiar voice with her ear against Anne's chest, that somewhat muffled voice she remembered from her childhood. Her mother's laugh was the same, her intonations, her energy. Seventeen years disappeared in the blink of an eye.

Because she fainted upon first hearing the news, she had made Fallon recount the story though Gideon already heard it, and Rathnar, of course, knew it. It had been Syldonia's idea, inspired by her son's and his friends' playmaking.

"We used one of your theatrical devices," Fallon said, "and filled pig bladders with blood. Our only error lay in keeping you in ignorance."

"We did not think you children could be convincing enough," Anne said, and Lauren had to concede that she had a point. A child could not truly understand the horror in witnessing a parent's murder. So they decided it best to keep it a secret, which should have only lasted a few minutes at best.

"But I underestimated how much the three of you would be affected," Fallon said. "You scattered and disappeared into the wind within seconds. I failed you all. And you have suffered much these many years."

Lauren would certainly not dispute that, but snuggled in her mother's arms she could almost forgive it. Were it not for her worry over John, she would have been content to stay there forever. Anne, of course, was mortified to learn that John had been within touching distance and was now gone again.

"I even caught just a glimpse of him when he visited the temple. But I thought him Gideon and paid him no heed."

The real Gideon was uncharacteristically silent, too overwhelmed by the surprises of the day to employ his usual loquaciousness. Lauren saw him and Fallon exchange occasional glances of curiosity, while Gideon accepted cup after cup of mulled wine. The last cup in question was dropped to the ground when none other than Lady Syldonia made her entrance. Lauren was touched to see Gideon so overcome with emotion; he knelt and kissed the hem of her exquisite dress, a shimmering gown of aquamarine. Lauren stood long enough to embrace the woman who was like enough to be her aunt before returning to her mother's lap, and this scene of filial affection caused a spasm of pain over the Selphyn princess's face. Thinking no doubt of her son, Syldonia joined her brother at the mantle, embracing him solemnly. Lauren saw the tear that leaked down her cheek, and snuggled in closer to Anne.

The wind picked up and howled, pushing trees and a loud hammering of rain against the windows. Fallon's face, illuminated by the fire, tightened. "They are in this storm, on *Transcendence*. I pray it is not as violent there as it is here."

"Myra is looking for them," Syldonia said.

Fallon turned to Lauren. "Myra is Syldonia's dolphin."

"Was she among the dolphins we played with that day?"

Lauren looked up at the sound of this new voice. Miranda, whom she now understood was one of her brother's players, entered the room, having stayed away to give everyone a chance to reunite. She sat down on an ottoman, a glass of wine in her hand. She was dressed in a yellow gown that complimented the color of her hair. Lauren, hungry for details about her brother, eyed the girl intently.

She saw the bruises on her throat from Fallon's near strangling and winced.

"Yes. She was among those dolphins," Fallon said, smiling at her. His eyes too seemed to light on the bruises, for he quickly frowned and averted his gaze. Gideon, slouched down far in his chair from too much wine, eyed Miranda rather rudely.

"So you were Helen."

Miranda blushed. "Yes."

"You resemble her. But you are fairer than she."

"But no less trouble I am sure," Fallon said. "I will forever be smarting from her and John's clever deception. We were all quite duped."

Miranda launched into a long explanation of bribery and threats, of the hold that Leonardis had over John, whom she called Jonathan. She painted a good picture of a group of innocent actors forced to be political pawns, and while Lauren believed her – the alternative being that she distrust her own brother – she wasn't sure Fallon was taking it in, having been deceived once before.

"But had you seen his face yester-morning, and heard the earnestness in his voice, you would have no doubt as to his sincerity in keeping Kassandra safe. I do believe he will do all he can to protect her, though there are those in our group who will oppose him."

Rathnar's attention finally caught, the Selphyn turned to look at Miranda for the first time since their arrival. "How many of them will oppose him? All?"

"Well, Sebastian certainly will, our Brother Dominick. The actors who played soldiers more than likely, and of course the assassin. Gregory is just a boy, no doubt caught up in the romance of it all, and Thomas…he is certainly vehemently opposed to the Selphyn, but I believe he lost his heart to Kassandra. I imagine his loyalties are torn."

Fallon and Rathnar sighed in unison. Lauren could certainly see the family resemblance between the three siblings, and if Rathnar had been sporting the natural color of his hair, they would have looked like triplets.

"I will go back with you as soon as *Transcendence* returns," Fallon said, and everyone stared at him.

"You cannot mean it," Rathnar said.

"Why not? You can dye my hair, paint my face. If you can masquerade as a human, then so can I. If she is still alive, John will need our help. And I feel that the Day of Reckoning is near. John could be our man."

Lauren blinked, her brow kneading. Though this sounded hopeful for John's future, she still wasn't sure she liked the sound of it.

"The Day of Reckoning is a myth," Rathnar said. "There will never be a day when we are welcomed home."

"Miken's other prophecies have been fulfilled. I see not why this one–"

"And you believe in faeries too."

Fallon's mouth dropped. "You *have* been away too long."

Lauren said, "Mother, you will come, will you not?"

"Of course. I will not be separated from you again, nor miss another chance to find John."

Lauren's heart surged. She glanced at Rathnar, his gaze lost again in the fire. There was only one loose end.

"I cannot keep my eyes open another second," Anne said. "Share my room with me?"

Lauren was only too delighted to acquiesce, and after goodnights were exchanged, she followed her mother – her mother! – to her chamber. They changed into their nightgowns, grinning at each other. Anne pulled back the coverlet for Lauren. Lauren stared at the sheet and pillow, suddenly immovable.

"Mother, I – before I retire with you…there is something I must attend to."

Her mother's face flooded with warmth. "Is it Gideon?"

"No, no. It – may I tell you of it in the morning?"

"Certainly. Thousands of times I have dreamed of giggling with you in the wee hours over a handsome face, or cradling you in the midst of a heartbreak. I suppose I can wait but a few more hours."

Lauren threw her arms around her mother, and then slipped out of the chamber, still in her nightgown. The stone floor was freezing on her bare feet, and she wandered halls glowing with torchlight for several minutes before admitting defeat. Fallon found her, and after listening to her stammering query, he smiled and gave her directions, stooping down to kiss her cheek.

"How glad I am to see you," he said. "You know not how much."

"Thank you."

"And I shall love you even more if you can give him some solace. For I cannot."

She felt her face burst into flame, and hurried down the hall before he could say anything else. When she reached the door in question, tall and made of heavy oak, crossed with black steel beams, she hesitated, fist in the air. She was quite beyond the bounds of propriety, standing there in her nightgown and bare feet. And yet she knew she would not sleep until she had had her say.

She knocked lightly, and he answered the door so quickly that he must have been standing right there. Waiting, perhaps?

She trembled under his gaze as he stared at her in that frank, intense way of his that always unnerved her. Two candles were glowing on the bedside table, and his window was open a crack so that the wind was billowing out the blue drapes. One reached across the room and caressed the bed, while the other brushed against a wine decanter. The candles flickered and almost went out.

"I have something I wish to say."

He stepped aside to allow her to enter. She was aware her breathing was very shallow. Her eyes darted to his wounded shoulder; the sling was gone and she could see the bandage peeking from behind the collar of his shirt.

"I misjudged you. I – I was harsh, angry. I said some things that were – they were unforgivable. And yet I stand here and implore you to forgive me nonetheless, though I am undeserving."

His dark eyes were glassy and unblinking. "You were not told the truth. You were led to convictions that anyone in your position would have made. And it is I who must ask for your forgiveness. I could have told you a thousand times – I did in fact nearly do so a thousand times – and yet I felt it to be a betrayal of my people. I felt I did not have the authority to make that decision, though my heart cried out against my judgment."

Her nod was circular. "Yes. I understand. Perhaps then we can forgive each other, and start anew. As friends."

She held out her hand. A smile caught at the corner of his mouth as he took it and shook it. "Yes."

"Yes. Friends. Well. That is what I came to say. And I am satisfied. I bid you goodnight."

As she turned to leave, he leaned over her, his arm above her shoulder, to slam the door shut. She stood unmoving, staring at the closed door, her breath coming in short bursts. He took her by the shoulder and spun her around to face him.

"You are not going anywhere."

"My mother—"

"Will be happy to see you at breakfast."

And then he simply engulfed her. Her last coherent thought was how lupine he looked and felt, with his eyes glowing and the feral tightening of his muscles, as if Stojak had taken possession of his essence. His skin, on his lips in particular, was scalding, and as his hands grabbed fistfuls of her hair and she tasted and smelled him, she knew she was done for. He threw her down on the bed with his one good arm, but she was already completely enraptured, groaning and gasping, as the world tilted and caught on fire.

THIRTY-ONE

THE FIRST NIGHT he spent on the floor outside the door of the captain's cabin, his sword drawn across his lap. At some point all but Gregory came to argue or plead with him, reminding him of his loyalties, past grievances, and at the very least, Leonardis's threats. He had nothing to say to them, especially Sebastian who ranted scripture and actually accused him of being possessed. Kassandra, sleeping at Uthen's invitation in his cabin while he joined the crew below, was under Jonathan's orders not to answer the door to anyone who wasn't he or a Selphyn. He gave no explanation, but nor did she ask for one as she nodded gravely before closing and locking the door.

He dozed off several times from the lulling of the boat, his head jammed between the door and the frame. In the middle of the night the sole of his boot was kicked; he jerked awake, scrambling halfway up with his sword extended. He saw Thomas and slumped back down to the floor, bleary-eyed.

"I want to speak to her."

"No. I will not let anyone in unless he is a Selphyn."

"Which counts you in then."

Jonathan saw that an insult was intended, but it fell flat. Thomas sighed. "Please. I want to know her mind. I – I have to make a decision–"

"No. I have made the decision for you. I will not allow her to be harmed."

"You know I love Miranda well. But to stake our country's future on one person–"

"This is not about Miranda. Not entirely anyway."

"And so then after a night of drinking and carousing, finding spirit animals and such, you are now so changed? Can you be so foolish?"

Thomas stopped when he saw Jonathan look over his shoulder. Thomas stepped out of Richard's way as he came to stand in front of Jonathan, his hand resting on the pommel of his sword. "As soon as I see an opportune moment, I will take her. If you insist on trying to stop me, I shall simply dispatch you as well. My mission is quite clear, and none will stand in my way. Sleep here, if you will, or be comfortable. Either way makes no difference to me when I decide to act."

When Richard was gone, Jonathan turned a tired eye on Thomas. "If we both were to—"

"No. I will not – this is madness."

Five minutes after he left, Uthen found Jonathan asleep once again. "Gideon. Go and rest. I will take a shift."

"Who told you?"

"Horatio. It is noble of you both to worry after her Highness."

Jonathan stood carefully, holding his back when it spasmed. "One of the soldiers—" He stopped, realizing how careful he needed to be. "Not all of them are convinced that bringing the princess home is best for our people. They are the king's men, yes, but…they are oft confused by their loyalty to him and to the country. Usually the two are not divided."

Uthen nodded, and Jonathan saw Belcastro peeking from behind his boot. "Fallon feared the same. Thus, I regret, an extra precaution was taken. I am very sorry."

Jonathan waved it off. "The fault lies with Fallon, not you." He shook Uthen's hand. "Thank you. And no matter what anyone may say, do not allow any humans entrance. I really do not know whom to trust."

"I understand. I do not hold it against you; nay, I esteem you well for your honor. I shall keep watch. Get you to bed."

When he awakened he half feared he would find Uthen lying in the corridor, his throat cut and the princess missing. But all was well; she was breaking her fast with the captain and Jonathan was invited to join them. The day passed uneventfully, and Jonathan enjoyed himself up on deck, a luxury he had denied himself on the journey to Rowan. Though she was surrounded by the Selphyn crew, he still kept an eye on Kassandra as she watched the waves under a sky blanketed by increasing clouds. Every so often she caught his eye and gave him a nod or knowing smile, some kind of simple acknowledgement or gratitude. And when Thomas tried to speak to her she inched closer to Jonathan until Thomas gave him a filthy look and surrendered.

When the rain first started it seemed innocent enough as large, infrequent drops landed on deck, darkening the wood. There was a loud rumble of thunder, and when Jonathan scanned the horizon he saw the clouds lighting up with distant lightning. As soon as the wind picked up, the clouds opened and released a blinding downpour. The ship pitched sideways under a large swell, and the crew began shouting as men crawled up the rigging to tie down the sails.

Gregory, playing lookout in the crow's nest with the cabin boy, scrambled down at Jonathan's frantic shouting, his face pale and soaked when he landed on deck.

"They are sending everyone below," Jonathan said. "Get yourself safe."

He found Kassandra holding onto a mast, her hair plastered to her face. He took her arm and shielded her against him from the wind as they ran to the captain's cabin at the stern. He went in with her to make sure there were no assassins lurking in corners, and then gave her a fleeting kiss on the cheek.

"Stay here, lock the door. It is more imperative than ever that you do not admit anyone save Uthen." He reluctantly added, "Including myself." Her eyes widened as she nodded. The ship pitched again and they both fell against the wall. A compass and sexton fell off of Uthen's desk, and Jonathan saw a whole new threat in all of the sharp instruments and blunt objects that could become deadly projectiles in a storm. The bed, at least, was bolted into the floor along with the rest of the furniture. Kassandra took refuge on it, holding onto the headboard for balance each time the ship rocked over a swell.

By the time he made it back on deck to help the crew, he was thoroughly seasick. He looked for a job to do that required no nautical experience and as little grace as possible as he could not walk in a straight line, and was directed to the buckets to help the seamen rid the ship of water. Grateful for the menial task, he set to work filling buckets and hurling the water over the side. With each new wave that crashed on deck, however, he and seven other Selphyn men were back standing in knee-high salt water. He lost his balance and fell more times than he could count, cowering once or twice when the lightning and thunder crashed simultaneously right over their heads. He paused twice in his frantic bucket-filling to vomit overboard; as he was righting himself after the second time the ship pivoted violently and he fell backwards. The water, sliding down, did not cushion his fall, and his head rapped soundly against the planks. Then he was sliding, upside down, toward the opposite railing, buckets and crates sliding with him. A loose rope of rigging saved him from being thrown overboard; he clung to it, head throbbing, and hauled himself up as the ship was righted. Then he was back in position, throwing buckets of water overboard.

In the two hours of remaining daytime he did nothing but fill and throw buckets, fall, slide and fight for balance. He had no time to check to see if his human companions were safe, or if Kassandra was still in one piece in the cabin. There was no one to guard her as all Selphyn hands were needed on deck, and Uthen was busy screaming orders and tying down the rigging. Now that it was dark, and everyone was frantic, Jonathan knew Richard would try to strike. It was the perfect time to conduct a murder, when accidents could and would happen. Already they had lost two Selphyn sailors to the unrelenting waves; Jonathan had seen one of them go down, his head bobbing before a murderous swell slammed him down and drenched the ship. When he managed to pull himself back up by the railing, the Selphyn was gone.

Now it was completely dark and the storm showed no signs of abating. A huge gust of wind snapped the topgallant mast; it came crashing down and was caught, just before impaling a crewman, by the rigging. He was reluctant to leave his post, but he knew he was needed more at the cabin. Throwing over one more bucket, he clambered across the deck, through throngs of yelling, desperate Selphyn, to the stern. The cabin door was open.

He went in and yelled for her anyway, his throat seizing so that his voice was strangled. When he came bursting out, Thomas was there, drenched and pale. "He has her. He held me at knifepoint and bade me call for her with instructions for safety." His face twisted. "She trusted me."

Jonathan started to run and then, realizing that Thomas was not following, spun, falling against a post as the ship tilted. "For the love of God, will you not help me?"

"It's for the best, Jonathan! I only regret my part in it; she will die thinking I betrayed her."

"*Knowing* you did, you mean! If you let him kill her, you are betraying her!"

Thomas's face crumpled as his shoulders heaved. "We must not – we cannot–"

"To hell with you!" Jonathan screamed over the wind. He ran back the way he had come, desperately scanning the deck for any sign of her. All he could see were the dark outlines of Selphyn men falling, grabbing ropes, filling buckets. The rain stung his eyes as he ran, calling her name as the wind swallowed his voice. A wave knocked him down, and as he scrambled for purchase on the slick planking he saw them. Richard had his arm hooked around the railing, his left hand a hold of Kassandra's wrist. She was on the ground, her feet pointing in the opposite direction, the water rushing, as the ship regained balance, over her face. Richard hauled her up just as Jonathan grabbed a loose piece of planking to pull himself up. He drew his sword as he ran toward them; Richard caught the movement out of the corner of his eye. A dagger flashed in his hand, and he would have stabbed her if not for the giant swell that reared up like the hand of God and came crashing down on them.

For a moment everything was underwater, and Jonathan literally swam over the deck in the direction he had last seen them. When his head broke the surface and he stood, the water was now thigh-high. Richard was standing up as well, but empty-handed: there was no sign of Kassandra. There was nothing Jonathan could do but hope she had not been swept off, as Richard was advancing on him with his rapier drawn.

Jonathan swung to parry the cut, horrified when he realized how spent his muscles were from throwing buckets of water for hours. His arms screamed with each thrust and parry, and the rocking of the ship made balance impossible. Several times they lost contact as they slid across the wood. Jonathan even held onto the rigging with his left arm while he frantically parried Richard's blade with his right. It was Jonathan's first real duel; the countless bouts heretofore had been staged, fought with blunted blades. And how many duels had this seasoned assassin fought in his lifetime, with his scarred face and hardened eyes? Undoubtedly more than Jonathan's choreographed ones.

The ship tilted at an obscene angle; for a moment Jonathan hung in the air, staring at the railing that was now below him instead of beside him. Then his hand slipped from the rigging, and he fell. He steadied his arm to catch the railing before he fell overboard, when Richard threw himself into Jonathan's path. They crashed together against the railing, and when Jonathan lost his rapier to the waves, he felt the horrible, searing pain in his side. He screamed and looked down at Richard's rapier embedded in his flesh. He saw the glint of Richard's teeth, exposed in a smile, and with all the strength he could muster, he kicked the assassin the chest, and then clung desperately to the railing.

The ship came falling back down, and Jonathan had his right foot and arm cradled in the railing to keep him from sliding. Richard, who had not fallen overboard as Jonathan hoped, rolled toward the center of the ship. Jonathan wrenched the rapier from his side with another scream and threw himself forward, hunched like a beetle, after Richard. Richard stood, seeing him coming, and braced his arms, ready to wrestle. He would have no doubt easily wrenched the sword loose from Jonathan, had there not been another terrible wave.

This time Jonathan kept hold of the sword as he was knocked over. He thrust blindly in three different directions, the third thrust yielding to flesh. He reached out with his left hand, wincing at the pain in his side, and grabbed a handful of Richard's shirt, using it for leverage as he stabbed deeper with his right hand. All sound was muted by the water over their heads, but he did hear the satisfying though muffled grunt. It would have to be enough.

The ship tilted, yet again, and he held onto a rope with his cheek pressed against the wood, watching Richard's body roll where it came to a stop at the railing. When it rolled back, coming to a rest just a few feet from Jonathan, the arms flung out limply and then did not move. Jonathan heaved a sigh and forced himself to stand. He called out Kassandra's name just once before he was knocked backwards by another pair of hands.

Incredulous, he scrambled under the weight of this new attacker, but in his weakened state his efforts were infantile against the heavy bulk. Hands locked around his throat, squeezing, and he was forced to look into the eyes of his oldest friend. Sebastian's face, barely visible in the darkness, was a mask of madness.

"You would help her to the throne," he growled, as Jonathan fought and clawed under him. "Then you would help them bewitch everyone, showing us some false idol to make us believe! They would have you be their savior. They would have you trick us! I will not let you. Forgive me, but I cannot let you."

Jonathan's vision pricked with colors and light as his body went numb. He felt his arms drop and his legs stop kicking as everything went black, but at least he could no longer feel the pain. Then abruptly the hands around his throat fell away, and he took a choking, panting breath that filled his lungs with fire. As his vision began to clear, he felt something hot and thick fall on his face. Then he saw it: the river of blood washing down Sebastian's face and dripping onto his own. Sebastian's eyes went still, his mouth hanging open, before he fell forward, his entire weight crushing Jonathan. Blood poured onto Jonathan's neck and into his ear, and another wave crashed down onto the boat, mercifully knocking Sebastian off of him. He struggled to his knees in the water, still coughing and wheezing. He could barely see and it was all he could do to stay conscious.

"Oh, God. Oh, God."

He looked up and saw Thomas standing over Sebastian's body, the silver Selphyn axe in his hand. A glance back at Sebastian revealed the split in his crown. Jonathan fell forward and caught himself so that he was on all fours. The pain in his side came back with a vengeance.

"Where – where is Kassandra?" he said, his voice ragged. Thomas took no notice, still rooted in place at the sight of Sebastian's body.

"I did not love him, to be sure, but now…" He threw a look at Jonathan. "Why could you not just leave well enough alone? You have made me a murderer."

"Where *is* she?"

But there was no response, forcing Jonathan back to his feet. He was limping now from a sprained ankle and had to lurch about, clutching his throat. He finally found Kassandra huddled behind secured crates, her arms wrapped tightly against one with her eyes firmly closed. He gasped her name and she opened her eyes, her mouth dropping.

"Are you all right?"

"Yes. But you–"

"No," Jonathan said. "Not all right."

Uthen found them, his face stricken. "What happened?"

As Kassandra explained it, shouting over the wind, Jonathan put his hand down on a crate and stooped over, grateful for this small reprieve. Then Uthen was shaking him.

"Is she out of danger? Or–"

Jonathan shook his head. "Some of the others – they were relying on Richard to kill her. They may – they may come after her themselves when they find he is dead."

Even in the night and rain, Jonathan could see how dark Uthen's face became. "Who are you?"

"It does not signify. You must help me keep her safe."

The captain shook his head, his soaked locks flinging water. "You cannot stay here. It is too dangerous for her. If I cut loose the longboat, can you go with her?"

"Yes."

Uthen looked up. "Believe it or not the storm is beginning to let up. You may be all right yet." He looked over the ruins of his ship. "I hope I can say the same for us."

Kassandra sat in the longboat as they lowered the ropes, and

Jonathan went back below deck to grab his satchel. From the supply hold he grabbed several apples and two canteens of fresh water, bleeding everywhere he went. From the deck he tossed the satchel down to Kassandra.

Uthen put a hand on his arm. "Can you jump and then swim?"

"I think so."

He handed Jonathan a compass. "Head due east for Zirnich."

"If I die, what will happen to Miranda?"

Uthen's voice lowered. "You mean Helen?"

"Her name is Miranda."

Uthen's shoulders dropped. "Leave word at the Swan that you have arrived safely. If we do not get word, I will assume the worst. I'll see her safely home."

"Do you swear it?"

"Yes. Get you gone."

He no sooner turned to leave than Thomas seized him by the shoulders. "Go then and take her. But know this: I will be there in Diernioch before you. I will be waiting. And I will not let you bring her back."

Too exhausted to argue, Jonathan said, "Then I shall see you in Diernioch. Until then."

He jumped into the waves, sinking much farther than he anticipated. When he began kicking, the pain in his side ripped through him. He flailed, sinking more than rising, and his lungs, not yet recovered, were already burning. He realized now there was no way he could make it to the surface. Still, he gave it his all, gritting his teeth against the pain in his side. Just as the familiar fogginess began to retake his mind, he felt something smooth glide under his hand. Thinking shark, he sucked in a mouthful of water and resumed flailing. Then the bottlenose pushed into his hand, and he melted with relief, gently enfolding himself over the back of a dolphin.

Kassandra helped drag him onto the boat as he threw up alarming amounts of water, the salt waging havoc on his nose. The ropes on their boat were cut free from the ship, as he lay on his back, choking and gasping, he could see *Transcendence's* figurehead bobbing sickeningly in and out of the waves. Someone waved, but Jonathan could not move. His last thought, before sinking into oblivion, was that Salsima's princess was soaked to the bone, bedraggled and almost murdered, rowing her little heart out as her would-be hero was passed out cold, completely useless. It would have to do.

THIRTY-TWO

WHILE HE SLEPT, he joined minds with the horse.

In this young, vibrant body, he felt no pain or exhaustion, only jubilance for life. As the horse welcomed him in he cantered around his corral, throwing his head and neighing. Time did not control him here; they may have galloped like that together for hours or minutes before it was brought to an abrupt end by a thrown rope.

The horse, used to this degradation, slowed and then came to a stop, holding still in order to be saddled. But Jonathan resisted as the mere thought of being restrained through this magnificent animal was not to be borne. His energy created discord and the horse threw his head and dodged the saddle in mid-swing so that its momentum carried it all the way to the ground. There was a curse, and through the horse's eye Jonathan caught sight of a dark-haired man in fine clothes. In spite of his hatred of this man, this captor of his friend, Jonathan was grateful for the clue provided. The horse he sought was owned by a rich man, a nobleman perhaps, on a large estate. Through his several rotations in the corral he had caught sight of what appeared to be vineyards set apart, and now with this newest clue he deduced his horse was more than likely residing in one of the noble estates in Sterling, the next town east of Zirnich.

The man tried again to swing the saddle on, and the horse, operating on Jonathan's strong negativity, danced again out of range. A riding crop smacked the horse's neck, and Jonathan felt this pain as the horse reared.

"She's in a foul temper," the man said, words which the horse undoubtedly did not understand though Jonathan could. "You saddle her."

"But sir. You are the only one whom she will allow to–"

"Do it!"

The pronouns hit home and Jonathan reeled. *She, her.* His horse was a mare.

Had he been in his body he would have burst out laughing in his folly. In his masculine ego, it never occurred to him that this magnificent creature, so strong, passionate and virile might be a female. Uthen's fox was male, as was Fallon's raven. He made an assumption, albeit unconscious, that the animals shared the gender of their human mind-links.

As he wallowed in the amazement of his discovery, he missed the riding crop sailing down again, this time wielded by a groomsman. As Jonathan's rage surged through her, the horse reared up again, aiming her hooves at the groom. He shrieked and leaped out of the way just in time, only to be bitten hard in the thigh. The harness was yanked in the other direction, and Jonathan realized the horse's master had a hold of her. The riding crop smacked her between the eyes, and Jonathan felt the ecstasy of her full strength as she reared back, roaring out a neigh of indignation. The rope pulled free and she ran, roped but unsaddled. Three more servants were called, and she danced and threw her head as each carried a rope and a crop. Jonathan balked and the connection was broken.

He opened his crusted, swollen eyes and stared at the sun directly overhead. He groaned and closed them again when the pain in his side ignited. He heard the gentle lapping of the waves and the rhythmic rowing, and remembered where he was. He tried to sit up but could not; his movements alerted Kassandra who stopped rowing in order to hold the canteen to his lips while he drank.

"I did not think you would live."

"Nor did I," he croaked, his throat still ragged.

He managed to rest his weight on his elbows, his body on fire, and looked around. The sky was mostly clear, with only a few scattered clouds. The sea was beautiful but immense; the mainland, he could now see, was still far.

"*Transcendence?*"

"I lost sight of her last night," Kassandra said.

"And have you been rowing all this time?" Jonathan said, deeply ashamed though there was little he could do about it.

Kassandra grinned. "I have had some help."

He followed her gaze and saw the two dolphin heads bob to the surface, ropes tied around them that were connected to the longboat. The sight of them was thrilling, almost akin to beholding a faerie. As if on cue, a small, furry body edged its way up on Jonathan's good side, the lupine head plopping down on his shoulder.

"A stowaway," Kassandra said, and Jonathan grinned through cracked lips. The movement revealed how sunburned he was – every muscle tick in his face was excruciating.

"At least I am among good friends." He looked meaningfully at Kassandra, and she smiled, laying a hand on his arm.

"I am beholden to you for saving my life. You are a true friend, Gideon."

With no sight of another ship and so far from land, Jonathan felt almost as if they were the last two people on earth. He made a decision. "You were best to call me Jonathan."

She stared at him as Zartha yawned lazily, burrowing her nose in Jonathan's neck. Without prompting, Jonathan told her the long, sordid story, pausing occasionally to take a drink, cough, or simply catch his breath. When he finished he was completely hoarse and could barely stay awake. He saw Kassandra's face in profile as she resumed rowing, her jaw set.

"Then you were very brave," she said at length, "going against your friends and the commands of your betters. Very brave, and I owe you my life."

"And I owe you mine. Thank you for caring for me."

They bobbed along in silence that was interrupted by the dolphins' chirping. He reflected on everything that had transpired over the last few weeks, ruminating over Sebastian's death. He mourned the Sebastian he knew as a boy, the Sebastian that played his kings, wizards, fathers and villains. That Sebastian had been lost to him long before last night.

When he felt brave enough he tentatively reached down toward the wound in his side. Rough material, perhaps from Kassandra's petticoats, was tied in place, crusted with dried blood. As he continued probing he found a layer that was soaked with fresh blood, and he did not dare investigate further.

"That will need stitching in Zirnich," Kassandra said.

"A quick stitching then. We must—"

She looked at him over her shoulder. "You cannot travel. Not for several days."

"We have to get there before the others do. Otherwise they will stop us—"

"It will be all right. You cannot ride like this. You must give yourself time to heal."

At the mention of the word ride, he remembered his recent encounter with the horse. "I have to find my animal link, the horse. I cannot go back without her. Will you help me?"

Kassandra smiled. "I would never stand between a Selphyn and his totem animal. Of course I will help."

He did not rebel against her choice of words, but let the label wash over him to see how it felt. *Selphyn*. The word contained two-hundred years of fear, hatred, revulsion. And yet, as he was learning, most of it was due to misconception. If only Fallon had not ruined everything by taking Miranda. He had just started liking the Selphyn king.

The present threat now, however, as inconceivable as it seemed, was Thomas. Thomas, his closest friend, whose banter and humor he sorely missed. He could not exactly pinpoint the moment their friendship turned sour, though the catalyst must have been the moment when he revealed his Selphyn blood. He thought that Thomas, more than Miranda, would be somewhat understanding. By all appearances Thomas was the most offended of all of them.

The dolphins chirped again and Kassandra stopped rowing, rubbing her arms while the dolphins pulled. Jonathan said, "Friends of yours?"

"Oh, yes. The one on the right is Myra. I have known her since I was a child."

Myra. The name tugged at a memory, and then suddenly he had it. He saw Syldonia splashing her feet in the surf next to his, the dolphin leaping up to chirp and dance for him.

"That was Syldonia's dolphin!"

"Yes. She – she stayed with us, these many years."

"My God. How she must miss Syldonia. I am so very glad she found me yester-night."

He lay back down, content for a moment in the swirl of memories. He was rocked to sleep, and dreamt of being rocked in his mother's arms, another memory long dormant. And he escaped, once again, from the pain.

THIRTY-THREE

WHEN UTHEN RETURNED with his storm-ravaged ship, broken topgallant and all, he received the news with a brave face that he had to immediately turn around to go back to Zirnich. Lauren felt for the captain, whom she took an instant liking to after seeing him murmur affectionately to his fox. His clothes were torn and ragged, there were dark circles under his eyes and his hair was a windblown rats' nest.

"I am sorry my friend," Fallon said as they met him on the beach, all packed and ready to go.

"I thought as much. *Feared* as much, if I may speak plainly. I was accosted by a human captain begging for forgiveness for taking humans to Salsima despite having a Selphyn onboard...after I dragged the story from him I began to understand what may have happened. And our friend did not deny he was not whom he purported himself to be."

He gave commands to his exhausted crew to re-board *Transcendence*, and there was a very un-Selphyn-like chorus of groans and curses. They were a mess of bruised and cut faces, bandaged limbs and tired eyes. As they stomped back into the surf, Uthen swept Syldonia into his arms, kissing her soundly. Lauren gasped, and then smiled as she watched the lovers stare into each other's eyes. Syldonia was positively glowing.

"You are not coming?" Uthen said.

"I am indeed. Through Myra's eyes I saw that he means to help Kassandra. And so I will help him: he may very well need my authority as to her parentage to fight off the likes of Thaddeus and Leonardis."

"But the king—"

"Can go hang."

"Dearest, I must advise against this. The danger—"

He broke off when she stood on her toes to whisper something in his ear. Whatever secret lover's promise she imparted to him had its effect, for he grinned and squeezed her, kissing her again. "I understand," he said. "Of course you must go."

Lauren marveled at the healing power of love: Uthen shed his slouched, exhausted posture as his eyes brightened. He led Syldonia by the hand toward the surf, where she lifted her dress over slender, delicate ankles and calves, and together they splashed toward the ship, smiling at each other.

The scene reminded her of her own sensitive situation, and she felt her face grow hot, wondering if Rathnar meant to put on a similar display of affection. She was deeply embarrassed by her transgressions, knowing full well that everyone else was aware of them. Over dinner, walking through the garden or talking by the fire she and Rathnar could hardly keep their hungry eyes off of each other, and Lauren caught the amused glances exchanged by the others. That her mother seemed delighted did nothing to ease her discomfort, and Fallon's gentle teasing was almost too much to bear. Only Gideon was scandalized, and took every opportunity to voice his disapproval.

Even now, as she stepped independently into the surf without looking back, she heard him say, "What is this? No escort from your heathen lover?"

She clamped her jaw shut and hoisted up her skirts, drawing in a sharp breath through her nose when the cold water swirled around her ankles. She felt Rathnar's searing gaze on her back but refused to turn.

"Your complaints are growing tedious," she heard him say.

"You'll forgive me if I offend," was Gideon's sardonic reply, and she rolled her eyes.

"I must agree with my brother," Fallon said. "Are we to endure this bitterness all the way to Zirnich?"

Gideon laughed. "My Selphyn friends do not find me agreeable. My heart should stop with grief."

"A shame you did not meet the other Gideon," Fallon said, presumably to Rathnar. "He was far more affable."

There was no response, and Lauren smiled.

They boarded the ship, and Lauren's eyes lighted on evidence from the devastating storm. Shivers with deadly points poked up from the planking, chunks of railing were missing, and masts and rigging hung limply. The sails were dropped, revealing one rent with tears, as if from the claws of a monster.

"...And he fought off her would-be assassin most gallantly," Uthen told Syldonia, and Lauren beamed with pride. "Did Myra see them safely to shore?"

"Yes. But he was much wounded. They may yet be in Zirnich when we arrive."

Lauren was almost too afraid to hope; she had been disappointed too many times, having missed her brother at the last moment.

"What of the others?" Fallon asked.

"I did not know who among them was her ally or foe. I told them so, and let them all go. Forgive me. I had not the heart to take further action against them."

Fallon nodded. "We can only hope they will not interfere." Tiben landed on the king's shoulder, cawing. "There you are, my friend. I can hardly go without you."

Lauren glanced at Rathnar and saw him watching the raven wistfully. "Will Stojak be there to greet us when we arrive?"

"Yes," Rathnar said, and Lauren felt a stir of apprehension at the prospect of a more formal meeting with the wolf, almost as if she were being introduced to in-laws for the first time. She worried that if she did not meet with his approval, Rathnar would suspect she was unworthy.

"I very much look forward to having the honor of meeting him," Fallon said. "Do you still miss Vyngara?"

"Everyday."

Lauren started and then relaxed. Vyngara was undoubtedly another wolf, Stojak's predecessor, and not a rival. In spite of knowing his reputation for being well feared, Lauren was apprehensive to have him back in court, surrounded by the lovely noblewomen. Regardless of whether or not they returned his sentiments, he could still desire them.

Ever sensitive to her moods, Rathnar turned to her, his eyes boring into hers. "Why do you frown?"

She felt the blush creeping up her throat. "I was thinking of the beautiful women of the court. One day you will open your eyes and realize there are far better—"

She was cut off by a chorus of guffaws, the two Selphyn men aghast, Gideon disgusted. They all began talking at once.

"I would advise him to sell where he can. He is not for all markets," Gideon said, while Fallon's reaction was the opposite.

"Where would he find a lady lovelier than you?"

Rathnar seized her shoulders. "Will you not see what is right in front of you? No other woman exists for me. They are weeds in this garden where there is but one rose. And oh, but her bloom would bring me to my knees were I to bask in her beauty for too long."

"Ugh. I am ill," Gideon said, and Lauren's mother and Miranda each smacked him on the back of his head.

Lauren laughed and Miranda winked at her. The two women

were best of friends, discovering a kinship in their respective relationships with John. They each wanted to know all about the other, gleaning whatever information about John they could. Miranda wanted to hear all about his exploits as a boy, and Lauren sought to know what he was like as a man. She was by equal degrees delighted and jealous by this recent development of love blossoming between her brother and this beautiful woman, who had acted with him on stage, something Lauren could only dream of. That detail was particularly hard to digest.

But they were entertained the rest of the afternoon, sailing on thankfully calm waters, by Anne and Syldonia telling stories of their days at court with the three children. They carefully skirted past any reference to the pain they suffered, and Syldonia was able to talk about Edward without tears in her eyes.

In the evening Rathnar showed Fallon and Syldonia how to mix and apply the white face paint. Having done his own face in demonstration, Lauren sank in disappointment to see the pale, waxy skin, longing for the vibrant hue of his natural color. Fallon and Syldonia were likewise rendered ghostly by the paint, but refused to dye their hair, hiding it instead in hoods. They would need their natural color to speak for Kassandra to the king and queen.

That night, under a clear, warm sky, Lauren slept in Rathnar's arms on deck, secure knowing her good friends and her mother were sleeping below. Again, the only thing missing from this scene of perfection was John. This time, however, she knew he was within reach. This time she would not let him get away.

THIRTY-FOUR

THEY HAD VERY few possessions among them and no money as the storm had thrown everything into chaos. They had only the clothes on their backs, their horses less the two that were killed in the storm, and Thomas's silver axe. He was only too happy to get rid of that as its presence only served as a reminder of his grisly deed. He sold it but was given little for it as the merchant in Zirnich traded with the Selphyn regularly and already had many of their silver works of exquisite craftsmanship to sell.

And so this company of players, in spite of missing three of its key members, did what they did best: they put on a play.

The innkeeper of the Swan was only too happy to accommodate them as very few traveling players had come through Zirnich. Gregory ran through town, ringing a bell and shouting, heralding the performance, and soon they had a decent-sized audience of some one-fifty or two-hundred people. Without Jonathan and Miranda, however, they were disadvantaged, and could only do select scenes. Thomas chose *William and Elizabeth*, as Rothford was always a crowd-pleaser, and this play had romantic and comedic elements that would be popular. Thomas played the clown and earned a good many laughs, while Gregory was once again reduced to playing Elizabeth.

They finished the scenes with a jig and some juggling, and after Thomas shared some of the profits with the innkeeper, they were begged to stay and do another performance.

"Wonderful, most wonderful," the innkeeper said, pumping Thomas's hand and ignoring his protestations. "And see, they are all coming into my establishment for beer and wine. You are good for business!"

"A shame the man upstairs is too ill to come down and enjoy it," a woman said, presumably the innkeeper's wife. "But that wound will keep him abed another day or so, to be sure."

Thomas's interest was snared. "Is he traveling with a young lady?"

"Yes, yes, his niece he says. Pretty thing. A shame, really, that they missed it. I hope at least they left their window open to hear."

Thomas felt a surge of adrenaline, thinking of Jonathan just up the stairs, listening to his actors perform outside, no doubt terrified of discovery. He looked up at the ceiling, imagining him just on the other side with Kassandra. It would be only too easy to take her from him, what with the eight other men in his company who would be only too glad to help. When they learned he helped her escape they had been enraged, demanding blood. Jonathan signed their death warrants as far as Leonardis was concerned. At the very least, they could never again perform in Salsima.

He sighed, his shoulders sagging. "I am very sorry. But we must be on our way."

He threw a passing glance at the ceiling. He would reckon with Jonathan, but not until his friend was recovered enough to make it fair.

* * *

Lord Bartholomew Riordan was awakened from a sublime afternoon nap by incessant knocking. His servant answered and then reported that the fellow and young lady at the gate refused to be turned away. They would speak with the master of house whether he would have them or no. Bartholomew refused to be bullied and would not give them entry, but met them at the gate. From a distance he was startled, thinking he saw Gideon and Lauren. Upon closer inspection he saw the man had longer hair than Gideon, and the woman was much younger, with auburn hues in her hair. The fellow was in obvious pain, holding his side and standing awkwardly. The weariness in his eyes along with his condition promised of intriguing tales to be told by the fire, but Lord Riordan had no patience.

"What is your will?"

"I think you have a horse?" the fellow said, and Riordan narrowed his eyes. "A mare. Black, beautiful. Powerful and wild. You have this horse, yes?"

"I may."

"I wish to buy her."

As he fumbled with a fat purse at his waist, Riordan let his gaze linger on the young woman. She was fresh and lovely, no more than seventeen. Perfectly delectable. Perhaps that fireside tale was in order after all.

"She is not for sale," he said, without taking his eyes off the lady.

"You see I have brought you much gold," the man said, and the desperation in his voice called Riordan's attention back to him. He was actually trembling. "Enough gold to buy twenty horses."

"That mare comes from a long line of champions. From Lansing. But you must know this, else you would not be wanting her."

"I care not if she is a decrepit nag. I will have her, champion or no. Please, do but count this gold–"

"You are not listening. I say she is not for sale."

Riordan watched with fascination as the fellow's emotions played out an intriguing drama across his face. One would think this horse a matter of life or death. His attention thus diverted, he was not aware the woman had drawn a dagger until it was resting across his throat.

He was astonished to see she was in earnest, her eyes, so soft and innocent a moment ago, now hard. "Take the money. Give him the horse. Now."

They were interrupted by a loud pounding noise. Without moving his head, Riordan swiveled his eyes in the direction of the stable. They heard it again, the scraping and pounding, followed by the loud, angry neigh of his prize horse. His mouth started to open when her hooves broke through the wall. Bursting through as if the stable were on fire, the mare leaped free of the wall and came galloping at full speed toward the gate.

The man's transformation was amazing. His face lit up like the sun as he lurched forward, running with obvious agony toward Lord Riordan's horse. Bartholomew and his female captor watched, mesmerized, as the two collided. The man burst into tears, throwing his arms around the mare's thick neck while she actually pulled him against her with her chin over his shoulder. She nuzzled the back of his head, whickering softly and gently nibbling at his ear. The fellow, in the meantime, was still sobbing, clutching the horse as if she were a long-lost love.

Riordan guffawed as the man slid onto his completely compliant horse – without a saddle! – and gave her the gentlest nudge to set her in motion. Riordan had never been able to ride her without a struggle, and certainly not without a saddle and bridle. She was now as gentle as a newborn.

She came galloping toward them, sliding to a stop with a toss of her head. The man held out an arm to his female companion, who pulled the dagger away from Bartholomew and slid onto the horse's back behind the man. She leaned forward and cut his purse free, tossing it to the ground at Riordan's feet.

"What is her name?" the fellow asked.

Riordan swallowed, still in shock. He had not thought to be so distraught by an animal's behavior again since the black wolf attacked him the night his three prisoners escaped.

"She is called Zephyrine." Because it seemed to mean so much to the man, he added, "It is Lansingese for *wind*."

"Thank you. It suits her well."

Bartholomew could only nod in bewilderment as his horse took flight, running with a grace and majesty he had never really appreciated until that moment.

THIRTY-FIVE

AFTER ALL THE rain they endured riding to Zirnich, the return trip proved to be almost the exact opposite. Midsummer hit with a vengeance, and they endured sweltering temperatures that lingered well after sundown. Because Syldonia in particular was still so striking, despite the white face paint, they camped more often that not, staying clear of inns. But the heat took its toll on the disguised Selphyn, melting their face paint so that their features appeared mottled and drooping. Frequent reapplications were necessary though they met few others on the road.

Making their journey more endurable were their animal companions. Stojak had indeed joined them in Zirnich, reuniting with Rathnar with so much affection and tenderness that all who looked on, save for Gideon naturally, blinked away tears. The wolf stayed close but out of sight when they passed through the larger cities, with the exception of Sterling. In case Bartholomew had orders to recapture them, the wolf was in plain sight to encourage him to keep his distance. They were able to pass through town unmolested.

In addition to Stojak were Tiben and Belcastro. Uthen refused to be deterred, and accompanied them with his fox while his crew remained behind, manning and repairing *Transcendence* until they returned. The animals were not only tolerant of each other, but affectionate. Once the horses were used to them, they too interacted with them, often nudging the fox or wolf with their noses. Lauren felt more secure with the animals keeping watch while they camped in the woods, and twice Stojak actually left his master's side to push himself under her arm. She slept with her nose in his fur, and when Rathnar found them curled up together in the morning, he looked more content than Lauren had ever seen him.

When they reached Elkyn, the last city before Diernioch, they paused to construct a plan. Without knowing whether or not John and Kassandra were already there, it would not do for them to barge into court only to be beheaded. Someone needed to infiltrate the court to find out what was going on.

Miranda volunteered her parents' home to house the others while Gideon and Rathnar presented themselves to the king and tried to affect an air of normalcy. Lauren did not want to be separated from Rathnar, nor did she want to miss another opportunity of seeing John, but Rathnar was insistent she remain in Elkyn. He did not know how much Leonardis had guessed, but after setting loose his hound Bartholomew on them, he obviously knew enough to be dangerous. He would not let her put herself in danger until they had the upper hand with Kassandra in place. The fact that he was putting himself in danger did not perturb him while it infuriated Lauren.

Rathnar kissed her before they left, his first public display of affection. For once she was not embarrassed by what everyone already knew, but rather let her tears flow unabashedly. Stojak was glued to her side, which provided much comfort though she refused to give Rathnar the satisfaction of seeing it.

He spoke into her ear and she closed her eyes so she wouldn't have to look at Sir Francis, Spymaster. It was Rathnar she loved. "When this is done, I will take you from here. And though it is not of my custom, I will marry you if it will make you happy. It matters little: you will be my companion for life with or without ceremony."

The fact that he had not asked but rather instructed was something about him that she loved though it contradicted the independent woman he would have her be. She preferred being swept away by his insistence, his force, his desire. She thought of the way he slammed the door closed over her shoulder the night she came to his chamber, and shivered; it was exactly this force of presence that she made her melt. She said nothing but gave him her answer with her eyes.

He started to walk away and then turned back. "If I see John, I swear to you I will do all I can to protect him."

She did not trust herself to speak and so nodded, and her mother squeezed her hand. With tears in her throat she called out to Gideon.

"Look out for him, please."

Gideon narrowed his eyes as if annoyed. She wished she knew if she could trust him, but even after all they had endured together, he was still a slave to his ego, emotional whims and excuses for tirades. She did not think their friendship, such as it was, could trump those things that motivated him, and if he were sufficiently goaded she feared he would betray Rathnar without thinking.

Stojak whined and she stroked him behind the ears, grateful to have this part of Rathnar. She looked up at Miranda and smiled.

"Will your parents object to a wolf, do you think?"

* * *

Gideon hoped Kassandra was already there, so that all that would be required of him would be to step forward and receive his accolades and commendation, perhaps even rewards, for his part in her rescue. Though he did not exactly rescue her per se, he would certainly inform the king of his concern and the wild excursion he went on to ensure she was returned to her parents.

Finishing his thought out loud, he said to Rathnar, "If all goes well, I will not betray you as long as you disappear once your part in this is finished."

Rathnar's face was impassive. "I do not intend to remain."

Gideon could not resist a sneer. "Because of *her*?"

"In part. Being reunited with my family revealed to me how far under the influence of humans I have become. I wish to go home, and revive my spirit."

"How noble."

As usual, Rathnar was not cooperating in rising to Gideon's bait. His equanimity always made Gideon feel inferior because of his own inability to contain his emotions. For once he would like to see Rathnar unhinged.

At Gideon's insistence they stopped first at his estate to see Helen. If there was any court gossip Helen would know it, and he had some atoning to do for his abrupt departure in now what seemed like another lifetime. She did not disappoint him with her reaction.

"You louse!" She threw a wooden spoon at him. "You have been gone for weeks without a single word! How dare you!"

"My love–"

"The court is in an uproar, the king ranting, myself left to die with worry–"

"What has the king said?"

"Why, that you are ungrateful, despicable–"

"What–"

"Always in trouble, always–"

"Mistress Helen," Rathnar said, and Helen's mouth snapped shut. She bobbed in a curtsey. "Have there been any...intrigues at court? Any odd visitors?"

"No. But my mistress is on edge, fearing conspiracy. Leonardis and Thaddeus are acting strangely, and what with that playwright gone missing..."

"Still missing?"

"Oh, aye. But not from a lack of her trying to find him. She thinks he's the king's bastard, you know."

"Yes, yes." He turned to Gideon. "In all likelihood, he is not here."

"We should make an appearance, get back in their confidences."

Rathnar nodded. "There are those I can question…"

He trailed off as Gideon watched him, fascinated. "What? The nefarious spymaster has lost his spine?"

But Helen stepped in between them. "You do not mean to leave me again so soon?"

Gideon kissed her cheek. "Forgive me, dearest. Duty calls."

She pounded on his shoulder. "You are a right louse indeed! Son-of-a-stinking-whore."

"And this is the reception for me, after being imprisoned for days in a wine cellar?"

Helen burst into tears and threw her arms around him while Gideon felt Rathnar's impassive gaze. He felt the familiar resentment stirring, of being the object of Rathnar's calm judgment whenever he lost his temper. If Rathnar would only speak, insult or chide him, he could unleash his fury. But this silent contempt was maddening.

They walked to the palace from Gideon's estate, the sounds of the playhouses carrying over in the wind so that they heard snatches of lines and scattered applause. It naturally reminded him of his rival, the fool that impersonated him. It little mattered that the man in question was being lauded as a hero by Fallon, having proved himself by risking his life to save Kassandra. Gideon still had a score to settle with him, and did not care that his deceit was forced upon him by Leonardis.

The king and queen were hearing petitions when they arrived, a perfect setup for Gideon to make his dramatic return. They were accosted by courtiers in the audience chamber, demanding to know the circumstances behind their long absences. Gideon spotted Thaddeus, and took great satisfaction when the chancellor's face went pale. He hurried from the room, ostensibly to alert his co-conspirator that Gideon was back. And knew everything. Oh, yes, when this all came to a lovely head with the return of Kassandra, King Edward would know exactly whom to blame for her near death.

The king spotted them and waved them over. Gideon have him an indulgent grin, glancing at Rathnar to see the disguised Selphyn's face still impassive. It was one of his trademarks, this calm in every situation, usually the first method used to intimidate traitors into talking. Rarely did he need to use more drastic measures. The placidity, for some reason, brought many to tears.

A crowd parted to give them space, and there was a hush over the audience chamber as they stood front and center before the dais. Gideon saw that the king had noticeably aged in the time he was gone, and was pale and somewhat slack in his posture. Lydia looked overtired, and completely uninterested in Gideon's presence. Her eyes were honed in on Rathnar, no doubt eager for word of thwarted conspiracies. Gideon quietly seethed.

Ready to launch into a long and hyperbolized rendition of their adventures, Gideon opened his mouth only to be muted by the king's narrowed eyes. "And is this our favorite courtier? Our belated and careless Gideon? And where have you been these past weeks, with no regard for your friends and peers, for your king? What have you to say?"

Gideon's jaw dropped and no sound issued forth. Edward's eyebrow shot up.

"As I thought. You have nothing to say for your much changed behavior, your foolishness. That our secretary Sir Francis has brought you back, errant knave that you are, is no surprise to us. We received word, Sir Francis, of your triumph in Chauncery. Our good queen's cousin is vanquished, and we have seen the traitor's letters written in his hand to prove his guilt. A band of his conspirators awaits our judgment in the Tower, and word has spread, throughout our land, of the justice wielded by your hand alone. Our country is safe, and to you we offer sovereign thanks."

Queen Lydia stood, adding insult to injury, and walked to the end of the dais so that she stood in front of Rathnar. She lifted a heavy gold medallion from her neck and held it suspended in the air as one might a hoop for a jumping dog. "Accept this gift on our behalf, and with it our eternal gratitude."

Rathnar, to his credit, finally looked unhinged. His face dark, he knelt on one knee and bowed his head as Lydia slipped the medallion around his neck. King Edward said, "For you I offer the dukedom of Reine. Rise, Duke Francis Rathnar, and accept your commendation that is due your person."

He started to rise, to turn and face the audience who would soon erupt in raucous applause. Gideon could feel it brewing in his stomach, felt it rising like acidic bile up his throat. He knew he could not stop it, even if he wanted to, and in that moment he did not wish to stop it, not in the slightest.

He threw out his arm to gesture, his voice booming and filling the chamber before the applause could begin. "This is your great hero? *This* man? Nay, I cannot call him so, for he is not. He is a *creature*, a monster whom you yourself have banished from this court, from this country. Like a worm in the bud he has been hiding, disguising his true nature while making fools of us all!"

"You had better speak plainly," Edward said through clenched teeth. "And it had better be worthwhile or I will have you thrown out."

"This *thing* is a Selphyn in disguise."

Oh, how he reveled in the gasps of the audience, letting it wash over him like an actor receiving his accolades. Faces swiveled to get a good look, and Gideon knew what they would be seeing: the angled face, sharp cheekbones, the white, pasty skin, the things that were now so obvious to Gideon as to never allow him to see anything else. Only the king laughed, though there was hatred in his eyes, a hatred for whom it was unclear.

"You take your petty jealousies too far. That is a serious allegation, and should not be made in mirth or envy–"

"Ask him," Gideon said. "Ask him, and learn his answer."

Only then did Gideon turn to look at Rathnar, to see him with his head bowed, eyes locked on the floor. He was not staring at him with incredulous wrath, or shouting protestations. Gideon's smile faltered.

"Well, Sir Francis," Edward said, "you hear this monstrous claim. What say you?"

Slowly Rathnar lifted his head. "What shall I say, my lord?"

"Why, say this is some joke or cruel trick." Edward's laugh was now tentative. "Tell us – tell us…"

When Rathnar said nothing, the king darted a desperate look at Gideon. "You jest, do you not? Why did you make this outrageous claim?"

Gideon forced a smile. "A jest, a poor, ill-humored jest. As you did call it, your Majesty, my envy made a fool of me."

Edward looked back and forth between them, at Rathnar's quiet, dark expression and Gideon's fierce blush and fidgeting fingers. Finally his gaze rested on Rathnar's face, and his lips parted.

"A cloth and water. Someone bring me a cloth."

There was scrambling among servants, guards and courtiers; a liveried guardsman was the first to produce a handkerchief and a bowl of water. He held it up questioningly to the king.

"Wash his face," Edward said without taking his eyes off Rathnar.

Both Gideon and the guardsman swallowed hard, the former intercepting the latter. "This degradation is not necessary, my lord. I spoke in jest–"

"Stand clear. Guardsman, proceed."

Gideon stepped aside, watching, his heart in his throat, as the guard lifted a trembling hand, the handkerchief dripping water on the floor. It splashed near Rathnar's feet, turning the faded red marble crimson. When the guard faltered, clearly terrified that Rathnar would kill him then and there, Rathnar snatched the cloth from his hand and dragged it down his cheek. The white paint ran in rivets down his face; women screamed with some actually fainting, and the men bellowed. The king half stood.

"Look to the king!" someone shouted, and Lydia slumped in her chair. "The queen swoons!"

Edward pointed a finger, his arm shaking. "Arrest him!"

Rathnar did not resist, and allowed the guards to bind his wrists behind him, the streak of gold visible on the side of his face. "The Day of Reckoning is nigh," he said, and Gideon shivered.

"I will see you beheaded at dusk!"

"So be it. I will not die in vain."

Gideon threw himself on the steps of the dais. "Sire, I beg for mercy on Rathnar's behalf. Banish him or imprison him, but do not forget the many years of service, the countless number of coups and treason he has thwarted–"

"The punishment for a Selphyn to enter Salsima is beheading. I will not make an exception!"

"What if I told you – what if I said Rathnar is responsible for restoring your daughter Kassandra to you–"

Edward's face turned purple. "How dare you say her name. How dare you mock our loss."

"She is not dead! The Selphyn–"

Edward grabbed his collar, lifting him off the ground. "One more word of this, and I will see your head mounted next to his."

He dropped Gideon and pulled his heavy doublet back from his throat, as if he himself were choking. He put a hand on the arm of the throne, sweat droplets popping out on his brow, his face red. As he recovered he helped Lydia, pale and trembling, to her feet. Gideon tried to follow, chasing after their heels like one of Edward's greyhounds. Pikes crossed in front of him, denying him further access. He spun, looking for Rathnar, but the guards had taken him away. Then he was seized by Leonardis's long bony fingers, the treacherous nose just inches from his own.

"What in the name of God is going on?"

Gideon threw him off. "You think I will answer to you? You, a traitorous blackguard?"

"I heard you mention the princess. What do you know? What have you seen?"

"Everything. Get out of my way."

He ran out of the audience chamber, shoving and pushing against the flow of petitioners and courtiers. The bright sunlight outside was blinding as he desperately searched, as if he would actually see someone who could help him. Only a convergence of Kassandra with Rathnar's siblings could help him now, and he realized, with horror, that he did not know how to find any of them. Had Miranda said her parents' name, or where to find them? Had she told Rathnar while Gideon was distracted, painting himself in glorious robes that were now rent and soiled by his temper?

He ran toward his estate to collect his horse, deciding he would ride to Elkyn and make inquiries everywhere until he found her family. Even as he ran, sweat pouring into his eyes, he began to picture their faces when he confessed to what he had done, seeing clearly the reproof and recrimination shining in their eyes, their staggering disappointment but not their surprise. To them Gideon would have acted in his normal fashion, staying true to his nature. They would never believe that he attempted to rescind his words, take it all back. He was, after all, just being Gideon.

THIRTY-SIX

THEY KNEW EACH other well enough by now, having spent some eighteen days in each other's close company, to gauge and interpret each other's moods, thoughts, and expressions. For three days at the Swan she sat at his bedside, attending to his fever and his wound. She read to him from the Book of Miken he brought with him in his saddlebag, or from a book of poetry they found on the shelf. On the afternoon Jonathan's actors arrived, they sat still on the bed, almost too terrified to move or breathe loudly, lest Thomas or someone else hear them and drag them out. The casement was open, and they listened to the players recite scenes from William and Elizabeth, as Kassandra wept hearing Thomas's voice. Then there had been the days spent traveling, camping near each other under the sky or even sharing a room at various inns. They were now completely at ease with each other, and very respectful of each other's thoughts and moods. So when Jonathan sat on Zephyrine's back, watching the sun go down behind the castle, Kassandra put her hand over his. He looked at her, on her gray mare, and smiled.

"You are very conflicted about returning."

"Yes. I will have to speak to someone, answer to someone...I cannot very well leave you at the gate and make a quiet exit. And yet, before, I had imagined doing just that. 'Here is your princess. I bid you good day.' You look very like your mother, but they will be unwilling to take our word for it. We need Thaddeus to stand before the king, and acknowledge you."

"But Thaddeus is conspiring with Leonardis—"

"Yes. But you do not know Thaddeus. It is not in his nature to be dissembling and treacherous. If we can but get him alone, I know I can convince him to help us."

"How?"

He looked at her, smiling wistfully. "We shall go to the gate, and ask for him. I know not how else to do it."

Zephyrine tossed her head and he patted her neck. "I know. You feel my fear."

He thought of the last several days of enchantment, of riding this magnificent creature, sleeping next to her, talking and crooning to her. He imagined their connection as akin to that of twins. There was never any period of awkwardness as they learned to know each other; there was already such a strong foundation of intimacy that they instantly knew every twitch, sound and feeling of the other. Though he and Kassandra had developed a strong relationship, there was still no comparison between the connection he had with her, and the one he had with Zephyrine. The horse was, indeed, his twin, if only in a spiritual sense. The moment he had to part with her, which was imminent, he knew he would be a ball of anxiety. But one could not ride into a castle on horseback. Propriety would force him to stable her, as if she were some lowly creature unworthy of sharing the same space as a human being. Or Selphyn being, for that matter.

"But there is a strong chance, is there not, that Thaddeus will not hear you? That he will simply send for Leonardis and…"

"I have…a card to play. And if things do not go as I hope they will, I will play it, though it will cost me everything I have fought for. But stand assured – he will not harm you. If I play this card, he will do whatever I ask of him."

Kassandra's eyes widened. "You have knowledge of some scandalous act, perhaps?"

"No. It is far better than that. But wait and see, for you will hear all if I must go there."

He took a deep breath as the last of the light died, sinking behind the mountains. "Are you ready?"

She nodded. "Yes."

"Then let us go."

* * *

Miranda's parents, Henry and Matilda, treated her guests, particularly the pale-faced ones, with great care, as if they were exotic creatures – if they only knew! – and for the most part left them to their own devices. They were tolerant of the animals once they were convinced of their lack of ferocity, but they went out of their way to avoid them. Matilda showed them to their rooms upstairs, glancing back at them over her shoulder with wide, apprehensive eyes.

The women were to be crowded in together in one room, with Fallon and Uthen occupying their own. Lauren and her mother would share one bed; Miranda and Syldonia the other. Lauren tried to imagine what this would be like, sleeping in an ordinary house while looking across the room to see Salsima's most celebrated woman. In the forests and under the stars it had not been as surreal, for Syldonia did not stand out, being so much of nature herself.

At dinner they crowded around the Faulkner table, staying quiet while Henry and Matilda studied them. Lauren was restless and had little appetite, worrying about Rathnar and fearing another missed opportunity to find John. As the afternoon waned into early evening, Stojak grew increasingly apprehensive, first whining and then digging at the bottom of the door. Henry suggested the call of nature, but Lauren knew otherwise.

"Something is wrong with Rathnar," she told her mother as Miranda helped Matilda clear the table. Fallon, having watched Stojak intently himself, agreed.

"I will find him—"

"And get yourself arrested," Lauren said. "Stojak and I will go."

She would not hear her mother's protestations, nor would she confess that she was deeply relieved that she had an excuse to go after him. Now she could look for John, and offer Rathnar any assistance, rather than remaining there, idle and anxious, doing nothing to help.

She set off on her dun mare, Stojak trotting at the horse's heels. She realized, when Stojak took the lead, that she needn't have worried how she was going to find Rathnar. The wolf knew exactly where he was.

THIRTY-SEVEN

HIS FRANTIC SEARCHING proved fruitless. Apparently maidens with yellow hair named Miranda were not entirely uncommon in Elkyn, and while one wool merchant knew of a Miranda in Diernioch who was a player, he did not know of her belonging to any parents in Elkyn.

With only minutes remaining until dusk, Gideon rode back to Diernioch, planning to beg once more on Rathnar's behalf, or bully Leonardis into intervening. Both were unlikely to help, but there was also a chance that Kassandra had arrived during his absence, and surely, in the madness following that event, he could easily spring Rathnar free.

He leaned down close to his horse's neck, giving him full lead as the sound of hooves striking the cobblestones rang out. Merchants, carts, passersby and houses blurred in his peripheral vision, melting together until they resembled nothing but blots of colors and shadows. Smells hit his nose and then retreated just as suddenly: cinnamon, horse dung, garlic, melting steel, the contents of emptied chamber pots. His eyes stinging and watering, he closed them for a moment, aware now of the horse's muscles moving and straining underneath him and the sound of his labored breath as he lurched up the street, carrying his master's dead weight. When he opened them a trio of barefooted children ran into the street; he snatched at the reins, leaning backward. The horse slid on the cobblestones before his legs began scrambling for purchase. By some miracle he maintained his balance, and once the urchins were safely out of the way, Gideon sharply kicked his belly to get him back up to speed. They darted in between playhouses and bear pits, hearing the muffled roar of the poor beasts as they fought off dogs. And all the while the sun was dipping, extinguishing the light like soft breath on a lighted candlewick.

At the gates he slid off before the horse was completely stopped, leaving him there, panting and wheezing, for the groomsmen. Ignoring the greetings of the sentries, he ran, feeling as though he were in that all-too familiar dream where he was trying to run or fight but lacking the strength, trapped in slow motion. Then he was shoving through the enormous crowd, the bloodthirsty people eager to bring down the man who owed his success to intimidation.

Peddlers sold them concessions, as if they were in the playhouse, and children were perched on their parents' shoulders to avoid missing any blood.

He fought his way to the dais just as they were bringing Rathnar out. Somehow his hair was reverted to its natural color; it hung loosely past his shoulders, as soft and golden as a maiden's. He was wearing crimson silk, shockingly thin and immodest as his torso was clothed only in a vest, his chest and stomach bare, as were his feet below the tapered ankles of the billowing trousers. His wound was stripped of dressing, swollen and black, its rawness a silent herald of recrimination of Gideon's betrayal. Gasps and cries rippled through the crowd as the tiger stood before them in all of his natural glory, free from any disguise. His head was half turned, and Gideon saw his eyes outlined in black kohl. He was a completely altered creature, a beautiful, almost angelic thing whose height now leant him a certain grace rather than awkwardness.

"What is this?" the king bellowed, and the crowd fell silent. "What are these weeds?"

"Prisoner's last request, sire," a guard said. "Chancellor Thaddeus granted permission."

The chancellor in question was standing behind the king's throne, dressed in emerald robes. "He wished to die with the dignity of his custom, your Majesty. For his many years of loyal service, I felt it well to grant his request."

Whatever the king's response was, it was drowned out by the crowd's cheers upon the entrance of the executioner, who was hooded and masked, his axe gleaming in the torchlight. Gideon glanced at Thaddeus; the king's brother caught his eye and slowly shook his head, warning him to stay silent. He pushed through the crowd to reach the executioner. His fingers shook as he fumbled with his purse, finally managing to untie it while the executioner waited. He slammed it against the hairy, bare chest, and it was so quiet that everyone must have heard the coins inside clinking together.

"Do it in one stroke, I pray you. I'll have none of your three sloppy attempts as with Lady Jane. If it takes more than one, I will kill you myself."

The executioner tossed the purse and caught it, smiling. Three of his front teeth were missing. "That scrawny neck will give me no trouble."

Gideon narrowed his eyes. "Lady Jane gave you enough trouble, and she was but a slip of a girl."

"I'll have him straight. Let me through."

He turned to face Rathnar. The Selphyn's eyes were clear, a dark, vivid blue that all but glowed without the stark white paint framing them.

"Forgive me. I did not – I did not know–"

Rathnar leaned forward, his voice low in Gideon's ear. "Grant me but one request, and all is forgiven."

"Name it, and it is done."

"There is money in my chambers, inside a wolf statue. Find it, before they come ransacking. Give it to Lauren, and bid her care for herself and Stojak."

"I—"

"If you do not, I will return to this earth as some hideous viper coiled in your boot, your doublet."

"I swear I will."

"Tell her I love her. Tell her…I am sorry about John, that I could not tell her the truth about him. But I thought it best…she will know. Just tell her I am sorry."

"I do not understand."

"No matter."

"Enough of this whispering!" the king shouted. Someone pulled Gideon back. His throat constricted as the king ordered the executioner to proceed.

Rathnar knelt before a wooden block, his hands bound behind his back. His hair fell forward, eclipsing his face. Gideon turned before he would have to see him lay his head down on the block. He heard nothing but the roaring of blood behind his ears.

"STOP!"

He threw his head up, incredulous. The executioner's axe, raised and poised in the air, froze. Rathnar, his face down and facing the audience, opened one eye. The crowd parted to make room for Lauren as she ran, hair flying and tears streaking her face. Gideon stumbled backwards to give her room as she fell to her knees, lifting Rathnar's face into her hands. She stroked his hair, his face.

"You are so beautiful. I love you," she said, and pulled his head forward, kissing him. The pain in Gideon's throat was almost unbearable as his vision blurred. A guard grabbed her arms just above the elbows, yanking her to her feet so that she tripped backwards. By chance she fell into Gideon's arms. As the executioner tilted back his axe, Gideon instinctively threw his arm around her head, pressing her face against his chest to shield her. There was a whoosh, the sound the crossbow bolt made just before it hit Rathnar on the ship, and Gideon squeezed his eyes shut. He heard the terrible noise of crunching bone and the axe blade hitting the block, and squeezed Lauren as she dug her nails into his stomach, yelping.

In the instant before the crowd erupted into cheers and applause, the air filled with the horrible, wrenching sound of a wolf howl so piteous and anguished it were as though the wolf's heart was being ripped from its body. Lauren stiffened in his arms.

"Lauren—"

She pushed back from him, her face soaked with tears. "Do not speak to me."

"Please. I tried—"

"I know you did this. I *know* you did. And after he saved your life."

She ran from him when he tried to catch her wrist, and then was swallowed up by the crowd. Remembering his promise to Rathnar, he fought through the people cheering, each one of whom he wanted to pound in the face.

He found the wolf statue easily enough in the Selphyn's chambers. Made out of thin plaster and painted black, it broke with one pound of his fist and an eruption of gold coins flowed out. As he pocketed the vast multitude of coins into his doublet, his eyes lighted on the strip of wolf fur on the pillow and his eyes flooded. The door swung open.

"I would have some conference with you in my chambers," Thaddeus said.

Gideon angrily wiped his eyes. "I have nothing to say to you."

"Oh, but I think you do. And I think you would rather say it to me than my brother Leonardis, yes?"

Clearing his throat, Gideon swallowed. "Please. Please, just leave me be."

"You will come to my chambers now. Or I will have you arrested on suspicion of treason. And it will not take much to convince their Majesties, will it?"

Gideon slowly rose to his feet. At the threshold of the door he raised his eyes and met Thaddeus's gaze just as there was another anguished howl outside. Gideon shuddered. "Lead on."

THIRTY-EIGHT

AFTER THE SECOND terrible wolf howl that spooked the horses, Jonathan and Kassandra stood at the gates, watching with amazement the crowds of people pouring out from the castle. The guard who was questioning them paused to watch, and Jonathan said, "What is happening?"

The guard stared at him as if he had sprouted another head. "Have you not heard? Sir Francis Rathnar was just executed."

Jonathan went cold. "What?"

"He was a Selphyn. Does that not just beat all? The queen's spymaster? A Selphyn?"

The guard laughed, and Kassandra pushed into Jonathan's arms, burying her face against his shoulder. He realized then that while she had never met Rathnar, she would be grieving for Fallon's sake. He stroked her hair while the guard's smile dropped.

"What business have you then, if not to see the execution?"

"I have business with Chancellor Thaddeus."

"That so, eh?"

"Yes. Please tell him John Warden is here. With a lady. He will know."

A groom appeared at his side and reached for Zephyrine's reins, the reins he reluctantly fastened on her to avoid unwanted attention. She threw her head and reared, neighing. Jonathan calmed her with some soothing words as his stomach filled with dread. The moment had come where he would have to part from her, leave her in some stranger's care, lock her up.

"She will allow none but I to lead her," he told the guard, and grabbed the reins of Kassandra's horse as well. "Stay but a moment. I will return."

He pulled the horses to the stables, and as he entered, every horse inside threw its head over the stall door to peer at him. He felt them with a curious shiver just under his skin, like the prickling of a memory just beginning to emerge. They tossed their heads and whinnied at him as Zephyrine answered. They strained to get at him as he led each horse to a stall, lingering a moment with Zephyrine to pat her neck. She pushed her nose against his cheek.

"Just for awhile. I will not abandon you."

He just closed the stall door and threw the bolt into place when a cloaked figure swept into his path. He threw back his hood, and in the dim torchlight Jonathan recognized Thomas.

"I thought I might see you here," Jonathan said, his voice tired.

"The others wanted to come. They are eager for your blood, you see. But I bade them remain so that I may talk sense to you, if you would but hear it."

"Save your breath. There is naught you can say—"

"I will not let you bring her in. I cannot."

"And I have heard this before. Stand aside."

Thomas put his hands on Jonathan's shoulders. "I say you will not—"

Jonathan threw off his hands and shoved him backwards. The wound in his side screamed. "I have had enough of you!" He stormed past him, nearly knocked off his feet when Thomas lunged for him, catching his arm to swing him around.

"Why do you do this? If not for Miranda, why?"

Jonathan closed his eyes. "If this be the only way to silence you, then so bet it. I do it so that I will not have to take the throne."

Thomas's laugh was like a fox's bark. "Not this sorry business of you being the king's bastard."

"No. I am not the king's bastard."

"So say I! You are not even John Warden."

Jonathan threw him a look. "What?"

"I say you are not John Warden! Everything you told me is a lie. Every—"

"How know you this?"

"It little matters. Now what foolish story will you contrive?"

Jonathan straightened. "If I do not see Kassandra rightfully home, I am, next to his brothers, the king's closest heir, and only logical choice for the throne. And I will have none of it."

The two men stared at each other as the horses restlessly pawed the ground and snorted. Jonathan let their familiar, soothing smell wash over him, and his trembling subsided. Thomas's face was slack.

"What...what are you suggesting?"

"Understand it in what sense you will. I have no time for you."

He brushed past his friend who, this time, made no effort to stop him. By the time he rejoined Kassandra, the guard had returned.

"Chancellor Thaddeus said he will see you in his chambers."

Jonathan looked at Kassandra. "Shall we?"

She nodded, sniffling. He took her arm, and led Salsima's princess home.

* * *

Thomas watched them go, his arms hanging limply at his sides. His mind felt thick and foggy, as if in sleep, and he felt he must be dreaming indeed when he saw the woman walking toward him, the black wolf at her side.

They came out of the darkness, she in her black cloak and the wolf with his yellow eyes shining. Thomas thought of the terrible howling he heard some moments ago, and thought he now knew the source of it. The woman was having trouble walking. She lurched and staggered, as though drunk, and each time she faltered, the wolf stopped and waited for her to regain her balance. Once she dropped to her knees, and the wolf lay down in front of her. She encircled him with her arms, sobbing into the fur. Thomas's mouth dropped open.

He took a step forward. The wolf lifted his head, and uttered a low growl that turned into a snarl, teeth showing, as Thomas approached. The woman lifted her head, wiping her nose.

"May I – may I offer some assistance?" Thomas asked, keeping a wary eye on the wolf.

"No. I do not think…"

Thomas took another step. The wolf looked at his mistress, as if gauging her reaction to the stranger before deciding whether or not he was going to rip out Thomas's throat. "I cannot, in good conscience, leave you to your misery. May I take you somewhere? Find someone for you?"

"If you can take me to John Warden, by all means do. Otherwise, there is none whom I seek."

Thomas froze. "J-John–"

She threw her head up. "Do you know him?"

He tread carefully. "Do you mean the playwright who oft goes by the name Jonathan Wilder?"

"Yes! That is he. Do you know where he is?"

"Yes. He was here moments ago; he is now in the castle."

She jumped to her feet, agitating the wolf who was following her every move anxiously. "What! How can – oh, God–"

"If we but wait a little, he may emerge again."

She dropped her head. "I have waited this long. A few minutes more will not make much difference."

She stood next to Thomas, her dark hair falling in disheveled clumps around her shoulders. The wolf sat on her feet. Thomas stared at them, wondering if the night could possibly get any stranger.

THIRTY-NINE

JONATHAN LED KASSANDRA down the dimly lit corridor, chilled in spite of the warm summer night. As he walked he was flooded with memories of galloping his wooden horses down the stone hall, pushing Lauren in a poorly constructed wagon of his own design, mock swordfights with his mother. He could almost hear the echoes of three children long gone, and felt their loss weigh on him heavily. Kassandra, ever observant, squeezed his hand.

They were admitted once again into Thaddeus's antechamber, the walls lined with dark wood and shelves. Though he had visited this room since his childhood, on the day that Thaddeus questioned him following his disastrous outburst in court after *The King of Salsima*, he was calmer now and took in the room's effects with a much more grounded attention. Much was the same since he graced the room as a child: the same mahogany desk sat at the far end, along with the same plush armchairs that were a hideous orange color. The one nearest the door still had a gaping hole revealing stuffing; Jonathan himself had rent that material with a dagger. His gaze thus engaged, he could not help but notice the gentleman occupying that seat, who was definitely not Thaddeus.

The king's chancellor was standing with his back to the door; he turned when they entered and stared at them. The guard closed the door behind them, at which point Thaddeus let loose a loud breath.

"You brought her. You brought her here. Are you such a fool? I believe your directive on this matter was quite clear. She is beautiful. Perhaps you've fallen in love. You are but passion's fool."

Jonathan shot a look at the man sitting near him. "Ought we not to have this conversation in private?"

"This man knows everything. He may remain. You ought to know him."

Jonathan studied the man, the blond hair, green eyes. He recognized him as the man who jeered at him in court. The gentleman regarded him with a tired expression, his chin resting on his hand.

"I think I have something that belongs to you," Jonathan said, pulling off the signet ring. Gideon Ambrose slipped it on without looking at it. Then he stood and abruptly backhanded Jonathan across the mouth, so that the ring in question with its miniature heron tore at his lip. He touched it and winced, his fingers coming away bloody.

"That is for assuming my identity," Gideon said.

"I suppose I had it coming."

Gideon raised an eyebrow, clearly surprised. The small bit of effort he displayed seemed to exhaust him, and his shoulders fell as he slumped back into the chair. Kassandra had his attention now. He drank her in, as did Thaddeus. Jonathan waited while they made their study.

"What do you expect me to do?" Thaddeus said. "You cannot expect me to allow her to remain."

"But I expect just that," Jonathan said. "We were wrong about them."

Thaddeus laughed. "Oh, that is rich. And coming from you! When you were there. You saw him slay your mother just as I saw him slay my wife. And you say we are wrong."

"I do not condone what he did. But I understand it now. I think."

"What evil potion did they slip into your wine?"

"Nothing but a good dose of reality." Jonathan took a breath. "Will you help her? Help me? Will you see her rightfully restored to her parents?"

Thaddeus stared at Kassandra as he answered. "You know I cannot do that."

"Will you do it for me? An old friend?"

Thaddeus's gaze swiveled in his direction. "That was some time ago. You were but a lad. I think you know our ties were never that strong."

"Then will you do it for your son?"

Thaddeus's face went dark, and his chin trembled, no doubt with restrained obscenities. "Get out. Leave her here for Leonardis to deal with, but get you gone. I will not look on you, nor think on you, ever again."

Jonathan reached back and pulled the ribbon free that held back his hair. It fell forward, a golden cascade that no doubt revealed Zephyrine's mane hair that was braided in it. The small torches on the walls threw shadows over Thaddeus's face, tricking Jonathan into believing his expression changed. He took a step forward and Thaddeus actually hissed.

"What mean you by this? Mean you to mock me with my son's death, by revealing your close resemblance to him? I should rent those looks with my sword."

"Look at me. *Look.* And tell me I am not your son."

Gideon gasped sharply, and Kassandra's hand, still in his, tightened. There was a long stretch of silence.

"I – I saw…I saw the body."

"You saw a body disfigured by the plague. When I finally came back for him, back for John, he was already dressed in my clothes." Jonathan smiled ruefully. "Belike he knew and made it easy for me, so as not to catch the contagion. When I saw him lying there, hair like mine, of my same stature…I saw that I could take his life, and he could have mine. I took his name, though I was advised wisely not to use it. And I was free. Free from the throne filled with incest and brutality. Free from a name I despised."

Thaddeus shook his head. "You mean to manipulate me. This is but some trick…"

Jonathan's tongue darted out to stop the trickle of blood from his lip. "Ask me something then. A question only your son would know."

Thaddeus face flooded suddenly with hope. "Do you bear a scar, on your left hand at the knuckle–"

Jonathan thrust his hand forward before Thaddeus could even finish the question. In the weak light the tiny crescent scar was visible on the knuckle of his index finger. "From the knife I used to carve my mother a necklace for her birthday."

Thaddeus stumbled forward, putting both hands on Jonathan's cheeks. "You have her eyes, her cheekbones…yes. My God, dare I hope? You are – you are my son–"

He crushed Jonathan in his embrace, his tears falling into Jonathan's hair as his entire body heaved with wracking sobs. Jonathan hesitated before returning the embrace, releasing, at last, his resistance and going limp in his father's arms. He closed his eyes to allow his father's storm of tears to rage uninterrupted, and kept them closed as his father rained kisses upon his brow. "Edward, Edward. Oh, God. Why did you not tell me? I lived in grief, such a terrible, wrenching grief…"

"I blamed you. For a long time I blamed you for never interfering. I know he is the king, but you never once stood up to him to defend her." Jonathan pulled away and wiped away his own tears. "But that is past now. I understand. I – I forgive you."

This only provoked a fresh onslaught of tears and blubbering apologies. Jonathan stroked his father's bent head, marveling at the multitude of gray hair that was now present. A movement caught his eye and he turned just in time to see Gideon kneeling at his feet. He started, having forgotten all about the courtier, and broke from his father's embrace.

"Thrice welcome, Prince of Salsima."

"Oh, do get up. Do not call me that. I – please, I beg you."

Gideon straightened, his eyes glassy. He pointed with a trembling hand at Jonathan's mouth. "You will – you will forgive – Oh, God, I have struck a prince–"

Jonathan waved his hand dismissively. "I said I had it coming. Prince or no."

Kassandra was beaming at him, her face streaked with tears. "Cousins! Why so we are." She threw her arms around him; he caught her with a groan as the air was knocked out of him.

"Yes, cousins," he said, "and I love mine well."

Thaddeus moved in, his arms outstretched as if to encircle them both, when the arras, bearing the Boussard crest of the black falcon, was thrown aside. Leonardis, dabbing his eyes, sighed dramatically. Jonathan stepped in front of Kassandra protectively.

"I am ecstatic to have my nephew restored to me. I truly am. But very sorry indeed to have it so under these circumstances."

Thaddeus's face crumpled. "Forgive me, my son – in the joy of our reunion, I did forget me that Leonardis was there to overhear our conference."

"Just as well," Jonathan said. "Now he understands why – why Kassandra must stand heir to the king."

"So that you may skirt your responsibility?" Leonardis tsked. "That is a poor reason. I am afraid I must detain you two for questioning–"

Father and son had the same thought simultaneously. Thaddeus threw his generous girth against his scarecrow of a brother who stood not a chance. He was flattened against the wall while Jonathan snatched Kassandra's hand. As Leonardis shouted, albeit strangled, for the guards, Jonathan threw open a panel next to the fireplace and pulled Kassandra in with him. Meant to be a secret from small, prying eyes, young Jonathan had nevertheless found this hidden chamber, constructed as a passageway between Thaddeus's chamber and Syldonia's as a way for her to escape the king.

It was dark and filled with cobwebs; Jonathan, in front, ran blindly, swinging at invisible webs that covered his face. Kassandra yelped and stumbled against him. "It crawled on me!"

"And me. Here. We are here."

It was dark in Syldonia's boudoir, but not so much that Jonathan could not see how it had been enshrined, meticulously cared for. Her pink chair was pulled back from the vanity table covered with brushes and clips, as if waiting for her to retake her seat at any moment. He would have loved to take up the seashells on our bureau and finger them lovingly, but there was no time. When they burst out of the chamber, the guards were at the far end of the hall, barging into Thaddeus's chamber. One saw them and yelled.

Kassandra hiked up her skirts into one hand and kicked off her shoes. Jonathan took her free hand and ran as fast as she could keep up down stone corridors, relieved his memory served him as well as it did. Soon they would find an exit with a direct route to the stables. He felt Zephyrine's alarm at his fear, which only compounded it, but her agitation lent him strength. He could almost imagine that he was back in her body, racing in the moonlight.

Outside they ran, first over dew-dropped grass and then sharp pebbles, evidenced by Kassandra's cries from her bare feet. Jonathan's lungs were on fire, and the pain in his newly healed side was flaring with a blinding intensity. Yet the stables seemed still so far away. He thought he could see two figures standing in the moonlight; one of them appeared to have a wolf as a companion. The other figure trotted forward, and Jonathan recognized Thomas's posturing.

"My horse!" he shouted, allowing a fleeting sense of relief when Thomas darted into the stables. He could hear the guards yelling for more guards; soon they would be overcome. By the time they ran into the stable, Zephyrine was free, rearing up and throwing her hooves. As she came crashing down, dangerously close to Thomas who had to leap out of the way, Jonathan swung up onto her back. Thomas pushed Kassandra on behind him.

"Where will you go?"

"The cathedral," Jonathan said, grabbing a fistful of Zephyrine's mane just as she lowered her head and charged out the door.

"Godspeed!" Thomas yelled, and the other figure, the one with the wolf, was almost trampled as she tried to step into the horse's path.

"Wait!" the woman called, but Jonathan was certainly not going to stop now.

He gave Zephyrine full rein down Diernioch's cobblestone streets, and, leaning forward, closed his eyes, and linked his mind with hers. It was dangerous, leaving his body precariously balanced and unattended, but enough of his mind remained to keep his fingers firmly locked in her mane. Now he could direct her with his own thoughts, galloping down the proper streets and dodging flower stalls and the like. He could hear the pursuit of guards behind them as their horses' hooves struck the stones, and his sense of smell was acute, overwhelming him with the pungent aromas all around.

He dove back into his own body once they reached the stairs of the cathedral, just in time for him to jump down and run to the door, pounding on it when it proved locked. Kassandra slid down and joined him, glancing anxiously back as he slammed the heavy iron knocker again and again. He heard the rattle of keys and turned to Zephyrine.

"Run! I will find you later."

The mare launched into a full gallop, and only when she had disappeared around the corner did Jonathan heave a sigh of relief. Then the cathedral door opened, and an elderly monk stared at him.

"Sanctuary, please."

"Of course, my son, all are welcome—"

Jonathan shoved him backwards to allow himself and Kassandra room to enter. Then he slammed the door shut and snatched the monk's keys from him to lock the door. Rich incense filled his nostrils, and the vast, arched and domed cathedral was alight with hundreds of candles. St. Miken stood on the altar, carved from stone, his wings stretched as if in midflight.

"Patience, dear boy," the monk said, and Jonathan got a good look at him.

"Brother Dominick?"

"Do I know you?"

"Listen, I beg you. Many years ago you provided sanctuary to two boys and unlocked the trapdoor to allow them to hide—"

"No, no. Never again. A boy died down there. I will never—"

"Brother, the king's men are after us. His own brother — they will not heed sanctuary here."

"They must. This is God's house."

"And some of these are godless men. Please. Let us down there. Just for one night. I beg you."

Three minutes later Jonathan led Kassandra down a narrow, spiral set of stairs into a dark, vast chamber that reeked of must and decay. Their torches revealed the ruined Selphyn temple: broken angel statues, cracked arches, crumbling pillars. A beheaded statue of Miken lay on its side, the head larger than Zephyrine as it stared at them with sightless stone eyes. Here were more spider webs, and a scurrying sound revealed rats. Kassandra clung to his arm.

"Well. And did I not promise you conditions fit for a princess?"

After a moment she smiled and then laughed. They heard voices up above and each shivered. Jonathan strained to hear but could make nothing out through the stone ceiling that was the floor of the church above them. The trapdoor swung open, and Kassandra threw her arms around Jonathan, burying her head against his chest.

"This yonder fellow swears you will see him. He too knows of the secret chamber—"

"Thomas?" Jonathan called, closing his eyes when he heard Thomas's voice answer back. "Thank God. Yes, Brother, it is all right. Send him down. Let no one else, I beg you."

As Thomas climbed down the stairs, Jonathan blinked with astonishment. The woman, and her wolf, climbed down behind him, each person carrying a torch. As Thomas approached, the woman rather rudely pushed him aside, and advanced on Jonathan as if she meant to kill him. She inspected him by torchlight, her eyes scanning every inch of his face. Her frown deepened.

"You are not my brother."

Now he took in her fine, dark hair, her brown eyes and rather lovely mouth. "Lauren?"

Her eyes widened. "John? Is it you? You do not…you do not seem yourself."

"Oh, God, have you followed me only to – oh, Lauren. I am so sorry. John is dead."

The torch in her hand shook. "No. I will not accept this. Not after – no. I refuse."

"I am sorry, indeed, but–"

Thomas appeared next to them, smiling, his hands grabbing hold of Lauren's elbows. "Lauren. Oh, it is – it *is* you. Lauren! It is I – it's John!"

She gaped at him before her mouth erupted into a huge grin. "It *is* you! Oh, John!"

"My sister! You are she."

They thrust their torches into Jonathan and Kassandra's free hands in order to throw their arms around each other, reenacting Jonathan's recent encounter with Thaddeus as they sobbed and rocked back and forth in each other arms. Jonathan watched them, his mouth hanging open. Finally he could stand it no longer, and after he and Kassandra found holders for the torches, he parted the two figures caught in a tight embrace.

"Wait, wait. John? You? You cannot be. I saw the body—"

"It was not I!" Thomas said, still beaming. "I grew fearful when you did not come. I banged on the door and the monk released me. I searched for you, in vain, and when I returned, there you were – or so I thought! – lying there dead of the plague."

"But if that was not you—"

Thomas shrugged. "I know not then. A beggar boy perhaps, or a thief also seeking sanctuary? He found your fine, rich clothes and put them on…"

"And died, poor thing."

"And yet," Thomas said, laughing, "I would not have it any other way."

Jonathan tried to pick them both up but the pain in his side prevented him. Instead he threw his arms around Thomas. "My wonderful friend John." Then he hugged Lauren, who was looking very confused. "And my wonderful friend Lauren! How glad I am to find you both!" He turned back to Thomas, laughing. "Though I had you with me long enough, and never knew. How came you by this dark hair and eyes?"

"They both changed colors the year my voice did. But look at the amazement on my sister's face. She knows not who you are."

"Though I may guess," Lauren said. "Prince Edward? Back from the dead?"

He shook her hand. His face was close to splitting he was smiling so wide. "I am he. Very glad to meet you. Oh, and here, you must meet my cousin, Kassandra, another ghost back from the grave." A thought occurred to him and he whirled on Thomas. "You know, of course, what this all sounds like?"

Thomas made a sour face. "Egad, *Two Brothers of Elkyn!* I always mocked it for its idiocy." He sighed, quite happy. "Now if our mothers could just resurrect, all would be well."

Lauren's eyes lit up, and she actually hopped in place. "Oh, my goodness. Wait until you hear my news!"

FORTY

THOMAS WANTED TO go to Elkyn immediately and bring them back to the cathedral, but after surveying the situation he reported what Jonathan already knew, that the soldiers were waiting for them outside.

"They will have to leave when mass starts tomorrow," Jonathan said, "and you can slip out then." He was horribly jealous that Thomas would see his mother first, but there was no way he or Kassandra could leave with all of Diernioch looking for them by now. "And when they report back to Leonardis, he will come here himself and force his way in, sanctuary be damned. You will have to move quickly."

After making their plans they stayed up most of the night talking. Lauren told them about her adventures with Gideon and Rathnar, concluding with the evening's terrible events that orphaned Stojak. What she left unsaid was plain enough in her eyes, and while Jonathan tried to focus on her loss, he could not stop thinking about his mother being alive, and Miranda with her, only minutes away. It was almost too much to bear, knowing both of them were so close but out of reach. It was unanimously concluded that Syldonia knew Jonathan was really Edward, after she sent her dolphin Myra after the ship to help him.

"It explains why she was so wonderfully happy," Lauren said, "and insisted on accompanying us. And no one – no one wanted to tell me you were not John."

"I am glad they did not," Thomas said. "You may not have come otherwise."

She hugged him for the twentieth time. Over her shoulder Thomas exchanged a look with Kassandra that Jonathan caught. The two of them had said little to each other, but the tension between them was almost palpable. Jonathan wondered what would happen if he and Lauren made themselves scarce.

Displaced again from his mistress's lap, Stojak waited until Lauren was sitting again before putting his head back in her lap. Jonathan hoped Zartha, still in the saddlebag on Zephyrine's back, was all right. He knew the horse was, having dropped in on her thoughts several times since he sent her running off into the dark. She was in the Priory stable, visiting the horses in their stalls.

When it was Jonathan's turn to speak, he started with Zephyrine, describing in detail the ritual that connected them. He could not describe their bond, but when he tried, Lauren's eyes filled with tears and she stroked Stojak behind the ears. He almost could not bear to look at Stojak, not wanting to dwell on how devastated the wolf must be after losing his connection to Rathnar. Losing Zephyrine, or vice-versa, was not something he could even contemplate.

Lauren listened with stark envy as Jonathan and Thomas entertained her with stories from their years together in theater. Apparently each of them had the same idea, of finding sanctuary within a company of players following the "deaths" of their mothers. Only Lauren could not because of her gender, and Thomas started late after first falling into the convenient trap of drink.

"Had you not approached me that night," he told Jonathan, "I never would have found the strength to join on my own."

They talked until they were hoarse, and then made rough pillows out of their cloaks and doublets. The floor was unforgiving – cold and hard – and Jonathan did not think he would ever actually fall asleep. As the last light of the torches died out, he heard and then saw Lauren sobbing next to a fallen pillar, her face buried in Stojak's fur. The wolf was licking her hand, over and over, softly whining.

He turned his face away, unable to watch them. Remembering he would be seeing his mother in a few short hours, he closed his eyes and fell asleep after all while trying to remember exactly what she looked like.

He was awakened at dawn by the loud ringing of bells. When he opened his eyes and sat up, groaning with the shooting pain in his side, he could barely hear the bells through the thick ceiling. He realized he must have joined minds again with Zephyrine in his sleep, and it had been through her ears that he heard the bells that awakened him.

He dozed off again until he heard the muffled singing from the choir announcing the beginning of mass. He awakened Thomas, who grouched and shrugged his hand off. Jonathan said, "Go get our mothers!" and Thomas was instantly awake, grinning. Jonathan watched him climb up the stairs with Lauren and Stojak in tow, smiling when he thought of the parishioners seeing two people and a wolf come out of the floor in the middle of the cathedral.

They were no sooner gone than the trapdoor reopened, revealing a pair of doeskin boots dyed green. Jonathan straightened and went for his sword, relaxing when he recognized Gideon coming down the stairs.

Upon reaching the landing he started to kneel; Jonathan caught him.

"You need make no show of obeisance to me. No one else must know it is I."

Gideon ran a hand through his hair. He looked terrible. "I was hoping to find Lauren."

"She and her brother sent for the others in Elkyn."

"Her brother?"

Jonathan sighed and settled down to tell Gideon the whole long story. When he finished Gideon simply looked exhausted rather than amazed. "I have some atonement to do."

Jonathan could barely stand to look at him when he was done explaining his part in Rathnar's death. The uncle he had barely known, in his intimidating guise as Sir Francis, would now never be made real to him. And he could never assure him he bore him no ill will in his failure to collect the children following their mothers' feigned murder.

"I hope you will allow me to help you and Kassandra both," Gideon said. "Though my motivation has changed, I still want to see her on the throne. And I want Leonardis to fail."

Jonathan accepted his offer, and in his growing agitation, he withdrew from conversation and stared impatiently at the closed trapdoor. When mass was over he began pacing, knowing it was now a race between his friends and family and Leonardis. When the door finally opened he held his breath, his heart pounding. Then he saw the pair of green shoes hurrying down the stairs, and the hem of a sparkling gown.

So he wouldn't knock them both down the stairs, he waited at the bottom while his mother hurried down. She leaped off the bottom step and landed in his arms; he squeezed her until neither of them could breathe. When he lowered her she grabbed his face and stared at him, while he took in her ageless one, relieved to see she was free of the white paint Lauren warned him of.

"My God," he said, his chest constricting. "You have not aged. You are as beautiful as ever."

"And you – oh–" She could not finish and hugged him again. Over his shoulder he saw the procession slowly descending: Fallon, Uthen (carrying Belcastro), Thomas, Anne, Lauren and Stojak. The last to descend was Miranda.

She kept a polite distance while Jonathan and his mother wept and embraced, exchanging apologies and forgiveness. Finally he could no longer stand it, and squeezed his mother's hand.

"Wait but a little. There is another whom I must embrace."

Miranda met him halfway, and while she made as though to throw herself into his waiting arms, she caught herself and fell to her knees instead.

"Your Highness—"

He yanked her to her feet. "You will never, *ever* kneel before me. I am not your master, for you shall forever be mistress of me."

She threw her arms around his neck and kissed him fiercely in spite of the group of onlookers. Thomas held his mother's hand and had his free arm around Lauren's shoulders, all of them watching with tearful smiles. The three animals -- Belcastro, Stojak, and Zartha, freed from Jonathan's saddlebag -- frolicked at their feet, energized by the excitement. Jonathan no sooner parted from Miranda than he was swept up in yet another embrace.

"Edward," Fallon said, kissing his brow. "Dear nephew, how glad I am to call you so."

"Uncle, I found her," Jonathan said. "The horse – I found Zephyrine."

"John and Lauren told us all. I could not be more thrilled for you."

They hugged again. "I loved you well enough before," Fallon said into his ear, "and now that I know it is you...my love knows no bounds, and could not be greater were you my own son."

"Will you make me weep yet again? Though I will confess to you how relieved I am to lavish all my goodwill and love on you without restraint. How glad I am to have no reason to withhold it any longer, bursting from me as it was anyway against my will. But now, I shall swoon from all of this wonderful emotion. I cannot hear tale of one more shred of good news."

"Would that your Uncle Rathnar were here," Fallon said, and Jonathan released him.

"I am so sorry."

Fallon shook his head. "We will pay him proper homage when the time is right. But now, I would not spoil your reunion with your mother."

Jonathan spun the mother in question in a circle while she clung to him. "My mother! I shall never tire of saying the word. My God, I cannot believe it, though I was told and can see you with my own eyes." He laughed. "I will be the envy of all of Salsima – the beautiful, exalted Syldonia is my mother. Mother, you must tell me all. I will hear everything!"

She kissed his cheek. "As will I of you! But first I must introduce you to someone very special to me, though you know him as the captain of *Transcendence*. Know him now as your mother's companion."

Uthen cleared his throat and bowed. When he straightened, Jonathan saw the look that passed between him and his mother.

"Well met, Uthen," Jonathan said, shaking his hand. "There is no one more worthy to whom I would see my mother…betrothed? Contracted? What say you?"

"Companioned," Uthen said, "though there exists no word worthy of our love."

They then explained how they had been in love since before Syldonia wed Thaddeus. Jonathan was genuinely glad for them, and had a sudden, wild desire to be the product of their union, rather than the forced one between her and Thaddeus. The thought gave birth to another, and after Fallon embraced Kassandra, inquiring over her health, Jonathan grabbed his uncle by his forearms.

"Uncle. I am ready to give myself over to my Selphyn blood. I wish to return to Rowan with all of you, and, if Miranda will consent to accompany me, raise a family with your blessing. Start a theater company. There is naught to impede me now. All resistance, with the return of my mother, has vanished. I renounce my human blood with abandon."

The silence fell over them, and though it made no sound, Jonathan's ears ached as if standing in the midst of an explosion. The smile on Fallon's face froze and then slowly dropped, forming a tight line. Jonathan surveyed the faces of the others, and saw the same look of tension mirrored in his mother, Thomas and Miranda. When Miranda's eyes dropped, he gave Fallon a demanding look.

Fallon reached up and put his thumbs on Jonathan's temples, his fingers in his nephew's hair. "My heart rejoices to hear this declaration. But, dearest Edward, you are a peer of land. You have a responsibility—"

Jonathan jerked out of his hold. "No. I will not hear this from you. Not *you*. Not after your lectures of enslavement and bondage. For you know if I assume the throne I will be so enslaved. Kassandra is here – it is she who—"

"Edward. Your return is like a gift from Miken. The people will be skeptical, perhaps even hateful, when Kassandra takes the throne because of her upbringing. If you marry her—"

"No. No, no, no. I love Miranda. It will be she I marry, she alone. You cannot ask me – you cannot expect me—"

He broke off when a painful lump in his throat surfaced. He threw a glance at his mother and saw the same look of pity. "God, Mother, not you too." He fought back the tears, mortified at his weakness.

"I am not asking you renounce your Selphyn heritage," Fallon said, "but to disguise it for a year or two until—"

"A year or two!"

"And then release it gradually, after the people—"

"And what of Zephyrine? Must I hide her too, and my love for her?"

Fallon's jaw tensed. "For now, she must just be a horse."

Jonathan's head snapped back and forth in rapid succession. He felt, for an awful moment, that he was again ten years old. "You made me this way! You cannot expect me now to renounce…you *made* me this way."

"And rejoiced in your transformation when I thought you Gideon. But now you are Edward, and you bear a responsibility—"

He grabbed Miranda's hand, squeezing hard. Her eyes were bloodshot. "What say you, Miranda? You will simply relinquish me? Forfeit our love?"

"I am but one voice. My needs cannot compare with those of Salsima. If I must give you up I shall, but will love you always."

"Will no one fight…fight for me? Can no one see how…" He wanted to say, *How much this will destroy me*, but felt he had already degraded himself enough with his emotional outburst. Gideon took a step forward; he saw in the courtier's face that he meant to pledge his loyalty. Jonathan shook his head and Gideon nodded. There was no point in Gideon promising what was not in his power to give.

He sat on a broken pillar, drained, holding his head in his hands. His mother sat next to him, his hand in hers. The others gave them space, breaking off into small groups to talk. Jonathan saw Gideon take Lauren aside before dropping his gaze back to the floor.

"I once felt as you did. I was wildly in love with one man, but given to another in marriage. I felt it my duty, in hopes it might bring peace between our people."

"And you see how well *that* transpired."

"But with you, it will be different. The entire country deeply mourned the loss of their prince and princess. To have to both back again…"

"I am half-Selphyn. Why should I reassure them?"

"You were raised as a human, while Kassandra was not. Together the two of you balance each other."

"But there is more…" Jonathan said. "You do not know what it is like for an actor to renounce the stage. You ask me to give up everything that is dear to me: the theater, Zephyrine, Miranda. It is too much, what you ask. My heart will break."

"But I will be here to help you, and Fallon. Someday, thanks to your guidance, the people of Salsima may tolerate our return. Please, Edward. I would not ask if I did not think it dire."

Jonathan raised his head and saw Fallon staring at them. He swallowed hard. "You have, I suppose, some grandiose plan?"

Fallon bowed. "Of course."

FORTY-ONE

"TOMORROW IS THE Feast of St. Miken," Fallon said, "and your king will open his court for petitioners. Your mother and I will make a grand entrance. Then we will introduce you and Kassandra. No one will doubt either of your parentages at the word of their beloved Selphyn princess Syldonia, not to mention that of your own father. You will announce your wedding plans. During the tearful reunion between parents and their daughter, you, Edward, will open the trunk."

For a moment Jonathan could only stare at him. "The trunk? Oh, yes. You brought it with you?"

"Yes. You will reveal whatever is inside to the court..." He drifted off, frowning. "With luck there will be more than just dust inside."

"I do not think I–"

Fallon put his hands on Jonathan's shoulders. "If not you, who else? Only he who is half-Selphyn, half-human can open this trunk."

"You hope."

"I *know*. This was written in Miken's own hand. You must trust me."

He looked from one set of violet eyes to another as Selphyn brother and sister stared at him. He wanted to clamp his hands over his ears and shut his eyes, screaming. He could not fight the intensity of those eyes, especially the ones belonging to his mother. After all these years of grieving for her, it was impossible for him to deny her anything. He was about to say as much when the trapdoor was flung open.

He threw up his head and unsheathed his rapier; Thomas followed suit while Uthen, the only armed Selphyn, drew a dagger from his belt. The animals were instantly on guard, and Stojak stood against Lauren's legs, his hackles rising.

"Can you keep Stojak calm?" Jonathan said to Lauren even as several pairs of boots came trotting down the stairs. "If he attacks, they will kill him."

"I will try." She knelt and put her arms around the wolf's neck, whispering in his ear. Uthen shot a look at Belcastro, and the fox sat down, ears pricked. Jonathan thought it odd that Zartha slid back into his saddlebag on the ground; he had credited her with more courage than that.

There were eight guards in all, and when they reached the landing they were obviously shocked to find themselves equaled in number. They formed a semi-circle at the base of the stairs, their broadswords extended, and looked anxiously from one face to another. Jonathan slowly moved forward so that he was blocking both Syldonia and Kassandra; his mouth dropped when his mother neatly stepped around him.

"Tobias? Is that you?"

The eldest of the guards, some forty years old or so, lowered his broadsword. The blood drained from his face. "Have mercy on me, O ghost," he whispered.

"I am no ghost," Syldonia said. "I fear you were the victim of a deception. I have lived, these many years, in Rowan. I am alive, as you can see, and well."

Tobias dropped to one knee, and Syldonia touched his head with all the grace and majesty she was reputed to own. "I remember when you were a young man. Your father was captain of the Royal Guard."

"Hawkins, your Ladyship. I am honored to have you recall."

"Yes, Hawkins. He was a good soldier and an even better captain. He was kind to me, and I remember both of you well."

Tobias looked up and saw his much younger comrades still standing, their mouths agape. "Kneel, you fools! You stand in the presence of Lady Syldonia!"

Jonathan smiled when he heard all of their kneecaps strike the hard stone in unison. After a moment of silence, Leonardis's voice called down from above.

"And where are my prisoners?"

When there was no response, he came down himself, sword unsheathed. He paused midway down the stairs and took in the scene. The last few steps he took slowly, his face gray. He walked past his kneeling men and stared at Syldonia, taking in her gown of sea-green silk, her golden hair in the torchlight, her violet eyes. He glanced at Fallon and Uthen but for a moment only before returning his gaze to Syldonia.

"I saw him kill you. I saw it with these two eyes. And yet you stand here before me…in all of your beauty and glory. I should think myself in a dream, and yet…"

"How unpleasant to see you again, Leonardis," Syldonia said. "My son tells me you were unkind to him."

Jonathan shrugged, unable to resist a playful smile.

"Ah, yes, perhaps I have been remiss."

"Remiss? Treacherous, I believe, is the word you were searching for."

"I have seen my nephew rise from the dead. Why not you?" Leonardis glanced at his kneeling captain. "Captain. You have not arrested your charges."

"Sir. I cannot do so in good faith, considering the circumstances."

"A Selphyn woman appears and suddenly you are incapable of arresting traitors? These two are imposters—"

"Sire. You told us they were impersonating Prince Edward and Princess Kassandra. And yet the Lady Syldonia lives. My lady, may I have your word that the man we seek is no imposter?"

"Do not ask—"

"He is my son. I swear it."

Leonardis's face turned purple as his captain shrugged apologetically. "Forgive me, my lord Duke, but I must take the lady at her word."

Jonathan saw the flap of his saddlebag lift out of his peripheral vision. A second later there was a blur of white in the air, in the same instant that Leonardis swung his sword in a wide arc toward Jonathan's head. Zartha missed the blade by a half-second, and fastened her jaws into Leon's throat. He fell backward, clutching the slender white wolf who weighed no more than a large rabbit, and smashed the back of his head against a marble statue. As he rolled away, revealing the bloody gash in the back of his head, they all saw the blood and bone matter on the hand and sword hilt of Miken the Archangel. The blood dripped onto his marble toes, cutting rivets through decades of dust.

A soldier ran to him, reaching as if to take his pulse. He drew his arm back. "He is dead. Oh, God, the king's brother, our good Duke—"

"Stop," Tobias said. "We can do without these obligatory tidings."

"But—"

"He was not loved. Let us not further insult him by feigning our grief."

"I think you are my hero," Jonathan said to Tobias, and Zartha trotted over, her tail wagging, and sat on Jonathan's feet. "Good – good wolf," he said, absently patting her head.

Tobias turned to Syldonia. "My lady, what – what shall I tell the king?"

"Nothing yet, if you please. We mean to make our appearance on the morrow."

"But...when we return without Leonardis—"

Fallon's face broke out into a smile. "Why not be our escorts tomorrow? You can keep her ladyship safe from those who might attack a Selphyn without knowing who she is."

Tobias's shoulders relaxed with relief. "Thank you. I should be honored to escort her ladyship."

"Can you guard us in the meantime?" Syldonia said, flashing him her sweetest smile. Jonathan grinned as the captain's knees literally went weak. All seemed to have forgotten Leonardis, who lay in a bloodied, macabre heap at their feet.

Tobias did a sweeping bow. "I am deeply honored. No one shall enter here without your consent."

Once the guards went back upstairs, taking Leonardis with them, the group in the ruins broke into nervous laughter. Jonathan threw his arms around his mother and pumped Fallon's hand, congratulating them both on their quick thinking. And of course Zartha reveled in everyone's attention and accolades. Embraces were had all around, but when Thomas moved toward Lauren to hug her, Stojak bared his teeth and uttered a low growl. Everyone froze save for Lauren, who knelt to look the wolf in the eye.

"Stojak! You know better than that. He is my brother. Will you not be friends?"

Thomas tried again, extending a tentative hand. Stojak actually snapped at him, and Thomas jerked his hand back. "What — I do not understand. He allowed me to embrace you yesterday."

Fallon approached, and the same thing happened. Stojak's fur stood on end as he snarled at his former master's brother.

"This is odd, indeed," Fallon said. He looked up at Lauren, really looking, and suddenly his face lit up. "I understand why our friend is being so protective. I see now what he has just begun to sense: you are carrying Rathnar's child. And the wolf has already bonded with it."

* * *

They would have made a fuss over her, Thomas and Anne especially, to ensure her comfort, but Stojak would not allow anyone to touch her. Gideon took the opportunity to help atone for his actions by fetching food, bringing Lauren the choice cuts of meat. He could not hand them to her, but rather was forced to leave them on the floor to ensure Stojak would not take off his hand. Stojak not only resisted taking the food for himself, but stood over it and wagged, looking at Lauren intently. She ate quietly, and Jonathan guessed she was still incredulous over her condition.

Thomas joined Jonathan on a pillar while they ate, watching the endearing scene of Lauren and her fierce protector as they ate side by side, the wolf waiting until she took a bite before taking his own.

"Are you following through with Fallon's plan tomorrow?" Thomas asked.

Jonathan's eyes glazed over as the question seemed to tap what little energy remained. "I do not see any other choice. They would guilt me into it, whether I would or no."

"Again I would switch roles with you. You could marry Miranda, and I, Kassandra."

Jonathan gave him a lopsided smile. "And would you be king?"

"If it meant marrying Kassandra, I would. And now that our mothers are back and I have spent time with Fallon, I – I see the wisdom in bringing them back. I would be proud to be the one who opened the gate for them."

Jonathan sighed and searched for Miranda, finding her sitting near his mother, the two of them in easy conversation. She caught his eye and smiled, and his heart missed a beat.

"And what about the theater?" he asked Thomas.

"Yes. That would be my only regret. I do not think... I do not think I could live without the stage."

Jonathan nodded, understanding him all too well. He patted Thomas's knee. "When I am king, I will build you the largest, most grandiose playhouse you have ever seen. Name it what you will, for it will be yours."

"He started building it, you know."

"What? Who?"

"Leonardis. He kept his word. I saw it when we rode into town. It is nearly half-done." Jonathan's stomach sank. "Oh, but if you could see it. The stage is done. I stood on it, and–"

"Thomas, please. I cannot bear this."

"Forgive me."

"You'll pardon me if I leave you. If this is to be my last night with her–"

"Yes, yes, go to her, by all means."

They both stood and shook hands. Thomas said, "Jonathan – or do you prefer Prin–"

"Jonathan."

"Good. I do not think I would ever be at ease with your proper title. I wanted to say that I have loved you ever, and I hope you will forgive my terrible behavior to you."

"Of course it is forgiven. I stole your name. You were right to be angry."

"I wanted to tell you, but…I was too angry to trust you."

"Yes. I understand."

He held out his hand to Miranda and she was in his arms in an instant. He pushed his mouth against her ear. "I would be alone with you, if you would consent."

Her eyes gave him the answer he sought, and they stepped carefully over fallen statues and broken pillars until they were enveloped by shadows. He was looking for a place to spread his cloak, when he saw a long sepulcher. Running his hands through the dust, he uncovered the ancient lettering engraved on the lid. He knelt and blew hard, revealing the engraved sword and angel wings.

"Miken's bones."

Miranda joined him, kneeling. "Someone you know?"

"Miken's bones – I was not speaking metaphorically. Fallon said – do you not recall? – that Miken's remains were buried here."

"Oh, God."

"Precisely."

They stared at the sepulcher in silence. Then Miranda whispered, "Would that I could properly feel the sanctity of this discovery. Yet…"

"Yet it is overshadowed by our looming separation–"

"Yes!"

She fell into his arms and they rolled away from Miken's remains that were all but forgotten. Jonathan lay down his cloak as they stretched on the unyielding floor. She was crying when he kissed her.

"Is it wrong to hate them for taking you from me?" she said.

"Do not hate them. I would have you love them because I do, even though they ask the world of me."

"Oh, I do not hate them," Miranda said against his shoulder. "But I am very, very wretched."

"I would not have you so for the world, not on our last night together. Be wretched with me tomorrow."

She smiled at him and he lost himself in the waves of her hair.

Hours later, when he could not sleep, he stared up the dark ceiling. An idea was taking root in his mind; when he gave attention to it, it blossomed and seized his other thoughts like a pernicious vine, draining them of sustenance until only this thought remained. He sat up, breathing deeply. Miranda did not stir as he covered her with her cloak, carefully retracing his steps back to where he had left the others.

All but his mother slept, and she was the one he sought. She was reading by candlelight, and when she saw him she lowered the book, which he saw was the *Book of Miken*.

"I am refreshing my memory of this prophecy," she said, "so that I might properly prepare you for tomorrow."

Grateful the others were out of earshot should they awaken while they talked, he sat down next to her and held both of her hands.

"Mother, I would ask something of you. A very, very large favor."

She smiled, and he remembered her wonderful leniency when he was child. She had never been angry with him, even when he broke her glass dolphin. His eyes swam.

"You know I would do aught you asked of me."

"Hear me first, for you may yet regret saying so."

He spoke for several minutes without pause, while she listened, blinking only twice during his monologue. When he finished she stared at him.

"You...you ask too much of me."

He tried to smile but his mouth turned down and trembled. He was dangerously close to tears. "You force me to dishonor myself by utilizing the only power I have." He held her gaze. "You *owe* me this, after what has passed."

She closed her eyes, and he saw a solitary tear fall down her cheek. "You know me well. Your weapon of choice is powerful indeed."

"I regret using it, truly I do. I hate to see you distressed. But..."

She nodded, sniffling. "Yes. I will do it." She smiled, somewhat ruefully. "But you are allowed only one use of this weapon." He grinned. "I will not have you manipulating me anytime you need something."

He threw his arms around her. "Thank you, Mother. I am sorry."

"And I. For everything."

He stood and bade her goodnight before finding his way back to Miranda. She awakened as he put his arms around her.

"Were you dreaming, my love? Nightmares?"

"No. They were good dreams. And I order you to have the same."

"Yes, my lady."

She smiled sleepily before drifting off again. He stroked her hair and sought out Zephyrine with his mind, finding instant solace in the warmth and love that was waiting for him.

FORTY-TWO

IN THE MORNING Thomas watched the Selphyn in their meticulous preparations for their dramatic entrance. He couldn't help but smile at this display of vanity for all of their natural inclinations and spiritualism. Fallon and Syldonia attended to each other with a precision comparable to apes grooming each other as they picked out each and every tiny bug. They straightened each other's clothes, adjusted loose curls, and touched up eye kohl. They were already blinding in their beauty, wearing matching gold silk, and Thomas nearly told them that no one would notice a stray strand of hair.

When they finished preparing each other, they moved onto Kassandra. Syldonia styled her hair, sweeping it up in an elegant pile on her head with a cascade of carefully arranged ringlets. Fallon draped a teal cloak around her shoulders that complimented her silver-and-black gown and brought out the color of her eyes. While she sat rigid under their administrations she occasionally threw glances in Thomas's direction. They had hardly spoken since their reunion, and Thomas hoped he could attribute it to a necessary distancing from her affection rather than the result of his ill behavior in Rowan. She had accepted his apology graciously, but without much feeling. It was absurd, however, to brood over such things when she would soon be married to his greatest friend.

Jonathan and Miranda were missing; they pleaded a need for privacy while they prepared for their appearance at court. When they did reappear, Miranda was stunning in blue and cream, while Jonathan was unaccountably hooded and wrapped up in a cloak.

"What is this?" Thomas asked. "Your mother and uncle will never approve of this poor fashion."

"I am making a grand entrance," Jonathan said.

"Ah. I see. As you stand before their Majesties, you will tear aside your cloak, sweep up your arms and declare your identity in a deep, booming voice."

"Something like that, yes."

Fallon joined them, dropping a hand on Jonathan's shoulder. "Edward, I have a favor to ask – you are not attending court wrapped up like a pastry?"

"I told you," Thomas said.

"Only until I hear my cue."

"Ever the actor," Thomas said with a grin.

"Well. I hope you are dressed exquisitely underneath, as befits a prince of the realm."

"I will be dazzling."

"Excellent. Now. May I impose upon your good humor and ask to borrow Zephyrine and Zartha? They will make an excellent finishing touch to my appearance."

"You have my blessing, but the decision is theirs."

"Thank you, nephew." As if on impulse, the Selphyn king pulled Jonathan in for a hug while the latter kept his arms inside the cloak. "I see you will not grant me even a glimpse. Very well. I will prepare to be amazed."

They gathered outside the cathedral, blinking and shielding their eyes from the intrusive sunlight as they positioned themselves in a procession. Fallon, a striking figure indeed with his signature purple coat, rode Jonathan's magnificent horse with Zartha trotting alongside, and Tiben perched on his shoulder. Syldonia, her gold gown blindingly reflecting the sun, rode an exquisite white mare at her brother's side, her hair swept up with combs. Directly behind them rode Kassandra, but Jonathan insisted on walking with the others. Stojak and Belcastro were included; the latter giving them little choice as he refused to be separated from his charge. He did, however, allow Thomas and Anne to link elbows with Lauren, though he was constantly craning his head back to make sure his mistress was safe. Their procession caused quite the stir. People gathered on the street to watch them, many dropping milk jugs or tools in their amazement. Several recognized Syldonia, and three women fainted while many others darted out to kiss the hem of her dress, their faces wet with tears. No one dared to approach Fallon, and no one recognized Kassandra, but, understanding her importance, stared at her intently.

Several people ran ahead to the castle, undoubtedly to report to the king what was rapidly approaching. Tobias with his promised entourage of guards led the way up the cobblestone streets, snapping orders to the guards at the gate who might have detained them. One such detainer wore a harp on his back; he pulled it free to sing one of the more popular ballads honoring Syldonia to the lady herself. He trotted alongside her horse, his voice and harp jarringly off-key as he tried to keep up. Syldonia gave him a look and Thomas lunged for him.

"Are you, by chance, Horatio, the king's harper?"

"Even he, good sir. Kindly unhand me that I might shower her ladyship with–"

Thomas shoved him so that he tripped over his own feet. The man was pox-marked and nearly bald with the longest nose Thomas had ever seen. He was gravely insulted that he was chosen to portray such a distasteful character.

As they crossed the bridge and neared the portcullis, Thomas looked up and saw the mounted head. The kites and crows had been at the eyes, and dried blood, black on the iron, coated the rod. He pulled Lauren against him, cradling her head.

"Do not look."

He felt her nod, and luckily Stojak was distracted and missed it. Fallon, however, saw, his face dark. He whispered something to his sister and she turned her face away, closing her eyes. Gideon never took his eyes off of it, a penance, Thomas guessed, of his own imposing. He was handsome in his dark-green doublet and matching boots, but was no match for his Selphyn companions. Only Uthen chose obscurity, dressed in simple gray with his happy fox trotting alongside.

They rode and walked into the open audience chamber. The king and queen were already standing, waiting for them with faces carved from stone. Voices hushed so that the only sound was the echoing hooves of the three horses, with Fallon and Syldonia still riding at the head. Thomas spotted Thaddeus standing next to the king, and as Syldonia approached he broke his stoic stance and ran to her horse. He touched a slender ankle before his hand was batted away by Tobias.

"You forget yourself, sir!" Thaddeus said. "My lady – my love, you live?"

"You will keep your distance from the Lady Syldonia unless she requests your presence," Tobias said, his face impassive. Thaddeus glowered at him, and when he turned back the horses had passed him. He grabbed Gideon out of line and pulled him off to the side, where Thomas saw him question the courtier with a red, blotched face.

The king and queen were pale, but stately in their tight faces. King Edward's eyes swiveled back and forth between brother and sister, and he waited until the procession came to a halt before speaking.

"What means this?"

Fallon spoke. "Gracious lord, my sister and I come before you this day to present you and your queen with a gift."

"You – you are returning your sister to us?"

Fallon laughed but Syldonia's eyes narrowed. "Ah. A goodly joke, that," Fallon said. "I revoked that gift long ago when you abused it."

"How came she to be alive?"

Fallon's mouth pursed with impatience, and he made a dismissive gesture. "That were better accounted for another time. We have more pressing business. Your honored Majesties, many years ago I made a dreadful mistake and committed a vile act out of grief and vengeance. I come now before you to atone for my wickedness, and return what is rightfully yours. I hereby present you with your daughter, Princess Kassandra, who has lived these many years with us."

Brother and sister pulled their horses aside, and Kassandra slipped from her saddle. Thomas held his breath as she walked up to the dais, sweeping low into a curtsey.

"Good Mother and Father, I have waited long for this happy day. I am honored to make your acquaintance at last."

For a moment no one moved, not even a rustle of skirts. Kassandra slowly rose up from her curtsey, and stared at her parents. The queen made the first move, taking one step and then another down the dais. Her breath caught in her throat, and as she lifted her hands to her face, Kassandra threw herself into her mother's arms. The king was still too stunned to move, even after his wife declared over and over again, between sobs, that the lady was indeed her daughter.

"I – I do not understand."

Fallon's eyebrow arched in annoyance. "I took her, my lord. Now I am returning her. It is not so complicated."

"She – you – she–"

"Gracious," Fallon said under his breath. He looked at Syldonia. "Would you?"

She launched into a more detailed explanation, and Thomas's gaze slid over to Jonathan, who was still cloaked and hooded, awaiting his "cue" which Thomas knew was rapidly approaching. His heart hammered in empathetic anxiety for his friend, and he was vaguely aware that the king had finally moved to his wife and daughter to embrace them both.

"And we are not finished, your lordship," Fallon said. King Edward threw up his head with alarm. "There is one other who is here today, returned from the grave as it were. And this one was a surprise even to me. His mother and father, both present here today, will vouch for his parentage. I present to you your nephew, Prince Edward Boussard."

This was it. Thomas smiled to give his friend encouragement, when Jonathan abruptly shoved him into the aisle. He wind-milled his arms to keep his balance through the gasps of the audience, and when he righted himself, Fallon was staring at him. Both of them looked at Jonathan, whose hooded head gave the slightest nod.

Thomas snapped his head back to the king, who was waiting. He took several gasping breaths and dropped his head in order to think. He closed his eyes and summoned his focus. When he raised his head, he was Prince Edward.

He bowed. "Gracious king and queen. I am very glad indeed to be restored to you, and in particular to my loving, patient and understanding father."

He glanced at Thaddeus, whose face was a mask of stone. Gideon, standing next to the chancellor, gaped like a fish. He took a step forward and Thaddeus threw his arm across his chest to prevent his advance. Thomas swallowed hard.

The king was shaking. "I do not – I do not–"

Fallon sighed. "Yes. You do not understand." He looked at Thomas with a raised eyebrow. "Perhaps, nephew, you would care to tell your story."

"I will tell it," Syldonia said, and Thomas melted with relief. She slid from her horse and joined Thomas at the dais, putting a hand on his shoulder without looking at him. She cleared her throat.

"Many years ago my son and his two friends witnessed what they understandably thought was the brutal murder of their mothers. They were not warned in advance, so as not to ruin the illusion, a decision that was made in folly that I will never cease to regret. In their fear, grief and confusion, they scattered. John and my Edward took refuge in the ruins under the cathedral, while Lauren sought employment with Duchess Isabella. Days passed, and Edward was forced to find food and provisions. He left John alone, and was subsequently locked out of the cathedral for several days. By the time he returned, John was dead, his body ravaged beyond recognition by the plague. By chance he was wearing Edward's clothes, and your prince saw an opportunity to put to death his princely persona, of which he wanted nothing more. But like us, he now sees it is his responsibility to his family and people to take his place as prince, and marry your daughter Kassandra if you will give your consent. One day they will together rule this country with grace, wisdom and courage."

"A match well-made indeed!" Queen Lydia said. "We could not hope for more."

Thomas's head made a circular nod. He was aware his mouth was open and closed it, trying to smile.

There was a rustle of skirts, and Thomas looked up to see Duchess Isabella, undoubtedly unaware she was recently widowed, elbowing her way to the dais. "If John is dead and this is Prince Edward, what of the man who called himself Jonathan Wilder? Who and where is he?"

Thomas was only too glad to step back for Jonathan, who pulled aside his cloak and let it fall in a puddle at his feet. Isabella threw her hands up onto her face and screamed before falling backwards in a dead faint. Thomas guffawed and turned to Jonathan. "Oh, God," he whispered.

Jonathan stood before them in all of his Selphyn glory. He was wearing bright red silk in Selphyn fashion, with nothing covering his chest but an open vest, the onyx horse in plain sight just below his collarbone. His long cloak had obscured his bare feet, which were now visible for all to see below the tapered ankles of his silk trousers. His hair was down and loose around his shoulders, the braided black horse hair striking against the gold color of his hair. His eyes were outlined in black kohl, his skin subtly darkened with some kind of golden paint. He grinned broadly and bowed.

Syldonia said, "May I introduce to you all, my other son, Siobhan."

A laugh of absurdity burst from Thomas, which, echoing in the court, sounded like a donkey bray. "Brothers!"

"And who is his father?" This from Thaddeus, who finally broke his silence. His eyes were red-rimmed and filled with pain and rage.

"I am."

Another gasp as the audience took in the fourth Selphyn present, the handsome and charming Captain Uthen. He joined Syldonia and linked hands.

"I loved him before I knew you," Syldonia said, "and I loved him after."

"I suppose then you met with him in secret during the sanctified time of our marriage." Thaddeus's eyebrows quirked as he waited for her response.

"Sanctified, was it? You had no objection to sharing me with your king." Before King Edward could respond, she added, "He was conceived before you and I were married. The Selphyn age more slowly than humans. And like my brother Rathnar, he came to Salsima in the guise of a human to be near me, and chose to remain here after my feigned death."

King Edward looked over Jonathan fleetingly but with obvious distaste before turning his attention back to Thomas. "You do not much resemble your mother, nor the young boy I remember."

"My hair and eyes changed the year my voice did," Thomas explained, yet again, grateful to say something finally that was the truth.

"What say you, Thaddeus? Is this your son?"

All eyes turned to the king's chancellor, who had his gaze on Jonathan rather than Thomas. There was a pregnant pause in which father and son stared at each other. Finally Thaddeus released a breath, and turned to the king.

"Yes. He is my son."

"Then be welcome, Prince Edward," said the king, and held out his arms as if to embrace Thomas. Fallon flashed him a lupine grin.

"Oh, but we are not finished with you, your Majesty."

FORTY-THREE

THE TRUNK FALLON pulled from Zephyrine's hip was much smaller than Jonathan had envisioned. It was wooden and completely free from embellishment or decoration. It resembled a box in which one would toss books or old papers. Not some ancient relic meant to unite two races at war.

Fallon put the trunk on the bottom stair of the dais.

"Before he died, Miken prophesied our people would be conquered by humans, our lands taken, our presence banished. He also prophesied that centuries later there would a Day of Reckoning, when it was time to show the world that Miken was in fact a Selphyn, a being of love and nature, and not born of a human." When the king began to sputter, Fallon spoke over him like a rake over leaves. "That day has come. With our half-Selphyn prince ruling with his Selphyn-raised wife, you will all have a chance to learn that our customs are not threatening, our beliefs free from violence, our philosophy based on love, equality and freedom. But first you must learn that Miken was one of us, and your so-called *Book of Miken* a terrible adaptation of the original. Whatever lies in this trunk, Miken said, would free you to accept the truth."

Fallon paused, and for once Jonathan could see he was at a loss. The prophecy called for half-Selphyn and half-human. If this proved true and Thomas attempted to open it...

"Uncle," Jonathan said, "may I open it? I understand only a full-blooded Selphyn can, and I would be honored beyond words to be he."

Fallon's eyes half closed with relief and gratitude. He gestured for Jonathan to approach. "I should be glad to give you that honor, nephew."

He knelt and ran his fingers over the lid and the clasp. It looked simple enough as there was no lock, but he was not about to question Miken at this point. He lifted the hasp and pushed the lid back, grinning. There was material inside, the color of an antique map. He touched it gingerly, remembering Fallon's fear that all was dust. Though it was whole now, there was no guarantee it would stay that way once he lifted it and exposed it to the air. It was thin like muslin. He pulled it up gently, catching glimpses of an outline in a dark, reddish-brown color. The color of old blood. He understood now what it was. Once it was fully unfolded, he held it high above his head, rotating so that everyone in the audience chamber could see it. Several people, men and women, wept; a handful even fled. The rest of them knelt, including Fallon and Syldonia. Then he turned to show it to the king and queen.

He watched the king's eyes as he registered the cloth in front of his eyes: the shroud that once covered Miken's dead body. His imprint was burned in it, and there was no ignoring the long, angled face with the chiseled features that marked him, undeniably, as a Selphyn.

The queen burst into tears, and Edward's hand crept up to his neck. He yanked at his collar, his face the color of a rotted tomato. Jonathan could hear his ragged gasps, and as his hand lowered to grasp his heart, his eyes rolled heavenward. Thomas leapt up the stairs and caught him just as he fell backwards, his great weight crushing Thomas beneath him. When Thomas managed to free himself and inspect the king's face, his stricken expression told them everything.

"Well, my friend," Jonathan said. "Are you quite ready to be king?"

Thomas's face went white. "Oh, God."

* * *

Pandemonium erupted all around her as Lauren watched the king fall, her expression impassive. She watched carefully as they rolled his giant body, fat drooping over the stairs, onto his back, making sure his eyes did not move. If they did, she wanted to plant a dagger into his heart to make sure he was really dead. When his condition was confirmed, her body sagged with relief, but no pleasure. She did not feel like Rathnar's death had been avenged, simply mollified, a temporary appeasement as if his loved ones were given sweets to soothe their grief.

She wanted nothing to do with the wailing courtiers, the grieving noblemen, the wretched queen. Isabella demanded Leonardis and it was announced that he too was dead, and Lauren's former mistress fainted yet again. Lauren would have nothing to do with these fools grieving over villains, when such a noble heart had been extinguished without so much as a tolling of a bell to mark the occasion.

She did, however, upon passing the dais, feel sympathy for

Kassandra, who had just been reunited with her father only to see him fall moments later. She was standing over her mother who was prostrate across her husband's expansive belly, her face stricken with her hands wringing. Recognizing another soul in need, Lauren grabbed the princess's hand and pulled her off the dais. Kassandra, despite their brief and unremarkable acquaintance, threw her arms around Lauren's neck.

Stojak endured this close proximity to his mistress with a whine of anxiety. Lauren pulled free to reach down and pat his head, his presence, once again, reminding her of her new responsibility. She put a hand on her stomach, wishing she could feel whatever Stojak and Fallon could sense.

There was a chorus calling for Prince Edward; for a moment Lauren forgot it was her brother they were clamoring for. All eyes turned in his direction and some hands even reached for him. He turned white and scrambled out of their reach; when he saw Lauren and Kassandra he snagged each of their elbows and propelled them out of the chamber.

In an empty hallway he slouched against the wall, panting for breath. "They already look to me for guidance. I – my God, I have been the royal heir for all of five minutes. I know not what they want of me."

Kassandra wiped her eyes. "We will – we will return together, announce a mass…a national holiday to grieve…"

Thomas brightened and took her hands. "Yes? And then?"

"And then…"

He pushed her hair back from her face and kissed her brow. "And then you will marry me."

She met his gaze. "Yes. I suppose I will."

Lauren, feeling terribly intrusive, did not want to move lest she disturb this scene, this moment that was about to happen that was long in coming. For too long had she watched her brother suffer in silence, brooding over the princess who had barely acknowledged him.

Both of them took shaking breaths, staring at each other. Finally Thomas – Lauren was under orders to stop calling him John – said, "I swear to you I did not know it would be thus. I did not know I would be thrust upon you, leaving you no choice but to wed me. And here you must despise me."

"I despise you? I never did."

Thomas closed his eyes. "Yet you do not love me."

Kassandra sighed, and Lauren saw the small smile playing at her lips. "We heard you reciting lines the day you performed *William and Elizabeth* in the yard of the Swan. Your friend Jonathan, before I knew him to be my cousin, did explain the story. A prince and princess, twins, separated after a terrible shipwreck–"

"I am well-acquainted with the story," Thomas said, and Lauren wanted to kick him.

"Yes, but allow me to tell it. Both are washed onshore, thinking the other dead. The sister, protecting her virtue, disguises herself as a boy, and seeks employment under that country's prince. This prince is forlorn – he must needs marry a princess, yet none has stolen his heart. Our heroine, because her country with his is at war, cannot reveal her parentage. But oh–" Here she stopped to place her lips on Thomas's neck, speaking in between kisses – "oh, how she pines for him in an anguished, secret passion, unable to confess her love."

Thomas's breath was coming in short, ragged gasps. "And – and absurd errors ensue over mistaken identities–"

"Yes…when the twin prince comes to town…"

"And it is revealed the war was founded on lies–"

"All is forgiven…"

"Brother and sister are reunited–"

"And," Kassandra said, taking him by the arms, "the princess reveals her gender, and her stature, and prince and princess are free to love each other–"

"With wanton, wicked abandon," Thomas finished, pulling her in for a kiss that made Lauren's cheeks go aflame. She smiled at them as she crept away, Stojak at her heels. They rounded a corner and Lauren sat down, folding her knees against her. A torrent of tears was building behind her eyes, but Stojak would have none of that. He pushed himself in between her chest and legs, lying over her stomach as if he meant to cocoon the life inside her. She squeezed him, chastised for forgetting her life was not over, but just beginning.

FORTY-FOUR

IT WAS DECIDED hours later, after Thomas and Kassandra announced a forthcoming requiem mass and holiday, that Lydia, now the Dowager Queen, would act as Regent until Thomas and Kassandra were married and crowned. There would be no festivities to celebrate the return of Salsima's prince and princess, under the circumstances, and those who were in on the monstrous switch that Jonathan had orchestrated converged together, taking a quiet banquet alone in the privacy of Thaddeus's chambers.

Jonathan sat across from Thomas and Kassandra, in between his mother and father. Uthen and Fallon were seated on Syldonia's other side, and Miranda was next to Thaddeus. Syldonia did not acknowledge the king's chancellor when he forced his seat near her, and Jonathan was not particularly enthusiastic about sitting next to him either.

"You have broken my heart," Thaddeus said without preamble.

"You know that was not my intention," Jonathan said.

"No? You renounced me. Replaced me with a Selphyn father. You rejected me, your heritage, your responsibility. I am undone."

"Is it not enough to have your son alive?" Syldonia said.

Thaddeus flushed and stared at his plate. "Where will you...will you not be near me? Or must I be content feigning love to a man who is not my son?"

"I will be near you. I would have us get to know each other again. Perhaps you can name me your Selphyn ambassador, thus ensuring my frequent presence in court."

"You mean you are not leaving for Rowan?"

"It had been my thought, yes. But with the advent of certain events...I find I am at liberty to pursue my dream of my own playhouse. I mean to stay, and hope that my mother and uncle will visit often."

Syldonia put her hand in his, while Jonathan felt the weight of Thomas's heavy stare.

"While I am grateful...I believe...for this turn of events, my heart breaks to hear you mention the playhouse. I must now renounce it."

Jonathan held his gaze. "Not entirely. I have a plan."

Thomas rested his chin on his hand and exhaled loudly. "Does it involve changing our names?"

Jonathan grinned. "No."

"What must I call you now? Sibo—Sinob—Siiiii–"

"Siobhan. And no, for I will not answer. Jonathan will content me." He could not resist a small smile. "Your Highness."

Thaddeus looked pained. "What…what experiences have you with state matters? What do you know of kingship?"

"No less than I," Jonathan said. "He was raised in court, just as I was."

"And John – Edward – Thomas? – likes people, whereas your son does not," Syldonia said. "This is an excellent quality for a king, would you not agree?"

"Well spoken, Mother," Jonathan said. "What say you, Father? Can you not forgive me for doing what I thought best for the realm? For me?"

Thaddeus pushed around a piece of chicken on his plate with his finger. "I will. If your mother will forgive me."

Syldonia smiled. "A fair trade, though it is an unnecessary one. I forgave you long ago."

Warmth simmered in Jonathan's stomach for the first time in hours. He looked down the table at his friends: Lauren and Anne, Kassandra, Gideon, confused but well, and at last Miranda. Miranda, glowing and smiling at him, her eyes sparkling in that wonderful, mischievous light he loved so well that promised a night filled with rapture. His heart positively swelled.

A rather large but bony body pushed its way into his lap as arms wrapped around his shoulders. "I have been trying to get to you all day," Gregory said.

"Where did you come from?"

"I came with the others."

"The others…the other actors?"

"Yes. We were all in court to see if you would come. They were all very surprised to hear you are a Selphyn."

"Oh, yes?"

"Yes. I think they miss you. Not as much as I do."

"Thank you, Gregory. But I think you are too big for my lap."

"But I wanted to ask you something."

"Yes?"

"With you and Thomas changing your names around so much, I wondered…well, who am I then?"

"You're yourself."

"But...can I not be someone else as well?"

"Very well. You may change your name if it pleases you."

"I think I shall still be Gregory. But...I would like to be your son."

Heat crept up Jonathan's throat. "Then who is your mother?"

"Miranda, naturally."

Jonathan looked up to see if she was listening. Her eyes were shining with tears.

"You understand, of course, that Miranda is too young to be your mother, as I nearly am to be your father."

"Oh, that does not signify. May I?"

"I do not see why you should not." Jonathan grinned, looking first at his mother and then his father. "Congratulations. You are grandparents."

Thaddeus shrugged. "I have heard stranger things this day."

After the banquet Gregory insisted on being swung back and forth in between Jonathan and Miranda, as if he were a lad of five instead of ten. They indulged him, smiling at each other over his head.

Gregory yawned. "May I sleep with–"

"No," Jonathan and Miranda said in unison.

"But you shall tuck me in and kiss me goodnight."

Jonathan rolled his eyes. "Only if you trot off to bed this instant, little scamp."

They had all been given rooms in the palace, Thomas's first hesitant command as prince. Jonathan was horribly disappointed, but not surprised, when his mother told him her plans. "Uthen, Fallon and I will be riding back toward Zirnich tonight. It is not right for us to stay here, and it may frighten those who still do not understand us."

"It is too soon," Jonathan said, following them outside and trying not, once again, to burst into tears. Like Gregory, he felt reduced to a child. "I have gone without you so long. I am loath to see you, all of you, leave so soon."

Fallon put a hand on his shoulder. "I think we will be back sooner than we hoped. And you know, you *know*, that you and your family are welcome in Rowan whenever you wish it."

"Thank you both for what you did for me today. I shall not forget it."

Fallon shook his head, smiling. "You shocked, horrified and amazed me. I am in awe of your courage, though some would call it cowardice. But no one could don full Selphyn regalia without a strong measure of courage."

"I wish Rathnar could have seen it," Syldonia said, and Jonathan nodded.

They all three kissed him, and Belcastro wagged his tail. Tiben soared down from a tree branch and lighted on Fallon's shoulder, squawking.

He watched the three Selphyn as they walked down a rocky path, the quartz pebbles glowing in the moonlight. With their matching heads of golden hair, shining silver in the night, they looked like a trio of faerie folk, three celestial beings gracing the earth with their presence. Jonathan wiped aside a stray tear.

"I came to tell you, that regardless of your name, you will always be Prince Edward to me." Jonathan looked up and saw Gideon approaching. "And as such you will have my undying loyalty and support, as well as my confidence."

"Thank you. My one and only command to you is to love your new king and queen, who will, I have no doubt, greatly bestow their favor upon you."

Gideon nodded. "For now it is Lauren's favor that I would have. I did as Rathnar bade me; I gave her his money and message, but she – she would not, *could* not even look at me. One day, perhaps, she will forgive me."

"Be assured of it. Her heart is too generous not to."

They looked at the stars, and the receding outlines of the three Selphyn.

"I suppose I will have to leave court. I have no stomach for courtly life. But out of all of this I will have Helen. I care not what my peers or parents think of me. I have seen too much pain to deny myself happiness."

"I am glad to hear it. And do not fret for your future. I have plans for you." He winked, which undoubtedly went unseen in the darkness.

"I am almost afraid to ask."

"You will enjoy it. I promise you. Ah, see yonder lady there, sparkling in the moonlight? The lovely one in blue and cream?"

"Yes."

"I must leave you now to claim her. She has been too much a stranger."

"I shall not impede you."

As he approached and swept Miranda into his arms, he checked, one final time for the night, on Zephyrine. She was in the royal stables, just drifting off to sleep. When she felt his soft touch, she instantly awakened, and blasted him with a surge of love.

He kissed Miranda's neck. "What say you, lady? Can you love a Selphyn?"

"I can, and do."

"That is excellent, for I have plans for you, dearest one. Be you ready for some quick changes: I will have you in and out of gowns – preferably out – and in wigs, crowns, jewels, swords and blood. You will be wooed, kidnapped, lost, married, rescued, adored, despised, arrested and acquitted. Be you ready, once again, to be a player."

EPILOGUE

SOME EIGHTEEN MONTHS following the death of King Edward II, the Raven opened and showcased its first performance.

Built in between the Crown and the Royal, the Raven playhouse was the largest. And well that it was so; at two o'clock on its maiden voyage every gallery was overflowing, and there was hardly room to move in the pit amongst the groundlings.

Jonathan came out on stage, dressed in a doublet and breeches, his hair tied back. There was loud applause and he bowed, quieting them with his hands.

"Welcome, dear friends, to the Raven! Happy are we to host you here for our first performance. I have an added delight, for it was whispered to me that we have special guests this afternoon." He shaded his eyes with his hand and searched the galleries, looking first in the noblemen's box. Syldonia, Uthen, Fallon, Thaddeus and Anne were there; he waved to them before continuing his search. "Where are you? Ah. There you are, disguised and hiding. We will have none of that. Ladies and gentlemen: I give you King Edward III and Queen Kassandra!"

Jonathan gave the audience two minutes to scream and applaud while the newlyweds shed their cloaks and stood. The couple was already so well-loved that they could not travel anywhere without being mobbed.

"My gracious king and queen, I am honored beyond reason that you have chosen to patronize our fine establishment. Relieved too, for I have a serious problem." There were groans of apprehension, and Jonathan, from across the pit, could see Thomas's face tighten. "When I learned you were coming, I thought it fitting to perform your Majesty's *favorite* play."

Thomas's eyebrow quirked. "Would that be, by chance, Rothford's *Two Brothers of Elkyn*?"

"Of course. I know how well you love this tale, of brothers separated, mothers dying, mistaken identities—"

"Only to be reunited, their mother resurrected, their ladies married, their dog's tail magically regrowing—"

Jonathan laughed. "Yes, yes. But here is my problem: I have not found, not in my vast journeys, anyone who can play your role with even a fraction of your talent. What am I to do? Shall I change the play–"

Thomas silenced him with a gesture. "I think I may have a solution."

"Yes? I will, of course, do anything your Majesty suggests."

"Why do not...*I* play the part?"

The screams were deafening. Jonathan once again gestured for silence. "But, surely, my lord, it would be unseemly for a king–" He was drowned out by booing. "All right, all right. Ladies and gentlemen: would you like to see your king on stage?"

He covered his ears, grinning madly. Thomas bowed, and gracefully leaped over the gallery railing. A group of soldiers followed him to the stage; Jonathan briefly took them aside.

"You are now townspeople, spear carriers, and, on occasion, trees. Be discreet and inconspicuous. I will have none of you sawing the air with gestures or improvising lines. Agreed?"

They nodded glumly, the only ones disappointed in the sudden turn of events.

Thomas hopped onto the stage, pumping Jonathan's hand. Through the curtains they could both see their fellow cast members, all new but two. Miranda waved, while Gideon and Helen, lately married, bowed and curtsied respectively. Gregory ran out and hugged Thomas's legs, dressed, at last, as a soldier. Jonathan finally had enough women to ensure that Gregory would never to have play one again. Thomas winked at the third woman, the one, besides his wife, who was dearest to him. Lauren blew him a kiss. At her feet was a chubby infant with golden hair. He was sitting next to a pile of costumes, yanking, very hard, on Stojak's ears. The wolf was a paragon of patience, occasionally licking the face of his charge and mind-link. The baby cooed and pulled out a handful of fur; behind the backstage area in the grass, Zephyrine contentedly munched from a bucket of oats while Zartha languished in the sun.

Over the cheers of the audience, Jonathan shouted, "Dear my lord, will you consider playing other roles as well?" The two men, "half-brothers," grinned at each other through the once-more deafening screams of assent.

"I should be glad to," Thomas said.

"Excellent. For I have here–" Jonathan paused to pull an ink-stained manuscript from his doublet – "a new play with a role that is perfect for you."

Thomas took the play and crushed it against his chest. Jonathan was touched to see the tears shining in his eyes. "Jonathan," he said quietly, "you are better than a brother. But prepare yourself: I am going to embrace you."

Jonathan gave him a face-splitting grin before picking him up off the ground, squeezing him, and spinning him around on the stage.

Acknowledgements

Many thanks to Michael Aiello, Sharon Belcastro, Peter Bish, Kathy Lopac, Kathy Sellers and Julia Stojak for reading early drafts of this novel, and for their wonderful encouragement. Thanks also to S.S. Bazinet for formatting assistance, and my parents, sisters, and Kat and Will Evans for their fantastic support.

To Aaron Falvey: may you always know the depth of my gratitude for helping me back on my path. Because of your overwhelming belief in me, I found myself. I love you.

About the Author

Ashley J. Barnard is the author of *Shadow Fox* (voted Novel of the Year for 2010 by Champagne Books), *Fox Rising*, *Night of the Fox* (Champagne/BURST) and *In Byron's Shadow*, as well as stage adaptations of *Sense and Sensibility* and *Persuasion* (Dramatic Publishing). She is a former staff writer for Fantasy-Faction.com, and lives in Phoenix, Arizona with her daughter Alexandria. Visit her website at www.ashleyjbarnard.com.

www.ingramcontent.com/pod-product-compliance
Lightning Source LLC
Chambersburg PA
CBHW051249260626
47162CB00002B/684